**Glendale Library, Arts & Culture Dept.**

3 9 0 1 0 0 5 5 5 7 7 9 4 8

D1006455

NO LONGER PROPERTY OF
GLENDALE LIBRARY,
ARTS & CULTURE DEPT.

# THE
# SAMARITAN

## ALSO BY MASON CROSS

The Killing Season

# THE SAMARITAN

## MASON CROSS

PEGASUS CRIME
NEW YORK  LONDON

M CROSS, MAS

THE SAMARITAN

Pegasus Crime is an Imprint of
Pegasus Books LLC
80 Broad Street, 5th Floor
New York, NY 10004

Copyright © 2015 by Mason Cross

First Pegasus Books hardcover edition February 2016

All rights reserved. No part of this book may be reproduced in whole or in part without
written permission from the publisher, except by reviewers who may quote brief excerpts in
connection with a review in a newspaper, magazine, or electronic publication; nor may any
part of this book be reproduced, stored in a retrieval system, or transmitted in any
form or by any means electronic, mechanical, photocopying, recording,
or other, without written permission from the publisher.

ISBN: 978-1-60598-953-2

10 9 8 7 6 5 4 3 2 1

Printed in the United States of America
Distributed by W. W. Norton & Company, Inc.

*To Laura*

# EIGHT YEARS AGO

## NEVADO HUASCARÁN
## YUNGAY PROVINCE, PERU

I watched Murphy as he crawled forward to the edge of the overhang and raised the binoculars to his eyes, training them on the spot a couple miles ahead, where the road emerged from the narrow mountain pass. He lay there motionless for a good five minutes. Long enough to allow a fine dusting of snow to cover his back.

"They're not coming."

"What do you want to do?" I asked. "Call it a day? Go home for hot chocolate?"

He twisted his neck to look back at me. "I don't get you, man. You seem like you're all about the hunt, and then when it comes to the finish, you get all . . . I don't know. Detached. What's the matter? I know you're not afraid."

"The hard work's done," I said. "You guys don't really need me for this part."

"And yet I notice you never turn down the opportunity to work downstream."

"I like the fresh air."

Murphy shuffled back and sat back down beside me, banging his gloved hands off his thighs to shake the powder off them.

"Too fresh for me. Hot chocolate sounds pretty good, in

fact. What the hell is up with the weather?"

"This is normal," I said.

"It was warm yesterday."

"That was El Niño. Yesterday was the aberration, not today. This is how it's supposed to be."

"I thought El Niño was Mexico."

"It happens all over South America."

"How do you know this shit, anyway?"

I shrugged, my eyes staying on the road a mile distant.

"No, seriously," he continued. "How do you know everything? Like, how do you know they're coming this way?"

"I don't know."

He stared at me for a few seconds and then shook his head. He looked to the road again and then down the slope to where it passed by us, fifty feet below.

"You think Crozier set the wires up right?"

"He knows what he's doing."

A pause. "I don't like him. Crozier."

My interest was piqued. For some reason, people didn't like to talk about Crozier. It was almost as though they were scared to address the subject. I'd had one or two brief verbal exchanges with the man, enough to decide I wanted to keep my distance. "He's quiet," I said noncommittally.

"He's not just quiet; he's a goddamn psychopath."

"He's on the right team."

"No, man, you don't understand. You hear about Baqubah, a few months back?"

"Sure. He took out five or six bad guys. It wasn't his fault about the hostages."

"It was six. You didn't see it. You didn't see what he did to them."

I turned my head and looked at him, waiting for him to

2

continue. Compared to the others, Murphy was practically a blabbermouth.

"I mean it. It was like they'd let Ted Bundy loose in there, man."

"He's a shooter. That's what he's here for."

Murphy paused, as though carefully considering what he was going to say next. "You've heard the story."

I had heard the story. I'd heard it from a couple of sources and wasn't sure whether to believe it or write it off as the equivalent of unfounded workplace gossip. That was the funny thing, though: with Crozier, you got the feeling anything was possible.

"I heard a rumor."

Murphy grabbed my shoulder and made me look at him. All of a sudden, he seemed to need me to listen to him. "It's the truth."

I paused, unsure of how to reply. And then I saw a glint of sunlight reflecting off glass or metal a mile distant.

"They're here."

**2015**
**SATURDAY**

# 1

## LOS ANGELES

People go crazy when it rains in LA.

It's a truism, just another of the unique quirks of character that grow up around any big city. But as is often the case, there's a lot of truth to the truism. Although Los Angeles is hardly devoid of rainfall, it is rare enough to qualify as an event when it does come. And for that reason, Angelenos just aren't accustomed to driving in the rain. That makes some of them lose their cool: driving too fast, or way too slow. Maybe taking tight corners at speed as though the conditions are dry. The fact that the city is built for desert conditions doesn't help, either. The drainage system is immediately overwhelmed, causing flooding and standing water. The rain grooves in the road surface fill up quickly and create a surface primed for hydroplaning. The statistics bear out the legend: traffic accidents spike by 50 percent when it rains. Crazy.

Kelly thought about this as she guided the Porsche 911 Carrera along the twisting strip of two-lane asphalt that was Mulholland Drive. The downpour flooded over the windshield as though she were in a carwash, the effect broken every second or so by the wiper blades sweeping back and forth on the fastest setting. At that moment, it seemed crazy to be driving, period. It seemed crazy no matter how careful you tried to be.

7

Kelly kept a tight grip on the wheel and hunched forward, as though the extra six inches of proximity to the glass would make a shred of difference. She'd lived in LA for most of her life, and she could never remember it raining like this. The speedometer needle danced just above twenty, which was as fast as she felt comfortable going with the steep drop to her right-hand side. Still, she'd been wondering if she should risk a little more pressure on the gas pedal, bringing it up to thirty, perhaps. She was worried about another car coming up behind her and not having time to stop. Somebody less cautious. Somebody going way too fast.

You'd have to be nuts to be speeding on a road like this one on a night like this, but that was the thing: people go crazy. She compromised and allowed the needle to climb to twenty-five. She breathed rapidly through her nose and tried not to blink.

Mulholland was a strange road, built a long time ago for a lot less traffic. It wound past the homes of the stars but also into darker, rural patches that felt like the precise middle of nowhere. Lots of sudden twists next to steep drops. Kelly wasn't overly familiar with the road under the best of circumstances, but tonight she might as well have been on the other side of the planet. It already seemed like hours since she'd left Sloan's. She risked a glance at the clock on the dash and realized that it had been only twenty-five minutes.

This had seemed like a good idea twenty-five minutes ago, when getting behind the wheel of Sarah's new toy had been an attractive proposition. Ten minutes later, when the heavens had opened, Kelly had immediately regretted her decision.

Ten or eleven miles from the bar to Sarah's place, give or take. She'd made good time in the first, blessedly dry, ten minutes—traffic was light on the 405 at this time of night, even in the automobile capital of planet Earth. How far to go, then? Five miles? Six? In these conditions, that could take her all night.

Kelly held her breath and feathered the brake as she took another corner that was a little tighter than it had appeared. It was difficult to judge, with the rain and the darkness. There were no streetlights up here, and the headlights illuminated a pathetically small patch of road in front of her before dissolving into the darkness. This was stupid, she thought again. This was ... crazy. She ought to pull off of the road at the next opportunity—one of the overlooks perhaps—and wait out the rain.

Only, there was no way to know how long the rain would last, and Sarah was counting on her. Sarah's dad would be home at one a.m., and if the Porsche wasn't in the garage, he'd check her room for sure.

Incredibly, the rain seemed to build in intensity, as though mocking her. The respite between swipes of the wipers was becoming less and less effective.

Kelly suddenly became aware that the radio was still on, tuned to a local classic rock station. "Black Hole Sun" by Soundgarden. The corner of her mouth curled upward for a second as she imagined what her own dad would have to say about that, about a record from the mid-nineties being labeled as "classic" anything.

And then she was jerked back into the moment. In the heartbeat between the pass of the wipers and the fresh sheet of water, the Porsche's headlights picked out a dark shape of something in the road, obstructing her lane. The wipers delivered another strobe-like snapshot of the road ahead, and she realized the shape was earth and rubble—a landslide from the slope on her left-hand side, leaving a dangerously tight gap in the road. Holding her breath, Kelly braked and aimed for the slender space between the pile of debris and the drop at the edge of the road.

*Sarah is gonna kill me*, she thought, as the driver-side front wheel crunched over a brick-sized rock while the drop loomed on her right-hand side.

And then the Porsche squeezed through the gap, missing the bulk of the obstruction and narrowly, wonderfully, keeping all four wheels on the road.

She exhaled in a short cough, grateful and guilty all at once, like she'd dodged a bullet. She skirted the remainder of the landslide, eyes peeled for oncoming headlights. Without taking her eyes from the road, she moved one hand gingerly from the steering wheel for the first time in ten minutes, reaching over to snap the radio off. Chris Cornell's voice winked out, leaving only the staccato beat of rain on glass.

*One less distraction*, she thought as she moved her hand back to the wheel. *One less—*

A loud bang pierced the rhythm of the rain like a gunshot, and she felt the rear of the car slide out from under her. *A blowout?*

The car was sliding to the right, toward the drop. Kelly yanked the wheel hard left. The vehicle ignored her, continuing its inexorable swerve toward a steep two-hundred-foot slope and oblivion. There was no barrier, because the road was relatively straight here. But that assumed your car was under control.

*Oh shit. Steer into the skid? Steer away from the skid? What are you meant to—*

As abruptly as the swerve had begun, it stopped. The steering wheel locked and the car righted itself, and Kelly leaned into the brake, hearing a nails-on-the-blackboard screech of metal as the Porsche hugged the very lip of the road and came to a full stop at the edge of the drop.

A brief moment of euphoria—she'd been certain she was about to die, and somehow she was still alive—and then a snatch of worry. Had she totaled Sarah's new Porsche? In the bar, Sarah had claimed not to know how much it had cost, but Matt had said something under his breath—with his usual mild disapproval—about a hundred thousand bucks or so. The rain battered down, unabated, as though trying to prevent her from thinking, from organizing her brain to the point where she might begin to piece together what had happened and what she might do next. But before she could start to think about the thousands of dollars of damage she might have done, those worries—and every other thought— were banished by the realization of a new danger.

She was sitting in an immobile vehicle, in the dark, in a rainstorm, on a narrow highway, next to a steep drop.

Frantically, she grasped for the door handle, finding it after an eternity and pushing the door open. She clambered out of the car and into the deluge. It was like diving fully clothed into a lake. She put a hand on her forehead to keep the rain out of her eyes and squinted at the road, looking one way and then the other. Seeing no lights, she reached back into the car and snagged the keys from the ignition, then scurried around the back to open the trunk, before remembering that this was a Porsche: engine in back, trunk in front. She made her way around to the front of the car again, hoping to find a coat, an umbrella, a tarpaulin . . . anything. Nothing. The trunk was utterly empty. *Damn it.*

She glanced again at the road, then circled back around the Porsche, inspecting it for damage as best she could. Miraculously, the bodywork looked to be unscathed, the silver paint job gleaming through the curtain of water. When she reached the rear driver's side wheel, she saw the real damage. The tire was shredded, to the extent that the rims of the wheel had partially cut into the road surface. The source of the unholy screeching as she'd lurched to a halt, she guessed. She cursed out loud this time and wiped rain out of her eyes again.

A flash of light made her jerk her head up again. Another car, a hundred yards away, though she couldn't yet hear the engine over the elements. He was headed straight for her. Kelly ran across the road and toward the direction of the oncoming vehicle, waving her arms and yelling. Dressed in a black halter top and jeans, she now wished she'd picked something more visible to wear. The car, a Ford, flashed by her, swerved when it saw the grounded Porsche, and narrowly missed clipping the rear driver's side fender where it stuck out into the wrong lane. The asshole had the temerity to lean on his horn as he continued on his merry way. Kelly prayed for him to hit whatever obstruction had eviscerated her tire, but the Ford continued past that point and cleared the landslide on the opposite lane before its taillights disappeared.

Kelly was soaked to the skin now. She ran back to the car and flung the door open once again. Her bag was on the passenger seat, looking somehow tawdry on the expensive leather upholstery. She grabbed it and sat down again behind the wheel, deciding to risk the danger of another car in exchange for a few moments' respite from the rain. They tell you to leave the car and stand by the road in a situation like this, but *they* weren't the ones getting soaked. She'd see the headlights in time anyway ... wouldn't she? She angled around in her seat and kept her eyes trained on the road behind her as she dug around in her bag, lifting and sifting the detritus that had accumulated in there and locating her phone by touch. Her hands closed around the familiar slim rectangle and she brought it out. There was no point in calling Sarah to tell her what had happened. Assuming she even picked up, it would only ruin her evening with Josh. AAA wasn't an option, either. Kelly didn't own her own car, and unless her manager spontaneously decided to double her paycheck, she doubted she would be buying one anytime soon. That left one option—her dad.

But when Kelly hit the button to activate the screen, it remained stubbornly dark. Goddamn Apple. Four hundred bucks for a phone and it couldn't give you more than eight hours of battery life, if you didn't use it too much. And she'd used it a lot in the bar—taking pictures, checking Facebook, calling Matt when he was late, Googling a cocktail recipe to settle an argument ...

Great. Dead car, dead phone. Could the night possibly get any worse?

Kelly got back out and entered the monsoon once more, looking both ways down the road. Nothing. She considered her options. She doubted she'd be physically capable of pushing the car over to the side of the road even on four good tires. With one of them blown out, there was no chance. She was stuck in the middle of nowhere with no coat, no phone, and pretty damn near no hope.

And then, a glimmer of light.

From up ahead, she saw headlights wink out and appear again as they cleared a bend in the road. She crossed to the opposite side again and this time stood as far out in the middle of the road as she dared. She waved her arms and yelled, much louder this time. The knowledge of the dead phone gave her hollering renewed urgency.

Fifty yards from her position, the vehicle began to slow as the driver spotted her. As it grew nearer, Kelly saw that it was some kind of pickup truck. That was good; he might have a winch or something to drag the Porsche off the road.

But she was getting ahead of herself—he needed to stop first. Kelly waved again, actually jumping up and down this time, worrying that this driver might pick up speed again and blow right by her like the last one. But he didn't. The dark pickup—it was impossible to discern even a vague color—pulled smoothly to a stop beside her, engine running. The driver's window rolled slowly down. Kelly peered into the darkness within. Between the rain and the absence of streetlights, she couldn't make out the driver.

"Hello?" she said unsurely.

Finally, the darkness shifted a little and a head appeared at the window. A man, she thought, although she couldn't be sure. A deep but quiet voice spoke out, almost lost beneath the sound of the rain.

"You need some help?"

The guy wore a dark blue or green baseball cap with no logo, the brim pulled down so that three-quarters of his face was in blackness, with only a clean-shaven chin visible.

Kelly swallowed and felt a chill that had nothing to do with her soaked clothing. She wasn't sure if it was the voice or the instinctive primal sense of unease that came from not being able to see his face properly, but all of a sudden she felt a strange urge to tell the driver that it was okay; she'd wait for the next car.

But that wasn't an option. On a night like this, she'd be stupid ... no, *crazy*—to pass up the offer.

"Yeah." She nodded. "Yeah, I really do need help."

# 2

## FORT LAUDERDALE

Saturday night, downtown Fort Lauderdale. It felt like I was a long way from the beach. Although the sun had gone down hours before, the bar felt noticeably cool in comparison to the outside. Too cool for my liking. Like stepping into a walk-in refrigerator. I paused by the door to survey the room, scanning for the important information.

It had a low ceiling and walls that had been painted black a decade or two ago. A relatively large floor space, sparsely attended for a Saturday night. Maybe a couple dozen customers. On the far side, the bar ran almost the length of the room, tapering off in a curve before it reached a corridor signposted for the restrooms and the fire exit. Circular tables adorned with candlesticks inserted into empty liquor bottles. I descended two steps from the entrance and started to cross the floor, scanning faces as though looking for a friend. Most of the clientele were arranged into couples and small groups, except for a lone blonde at one of the corner tables who'd looked up and then away again as I'd entered the bar. I didn't linger any longer on her face than on any of the others. Aside from her, the crowd was made up of an unremarkable mix of professional barflies and lost tourists.

The only alarm bell chimed when my eyes alighted on the dark-haired man sitting down by the jukebox. His eyes met mine, sized me up as I walked past, then moved away in disinterest. He had a broken nose and big hands. A fighter, though not necessarily a good one. He wore a leather jacket. All in all, a good match for the two very similar-looking gentlemen I'd seen loitering across the street outside. Interesting, though nothing to do with me. I filed it away for future reference and took a seat at the bar on the corner, adjacent to the fire exit hallway.

The position gave me the best view of the room. I let my eyes sweep over the faces once again and nodded as the bartender made his approach. I resisted the impulse to order a cold beer, opting instead for a soda water with a twist of lime. Nonalcoholic, but it looks enough like a real drink to avoid unwanted attention.

I sipped the soda water and tried to ignore the Europop blasting from the speakers five feet from my left ear: the single downside of my strategic position. I moved my head from left to right again, refreshing my picture of the room. The guy at the jukebox hadn't moved. My eyes moved to the northwest corner of the bar, where the blonde was sitting. Only she wasn't sitting now. She was up and walking diagonally across the floor to where I was perched.

As she got closer, I confirmed that her curly shoulder-length hair was convincingly—and therefore expensively—dyed. She wore blue jeans and a black blouse that showed some midriff and leather boots with three-inch heels. There was a small leather bag hanging from her right shoulder by a strap.

I averted my eyes and looked toward the door, as though expecting someone to join me any minute. The blonde stopped when she got to the bar and put her forearms down on it. She was at the stool next to mine, even though that meant she'd had to walk five paces out of her way to get there. Which meant she'd deliberately wanted to end up beside me. Which meant a change of plan.

She stared straight ahead as she ordered a shot of Stoli, but then turned to me and smiled.

"Hey."

I smiled in acknowledgment and tried to read her expression. Did she know why I was there? I supposed it wasn't outside the bounds of possibility that she'd realize someone would be looking for her, that she'd be on the lookout for a certain type. But that's the thing: I work hard at not being any particular type.

"I like this song," she said after a minute, then looked me up and down with a coy smile. "What's your name?"

I decided I had nothing to worry about. She didn't know who I was. She was just a party girl in a bar, acting interested in the lonesome stranger who just walked in. Emphasis on *acting*.

"My name's Blake."

"Cool." She nodded, as though a name meant anything at all. "I'm Emma. Are you here with somebody?"

She was overselling it like a life insurance cold caller ten minutes from the end of a bad shift. Nobody who looked like she did would have to try to pick up a guy in a bar. Nobody who looked like that would even have to approach the guy. So what was the play? I set my mind to work on the quandary; the mental exercise wasn't unwelcome. I decided to see where this was going.

"You tell me."

She smiled and put a hand on my left arm, just below the shoulder. I felt her squeeze a little through my shirt, as though testing it, and then I understood what she wanted me for.

She dropped her hand as the bartender returned, tossing a napkin on the bar and placing her shot glass on top of it. He glanced at my still half-full glass and I shook my head.

"And what do you do, Blake?"

I considered my answer and decided there was no reason to lie. "I'm sort of a consultant."

Her eyes narrowed. "What kind of consultant?"

"The usual kind," I said. "People pay me to solve problems they can't solve by themselves."

She laughed as though I'd cracked the joke of the century and slammed the shot in one. "You solve *problems*. Outstanding."

"I aim to please."

"And what would you say is the most important skill that goes into being a consultant?"

"Why? Do you want to become one?"

"Maybe."

"Then I guess I would have to say improvisation."

"Good." She leaned in close and whispered, the vodka fumes strong on her breath, "Do you want to get out of here?"

I glanced at the door, then back to her. "Right now?"

She nodded, and her tone changed to conspiratorial. "Listen. There are a couple of guys outside waiting for me . . ."

"Guys you'd prefer to avoid?"

"That's right."

"Two guys."

"That's what I said, isn't it?"

"Just making sure."

She laughed uneasily, as though I'd gotten the wrong idea. "I mean, there won't be any trouble or anything like that, not if you walk me to my car."

I saw the sudden fear in her eyes, the flash of concern that she'd put me off. That meant there was going to be trouble, all right. Probably a lot more trouble than she realized.

I sat back on my stool and took a drink of the soda, as though carefully considering the proposition. The bartender was dealing with customers at the other end of the bar. That was good.

"Where's your car?" I asked.

"Right outside. It's a red coupe."

*That* was true. I'd seen the little red Audi A5 coupe parked by the sidewalk twenty yards from the front door.

I leaned in close again, keeping my voice low. That was mostly for her benefit; nobody could hear me over the music even if I'd been yelling at the top of my voice.

"Okay, you're going to pretend that I've insulted you. You're going to get up and act like you're headed to the ladies' room. There's a fire exit along the corridor behind me. Use it and wait for me."

She looked taken aback for a moment, probably because she wasn't expecting her compliant muscle to start calling the shots. She got over it quickly, signaling acceptance with a brief, crooked smile that was the first genuine thing she'd offered since she'd started talking to me.

She pushed off her stool violently and stood up, rolling her eyes in disdain as she walked away. I was happy she hadn't overdone it by slapping me or maybe yelling. She was much better at acting pissed off than she was at feigning romantic interest.

I watched her go and waited for a few seconds. As I'd expected, the guy in the leather jacket got up from his seat and made a beeline for the corridor. He could read as well as I could. He knew there was a back exit. That's why he was in the bar while his friends waited out front. He glanced at me as he passed. I pretended not to notice.

I got up and followed behind him as he quickened his pace. The restroom doors were on the left-hand side, and the corridor vanished around a corner to the right, another sign for the fire exit pointing the way.

"Excuse me," I said.

He started to turn around, and I put all of my weight into

a short, rapid punch to the bridge of his nose. He screamed in pain and lunged forward, and I grabbed his head and smashed it down on my knee. He crashed down on the beer-stained carpet, unconscious. I glanced behind me to confirm the yell of pain had been masked by the music and crouched on one knee, patting him down. I found his gun in the inside pocket of his jacket. It was a Heckler & Koch HK45. Close to military spec—definitely trouble. I relieved him of it and tucked it into the back of my belt.

I moved quickly down the remainder of the corridor and found the blonde standing by the open fire exit. Her real name wasn't Emma, of course. Her real name was Caroline Elizabeth Church. She was twenty-four years old. Her Massachusetts driver's license listed her as five eleven, brown hair, brown eyes. Two out of three matched up with the person in front of me.

"My car's around the front," she said, oblivious to the altercation in the corridor.

"Forget it," I said.

I took her upper arm and pulled her through the fire exit and into a narrow, dingy alley. Dumpsters lined the wall, trash overflowing from some and strewn across the pitted concrete. The alley terminated in a dead end twenty feet to my right. Fifty feet to my left it opened onto the road that led off the main street out front. The buildings on either side were one- and two-story affairs: the blank rear walls of bars and diners and anonymous office buildings. If we were fast, we could come out on the street, circle the block, and get into my rented Honda without the two guys staking out the bar noticing. Assuming they hadn't moved from their earlier position, of course.

I started fast-walking toward the street, trusting that Caroline would follow. She didn't disappoint.

She trotted on her heels until she was abreast of me. "What the hell do you mean forget it?"

The mouth of the alley was still clear. I scanned the low rooftops on both sides. "The two guys out front—who are they?"

"Slow down!"

I stopped and faced her. "Who are they?"

She looked away. "Nobody. Just an ex-boyfriend. He turned kind of creepy. Won't leave me alone."

"Just an ex?" I asked, turning to walk again.

Caroline caught up again, surprisingly quick despite her heels. "Yeah. Why?" Curiosity in her voice. She knew I knew she was withholding information and was more interested in how I knew than in keeping her secrets.

"Because standard creepy exes park outside your house and post nasty messages on your Facebook page. If they're really brave, they might even try to get physical. They don't generally bring armed flunkies with them. Not unless they happen to have a couple lying around already."

"Who's an armed flunky?"

I took the gun out and held it in front of her in my palm. Her eyes widened. "I just took this from the third guy in the bar. The one you didn't know about. It's an HK45 Compact Tactical pistol. Costs about twelve hundred bucks. It's not an entry-level model. Who's the boyfriend?"

"Oh shit. He *said* he was gonna kill me, but ..."

We reached the mouth of the alley. I motioned for Caroline to keep back and kept the pistol low, finger on the trigger. I glanced around the corner and found myself looking down the barrel of another gun.

Which meant another change of plan.

# 3

Caroline's ex-boyfriend was the taller one of the two men I'd seen outside earlier. He looked in his mid-to-late forties, but in good shape, with jet-black hair and angular, handsome features. The combination of designer leather jacket, expensive hardware, and the dead, disinterested look in his gray eyes told me everything I needed to know.

He waved us back into the alley, off the street, and told me to drop the gun. I did as I was told. I watched his eyes and saw there was more going on than was first apparent: calculation, deliberation. That was good. It meant I wasn't dealing with an outright psycho. I slowly raised my hands, taking a second to glance down the street and confirm that he was on his own. I guessed the other one was still covering the front.

"What's this, Lizzie?" he asked, shooting a glance at the girl with the ever-expanding list of aliases. "New man already?" He spoke with the barest trace of an accent. If I'd had to guess, I'd say Serbian. Factor in his age and willingness to point guns at people, and it seemed like a reasonable bet he was a Kosovo veteran. The voice reinforced my impression of a calm, deliberate man. It also told me that he hadn't chased Caroline down purely on account of her feminine wiles.

"He's nobody, Zoran," she said. "Let him go."

He didn't look at her, kept staring at me, and I was pleased to see a hint of consternation on his face. We both had a problem: I was the one with a gun pointed in my face, but he was the one who had to decide what to do about it. An irrational man would shoot me and leave me to bleed on the sidewalk. If my estimation of this man was right, he wouldn't want to invite the potential consequences of that action, not without good reason at least.

Zoran hadn't taken his eyes from me the whole time. That was smart, because he hadn't given me the split second I'd need to take the gun from him. It also meant he hadn't been able to look down, to examine the gun I'd been carrying and perhaps identify it as the one belonging to his man in the bar. That left open the possibility that he might underestimate me.

Out of the corner of my eye, I could see Caroline tensing, as though weighing whether she could make a run for it. I hoped she wouldn't. It would likely be a bad decision for both of us, and particularly for me. No one said anything for a moment. I heard the low rumble of a northbound train on the Tri-Rail line a few blocks over.

"What do you want?" I asked the man with dark hair, fixing my eyes on his so he would know that this was not a rhetorical question. We were just two guys calmly discussing how best to resolve a mutual problem.

Zoran nodded at Caroline Church, still not taking his eyes off me. "I woke up two days ago and she was gone. So was fifteen grand cash from my apartment."

"Okay," I said. Then, without turning to Caroline, I addressed her. "Give him your car keys."

"What?"

"I don't give a shit about the car, friend," Zoran said softly. "I just want my money."

From the tone of his voice, I guessed he was lying and it wasn't really about the money. Or at least, not primarily. It was about the principle—a man in his position could not be seen to be ripped off in this way.

I nodded in Caroline's direction. "She spent last night in a hotel on North Andrews Avenue, checked out this morning.

If she still has your money, it's in the red Audi coupe around the front."

Caroline started to say, "How the hell do you—" then shut up.

And then she ran.

Zoran made a split-second calculation. The choice was staying with me or chasing Caroline. If he stayed with me, his money and his opportunity for redress would disappear once again. If he chased Caroline, he'd be leaving me with the gun I'd dropped. He made the smart move, the most ruthless move. But not quite fast enough.

As he pulled the trigger, I was already diving for the pistol.

A .45-caliber slug carved itself into the wall behind where my head had been a moment before. As I hit the ground, I swept the heel of my shoe hard into the back of Zoran's knee as I simultaneously picked up the gun I'd dropped. His knee buckled, and he fell as my fingers closed around the weapon. He fumbled his grip a little, recovered quickly, and started to bring his gun back toward my face. I smashed his wrist with my left fist as the gun discharged, the loud bang echoing and reverberating from the walls of the alley. Before he could take another shot, I had the muzzle of the H&K pressed into his forehead, equidistant between his eyes. His eyes brightened for a moment in surprise and then narrowed.

"Don't be an idiot," I said.

Mere seconds had elapsed since the sound of the gunshot, but I was keenly conscious of two sounds that marked the passage of time: Caroline Church's footsteps fading into the night and the sound of voices from the opposite direction. Now I was the one with the dilemma. Only that wasn't quite true. Zoran was the one who was going to dictate what happened: whether he lived or died.

His grip relaxed and the gun dropped from his right hand,

smacking on the pitted concrete. A rational man. I gave him an apologetic shrug and slammed the butt of the pistol into his right temple. Nonfatal, but enough to give me time to make a graceful exit. He'd thank me in the morning, once the concussion wore off.

I picked up Zoran's gun as he dropped to the sidewalk; then I glanced out at the street. Caroline had vanished. If she was smart, she'd forget about the car and the fifteen grand and vanish into the night. But then, her actions so far hadn't exactly been characterized by an overabundance of good sense.

The shouts from the street were getting closer, and I remembered the third guy, less than a block away, who would certainly have heard the gunshots. And he'd be the only person within earshot who wasn't using his cell phone to call the cops at that moment.

I pocketed the two H&Ks and moved quickly to the nearest Dumpster, pushing it all the way back to brace it against the stucco wall. Then I pulled myself up on top of it, caught my balance, and jumped vertically. I caught the edge of the roof with both hands and pulled myself up and over the parapet, rolling to my feet. From below, I heard a scream and loud voices. I crouched down and risked a glance over the edge to the alley below. Three people at the mouth of the alley, and one of them was Zoran's guy—the third man I'd seen outside the bar earlier. The other two were a middle-aged couple, tourists from the look of their clothes. The woman was doing the screaming.

"Oh my God, is he dead?"

The husband was crouched beside Zoran, checking for a pulse. The third guy was looking up and down the street frantically, his right hand jammed deep in the pocket of his coat. I ducked down and crawled back before he looked in the right place. I rose to my feet when I'd gotten far enough from the edge and started running back toward the line of units that housed the bar. The soles of my shoes were virtually soundless on the soft asphalt roofing, weathered by ten thousand sunny days. The roof was a long, flat rectangle, patched haphazardly and spotted with air-conditioning vents. It extended for a couple of hundred yards to the point where it intersected the line of units along the main road, of which the bar was one. Beyond the edge of that block, I could see the upper thirds of the palm trees that lined the road.

I picked up speed as I headed for the end of the roof, calling up a mental picture of the street outside the bar as I ran. I estimated that Caroline's coupe was parked at around the position of the tallest palm tree in my line of sight. She had a good head start, but I was taking the most direct route.

I covered the distance in seconds, grateful for the explosion of energy after the days spent on planes and in cars and sitting down in bars. I heard the peal of a police siren from somewhere behind me as I reached the edge of the roof and peered over the edge. My estimate had been dead-on. The red car was parked directly below me, and Caroline Church hadn't reached it yet.

She was approaching fast, though. Running barefoot and carrying her boots in her left hand as she dug the keys out of her bag. I turned and looked the opposite way down the street, expecting the third man to appear at the corner at any moment. Small knots of people were beginning to wander up the side street, drawn to the commotion a little farther up like iron filings to a magnet. No sign of the third guy, though. Not yet.

Caroline Church reached the car and fumbled with the key fob, finally finding the right button that made the lights flash and the locks disengage with a *clunk*. I took two steps back to give myself room and then launched myself off the roof, coming down on the car's roof and then sliding off to the sidewalk, between Caroline and the car.

"I'll drive."

She caught her breath, looked back up the street the way she'd come, and back to me. She looked irritated. "Who in the hell are you, mister? And how do you—"

"Hey!"

The yell from the other direction snapped my head around. Coming toward us at a run, right hand buried deep inside the jacket pocket, the third man. Obviously, he'd seen what had happened to his boss and had made sure to remove himself from the immediate vicinity before the police showed up.

I swung the door open and plucked the keys from Caroline's hand as I got inside. I put the keys in the ignition as Caroline got in the passenger seat and slammed the door. The engine purred to life as our pursuer reached us, getting close enough to slap the dented roof before I peeled away from the curb.

I reached across and pushed Caroline's shoulders down, hunching down myself and snatching glances in the rearview as I accelerated away. The guy was still on the sidewalk where we'd left him. He had not taken the gun out of his jacket. As we hung a left on the first corner, I guessed he didn't want to push his luck on what had already been a pretty bad night for his team.

I resisted the impulse to floor the gas pedal, even though the streets were quiet. It would take guy number three a couple of minutes to reach his car, if he even had one. By taking a few random turns, I could make sure the trail was nice and frosty by then. The last thing I wanted to do was draw attention to a car leaving the scene of a shooting. I navigated down a series of side roads before finding the South Federal Highway. When we'd put a mile or so between ourselves and the bar, I slowed down and started paying attention to the signs.

"Okay, who the hell are you? Really?"

"I told you."

"Bullshit. You're no consultant. And why have you been following me? Are you some kind of stalker? Is this how you get a thrill?"

I saw a sign for the A1A. Fort Lauderdale was brand-new territory for me, but I remembered from the day before that that route would take me where I wanted to go.

"You're welcome," I said. "You have a high opinion of yourself, don't you, Caroline?"

"You know my name? Of course you know my name." She frowned. "My dad sent you, right? What did he do? Pay you to kidnap me?"

I turned west onto the A1A and kept my eyes on the exit signs. Palm trees lined the route on both sides. Though I couldn't see it, I knew the Atlantic was dead ahead, beneath a dirty orange night sky.

"I don't kidnap people. Your father hired me to find you and to give him my assurance that you're safe. I'm not sure I can fulfill the second part. How about you?"

She said nothing, bit her lip petulantly.

"I'm betting that right now, going back to Boston and your generous allowance seems a little more attractive than it did. Seriously, you ripped off a Florida gangster for fifteen grand?"

"My dad stopped my allowance. A girl's gotta eat."

I saw the exit I wanted and came off the highway onto Sebastian Street.

"You gave a fake name in the hotel last night. The guy

who sold you the car didn't ask to see any ID. That's good. Did you tell anybody down here your real name?"

She said nothing for a moment, then grudgingly shook her head.

"That's good," I said. "If you're going to lie, be consistent. Okay, I'll get rid of the car and the guns. Like I said, I can't tell you what to do, but if you have more than two brain cells to rub together, you'll be on the first plane back to Boston with your father."

"My father's *here*?" She sounded horrified.

I saw the building I wanted and pulled the car to a stop at the curb, twenty feet from the front door of the Sunnyside Beach Resort. I took my cell phone from my pocket and dialed a number from recent calls. It was answered on the first ring.

"Blake—any news?"

"Mr. Church, I'm outside your hotel with your daughter." I glanced at her as I said this, half expecting her to make another break for it. Running was what she seemed to do best. But she didn't make a move, just rolled her eyes as she resigned herself to the lesser of two irritants.

"Thank God. Is she all right?"

"She's in one piece."

"Thank God. Thank *you*, Blake. You're worth the fee. You say you're downstairs right now?"

"That's right. If you want to come down, I'm sure the two of you can work something out."

"I'll be down right away."

I looked back at Caroline Church. I'd known her for all of twenty-five minutes, but already she'd cost me a year's worth of hassle.

"Make it quick."

# SUNDAY

# 4

## LOS ANGELES

The man in the baseball cap drove on through the night.

The rain had abated an hour before, leaving streets that shone with surface water. The man drove with caution, but not overcaution, aware that he didn't need to run red lights or exceed the speed limit in order to draw attention to a vehicle like this. All being well, there would be no trouble, though, because fortune favors the prepared mind. The spare had replaced the shredded rear tire, and he'd taken the time to confirm that there was no visible damage to the bodywork and that all of the exterior lights were operational.

There was still a quarter of a tank left, which was more than enough to get him where he wanted to go, with enough left over for the car's onward trip.

The clock on the dash read a few minutes to five, which meant he still had almost an hour until daybreak. As he neared his destination, he was careful not to let up his guard, keeping a watchful eye on the occasional cars that appeared ahead of him and in the rearview mirror.

People who do not live in Los Angeles like to complain that it all looks identical: an endless sprawl of street after street after street, all looking much the same. Not true. Just tonight, he'd driven past gated communities and through peaceful suburban picket-fence neighborhoods. He'd encountered

33

architectural marvels and the gray utilitarian concrete of 1960s apartment buildings. And now the geography changed once more. Overgrown yards, broken fences, gang graffiti. Apartment blocks enclosed by steel fences—gated communities of a different kind. Ageing duplexes with the street numbers spray-painted on the front. Here and there, the man saw properties that were better maintained, that had neat lawns and freshly painted doors. He knew most people would wonder why they bothered, but he understood. The simple pleasure of taking pride in yourself and your work while everything else went to hell.

The specific character of the neighborhood was a momentary distraction, and his eyes remained firmly on the road. If he was to be stopped by a traffic cop anywhere on the journey, it would most likely be here. The silver Porsche stuck out like a Michelangelo sculpture in a landfill. But that was exactly why he'd brought it here. It was how he'd be able to make the car disappear for a while.

He saw a short line of retail units—a couple of easy credit places, a vacant unit, and a liquor store. Two Hispanic men in their twenties were facing each other on the sidewalk. They looked drunk and were engaged in what was either a spirited debate or the beginnings of a fistfight. The bigger one wore a sleeveless shirt and his arms were coated with tattoos.

The man in the baseball cap pulled the Porsche over and put the brake on. He took a last look around the interior. The leather seats were spotless, nothing in the footwells, nothing in the glove compartment.

Leaving the keys in the ignition and the engine still running, he opened the door and got out. The two men had noticed him now, the incongruity of the Porsche and its driver distracting them from their disagreement.

34

"Hey, man," the one with the tattoos said. "Nice car." He said it as though he was weighing up whether or not he wanted the statement to be a threat.

The man in the baseball cap made no acknowledgment, other than to tug the brim a little further down over his face. As he walked past the two men, the tattooed one moved to intercept, grabbing his arm.

"I'm talking to you, man."

The man in the baseball cap stopped, looked down at the fingers curled around his forearm, and then raised his head again so that his eyes met those of the tattooed man. The guy blinked and his fingers snapped open as though spring-loaded.

He kept staring at him, unblinking.

The tattooed guy looked at the Porsche, with its engine running, and then his eyes moved all around, as if to say, *Look at this place.* "You're just going to leave that? Here? Are you nuts?"

"Luis, what the fuck, man?" the older one said, keeping his distance from the pair.

The man turned away from the two drunks and started to walk again, his strides carrying him along at a steady four miles an hour. He had taken less than two dozen paces before he heard the door of the Porsche slam shut and the idling engine roar to life again. He kept walking as he heard the tires peel away on the damp surface, turning and heading in the opposite direction. He kept walking as the sound of the powerful flat-6 engine built and then faded and then vanished into thin air.

The man in the baseball cap walked ten blocks north as the sky began to reveal the first hints of light on the horizon. Another mile or so and he would catch a bus and sit anonymously among the luckless Sunday-morning shift workers.

He'd alight a mile or so from the house and make the rest of the trip on foot.

And then? A shower, perhaps something to eat, and then sleep. It would be good to get some rest. It had been another busy night.

# 5

## LOS ANGELES

A Sunday-morning homicide and a hangover: never a good combination, Detective Jessica Allen thought. How did the Johnny Cash song go? Something about there not being a way to hold your head that didn't hurt.

Going to Denny's friend's birthday party had been a bad idea, but drinking as much as she had had been a much worse idea. This wasn't like her, but she realized it had happened a couple of times recently. It would be easy to blame the job, and she knew plenty who did just that, but she knew that wasn't it. She was drinking a little more because spending sober time with her boyfriend was beginning to feel like a drag. Probably not a good sign. She resolved to make some changes—easy to do with the headache as an incentive.

God, it was a bad one. Her head was throbbing so painfully that, perversely, catching a body dump out in the Santa Monica Mountains qualified as a break. It meant fresh air and a cool breeze instead of staring at a computer monitor for the next few hours.

Or at least, it would mean that, as soon as they got out of the damn car.

The sun had almost finished burning off the morning mist, and it was already clear and warm. Allen was pretending to look out the window as they drove north through relatively light—for LA—traffic on the 405. What she was actually doing was resting her eyes behind her sunglasses. She started to feel the welcoming pull of sleep and reluctantly fought against it, turning her head to look at her partner in the driver's seat.

Jonathan Mazzucco was a little older than she was; probably in his early forties, though she'd never gotten around to asking. He looked good, as he always did. Better than the father of a three-month-old had any right to, give or take some dark shadows under his eyes. Never a crease on his suit, never the hint of stubble on his unblemished face. His hair never seemed to get longer or shorter. It just stayed in its no-nonsense crew cut. Allen liked to joke about it; she'd ask him how the commute was from the fifties, but he never seemed to mind, or feel the need to respond in kind.

Mazzucco was smiling behind his own sunglasses. Either in amusement at Allen's fragile condition, or simply because he was enjoying being allowed to drive without his partner putting up a fight, for once.

"You take some aspirin?" he asked, without looking back at her.

Allen nodded. "Four."

"I don't think you're supposed to take four at a time."

"Trust me, I needed four. How much farther?"

They'd left the freeway and the city proper behind them now and were winding their way north up Mandeville Canyon Road. Mazzucco made a mental calculation. "Ten minutes. Can you hang on?"

"I'm fine."

"You look fine."

"Fuck you."

Mazzucco laughed.

Allen turned back to the window so that he wouldn't see her smiling too. She liked Mazzucco. He was one of the few she did like after six long months. Six months, and DC to LA was proving to be a more difficult transition than that simple exchange of initials would suggest. It wasn't that the other guys in Robbery Homicide were unpleasant, exactly. Joe Coleman aside, most of them were fine. But it was almost as though there were some kind of invisible force field that kept her separate from the rest of them.

Or perhaps it was more like a firewall, something that allowed the other detectives to interact with her and work with her but without letting anything extraneous through. At first this hadn't surprised her—it was the standard team response to a new recruit. It was even more to be expected with cops, who were more suspicious than average by profession. But as the weeks became months, she began to wonder if the frostiness was exacerbated by the fact that she'd arrived in the department with more baggage than most. There were times when she'd wanted to ask Mazzucco about it, about whether or not the other guys actively disliked her. And each time she'd realized how pathetically high school that sounded and dismissed the idea.

The road took an unexpected dip and shunted office politics to the back of Allen's mind once more. The wave of nausea rose and retreated, leaving an unpleasant thought in her mind like driftwood on a beach.

"This isn't a decomp, is it?"

"Nope. Day or two at the most, they said. And if it's one day, we might even have an idea of who it is."

"Yeah?"

Mazzucco nodded. "Sarah Dutton. Reported missing last night; lives up on Mulholland."

"How long was she gone before they reported her?"

"Since last night."

"So why do we know about it already?" Allen was curious. Contrary to popular belief, there was no official waiting period of twenty-four hours before you could report somebody missing, but that was generally still how it worked in practice.

"I guess Dad made sure it was on the fast track."

"Ah," Allen said. "She lives on Mulholland. So who's the father? Movie producer or something?"

"I don't think he's in the business," Mazzucco said. "Although I heard he lives in Marlon Brando's old house."

"That's novel. I was beginning to think there was nobody in this town who wasn't either a cop or an out-of-work actor."

Mazzucco grinned. "And how is the new boyfriend? Dave, is it?"

"Denny." She sighed. "I'm sure he's fine."

"Ohhh-kay." Mazzucco's eyebrows rose behind his sunglasses.

"No, really. Denny's great."

"But ..."

"But I think he'd prefer it if I were an out-of-work actor rather than a cop, you know?"

"Allen, there are some days I'd prefer to be an out-of-work actor rather than a cop. A lot of days."

Allen smiled and tucked a stray lock of blond hair behind her ear. The headache was way too intense to wear it in her usual ponytail. "How's Julia?" she asked after a minute. She asked only out of politeness, because he'd made the effort to ask about Denny. From the way Mazzucco's wife had sized her up the one time they'd met, she was pretty sure they weren't ever going to be getting together on a social basis.

"She's great," Mazzucco said quickly, unconsciously mirroring her lukewarm endorsement of Denny. Allen could always tell when Mazzucco and his wife had been fighting the day before. He was always a little quieter, less chatty. She guessed a cop's marriage was stressful enough—throw a new baby into the mix and it wasn't surprising things were a little tense. All of a sudden, Allen was grateful that most of her off-duty problems could be solved with aspirin.

Mazzucco slowed and took the turnoff for the fire road. The surface was rough and pitted for the initial stretch. A minute later, they saw a uniformed cop standing in front of the open gate at the point where the road turned into a narrow dirt track. He waved them down. The narrow-eyed stare told Allen that he was reasonably convinced of who they were by the make and model of their car but wasn't taking any chances. He approached the driver's window, which was already rolled down, and Mazzucco badged him.

"Detective Mazzucco, Detective Allen, RHD."

The uniform nodded and told them his name was McComb, out of West LA Division, and waved them through.

Mazzucco slowed to ten miles an hour or so as they passed through the gateway and onto the dirt track.

The scene was another half mile along the fire road. Two more marked cars and a coroner's van were jammed at the edge of the track in single file. The hill rose up from the road at a shallow gradient, and the focus of activity was about fifty yards up the slope. Mazzucco parked on the dirt shoulder and they got out and started the ascent. The earth was still damp from the rains the previous night as they picked their way up through the rocks and brush.

Allen breathed in and out through her nose, grateful to be

out of the car at last. She decided the pulsing headache was at least as much to do with caffeine withdrawal as it was to do with the hangover, and she regretted not having had time to get a strong black coffee before leaving headquarters.

There were four more uniforms up here, arranged around a nude female body. She was about five six, slim, had dark brown hair, and was facedown and smeared from head to toe with dirt. The coroner investigator was on his knees by the body, scraping dirt from the victim's fingernails into a plastic evidence bag. There was a small tattoo of a butterfly or a fairy or something in black ink at the base of her spine. Allen showed her ID this time and introduced herself and her partner. Then she opened her notebook and started jotting down the specifics of the scene for the report as the older of the four cops gave them the basics.

"Caucasian female, late teens to early twenties. No identification, obviously."

"What about that?" Mazzucco said, pointing to the ink.

The cop snorted. "Yeah. That'll narrow it down."

"Preliminary cause of death?" Allen asked, addressing the coroner investigator this time.

He didn't look up. "Slit throat, multiple stab wounds, partial strangulation. Some shallow lacerations to the face and upper body, too."

"She was tortured," Mazzucco said.

"For sure."

"Sexual assault?" Allen inquired.

"We'll do a rape kit at the morgue. Until then there's no way to be sure. No preliminary physical evidence, though."

"Okay," Allen said. "Can you turn her over?"

The coroner investigator waved at one of the uniforms for an assist. The two of them moved the body from its front onto its back, performing the maneuver with respect and

41

care, as though moving a living person who was merely unconscious.

The body was smeared with dirt on the front, too. There were puncture wounds and cuts all over her abdomen, many of them plugged with dirt. A pair of perfectly symmetrical diagonal cuts crossed her cheeks, as though tracing the paths of tears. The eyes were open, staring sightlessly up at the cohort of intruders. Allen thought they were gray, or a washed-out blue. Either way, they matched the drained colorlessness of the rest of her. The throat was cut deeply, from ear to ear. With one stroke, by the looks of it. No way was this a first timer. And yet the cut had strangely ragged edges to it, unlike the marks on the face and body. Allen had seen cut throats before, more than she cared to remember, but this one looked different somehow.

Mazzucco gestured at the dirt streaking the body. "Was she buried when she was found? Partially buried, maybe?"

The uniform who'd helped to turn the body pointed up the hill to where there was a fluorescent marker staked in the earth. From that point to this, they could see evidence of slippage, of overturned earth.

"The grave was up there," he said. "You can go have a look if you like. All of the rain caused a pretty good land-slide. You see that shit last night? Insane."

"Insane," Allen repeated, eyes still on the ragged gash in the girl's throat, which was somehow less out of the ordinary in this town than inclement weather.

"It was actually a good grave," he continued, in the tone of a connoisseur of such things. "Half of the goddamn hillside came down last night; otherwise she would have been one of the ones we don't find."

Mazzucco was nodding. The Santa Monica Mountains probably played host to more unofficial burial plots than

42

anywhere else in the United States. With the exception of the desert outside of Vegas, of course.

Allen, who'd been crouched down, examining the dirt-filled wounds in the body, stood up and looked around, headache forgotten for the moment.

"This isn't the primary crime scene, is it?"

The coroner investigator was already shaking his head in sympathy. Body dumps, particularly in an environment like this, were the toughest cases to clear. They left no crime scene and no trail. "Again, difficult to be sure. But no. I think it's the disposal site only."

Allen nodded. "Because it's a good dump site. Easy to reach, but a couple miles from the nearest homes. A closed gate, but no real security. Good visibility in both directions, lots of notice if anyone does decide to drive past. Let's get some more people out here to keep digging."

"You think there's more?" Mazzucco said. "More from this guy, I mean."

Allen was looking at the ragged gash in the victim's throat again.

"I guarantee it."

# 6

Allen swigged from a bottle of tepid water as she sat on the hood of the gray department-issue Ford Taurus and watched them digging on the hillside. They'd been out here almost three hours now, and it was a little after noon. She was thinking about details. About how funny it was how you could still remember so many details about something you'd

43

seen years ago, assuming that something left enough of an impact on you.

"Something on your mind?"

She started at the voice. Mazzucco was behind her, his jacket removed, arms folded on top of the roof of the car.

She screwed the lid back on the bottle and swallowed the last gulp. "What do you mean?"

"You think they're going to find more bodies up there? Courtesy of this guy?"

"Yeah, I do. Don't you?"

"Why?"

"Why do you think? It's an optimum dump site, and that wasn't the work of a first timer. A rookie could see that, Jon."

It was true. Everything they'd seen so far pointed to the body being the latest victim in a series, not a one-off killing. The torture wounds showed patience, deliberation, confidence. Restraint, even, if that wasn't an oxymoron. He'd been careful to keep the girl alive for a while. The killing stroke had been delivered with experience and with absolute resolve in one attempt. More than one person had commented on the professionalism of the grave. Luck was the only reason this body had been discovered. Add it all up and everything pointed to this being the work of an experienced killer.

But it wasn't the whole truth. The whole truth required more consideration before she let anyone in on it, even the man she trusted most in the department. All she knew was that there would be more.

"You're right," Mazzucco admitted. "I'd have told them to keep digging myself. I don't think they'd have needed to be told, to be honest. But the way you said it, the way you were staring at the body ... It wasn't just an educated guess. It was like you *know*."

Allen smiled and shook her head, feeling guilty as she did so. "Headache's making me pessimistic. Maybe they won't find anything."

"Maybe," he repeated, looking unconvinced.

Allen, uncomfortable with the expression on Mazzucco's face, turned away to gaze back up at the hill. The body was still in place, covered with a sheet. Soon it would be transported to the Los Angeles Coroner's Office for postmortem.

"The missing girl," Allen said. "Sarah Dutton, wasn't it?"

"Sarah Dutton."

"You think it's her?"

"I haven't seen a picture, but she fits: slim, white, brunette, twenty-two years old."

"Mulholland's close by," Allen said, drawing on her limited knowledge of LA geography. She pointed roughly north: "It's over there, right?"

Mazzucco smiled as though she was doing okay for a fresh transplant. "Sure, but we have to go around the long way. Mandeville dead-ends just before you get to Mulholland."

"Okay. Let's go talk to the father."

# 7

## FORT LAUDERDALE

If I'm looking for you, it could be for any one of a hundred reasons.

Perhaps you've done something you shouldn't have, or are planning to. Perhaps you took something that didn't belong to you. Perhaps you haven't done anything wrong,

45

but someone would like to know you're okay. The one constant is that I find the subject—the subject doesn't find me.

The job Conrad Church had asked me to do had been a straightforward proposition at the outset. Almost too straightforward for me to take an interest, in fact. The problems of rich guys and their spoiled, wayward rich kids aren't usually my area of expertise. I'm at my best when I'm playing for higher stakes than that.

However, not having anything else going on, I agreed to take the job when it was offered to me. As happens from time to time, a straightforward assignment had turned complicated. Church had been looking for a professional to find his daughter. Caroline was the wayward type but had never disappeared as effectively or for as long as she had this time, and he was starting to worry that something had happened to her. I met with Church and decided that he was on the level: he just wanted to make sure his kid was alive and safe. I gave him the usual terms: no interference, no questions, half up front, half on completion. He'd agreed readily and I'd gotten to work, appreciating the novelty of looking for someone who wasn't likely to be armed and dangerous.

It was early spring and still cold in Massachusetts, which to my instincts made it more than likely she'd gone south. It hadn't taken me long to identify a trail that confirmed that direction of travel, and as it turned out, she'd gone all the way south, to Florida. Church wanted to travel down with me. I reminded him of my terms but told him he was free to make his own arrangements, which he did.

I narrowed the location to Lauderdale and within twenty-four hours, I'd tracked her as far as the hotel and the guy who'd sold her the used Audi for two grand cash. Then it was a simple matter of cutting down the possibilities. It was a Saturday night, and there were only so many dive bars and only one of them had a red Audi parked nearby. Everything had gone smoothly, right up until the bar and the complication of Caroline's erstwhile boyfriend.

After reuniting her with her father, I had taken a walk down to a quiet section of the beach. There I'd wiped the two HK45s down and thrown them as far as I could out into the ocean, one after the other. I didn't worry too much about them washing up on the beach; they weren't mine, after all. Then I drove the Audi to a long-term parking lot serving the airport and parked as deep into the compound as I could get. I wiped down all the surfaces in the car and the touch surfaces on the exterior too, not forgetting the spot where Zoran's man had slapped the roof. I checked the trunk, the glove box, and beneath the seats, finding only a used lip gloss stick. Plus fifteen thousand dollars that I'd managed to forget all about. I removed both and locked the car, dropping the keys and the lip gloss in a trash can on my way out of the lot.

A shuttle bus took me back into town, and I got off a couple of blocks from my hotel. There were three charity thrift stores right by the bus stop. I split the cash into four wads by feel: three bundles of roughly four grand each, and a slightly smaller bundle making up the difference. I slipped a bundle of each through each store's mail slot and deposited the last one in the saxophone case of a late-night street musician. He didn't notice, or if he did, it didn't interrupt his interpretation of "Rhapsody in Blue."

Ten hours and a restless night later, I was walking into a nondescript diner on the opposite side of South Atlantic Boulevard from the beach. Most of the customers seemed to be sitting outside at tables beneath red and blue parasols. I passed them by and took a seat inside next to one of the picture windows. I ordered a cup of coffee and drank it as I stared out at the ocean. An Otis Redding song played through the diner's sound system. Not "Dock of the Bay," which would have been appropriate, but one of the lesser-known ones.

I'd received a text from Church to let me know that he and Caroline were safely aboard the eight-a.m. flight to Logan. As long as she dyed her hair back to brunette and didn't broadcast the details of her Florida adventure, I thought it was extremely unlikely they'd experience any trouble from Zoran.

It was funny: every time I let my mind wander, it drifted back to the look on his face as he realized I had the drop on him and that there was every likelihood he was about to die. A look of surprise. A look that said, *Wait a second. This isn't supposed to happen to me. There's been some terrible mistake.*

I wondered if that would be the look on my face when it was my turn. Everybody thinks they're invincible, until they're not.

Absently, I let my fingers play over the knot of scar tissue on the right-hand side of my stomach. A reminder of Wardell and Chicago, when my turn had very nearly come around.

The Otis Redding song finished and was replaced by Percy Sledge. Outside, on the street, a figure caught my attention. A heavyset, tanned man in his fifties. He was walking stiffly, as though in mild pain. He wore mirrored shades, a blue T-shirt that was a little too small for him, and knee-length shorts that were at least two decades too young for him. He carried a battered brown leather briefcase, just to complete the ensemble. I pretended to keep my eyes on the view, watching out of the corner of my eye as the man paused at the doorway and entered the diner.

A shadow fell across my face and I heard a familiar voice. "Getting sloppy, Blake. I snuck right up on you."

I kept my eyes on the view. "You're limping, Coop. Rheumatism?"

48

He laughed. "I sprained it playing racquetball. I approve of the location, by the way."

I looked up at last. "Easy commute for you," I agreed. "Or did you mean this place?"

"No, this place could be better. They don't serve liquor."

"It's eleven o'clock in the morning, Coop," I pointed out. He shrugged. I waved a hand at the chair across from me and he sat down.

"So you found the prodigal daughter. Everything go okay?"

"Nothing I couldn't handle."

"So I hear."

I smiled and said nothing. Nobody had died, and I didn't think Zoran and his guys would be filing a police report anytime soon. There had been nothing on the news about an incident involving firearms in a dicey neighborhood. I wondered if Coop had heard something from another source, or if he was just being Coop.

"So, this is an honor," Coop said, raising his bushy eyebrows. He was referring to how unusual it was for us to meet in person, the majority of our interactions being carried out over the phone or by secure email.

"It seemed silly not to meet up, since I was in the neighborhood."

"And it means you can buy me a drink to thank me for everything I do for you."

"They don't sell alcohol, remember? Besides, don't I thank you by paying you?"

"There is that."

"So what do you have for me?"

He smiled. "Same old Blake—straight down to business." He reached down and snapped the catches off the briefcase, withdrawing a thin plastic document wallet. "I got something."

"Black, white, or gray?" I asked. The question was standard. I like to know up front how legitimate a prospective job is, and that usually comes down to the character of the employer. A black or gray job isn't necessarily a barrier, but it's good to go in with eyes open.

He wavered a second. "Off-white."

"Off-white?" I repeated skeptically.

"It's a big company. They operate out of New Jersey. Denncorp. They make semiconductors or something."

"Who have they lost?"

"A senior accounts manager. They were cagey with the details. He jumped ship with some sensitive information, and they can't find him to have a discussion."

"So he knows they're doing something they shouldn't be, and they don't want him to tell anybody. What's their desired output?"

"Desired output? Jesus, you sound like one of them."

"Gotta match the terminology to the client, Coop."

"They want you to find him and bring him to them. Location to follow."

I shook my head. "They mean they want me to find him and bring him to a storage unit where they can have somebody beat him up. Or worse."

Coop shrugged. "It's a good offer ..."

"I don't work for bad guys, Coop."

"Bullshit," he said immediately.

"Okay," I agreed. "But I don't help bad guys do bad things. It's a rule."

"You got a lot of rules, Blake. Anyone ever tell you, you might be OCD?"

"Yeah. But only you."

He smiled as though he'd half expected me to turn this one down. He slid the document wallet back into the briefcase.

"Nothing else?" I asked.

"Nothing that would meet your stringent criteria, anyway."

"I probably don't want to know."

Coop didn't respond to that. He turned away from me and signaled the waitress, who strolled over and took his order. Iced tea.

"So what now?" he asked once she'd gone. "Some downtime, catch some Florida rays? You could use some sun, you know."

"I don't like to stick around too long after a job," I said. "But downtime sounds good. I'll stay tonight. Tomorrow I'll probably rent a car, head back home the slow way."

"And where's home?"

"Better you don't know."

Coop smiled again and turned his head to look out the window at the harbor and the calm expanse of the Atlantic. Another soul song kicked in on the diner's playlist: Sam Cooke's "Bring It on Home to Me." That song always reminds me of Carol, and I thought about our half-joking, inexpert waltz to that song, in a hotel room as the rain poured down outside. The night before the last time I ever saw her.

After a long moment, Coop spoke again. "It's funny, Blake, isn't it? How easy it is for two personable guys like you and me to maintain the illusion."

"What illusion's that?"

"The illusion that we actually know each other."

"I don't agree," I said after a second.

"You don't?"

I shook my head. "We don't know anything *about* each other. That's not the same thing. Where I live, where I came from . . . does any of that really matter? We know everything we need to know."

Coop looked back at me, a thoughtful, serious expression on his face. Eventually, he nodded in agreement. "I guess so." He looked back out at the sun and the sand and the Atlantic. "It's colder than here, though, right?"

"I'm sorry?"

"Home. Wherever you're from is colder than here."

I smiled and changed the subject. We talked for another twenty minutes and another coffee for me and another ice tea for Coop, but the conversation never became as contemplative or as strangely personal as that again. We talked about Florida, about music, about the election next year. About everything but ourselves.

After Coop had gone, no doubt to call somebody else about the off-white job in New York, I stayed awhile, watching the customers as the diner began to fill up for lunchtime. When I'd had enough of people, I turned back to the water and thought about the different places I'd called home. I thought about Carol.

I thought a little about Winterlong, too. About how I'd come from somewhere colder.


# 8

## LOS ANGELES

Walter Dutton's Mulholland Drive mansion was perhaps only a couple of miles or so from the makeshift grave across country, but more than half an hour by road. Maybe it was due to the fresh air, more likely it was just having something to focus on, but Allen's headache had cleared, meaning this trip was more pleasant. At least, as pleasant as a trip to interview a man whose daughter was probably dead could ever be.

Allen had seen homes like Dutton's before, but only on television. Like many of the palatial residences that lined the route, it sat a respectable distance back from the road, behind eight-foot-high stucco walls. She wondered if it really was Brando's old house. She'd caught the last half of *The Godfather* on TCM a couple of nights ago, but in truth she liked him better in his early roles: *On the Waterfront*, *The Wild One*—the pictures he made when he was still young and beautiful.

There was a security gate between sandstone pillars. The gate was wood veneer, probably over a steel frame. There was a keypad and intercom set into the pillar on the driver's side. Mazzucco pulled the nose of the Ford within six inches of the gate and then got out. He pushed the call button on the intercom and waited ten seconds before there was a burst of static and a crackly hello.

"Detectives Mazzucco and Allen, LAPD Homicide. We'd like to speak to Mr. Dutton."

There was a long pause. Allen started to wonder if Mazzucco would have to buzz again, but at length a response came. Sitting in the car, Allen couldn't hear it clearly over the static, but it sounded like *"Jesus."*

The static clicked off, and a sharp clunk heralded the disengaging of a heavy lock. The gates began to swing inward, painfully slowly. Mazzucco got back in the car and steered it through the gap as soon as it was wide enough.

There was a long, gravel driveway that snaked through well-tended gardens. Allen took in the verdant surroundings as they crawled up the drive and thought about the purloined water of Los Angeles that made these gardens possible, deciding that William Mulholland had probably earned his name on this prime piece of real estate.

There was a man waiting for them at the front door. Early fifties, dressed in gray slacks and a navy tennis shirt. He stood at the stop of the steps leading up to the door, one hand braced against a pillar supporting the porch roof. He looked as though he was debating whether he could trust his legs to carry him safely down the steps. Mazzucco parked and they got out, both detectives instinctively removing their sunglasses.

"Walter Dutton?" Allen asked.

The man nodded reluctantly. "What happened to her?"

Allen held up her badge. "I'm Detective Jessica Allen; this is Detective Jon Mazzucco." She nodded at the open door behind Dutton. "Could we go inside, please?"

Dutton released his grip on the pillar and motioned for the two detectives to step inside.

Mazzucco went in first. When Allen stepped across the threshold, she had to restrain herself from whistling. You couldn't just have fitted her whole apartment into Dutton's entrance foyer; you could just about have fitted her whole apartment *building*. It was a double-height space, with a marble-tiled floor stretching out for a couple hundred square feet. Black and white tiles, like a chessboard. There was a working fountain in the dead center, just before you got to the foot of two marble staircases curving languidly up in mirror images of each other. The staircases met at a landing that overlooked the entrance, at the level of a big crystal chandelier. Allen made brief eye contact with Mazzucco, and a telepathic message passed between them. *Wow*. Mazzucco might have been an LA native, but from the look on his face, this environment was as alien to him as it was to Allen. She composed herself before turning back to face Dutton, who was closing the door behind them.

54

"Let's get this over with, Detectives."

"Mr. Dutton," Mazzucco said quietly, "I think we ought to sit down before we—"

"My daughter is dead, isn't she?" Dutton snapped, some steel coming back into his voice in sharp contrast to his previous, almost whispered sentences. "What goddamn difference does it make if I'm sitting down when you tell me?"

"That's not confirmed yet," Allen said. "We need to—"

"*Yet*. Oh my God."

Allen decided to switch tack. Perhaps getting Dutton to do something was a better approach than trying to put him at ease. How could you expect to put someone at ease in a situation like this, anyway? "Mr. Dutton, do you have a recent picture of your daughter?"

He opened his mouth, as though about to rebuke her, and then sighed. "Wait a minute."

He walked across the cavernous foyer and through a twelve-foot archway that gave onto another vast room. Allen glanced at Mazzucco. He stared back, the look on his face saying, *Be careful*. Allen didn't know whether he was warning her to take care not to upset an emotional relative, or to take care not to piss off a rich and influential businessman. Probably both.

Dutton returned carrying a framed eight-by-ten photograph. He bypassed Allen without looking at her, handed it to Mazzucco. Mazzucco studied it, holding it in both hands. Keeping his eyes on the picture, he moved to Allen's side, so she could examine it, too. The frame was silver in color, probably *real* silver, and the photograph showed a confident, pretty young brunette wearing a gown and a square academic cap. She had blue eyes and was displaying two perfect rows of teeth. She looked a lot like the body they'd viewed an hour before. But then she also looked like a lot of other girls that age. Allen raised her eyes from the photograph to meet Mazzucco's, conscious of Dutton's expectant gaze on the two of them.

He didn't look sure, either.

Dutton cleared his throat. When he spoke, his voice was almost steady. Almost but not quite. "Tell me."

Allen opened her mouth, but Mazzucco tapped her on the forearm, indicating he wanted her to let him take the lead.

"We recovered the body of a young woman, not far from here," he said.

"It's her, isn't it? What happened to her? You guys are Homicide, so that means some son of a bitch killed her, right? Was it that Josh kid? That little ..."

Mazzucco was shaking his head. "Now, hold on. The body was ... We did not find any identification on the deceased. What time did you last see your daughter?"

"Last night, must have been six ... no five o'clock. She was headed down to Santa Monica. Some birthday party, I think. I was going out, too."

"You mentioned a guy named Josh?"

"Her boyfriend, apparently. I'm sure he'd have been there."

"We'll want to speak to him," Allen said. "What time did you expect her home last night?"

Dutton blinked and thought about it. "I got home around one thirty a.m. Her car wasn't in the driveway or the garage. Her curfew is eleven thirty."

"Her curfew?" Allen repeated, unable to keep her incredulity at bay.

Dutton's eyes flared up. "That's right, Detective. She has a curfew. While she lives in my house, she obeys my rules. Is that quite all right with you?"

"I'm sorry," Allen said, though she wasn't sure why she

should be. Dutton's daughter was twenty-two. Old enough to stay up past midnight.

"What kind of car does she drive?" Mazzucco asked quickly, as much to defuse the tension as because it was the natural follow-up question.

"A Porsche 911 Carrera Cabriolet. Silver. I bought it last December, for her birthday."

Allen felt the vibration of her phone in her pocket. A repeated, sustained pulse, which meant it was a call. She ignored it.

Mazzucco nodded and noted the information on the car down. "We're going to need the license plate."

"Of course," Dutton said, seeming to settle down again. "Your colleagues in the Missing Persons Unit already have it, but if it will help things along ..." He looked down at the marble floor and seemed to gather himself. When he looked back at Mazzucco, his voice was steady. "I've been calling her all night. Straight to voicemail every time. You think it's her, Detective?"

Allen remembered the tattoo. "Mr. Dutton, does your daughter have any identifying marks? Like piercings, or a tattoo, perhaps?"

He shrugged. "Sure. What kid doesn't, these days? Some kind of Chinese symbol, on her left shoulder." The way Walter Dutton said it, Allen could tell just how happy the old man was about that one. And then she processed what he had said and what it meant. She looked at Mazzucco, then back to Dutton. "She doesn't have any others? Like a butterfly maybe?"

Dutton's eyes narrowed. "Not that I know of." Then they widened again as a thought occurred to him. "A butterfly? On the small of her back?"

Allen nodded.

"It's not her," Dutton said, a complicated look on his face. A look caught between relief and shock. "It's not Sarah."

Mazzucco and Allen exchanged glances as Dutton hurried back through the archway and returned with another photograph, this one showing two young women, bathed in different shades of neon. This was a more natural, candid image, taken in a bar or a club. Sarah Dutton was on the right, recognizable from the graduation photograph they'd just seen. The girl on the left was recognizable too. There was no doubt about it this time. Allen had been looking at her face less than an hour before.

"Kelly," Dutton said. "Her name is Kelly Boden."

Dutton talked quickly. Their initial victim was one of his daughter's friends. Best friend, in fact. Like his own daughter, Sarah, Kelly was twenty-two years old, five six, slim build, with dark hair. He didn't blame them for the mix-up given the circumstances. He said he'd mistaken one for the other more than once with their backs to him.

As she was listening, Allen's phone buzzed again in her pocket. Just a single pulse this time. She took it out and read the three-word text message.

*Two more bodies.*

# 9

The second and third bodies had been in the earth longer than Kelly Boden, but neither for more than a week or two at most. The coroner investigator said he was fairly sure of that. Decomposition was more advanced in both bodies, but they were both still relatively fresh. There was a strong possibility that one of them was only a few days' dead. On that one, they found a couple of small twine fibers on the insides of the wrists, indicating she'd been tied up.

There was no doubt that both were the work of the same killer.

Both of the new bodies were nude, had been tortured, and had had their throats cut with the same ragged pattern. Both had similar cuts on their bodies, and both had the distinctive tear-patterned lacerations to the cheeks. The signature of the killer was unmistakable. The clincher was the profile—both were young, Caucasian brunettes of a similar build to Boden.

To Allen's surprise, neither looked like they could be Sarah Dutton, beyond those physical similarities. Which meant they still had one missing person and one missing car. She hoped it was a coincidence, but grim experience suggested differently.

They'd assured Walter Dutton that they'd find his daughter, but from the brief time they'd spent with the man, she knew he'd be on the phone to her superiors before they'd pulled out of the driveway. They had people interviewing her friends, speaking to the staff at the bar, and trying to establish when she was last seen. One point of interest: they hadn't been able to locate her boyfriend, Josh, as yet. But again, that could be a bad sign as easily as it could be a good one.

She watched as the two new body bags were loaded into the coroner's van. They slammed the doors, and the van bumped slowly back along the track toward the main road, its destination the medical examiner's office. She heard a rustle of activity and the soft clicking of digital camera shutters from above. The reporters and the paparazzi had gathered on a parallel dirt road overlooking the slope, and a helicopter liveried with the branding of the local Fox affiliate hovered overhead. A slightly overweight uniform in his early fifties shook his head as he watched the van disappear around the bend in the fire road.

"This guy's been a busy little critter, huh?"

Allen was about to respond, but stopped as she heard Mazzucco's voice calling out her name. She turned and saw him approach, replacing his phone in his jacket pocket.

"I got something."

"A detailed confession from a viable suspect?" Allen asked.

Mazzucco flashed a humorless smile in response. "A possible on one of the new bodies. We have to get a positive ID, but ..."

The cop standing beside Allen raised a hand to get Mazzucco's attention, stopping him mid-flow. "Maz, how's tricks?"

"Federmeyer," Mazzucco said, acknowledging the man with neither warmth nor antagonism.

"I know this guy from way back," the uniform said, turning to Allen. "He never writes; he never calls ... How's Homicide, slick?"

"Busy," Mazzucco said, and stared at Federmeyer until he got the message and grudgingly stepped away from the pair.

Allen looked at Mazzucco with amusement and told him to continue.

"A missing persons report that looks very good. Carrie Burnett."

"When did she go missing?"

"A week ago. Sunday night. You recognize the name?"

"Should I?"

Mazzucco smiled. "Me either. Apparently, she's on a reality show about some pop singer. BFF of the star."

When Mazzucco went on to relay the name of the star and the show, Allen realized she was dimly aware of this.

She shrugged it off. It would be another angle for the media, a unique selling point for the story of the killings, but it made no difference to their job. A victim was a victim, and it changed nothing about what they had to do.

Only, that wasn't quite true. Because it opened up another potential line of investigation.

"Could the killer have targeted her from the show?" she suggested. "Some kind of stalker angle?"

Mazzucco shrugged. "I don't know. Stalkers are focused. Who are these other victims? Kelly Boden wasn't on any TV show." He shook his head. "Gut instinct, no. These women all look alike. Same victim profile. That's the link."

"Maybe Kelly knew Burnett. Rich kids and celebrities mingle."

"Sarah Dutton's the rich kid. Kelly wasn't, going by her address."

"Where the hell *is* Dutton?" she said, going back to square one.

Mazzucco nodded along with her frustration. Too many tangents, too little evidence. And the clock was ticking. "This one is a bitch. Sorry, Jess."

For now, they had to assume the two girls had been abducted together. If Dutton wasn't here, that meant she was possibly being held somewhere. Maybe at the murder scene itself. That made finding Dutton the immediate priority, but so far there was no sign of her or the Porsche.

Allen sighed and came back to the reality show star. "Okay, tell me what we know about Carrie Burnett. Last Sunday would fit with what the coroner investigator said. Where was she last seen?"

"That's where it gets interesting," Mazzucco said. "She was last seen outside a club in West Hollywood, getting into her car with the intention of driving home. She was alone, it was nighttime, and she lives in Studio City. No sign of her since then. Or her car."

Allen felt an adrenaline jolt. The similar circumstances suggested a link that could well be borne out once they were able to trace Kelly Boden's last minutes. It did more than that: it suggested an MO. She started to work through the scenarios, conscious that Mazzucco had a couple of minutes' head start on her.

"What do you think? A hitchhiker?" As soon as the words were out, she knew it wasn't that. No female driver would stop for a random hitcher at night. Not in this century.

Mazzucco was shaking his head. "I don't think so. There's one other thing: the last person to hear from her wasn't a friend or family member. It was a dispatcher at Triple A."

"She had a breakdown?"

Her partner nodded. "Somewhere on Laurel Canyon Boulevard. No sign of her or her vehicle by the time the tow truck appeared."

"He's picking them up. Somehow he's finding female drivers in trouble and he's showing up like some kind of . . ."

"Good Samaritan?"

Allen raised her eyebrows. "More like a bad one. Can we get an ID on the Triple A driver?"

"I'm on it." Mazzucco took his phone out again and scanned an email. "Kelly Boden's father lives down in Reseda; somebody's with him. You want to go there now?"

Allen nodded at the suggestion, registering that Mazzucco was making a point of deferring to her as the primary, even though he'd made all of the breakthroughs so far. "Yeah, let's go talk to them. I'll drive."

They got into the Ford, Allen in the driver's seat this time, and pulled out onto the road. Seeing the two new bodies had crystallized one thing in her mind: she'd seen this killer's work before.


## 1996

It was a Wednesday, the last day of July. The midsummer morning sun was already high in the blue sky over Los Angeles, burning determinedly through the haze of smog. Though it was barely seven o'clock in the morning, the roof of the black Buick Century was already getting hot to the touch. He rested both palms on it, enjoying the sensation. He looked north, toward the Santa Monica Mountains, and thought about the day to come.

He heard Kimberley coming up behind him from the direction of the front door, trying to sneak up. He played along, pretended to be startled when she grabbed his shoulders and yelled, "Wakey-wakey."

He turned to look at her. She was wearing cutoff jeans shorts and a black Nirvana T-shirt. Her long black hair was tied back, the ponytail fed through the strap at the back of the Dodgers baseball cap she wore. The brim shaded her brown eyes but could not mask her excitement at the adventure ahead.

A plaintive voice trickled out from the driver's seat. "I'm gonna need gas money, you guys."

He ducked his head to look inside the car, at the source of the whine. Robbie was a scrawny, red-haired kid. He wore baggy mesh basketball shorts and a gray T-shirt with the slogan THE TRUTH IS OUT THERE. He'd met Robbie for the first time a couple of days previously. Robbie didn't go to their school; he was one of the other kids who lived with

Kimberley, here at Blackstones. He wasn't sure why she'd asked Robbie along on the trip, although he had a suspicion that it was because she wasn't comfortable being alone with him just yet. He didn't hold that against her. He was aware there were probably good reasons for people to feel that way about him.

"We heard you the first hundred times, kid."

"Don't call me that. I'm older than you. And Jason will be pissed if I return his car empty. Do you know what Jason will do to us if he's pissed?"

He opened his mouth to respond to that but felt Kimberley's hand on his shoulder again. Her face was tilted upward, the look in her eyes easy to read: *Be nice.*

"You're the boss, Robbie," he said, picking up his backpack by its strap and dumping it in the backseat.

Kimberley ran around the front of the car and got in the passenger side. "Are you ready? This is going to be great, I promise."

He got into the backseat and closed the door behind him. He thought she was wrong. He thought it was going to be *better* than great.

# 10

He drifted into consciousness to the sound of distant screams.

His dreams had been fragmented and confused, as they always were. A little of the past, a little of the present, a little of what he thought was to come. He kept his eyes closed and savored the thick aftertaste of sleep. Memories of a long, hot summer two decades before, and of one day in particular. In the dream, images and sensations from that summer's day had blurred and blended with more recent input. Last night. Darkness and rain and blood. Sunshine and a cool breeze and the creaking sound of an old sign hanging in front of an empty building. The kindred ways sunlight and moonlight glance off a blade

Dark hair and brown eyes. He knew he'd be seeing her again soon.

He opened his own eyes gradually, allowing them to adjust to the afternoon sunlight penetrating the narrow gaps between the blinds. Dust motes circled and whirled lazily in the light. As he allowed the world back in, he realized the far-off screams were not born of pain and terror, but of delight. Children playing in some backyard, or perhaps even out on the street.

He slid his legs off the bed and stood up. As was his routine, his hand reached for the photograph he kept beside him when he slept. He gazed at it for a few moments, the curve of a smile on his lips, and then replaced it on the table beside the bed.

He opened the door and walked naked across the narrow hallway to the opposite room. This had originally been the second bedroom, when the house had been a home, but now it was simply a place to work. It looked out on the backyard, which was enclosed on all sides by high bushes, providing quiet and privacy. There was a bed that had not been slept in in months or years, a squat two-drawer chest supporting an old-fashioned boxy television, and a desk set up in front of the window. On the desk were various tools and instruments and parts, grouped according to their uses. Some were of the digital and electronic variety and were new things, things that had been undreamed of in their compactness and intricacy even ten years before. Others were much more traditional and had not evolved or developed in a thousand years.

He had another kit to prepare, because he did not think it would be long until the next time. He sat down at the desk and started to lay out the tools and the parts he would need.

Before he got to work, he got up, walked back across the room, and switched on the television. He liked to have background noise while he worked. Music was his first preference, particularly oldies, but anything would do. Usually, he would switch the television or the stereo on, turn the sound down a little, and go back to the desk to work.

But today he didn't move. Today he just watched the screen.

A helicopter view of the place in the mountains. His place. Cops in uniform and cops in suits and cops in overalls, digging up the earth in his place. Taking something that belonged to him.

He stood there for a long time, the task he'd begun forgotten for now.

# 11

Allen and Mazzucco left the home of Kelly Boden's father with two things: confirmation of their hypothesis and an increased desire to catch the bastard who'd killed the three women buried in the hills.

Boden's father had identified Kelly from a photograph taken at the gravesite without hesitation. Allen had been reluctant to show him, given the visible wounds, but he'd insisted. He was an ex-cop, which made it a little more personal. He'd taken the news without hysterics but had quietly asked the detectives to do all they could to find the person responsible.

Just as they were leaving, he stopped them at the door to ask if they'd found Sarah Dutton yet. Mazzucco shook his head. "Not yet."

Boden's voice was muted, almost as though he were speaking to them from much farther away. His eyes were pools of blackness. "I hope you find her. Safe."

Allen did, too.

They got into the car, and Allen started the engine. She glanced across at Mazzucco, who was staring back at Richard Boden's closed front door, his jaw set. She knew he had the same desire as she did to catch this guy, of course. But he was also a parent.

In the time she'd been working with him, she'd come to take for granted that Mazzucco wasn't the kind of guy to go on and on about his family. He'd shown her the pictures right after his wife had given birth, of course. He'd given Allen and the others the obligatory details of time of birth and weight and that mom and baby girl were doing fine, but beyond that, you would barely know anything had changed, other than he looked a little more tired and spent a little more time checking his personal cell. Allen didn't blame him for not wanting the two halves of his life to bleed into each other, for his work to contaminate his home. But still, something like this had to hit Mazzucco in a way she couldn't fully understand.

"You ever think about what you would do, Jon?" she asked before she could stop herself. "If your kid was that age, if—"

Mazzucco cut her off mid-sentence, still looking at the door as he spoke. "I don't think about it. Ever."

After that, the conversation was sparser than was usual for most of the drive back downtown. They barely exchanged a word for the first ten minutes, each of them lost in thought. When Mazzucco grimaced and shifted in the passenger seat, Allen gratefully seized the chance for a break from the subject.

"*Tauruses*," she growled, in a passable imitation of her partner's voice.

The Ford Taurus was the department's anointed replacement for the old Crown Victoria, a venerable warhorse that had finally been put out to pasture. Mazzucco, at six two, was no fan of the reduced legroom in the new cars.

"Clue's in the name," he said, not for the first time. "*Los Angeles* Police Department. We spend half the shift in the car, so you'd think they coulda given a little more consideration to comfort."

"You're right. Maybe they'll go for limos next time they change the contract."

They reached the office of the LA County medical examiner just before three o'clock. The Medical Examiner was a very thin, very bald man in his sixties named Burke. He wore a white coat that was probably in the slimmest size available, but it looked baggy on him. On his hands were heavy rubber gloves with the cuffs turned up. He ushered Allen and Mazzucco into the mortuary where Kelly and the other two, still officially unidentified, women lay. The room was cold, in temperature and in color: a polar blue. Harsh fluorescent lighting bleached every shadow.

Burke located the correct drawers by their locker numbers and pulled them out. The three bodies, covered with thin green sheets, lay on sloping metal tables within each drawer. Burke ambled past the three drawers, unceremoniously whipping back the shroud from each corpse. Allen winced as she saw the most decomposed body, the one they'd yet to identify. The yawning tear in her throat that had practically decapitated her.

"Any further forward in identifying our victims, Detective Mazzucco?" Burke asked in a bored tone of voice that implied he didn't much care either way. He didn't look at either detective, but as usual, favored Mazzucco over Allen if he had to address one of them. Allen wasn't sure if he had a particular problem with her, but decided to give him the benefit of the doubt and assume he was just a sexist prick.

Mazzucco smiled and said nothing, deferring to Allen because it irritated him, too.

"As a matter of fact, yes," Allen said. She looked at the most recent of the three victims. "Kelly Boden. She was a waitress, worked at a pancake joint over on Sepulveda. We just came from talking to her father."

Burke shrugged. "One out of three isn't bad, I guess."

"It isn't bad at all," Mazzucco interjected, "considering the three of them came out of the ground a couple of hours ago. And as a matter of fact, we think we have an ID for this one, too. So I guess it's over to you, Doc."

Burke didn't flinch at the rebuke, but he did turn to look at them. "I daresay I'll have more to offer after the autopsies, but at the moment ..." He waved a hand at the three decimated bodies before them. "What you see is what you get."

"Meaning?" Allen prompted.

"Meaning you have three white women of roughly similar age. They've all been tortured with knives." He paused and let his dull, colorless eyes run over the three forms. "Minimum of five different types of blade, I'd say. The killer has a tool kit. Signature wounds on the cheeks make it clear that he is attempting to make some sort of statement ..."

"*Attempting?*" Mazzucco repeated, raising an eyebrow.

If Burke heard him, he didn't acknowledge it, just continued unabated. "And, of course, it looks like the cause of death is identical in all three cases. Throat opened in a single stroke, severing of the carotid artery. Exsanguination ensued; death would have been pretty much instantaneous."

Allen eyed the multitude of cuts on each of the women and wondered how instantaneous it would have felt to any of them after they'd been in this bastard's hands for a few hours, or however long it took him to do all this.

"Any doubt these are all the work of the same man?" she asked.

Burke shook his head in a way that implied he thought the question ridiculous. "No doubt whatsoever, Detective. It's not just the similarities in the wounds inflicted on these victims; it's the *way* they've been inflicted." He reached out and touched a gloved finger to the ragged edge of the throat wound of the nearest body. In the corner of her eye, Allen saw Mazzucco wince and swallow. She resisted the urge to do likewise.

"Look at the three fatal wounds," Burke continued. "Absolutely no hesitation, no practice strokes, just one quick, deep cut, right to left. We get a few slit throats every year, but never this ... practiced. Last time I saw anything like this was in Vietnam."

"What are you saying? That this guy could be military?" Mazzucco asked.

Burke shook his head. "Not necessarily. I'm saying it's somebody who's done it before. Somebody who knows exactly how to cut a throat without screwing it up."

*Somebody who's done it before.* Allen's eyes jerked across to look at the ragged cut across Kelly Boden's throat again. "You ever see wounds exactly like that before, Doc? Even in Vietnam?"

Burke paused and looked at the three bodies again, the bored demeanor evaporating for a moment. "As I said, the skill and resolve that went into these killing strokes, I've seen on the battlefield. But you're talking about the ragged pattern, aren't you?" He shook his head. "That is unusual. A cut like this—a quick, single stroke of the kind I described—should have relatively clean edges. These are ragged, as though the blade had a particularly pronounced serration, or the blade itself curved in multiple places."

Allen's brow creased. "Would you be able to give us an idea of what the blade would have looked like? Could make it easier to find a match."

The ME nodded, looking surprised to have stumbled upon two police officers with the capacity for independent thought. "Yes, given some more time. I've cleared my dance card for the three autopsies today, Detective. I hear this case is becoming quite the hot ticket."

# 12

"What do you think?" Mazzucco said as they stepped out into the fresh air.

"I think spending most of your time around dead people probably has an adverse effect on interpersonal skills," Allen said.

Mazzucco shot her a sarcastic glance and said nothing else until they'd gotten into the car.

"What do you think about our perp?" he clarified as Allen started the engine and pulled out onto North Mission, headed southwest back toward the Police Administration Building.

71

Allen pressed the button to roll down the window before she answered. She savored the breeze on her face after the olfactory cocktail of formaldehyde and bodily fluids.

"He's a sick son of a bitch. Burke's right, though. He's definitely done this before, and he'll do it again."

"And he's working on a pretty fast cycle, too," Mazzucco added. "Three victims in a couple of weeks, if the estimates are right. Three that we know of. So what next?"

"Next, we nail down the identification on Burnett and see if we can work out who number three might be. Maybe we'll get lucky on the prints, or maybe we need to look at missing persons again. She's been dead two weeks; somebody has to have missed her. I mean, she didn't look like a transient or a junkie or anything."

Mazzucco shrugged. "Difficult to tell for sure, the way he left them. No clothes, no personal effects, nothing to identify them beyond the tattoo on the Boden girl."

"And he's smart about DNA. The coroner investigator got jack at the scene: no foreign hairs, no skin under the fingernails. He's being careful."

"I think it's more than that. It's like he wanted to strip them of their identities, of everything that made them individuals. Like they belong to him now."

Allen narrowed her eyes and gave him a sidelong glance. "You sound like a goddamn shrink, Mazzucco."

He laughed. "We'll be dealing with the real thing soon enough; you know that. Serials equal payday to those guys."

"Great. So we pay eight hundred bucks an hour for some pen pusher to tell us we're looking for a white male between twenty and forty-five with a history of violent relationships."

The new Police Administration Building was only a couple of miles from the County Coroner's Office. Allen went along with the habit of calling it the *new* building, even though, of course, it was the only headquarters she'd known in this town. The LAPD had been based out of Parker Center for more than fifty years, and she expected it would take a decade or so for the new place a couple of blocks over on West First Street to feel like home, as far as cop folk memory was concerned.

She didn't have access to one of the rare and coveted basement parking spots beneath the PAB, so she parked in a more spacious lot a couple of blocks over. A lot of cops parked there, which had a drawback: people could wait around for you to show up. As she pulled past the barrier, she saw her partner's head snap around as they passed a familiar face on the sidewalk outside. The two exited the car, and she followed his gaze back up the ramp to where the man they'd seen stood. He was a little taller than average, and fairly slim. He wore a vintage T-shirt displaying the poster for the original *Evil Dead* movie, under a flannel shirt. He wore a skull cap, and a camera dangled from a strap around his neck.

"Shrinks ain't the worst we'll be dealing with," Mazzucco said as they approached the man. "These bastards bring it all out of the woodwork."

"Smith." Allen sighed. "Thought you'd be out in the hills," she stated as they drew level with him.

The man grinned and shook his head. "Got all I could use already. There's only so many shots you can take of guys digging, you know? Thought I'd try my luck with you, get myself a fresh angle."

Allen sighed. Eddie Smith was as bad as the rest of them, maybe worse, but she owed him one. That didn't mean, of course, that she couldn't be selective in how she repaid that favor.

"There's no angle, Smith. Just an unexplained death."

Smith angled his head. "Nice try. I got there just before

they found the other two. So tell me, is this a new killer, or somebody who's already on your radar?"

"No comment," Mazzucco said, brushing past.

"What he said," Allen added.

They left Smith standing on the sidewalk, staring after them like he knew something they didn't.

"Fucking new mutation," Mazzucco said under his breath as they reached the doors.

"Huh?" Allen asked, wondering if she'd misheard.

"Symptom of the modern world," he said, jerking his head back in Smith's general direction. "Used to be there was a dividing line between the paps and the on-the-payroll journalists. You could almost trust some of the traditional guys. Ever since print media started circling the drain, everybody's gone freelance, doing a little bit of everything. I don't know how to deal with this new hybrid."

"Kids today," Allen said, mocking only gently.

Smith ran his own crime blog, operating like a one-man news network. He linked to AP stories around the Greater Los Angeles area and cherry-picked the most sensational for featured articles. He'd built up a good network of sources and was reliably among the first responders to a big story, whether it was a celebrity overdose or a gang shooting.

After his path had crossed with Allen's a couple of times, she'd visited his website out of curiosity. His copywriting was okay, maybe good enough to be a staffer at a provincial newspaper, but his photography was the real deal. His fundamentals were solid in terms of light, composition, and all the rest of it; but more important, he had a war reporter's talent for capturing the aftermath of violence. He prided himself on showing images that the legitimate news outlets shied away from, and that was why his site racked up more page views than many a larger operation. *If it bleeds, it leads* was unspoken policy at most news organizations, but Smith actually used it as a banner tagline on his site. Allen didn't know exactly how paid advertising on websites worked, but Smith certainly seemed to be doing all right.

Most of the cops who knew of Smith hated him. They hated him because he was good at his job, and that meant sometimes he got in the way of their jobs. He'd got talking to Allen in her first couple of weeks in the department, at the scene of a supposed suicide: a lawyer who'd fallen sixty feet from a bridge crossing a dry river bed. Perhaps Smith had sensed a similar, if lesser, isolation in her when they met.

They'd exchanged pleasantries, and then Smith had casually dropped in that he'd noticed from his zoom shots of the body before it was covered up that there were scratches on the wrists. Not the kind that would suggest a different kind of suicide attempt, but the kind you get from being bound or handcuffed. Inconsistent with an open-and-shut suicide. Allen had caught this already, of course, but she warned him not to spread that around, whereupon he'd smilingly reminded her that it was a free country and a free press. No stranger to negotiating with journalists back in DC, Allen realized that a different approach would pay dividends. She'd asked him—nicely—to sit on this particular detail until they'd had enough time to look into the lawyer's background. Twelve hours later, they had the lawyer's wife in custody following a full confession, and Smith got to be first with the story anyway. Allen assumed that the gruesome pictures of the lawyer's body got him a lot of hits, or clicks, or whatever.

Allen shook her head in wonder as she remembered the case. The wife had doped the lawyer up with sleeping pills before tying him up and driving him out to the bridge. Every cop who'd come near the investigation had been openly skeptical at first, that a relatively slight woman would have been capable of leveraging her husband's two-hundred-pound frame over the barrier. Then they'd been just as openly impressed when the woman explained, proudly showing off her toned arm muscles. Pole-dancing classes, apparently. What a city.

"He likes you, you know." Mazzucco's voice brought her back to the present.

The thought had occurred to Allen. Smith had called her a couple of times after she'd contacted him – making the mistake of not withholding her number. Not about anything specific. *Just touching base*, he'd say. Then again, she guessed there were plenty of professional reasons why he'd want to cultivate open communications with a homicide cop. And if she was smart, she could make sure she benefited more than Smith did.

She hadn't told Mazzucco about any of this. She didn't think he—or any of the others—would be comfortable with her getting too close to somebody like Smith. But they didn't have to worry about her.

She shook her head. "Nah. He just thinks I'm an easy mark, 'cause I'm new. Nothing I can't handle."

Mazzucco stopped and met her eyes. "I hope you're right. Because this thing is already going primetime. Any hope we might have had of keeping this thing low-key just vanished."

# 13

They rode the elevator up to the sixth floor, where Lieutenant Lawrence was waiting for them. Lawrence was a well-built and well-preserved sixty, with a good head of hair that had retained much of its original color. The only things about him that betrayed the pressures of the job were the lines and bags under his eyes. The look on his face said they could skip the introduction.

"Congratulations, Detective Allen," he said. "Only been with us six months and you already get to be on TV."

"Just lucky, I guess, Lieutenant."

He watched her face for a moment, and she could tell he was uneasy about her leading on a high-profile investigation. Maybe because it was too early, maybe for other reasons. She wondered if he was thinking about taking it away from her. It would be bad protocol, but he had the authority. But then he looked from her to Mazzucco and seemed to shrug it off, beckoning the two of them over. "Come on in."

They sat down in Lawrence's office and thrashed out a plan of action over the next forty minutes. They kept it simple and focused, knowing that complexity and tangents and factors outside their control would be inevitable soon enough.

Goal one: find Sarah Dutton. Goal two: confirm the IDs on the remaining victims. Goal three: start chasing up leads, identifying suspects. As they'd anticipated, Lawrence had already engaged a forensic psychologist to produce a psych profile on the killer.

The final point was maybe the toughest one: manage the media.

"Let's keep it by the book," Lawrence said. "Release the basics: location of the bodies, number of victims, names when next of kin have been notified, not before. No speculation, nothing specific around cause of death. We're following a number of lines of inquiry. You know the drill."

Allen nodded, conscious of the need to feed the media without compromising the investigation. If they wanted to be able to sort the kooks from the genuine leads, they needed to keep the details under wraps: stuff like the fact they'd been buried, the fact they were all nude, the torture wounds ... and of course, those ragged, grinning neck slits. Allen's mind wandered to those ragged edges and then back to Washington.

"Allen?"

She snapped back into the present, feeling like she'd been caught daydreaming in class. She winged it, assuming she was being asked for general feedback.

"Sounds solid," she said. "We need to find Sarah, although I don't think any of us are expecting to find her alive now. Aside from that, the priority is establishing where these women were when they went missing, that and finding the vehicles. We know that, we're on track to finding out how he's abducting them."

Lawrence stared at her for a moment and then nodded. "Okay. We're already getting a lot of calls about this; looks like one of the victims was some kind of celebrity, whatever that means anymore. The chief's talking about a press conference, and he likes to have somebody close to the case up there with him. You up for it, Allen? You're the primary."

She nodded. "Sure."

Lawrence told them to get to it and picked up his phone as they exited his office, Allen closing the door behind them. Mazzucco almost walked right into Don McCall as he turned into the corridor. The solidly built, clean-shaven SIS captain was coming the other way, holding a paper cup of coffee, which he exaggeratedly swung out of harm's way.

"Whoa, easy there, tiger."

Mazzucco grumbled an apology and tried to keep going, but McCall tapped him on the shoulder with his free hand. An onlooker might have seen it as a friendly gesture rather than the deliberate invasion of personal space it was.

"I hear you two caught a big one. Need any help?"

Mazzucco sighed and met McCall's eyes. "Thanks. We got it."

McCall grinned and looked at Allen. "I bet. Watch and learn, Allen. Mazzy here will have the snazziest SharePoint environment set up in good time for the next body."

Mazzucco leaned closer, so their faces were inches apart. "You're right, McCall. Maybe I should go out and shoot a few unarmed suspects dead to get the ball rolling. That approach work better for you?"

The smile vanished from McCall's face. "That was ruled a good shooting, Mazzucco."

They were referring to the incident the previous December, not long after Allen had transferred in. McCall's team had had a couple of armed robbery suspects under surveillance in Crenshaw. They'd ambushed the two suspects in their vehicle and things had gotten ugly. The net result was two dead suspects—only one of them armed—and one dead civilian by the name of Levon Jackson, a twenty-four-year-old local resident who multiple witnesses said hadn't even been near the two suspects and their car. Had Jackson not had an impressive list of busts for selling crack cocaine, things might have gone a lot worse for McCall. But Allen had it on good authority that things never seemed to go all the way bad for McCall.

McCall opened his mouth to say something, then reconsidered as he thought of a more subtle way to get Mazzucco's back up, turning to smile at Allen.

"Good thing your partner's leading on this. I heard she knows how to get things done. That right, Allen?"

She didn't return the smile. "Your coffee's getting cold, Don."

McCall shrugged, met Mazzucco's eyes again with a cold stare, and then passed by them. He gave Lawrence's door a cursory knock and entered.

"I wonder what that's about," Allen said, watching as the door closed again.

Her partner shrugged. "Probably just asking again why it is they can't have tactical nukes."

"I guess he wouldn't still be around if he didn't have a use," Allen mused.

"That's one way of looking at it. It's assholes like him that give all of us a bad name."

They headed into the main squad room, where the orange light on Mazzucco's desk phone was flashing to indicate voicemail. Allen hoped it was the callback he was waiting on from AAA. He sat down at his desk to listen to the message, and Allen circled around the hub to her own desk, which faced Mazzucco's. In contrast to Mazzucco's neat, squared-away desk, hers was littered with assorted reports and stationery and doodled-on pieces of notepaper. She raised the handset of her phone and dialed a number. The call put her through to the Metropolitan Police Department of the District of Columbia. Allen cleared her throat and kept her voice low. She didn't want anyone else—even Mazzucco—to hear this until she was sure. She identified herself and asked for Lieutenant Michael Sanding in the Homicide division.

The call was transferred, and a minute later a familiar voice answered.

"Sanding."

"Hey, Mike. Got five minutes for an old acquaintance?"

"Allen," he said at once, his voice perking up. "How you been? You still in LA?"

"Yeah. I had to stop going when I realized they put an ocean right in my way."

"How are you doing?" He paused, sounding circumspect, like he wanted to know, but didn't want to ask her straight out. "You ... okay?"

"I'm great," she said briskly. "Be even better if you can help me out on something, though."

"Shoot."

"Two and a half years back. Body in the Potomac. Ring any bells?"

"You're gonna have to be more specific," he cracked, sounding happier on less dangerous ground. He was exaggerating about needing to be more specific, but only mildly. The line went quiet, and she could hear him tapping a pen on his desk, the way he always did when he was thinking. "Sure. Fall time. Homeless guy, right? Can't recall the name."

"There wasn't one. We never got an ID. "

"That's right. He'd been in the water a while, and there wasn't much in the way of physical evidence. I guess he wasn't missed. The body could have washed out to sea and nobody would have even known there'd been a murder."

Something about that sentence sent a shiver through Allen. It reminded her of something the uniform at the gravesite had said earlier, about the undiscovered dead in the mountains. That made her wonder how long Boden and the other two might have lain in their unmarked graves had it not been for the rain and the landslide.

"Hello?" Sanding said. "Allen, you still there?"

"Yeah. Sorry. Just thinking. The guy in the Potomac, do you remember anything else about him?"

"He had that weird slash cutting his throat. Like somebody had hacked away at it with a butter knife or something. The ME thought maybe it could have happened after he wound up in the river. Like he got caught on something that ripped the wound up more."

"Did you ever see anything else like that?"

There was silence at the other end. No tapping this time.

"Actually, yes. Maybe a couple of months before that. A snitch down in Columbia Heights. We found him in a boarded-up apartment; figured it was his homies did it. Looked like they'd found out he was telling tales out of school."

"How so?"

"He'd been tortured. It was bad, Allen. Maybe the worst I've seen."

"Throat cut?"

"Nah. Cigarette burns, missing digits, castration. His belly had been ripped open at the end of it, like he was literally spilling his guts. And the wound looked kind of like the one on the homeless guy." He paused; then his voice got louder again, like he was returning to the present. "What's this about, Jess?"

"I'm not sure yet," she said. "Thanks, Mike. I'll call soon."

She hung up before he had a chance to question her further and stared at the postcard she'd pinned on the partition separating their desks. It was kind of a joke, a reproduction of some fifties advertising art, showing a glamorous couple lounging on the beach. *Come to Los Angeles, California—City of Dreams!* She always got a kick out of that whenever she looked up from crime scene pics of some grisly murder. She stared at the vibrant colors and the upbeat sentiment, lost in thought.

Mazzucco's fingers tapping on the partition snapped her out of it.

"What?" she said, looking up.

"The shift runner at the Triple A branch confirmed the timeline on Carrie Burnett. They took a call from her last Sunday night, saying she'd broken down on Laurel Canyon Boulevard. The tow truck driver got out there pretty quick because they prioritize single women. When he made it to the scene, there was no sign of her or her vehicle."

Allen opened her mouth to ask about the driver, but Mazzucco stopped her.

"We've got somebody going to talk to the driver, but I think he's clean. The manager checked the record before calling me back. Turns out these guys all ride with an onboard digital video camera now, for security. He drove out to the scene and the car wasn't there. He made a call back to base and they told him to come back in. The tape backs up his account perfectly, as does the mileage on his truck and the fact he was assisting a different driver in West Hollywood a half hour later."

Allen thought about it. "Can we get them to check if there are any other no-shows? Anybody we can't account for?"

"Worth a shot."

Mazzucco's hand was on the phone to call the AAA guy back when it rang again. He picked it up and said his name, then listened. He said okay and thanked whoever was on the other end, and then hung up.

"We got confirmation on Carrie Burnett. Her prints were in the system for a DUI last year."

"Okay," she said. "We need to find Sarah Dutton, and we

need to know who the third victim is. I want to nail this guy, Mazzucco."

# 14

## FORT LAUDERDALE

Since I was temporarily in the position of having nowhere in particular I had to be, I spent a day exploring Lauderdale on foot, getting to know a little more about the geography of the place, in case the local knowledge ever came in handy again. I avoided the area around the bar from the previous night, but covered a respectable chunk of the city, taking in the sights and the sounds and the smells. By the end of the day, even though the sun on my face was pleasant after a long winter, and even though there was no pressing reason to leave, my feet were getting itchy again. It never feels right to stick around too long after I've concluded a job. I ate a large and satisfying dinner in a beachfront burger joint and then headed back to my hotel. I gave my room number at the desk, and the attractive redhead located my keycard and tapped a couple of buttons on her computer. "Have you decided if you'll be staying with us after tonight, Mr. Adams?"

I smiled and shook my head. I was planning on checking out in the morning and then Mr. Neal Adams of Lansing, Michigan, would be gone, never to be seen again.

"Back home tomorrow, I'm afraid."

She smiled and assured me the room would be available if I changed my mind. I paid for checkout in advance, just in case I decided to leave early, and ascended one flight of stairs to my floor. The second floor is always my preferred option: more difficult for somebody to break into, but easier to leave in a hurry than higher up. I slid the keycard into the lock and pushed the door open. I checked the couple of telltales I'd left to alert me to an intruder—force of habit, or maybe just superstition—and found the hair across the drawer in the bedside table and the tiny smear of toothpaste under the bathroom doorknob, just the way I'd left them.

Satisfied, I slid my jacket off and hung it up in the closet so it wouldn't get creased. I took the remote from the bedside table and clicked the television on as I walked into the bathroom and turned the shower on. As I took off the rest of my clothes, I could hear the news drone away in the background beneath the sound of the water hitting the shower tray. Something about an upsurge of violence in Kashmir. I couldn't help a grim smile at that. The more things change ...

I closed my eyes as I stepped under the powerful jet of water. I half expected to see Zoran's face again, the look of surprise on his face that had stayed with me, but instead my thoughts drifted much further back. The news report had drawn old memories to the surface. Memories of my own experience of Kashmir, a place where *sudden upsurge of violence* was just another term for everyday life. SSDD, Murphy had called it: *Same Shit, Different Day*. We'd accomplished what we'd set out to do in our brief sojourn there, but it had not gone smoothly. I'd begun to see things I didn't like in some of the other men, like Dixon and Crozier. Especially Crozier. I'd never really thought about it before, but Kashmir had been the beginning of a long journey that had culminated in Winterlong and me going our separate ways.

Ten minutes later, I emerged from the bathroom, toweling my hair dry. The news was still on, but the story had changed, moved closer to home. BREAKING NEWS, the bar along the bottom of the screen said. Which usually translates as news that broke eight hours ago, which we've been regurgitating ever since, adding some wild speculation and unconfirmed reports along the way. Los Angeles. Some new serial killer, three confirmed victims so far. *Same Shit, Different Day.*

My eyes lingered on the screen for a second, taking in helicopter shots of a crime scene in what looked like the Santa Monica Mountains. Then I turned my attention to my laptop, checking my options for the journey home. Although calling it *home* seemed almost dishonest, given it was a place where I spent less than four months out of every year. Maybe it was time to change that.

Earlier, I'd told Coop I was thinking of driving back. I said that for two good reasons: first, it gave him nothing to go on, the way a flight time or a specific airport might. I liked Coop, but I wasn't kidding when I told him the less he knew about me the better. I liked being at large in the world, as Neal Adams or Carter Blake or whoever. But I had good reasons to keep a barrier between all of that and the place I chose to hang my hat. When a job was over, I made sure the trail went cold long before it ever reached home.

The second reason was that I really hadn't decided how I was traveling back home. The more I thought about it, though, the more driving appealed. It would take a couple of days at least, if I was in a hurry. But I wasn't in a hurry. After all, what good was working for yourself if you couldn't take a little time off? I decided to toast that thought, opening the minibar and taking out a cold bottle of Heineken. I took a swig and looked out at the lights of the traffic on North Atlantic Boulevard and the black ocean beyond that. I began to relax for the first time in days, or maybe longer than that.

That was the ticket. Rent a fast car in the morning, maybe a soft top. I could make a week of it, decompress gradually, and maybe by the time I made it home, I would have worked out who I was when I was off-duty. The beer went down smoothly and quickly, and I started to think about another. I barely registered the excitable voice from the news trailing another major development.

"... source within the LAPD has told this station that all *three* victims were murdered in *exactly* the same way: their throats *brutally* cut. What's striking about these injuries is that they all seem to have been caused by the *same type of weapon*, which the police are speculating may be some kind of jagged, curved blade."

I froze, the bottle neck still touching my lips, and my eyes moved to the television screen. The reporter was live on the scene in LA; a caption on the screen told me she was Jennifer Quan, from the local ABC affiliate. It was still light over there, at the other end of the continent. She was clutching her microphone and staring wide-eyed into the camera like an elementary school teacher telling a ghost story on Halloween.

"The source added that these killings seemed to be almost *ritualistic* in nature ... Whether that means there could be some kind of cult or satanic connection to these murders, we can't speculate at this time."

I put the bottle down and swallowed the slug of beer that had lingered in my mouth. It tasted bitter all of a sudden.

It couldn't be. It couldn't be him.

# 15

## LOS ANGELES

"Who the fuck talked to the press?"

It was just after seven p.m. Allen had been waiting on a callback from Mike Sanding in DC when Ed Simon stopped by her desk and directed her attention to the screen on the south wall of the vast RHD squad room, where a peroxide-blond reporter was gleefully spilling restricted information on Allen's case all over the airwaves. Her reaction was instantaneous and loud enough to draw the attention of each of the half-dozen other cops in the room.

Most of them had the good sense to stay quiet. Joe Coleman, however, was not known for good sense. The pudgy, fifty-ish detective displayed a broad smirk beneath his graying mustache. He turned his eyes away from the screen, and the smirk widened further still when he saw the anger in Allen's face, his busy little brain obviously cueing up another wisecrack.

"What's the matter, Allen? Don't you—"

"Shut the fuck up, Coleman." Allen stared him down until the smirk faded and he sat back down.

The idiot on TV was blabbing away, telling the world that one of the victims had just been identified as reality TV celebrity Carrie Burnett. Allen thought that was stretching the definition of celebrity, but she wasn't surprised. Then the reporter went ahead and revealed that one of the other victims was Kelly Boden of Reseda. Jesus, they even had a picture of her. The standard type of social media selfie that always looks so inappropriate when plastered over TV screens and newspapers to illustrate violent death. The view switched to reporters camped outside Burnett's house, and another, much smaller group outside Richard Boden's place. Allen felt bad about that, but knew it was inevitable. At least she could take comfort from the knowledge that Boden would have no problem telling them where to go if he didn't feel like talking to them.

The door opened and Mazzucco walked in, carrying his phone. He took one look at the scene, the group of detectives staring in fascination at the screen, and looked at Allen. "What?"

She didn't take her eyes away from the screen.

"Tell me you have some good news."

"Depends how you define good," Mazzucco said, bouncing the phone in his hand. Then he looked back up at the screen, reading the ticker. "Ah, shit."

"Some ..." Allen cleared her throat and composed herself. "Someone has talked to the media." She looked at Mazzucco, waving a hand at the screen. "Not just talked. Sounds like they have every goddamned detail. Burnett, Boden's name and picture, the number of bodies, even the goddamned wound pattern." Her eyes widened in disbelief as the graphic changed to display the line: LAPD INVESTIGATES SO-CALLED SAMARITAN SLAYINGS. "Jesus!"

"*The Samaritan*," a voice across the room intoned in a deep, movie-trailer voice. "Your boy's a star."

"Shut the fuck up, Coleman," Mazzucco said without giving him the dignity of a glance. He turned back to Allen. "Who was it?"

Allen said. "This is guy-on-the-scene stuff, I'm guessing. One of the uniforms, maybe even one of the coroner investigators."

"There could be a silver lining," Mazzucco said as Sarah

Dutton's picture flashed up on the screen. They'd already been working with the media to publicize the search for Sarah, but if nothing else, that part of the investigation had just gotten a major ratings boost.

The blonde on TV continued. "Unconfirmed reports suggest that the search for this woman, Sarah Dutton, is related to the ongoing investigation. Anyone who knows the whereabouts of Sarah is urged to call ..."

Allen shook her head. "It's not worth it. We're not going to find her, are we? Not alive."

For the last couple of hours, they'd been chasing leads. Silver Porsches were being routinely stopped, regardless of license plate, leading to a lot of pissed-off rich people. AAA had come back with a list of no-shows for the past month, but all of the callers had been accounted for. They'd worked the phones and batted theories back and forth over too many cups of coffee. Allen liked to push Mazzucco to think outside of the box, Mazzucco tried to keep Allen focused on the sparse facts they had at their disposal. It was a relatively new professional relationship, and they were both still feeling their way, learning how to play to each other's strengths. Allen appreciated the back-and-forth, but she suspected they were both glad of the respite when Mazzucco had gone outside for a cigarette.

He was back now, though, and she realized he was holding his phone up for her to look at the screen. Another carefree social media profile picture of a brunette, slightly older than the others, but probably still in her twenties. She looked a lot like their remaining unidentified victim.

Allen's eyes flicked from the phone screen to Mazzucco's expectant face. "Well? Are you going to keep me in suspense?"

"Rachel Morrow, twenty-eight years old."

Allen's brow creased. "She's not famous as well, is she?"
Her partner shook his head.

"Rich?"

"Nope. I mean, she's an accountant—was an accountant,
I mean—so she was doing okay, but not exactly rich and
definitely not famous."

"We didn't get a hit off her prints, I'm assuming."

"Correct. This is from MPU. We'd have matched her
earlier today, but the missing persons report was only filed
yesterday. Her husband was out of the country for more
than a week. Got back yesterday to find an empty home."

Allen was incredulous. "He didn't speak to his wife on the
phone for a *week*? How solid is his alibi?"

Mazzucco shrugged. "I've heard stranger things, and
yeah. He was in Finland at some conference. Speaking slots
every day. He's in the clear, unless ..."

"Unless he paid somebody else to do it."

"Right, but why the collateral damage? The other two
vics, I mean."

The rest of the office was still watching the news. Allen sat
back down in her chair and mulled over the new information. "So if the husband's been out of the picture, who was
the last person to see her before she went missing?"

"She went for a drink after work on the tenth with some
people from her office. She had only one, and then she drove
home. Apparently, she had a headache. That was the last
anyone saw of her. She was on vacation the following week,
so she wasn't missed at work."

"Any idea if she made it home?"

Mazzucco shrugged. "Hard to tell. A patrol unit visited
the house yesterday when the husband called it in. He said
the house was locked up. No car in the garage, but none
of her clothes or possessions were gone, and there was food

rotting in the refrigerator. He checked their joint account and there were no withdrawals after the tenth."

"So she could have been snatched en route after the work thing."

"Sounds likely. That's the Samaritan's MO, right?"

"Stop it," Allen said, knowing she was fighting a losing battle against the moniker. "I take it there's no sign of the car."

"It's a blue Honda Civic and we have another bulletin out."

"We need to find the cars. We do that, maybe we get a line on our killer."

Allen's phone rang. She picked up and said her name. She tensed as she listened to the voice on the other end. Mazzucco was staring at her intently when she hung up.

"We found Sarah Dutton. Alive."

# 16

## FORT LAUDERDALE

They'd come up with a catchy name for him already. Of course they had. *The Samaritan*, because apparently he was preying on lone female drivers who'd broken down at night. Sometimes I wondered if the cops and the reporters got together in a room to come up with these nicknames. After all, it was in their mutual interest to create an attention-grabbing stage name. The news didn't give me much else to go on, but the mention of the ragged wound pattern, together with the location being LA, had been plenty.

When it became clear the news was moving comfortably back into regurgitation mode, I sat back down at the hotel writing desk and my fingers hit the keyboard of my laptop. I killed the browser window I'd had open and went to the website of the *Los Angeles Times*. Naturally, they were leading with the Samaritan story. The tone of the article was a little more sober than the reporter still emoting away on camera on the hotel's television screen, but the speculation was identical. They made sure to hedge their journalistic bets by prefacing it all with *News outlets are quoting unconfirmed sources ...*, but the details were the same. Three dead women: tortured, murdered, and disposed of. All with a unique, ragged slash wound to the throat.

If I closed my eyes, I thought I could picture exactly what that ragged slash would look like. I could picture the blade that made it.

Rationally, I knew that all this didn't necessarily mean what I feared it did. Just because the wound was the same didn't mean the killer was. There were only so many ways to kill a person, after all, and only so many weapons. Add to that the fact I'd been thinking about the past only moments before I saw the news report, and the reassuring, comforting explanation was that this was nothing more than a disconcerting echo, an unwelcome synchronicity. Like hearing a song on the radio that reminds you of an old flame at the same moment somebody says her name.

But the pattern fit: abduction, torture, murder. And it wasn't just that; it was Los Angeles. LA was home turf for him. However I explained it, only one thing mattered: the story on the news had tripped the silent alarm at the back of my head, the one that won't let me sleep until I've investigated further. Call it a sixth sense; call it intuition—either way, I've learned not to ignore it.

I opened up a second browser window and navigated to Google. I typed in two words—a name. As I hit return, I didn't know whether I truly wanted to find anything or not. I didn't really expect to get anything useful on just the name, so I wasn't surprised when I didn't. Some images showing half a dozen unfamiliar faces, presumably belonging to men who shared the name. An invitation to view the profiles of individuals of that name on LinkedIn. Even the website of a writer by that name, who apparently specialized in *sensual erotica*. I was pretty sure none of these links would give me what I was looking for.

I left the name in the search field and added *Los Angeles*. Fewer results, but none of them any use. Again, I wasn't surprised. The type of person I was looking for wouldn't be much of a social media animal. The type of person I was looking for would try to leave as little trace of himself as possible. Not so different from me, if only in that respect.

I retrieved my beer and took a long pull. I looked out of the floor-to-ceiling window at the black void of the ocean. I thought about the distance from here to California. It was the better part of three thousand miles. About as far away as you could get without leaving the continental United States. I thought some more, and then my hands returned to the keyboard. I deleted the first name and left everything else in the search field: just the last name and Los Angeles.

I got some more Facebooks and the website of a performing arts theater and some more random grains of sand from the Sahara of the Internet ... and one news article, second from the bottom of the first page. A news article about an event that occurred in the late nineties.

I heard an echo in my head from long ago. *It's the truth.*

I clicked on the link, and the alarm in the back of my head picked up in intensity.

94

# 17

Sarah Dutton had been found. Not a dead body, but a living, breathing potential witness. Sarah hadn't exactly been living under a rock for the previous twenty-four hours, but it seemed she'd been similarly cut off from the real world— ensconced in a three-thousand-dollar-a-night penthouse suite in the Chateau Marmont.

Expensive room or not, she was still in the twenty-first century. She'd made it to two p.m. before learning she was feared murdered and the subject of a statewide search, but she'd laid low for another few hours anyway. Allen didn't think that was particularly odd. She'd never been in that precise situation herself, of course, but she decided it might easily provoke panic in your average young lady. And besides, reading between the lines, Allen decided the fact that she had not been occupying the expensive hotel room alone might explain her hesitation.

The sun was all the way down by the time they got underway, and the evening traffic was typically sluggish. She and Mazzucco made slow progress on the drive back to the palace on Mulholland Drive. The house looked somehow bigger in the dark, the high walls lit from ground level by floodlights.

Walter Dutton was a changed man from their first encounter. Where before he'd looked unkempt and shaken, now he looked rejuvenated. He was dressed in a suit that Allen suspected wouldn't leave much change out of her monthly paycheck. From the moment he opened the door to them, he seemed impatient. Allen wondered if he was

95

overcompensating, embarrassed about his earlier show of vulnerability.

He ushered them back into the big living room, where there were two other people waiting. The first was another suited man with a silk tie and gray hair at his temples. Allen's time in DC had attuned her to certain indigenous character types, and she would bet that meager paycheck on this man being Dutton's senior corporate lawyer.

The other person in the room was easy to place without a detective's instincts—Dutton's twenty-two-year-old daughter, Sarah. She sat huddled in a stiff-backed antique chair, cradling her forearms. She was dressed simply, in contrast to the men, just a lavender blouse, jeans, bare feet. Her eyes were red, and she looked almost relieved to see two Homicide cops. A rarity in itself.

Dutton didn't offer the two of them coffee, didn't ask them to sit down.

"Detectives Allen and Mazzarello, correct?"

"Mazzucco."

"My apologies." He nodded at the lawyer. "This is Jack Carnegie, one of my legal team. And, of course, my daughter, Sarah. I understand you'd like to ask Sarah some questions. We'd like to resolve this as quickly as possible."

"We'll try not to take up too much of your time, sir," Mazzucco said. Allen was impressed: the sarcasm was so reserved, she doubted if it registered with any of the other three. "Perhaps it would be better if we could speak to Sarah alone."

Carnegie was quick off the mark, just as Allen expected him to be. "That's ... not gonna happen, Detective. You can ask Sarah questions, but only in the presence of Mr. Dutton and myself."

Allen looked at the daughter. "I think that would be Sarah's decision."

Dutton shot Allen a glare. Carnegie opened his mouth to object. Sarah cut him off. "It's okay. I want them to stay." Her voice sounded steady enough, but Allen caught the flicker of her eyes as they darted up to her father for approval.

Allen quieted the urge to escalate. It would only burn time, time they did not have. "Okay, Sarah, if you're sure. We're trying to catch the guy who did this to Kelly, okay? He killed some other people, too, and we're pretty sure he'll do it again. We need you to tell us everything you know, even if you don't think you know anything important. The smallest detail can help us out, okay?"

Sarah nodded and sat up straighter in the chair.

"Why don't you tell us about last night?" Mazzucco asked. "You were out with Kelly, right? Who else?"

The mention of the name of her murdered friend was enough to make the girl break into a sob. They waited for her to compose herself.

"Yeah. Just Kelly and me . . . and Josh." Her eyes dropped to the floor as she sensed her father's glare. Allen wondered if the curfew arrangement had been imposed not because of boys in general, but because of this boy in particular. "We had dinner at Mélisse, then a few drinks at Sloan's. I was planning on being back here for eleven or so. But then Josh wanted to stay out longer, and he said he could drive me home. Kelly wasn't feeling so good, so she offered to . . . I mean, she said she could take the . . ."

"Enough, Sarah," Dutton said with an audible sigh. He turned to the detectives. "I believe what my daughter is trying to say is that she wanted to spend the night with this . . . *Josh* character, but she knew I would know she hadn't returned home if I got back and saw that the Porsche was missing. In point of fact, that's exactly how I did know she hadn't returned and why I alerted the authorities."

Mazzucco's brow creased. "You wouldn't have noticed she wasn't here otherwise?"

"My daughter lives in the annex, down by the lower pool. She tends to sleep late on Sundays. Chances are I wouldn't have noticed anything was amiss. She was counting on that, and that's why I imagine she asked her friend to drive the Porsche home."

Allen felt a shiver of electricity and exchanged a glance with Mazzucco. She could see he felt it, too. Kelly Boden now fit snugly into the pattern: lone women drivers at night.

"Is that what happened, Sarah?" Allen prompted. "We need to be very clear on this. Did you arrange with Kelly for her to drive the Porsche home?"

Sarah kept her eyes on the floor and nodded reluctantly. "That's right."

Mazzucco flipped a page back in his notebook. "This bar, Sloan's. That's on Santa Monica Boulevard, isn't it?"

Sarah nodded.

"Was Kelly planning on driving straight back here?"

"She had to. She left around ten thirty. Right before it started raining. I remember being really worried about her. I tried calling her cell around midnight, just to check if she was okay, but it went straight to voicemail."

Allen and Mazzucco shared a glance. The Samaritan had probably started killing her by midnight.

Allen glanced down at her notepad and ticked off another question. "Were you aware of any problems with the Porsche? Any faults, any reason it should break down?"

Sarah looked confused. "No. It was new. I mean, I was low on gas, but I warned Kelly about it. I gave her a twenty to put some in the tank."

Mazzucco raised an eyebrow and made a note on his own pad.

They talked to Sarah for another half hour, but she had nothing else usable to give them, given that she'd had no contact with Kelly after she left the bar. After they'd run through the details of Saturday evening a few times, they asked Sarah to give them chapter and verse on her own movements between then and now. It didn't take long, and it was all easily checkable. One of the lower-priority tangents that could be checked out by one of the uniformed officers drafted in to help with what had already become a major investigation, along with an interview of the boyfriend. Allen didn't expect that to be of much use either, since they already knew his alibi: an alibi that would be corroborated not just by his girlfriend but by the security cameras at the hotel.

The interruptions from Mr. Dutton and his lawyer grew more regular and more impatient as they began to go back over the ground already covered, and so they wound up the interview. It had been worth the trip, because the two pieces of information Sarah had confirmed right out of the gate were golden: Kelly Boden's mode of transport and approximate whereabouts at the estimated time of her abduction. Dutton hustled them out the front door and moved quickly to shut it behind them, as though wanting to close the door on this whole episode. His haste irritated Allen, who couldn't resist a parting shot.

"One other thing, Mr. Dutton?"

"Yes?" He stretched the word out to a couple of syllables.

"Is this really Marlon Brando's old house?" she asked after a pause. She ignored the look from her partner.

Dutton shook his head. "No, Detective. That's a couple of miles from here. And smaller."

The door closed firmly, just short of a slam.

Mazzucco offered to drop Allen off at her place, since it was on his way. Allen agreed but said that she'd drive. As she started the engine and pulled out of the gate onto Mulholland, Mazzucco shook his head.

"Brando's house. Nice."

"He pissed me off," Allen explained. She thought for a second and asked, "You think that was a little weird? Bringing in a lawyer to babysit and all?"

Mazzucco considered. "Nah. I think he was a little rich, that's all. Rich guys like to cover their asses until they know exactly what's going on. They also don't like the little people knowing their business."

"So we know Kelly definitely had the Porsche and that she was headed straight for the Dutton place," Allen said.

"Not straight there. She had to get gas, remember?"

"We might be able to trace that, even though she probably paid cash. Gas station attendants tend to remember nice cars. Helps us to narrow the route down."

"So we have a pretty good idea what happened. This guy somehow got her to stop on the way, abducted her, and took the car." He took out his phone, scrolled to find a contact, and held it up to his ear. "Hi. This is Detective Mazzucco, RHD. I'm just calling for an update on a BOLO for a silver Porsche Carrera." There was a pause. "You're sure? Yeah, I guess you would, at that. Okay, thanks." He hit the button to hang up.

"Nothing?" Allen asked.

He shook his head. "They never found Burnett's BMW either. That's three for three."

"And we know they were all within a few miles of the dump site the last time they were seen. Burnett in Laurel Canyon, Boden heading for Mulholland Drive, and Morrow was close by, as well. If the abduction sites are all in the vicinity of the dump site ..."

"Then the kill site is probably within that radius," Mazzucco finished. "Probably a house, somewhere private."

"Do we know if Rachel Morrow broke down yet?"

Mazzucco made another call to MPU, having to wait a few minutes for the administrator to dig up the relevant file from the missing persons database. By the time he got off the phone, Allen was pulling the gray Ford to a stop outside her apartment building.

"She wasn't a Triple A member. We don't have a contract phone listed for her, either, so we can't tell if she tried to call anybody."

"The Triple A angle didn't pan out for Burnett anyway. But maybe there's another way they could have all come into contact with the same person. Maybe they all stopped for gas in the same place."

"Great minds think alike," Mazzucco agreed, smiling. Then he sighed and looked at his watch. "I'm going to head back to the ranch, test out some of these theories. We know the Porsche's tank was empty, but who's going to remember a Honda Civic from a week ago? I'll start calling around the gas stations en route from Santa Monica to Mulholland. Maybe I can talk to the people who were on last night."

"You asked the boss about this overtime?"

Mazzucco opened his mouth to respond and then realized what she meant, nodding sarcastically. "Julia's fine. I checked in with her a half hour ago."

"Couldn't resist. Sorry," Allen said. "Checking the gas stations is a good idea. I'll make a couple of calls, too. We need to get people canvassing the neighborhoods around the mountains. Maybe we'll get lucky and find his kill house."

She opened the door and got out. As Mazzucco circled the

car to get in the driver's seat, she looked at him, thinking about that call she'd just mentioned. "This is getting big, Mazzucco. I don't want anybody taking this away from us if we can help it. What do you think Lawrence will do?"

"When the feds knock on his door, you mean?" Allen's partner nodded. "We're one, maybe two more victims from that happening, I guess. But Lawrence has no love for the Bureau. He won't give it up without a fight. Why?"

"No reason."

Mazzucco smiled and started to get into the car. Then he remembered something, reached into his jacket pocket. He handed her a folded piece of paper.

"Almost forgot. Burke came through with the sketch of the knife."

Allen looked down at the piece of paper in her hand: a printout of a scan of a detailed pencil drawing. The drawing showed a knife about six inches long, the blade curved back and forth along its length. More like a dagger, in fact. Allen suppressed a shiver as she remembered the wounds that this knife had made.

Mazzucco got in the car and looked up at her through the open window as he turned the keys in the ignition. "Don't work too late."

"Right back at you," she said as he drove off.

As she watched the taillights disappear around the corner, Allen gave Lawrence and the FBI some more thought. Putting up a fight was one thing when the bodies all fell within your jurisdiction, because there was a gray area around exactly when the FBI had to get involved with a serial killer investigation and because the LAPD had more experience in that area than most departments in the country. But a case that crossed state lines? That removed all of that ambiguity with one stroke.

# 18

Allen swiped her security pass and entered the front door of her apartment building, her body on autopilot as her mind cycled through the known facts of the case. On a normal night, she liked to unwind after a shift by watching a movie: rom coms or westerns or action flicks, she wasn't picky. A nice, tidy fictional plot with all the loose ends tied up was an effective palate cleanser after the frustrations and unanswered questions of even a good day at work. She liked watching movies because they always had a definite ending; it didn't even need to be a happy one.

But she knew there would be no time for a DVD tonight. Tonight would be a necessary overspill of the day's work. As she climbed the four flights of stairs to her floor, she realized she'd left her phone on silent after interviewing Sarah Dutton. She took it from her inside pocket and smiled as she saw a missed call from a 202 area code—Washington, DC.

It was now just before ten thirty, and the missed call had been logged at 9:47, so she hoped Sanding would still be around. She hurried up the remaining steps, taking her key from her bag. She opened her apartment door and entered.

And stopped dead in her tracks at the threshold.

The door led into a short hallway: bedroom on the right, living room on the left, bathroom straight ahead. The door to the living room was ajar, and she could see the light was on in there. She thought back to this morning. Had she left the light on? Why would she, in daylight? Then she heard the noise of movement in the living room. Somebody walking across the creaking floorboard on the approach to the window and then the squeak of her venetian blinds being prized apart for a better view to the street.

Allen slipped her shoes off and began to move down the hall barefoot, taking care to avoid the other creaking floorboard outside of the bathroom. She took out her gun, slid the safety off, and cocked it carefully, so as not to make a noise. Then she held her breath and shouldered the door open, holding the gun in a two-handed grip, covering the small living room in a wide arc as she brought the gun to bear on the figure standing by the window.

"Hands on your head," she said, calm and clear, the four words issuing before she recognized the man skulking around her apartment.

"Jesus, Jessica! What the fuck?"

Allen sighed and lowered her gun as she glared at the tall, dark-haired man at the window wearing a dark suit. "I don't remember giving you a key, Denny."

"I used the spare, the one you keep behind the picture in the hall. You know, for a cop, your idea of security is lacking."

"Thanks for the advice."

"I was watching for you," he said, nodding at the window.

"I left the car at home today. Mazzucco dropped me off. What's up?"

Denny's eyes widened in surprise at that, and he just looked at her until it clicked.

"Shit," she said. "Dinner, right?"

"Yeah. Dinner."

"I'm sorry," she said, although she didn't really mean it. She was still too pissed at him for using the spare to get in. "We caught a big one today—three bodies buried out in the hills."

"Yeah, I saw that on the news. You're on that, huh?" Denny's statement of interest was about as sincere as Allen's of apology. In the three months they'd been dating, he'd consistently demonstrated a complete lack of curiosity about her job. Not that Allen would necessarily have wanted him to be too inquisitive, but most people she'd met seemed interested in the job, even if they just wanted to hear some horror stories. Denny, however, seemed to regard the work of a Homicide detective as no more interesting than if she'd been an assistant manager at a suburban McDonald's. The funny thing was, he loved talking about his own work. Whenever he actually got work, that was.

"I'm on that, yeah. It looks like it's going to be a tough one. I completely forgot about tonight."

Denny cocked his head insouciantly and sauntered across the floor to her. "That's okay, babe," he said, encircling her waist and resting his palms on her butt. "I can think of some ways you can make it up to me."

Their lips met, and Allen put her arms around his neck and then pulled her head back, smiling. "Rain check? I actually have a lot still to do tonight."

He stared back at her for a second, an amused look on his face that turned to shock as he realized she was serious. "Are you fucking kidding me?"

Allen's hands snapped down and she stepped back. "No, I'm not kidding. I'm looking for a psycho who tortured and murdered three women, and I have calls to make."

He shook his head. "Well, please accept my apologies for thinking I could spend time with my girlfriend when she's *off-fucking-duty*."

Allen rolled her eyes and turned away from him, walking across the room to the small galley kitchen where she kept the phone and the Chinese menu. "That's not how it works, Denny. We've done this before."

She heard a snort. "You're damned right we've done this

before. How many times is this? You care about these fucking cases more than you care about us."

*More than you care about* me, *you mean*, she thought. "I'm not gonna be much fun to be around tonight, Denny," she said, scanning the menu. She read through the options every time, although she always wound up ordering the same thing. "Why don't I call you tomorrow? We'll do whatever it was you wanted to do tonight."

"Whatever ..." Denny stopped and stared at her for a second. Then he made up his mind, turning and walking to the door. "You know what? I don't need this shit. See you around, Jessica."

He slammed the door to the living room, and Allen quickly called out his name.

The door opened again and his face appeared, scowling petulantly. "What?"

"The spare key?"

Denny shook his head once again, dug a hand into his pants pocket, and pulled the key out, throwing it at the coffee table. He slammed the door again, and a moment later there was a louder slam as the entrance door got the same treatment.

Allen's eyes stayed on the door for a moment and then dropped to the phone in her hand as she considered her next move. It didn't take her long to decide: spicy beef chow mein first and then Michael Sanding.

# 19

## FORT LAUDERDALE

The name was Dean Crozier.

I'd worked alongside him. I'd seen bodies like the ones described in LA once before, and I'd heard about others. The clincher was the archived news story from the nineties: a husband, wife, and their seventeen-year-old daughter found butchered in their beds in their Santa Monica home. There was only one survivor: the sixteen-year-old son, who had apparently been across town at the time of the murder. The authorities had been very interested in him but had never been able to prove anything. The family's name was Crozier.

The rumors had always been passed around the team in quiet voices: that Crozier had killed his family. None of the others seemed to take it particularly seriously, and I'd been inclined to agree at the time. I thought it was probably bullshit, that Crozier himself was most likely the source of the rumors and was simply burnishing his mad dog credentials. Or maybe I just wanted it to be bullshit, because otherwise I'd have to look a little more closely at what exactly I was doing in an outfit that saw fit to employ a man like Dean Crozier.

I'd traveled light on the way down to Florida, but the urgency of my trip to the West Coast meant I'd have to travel lighter still. Taking a gun was out of the question. Even if I could somehow get it through post–9/11 airport security at both ends of the trip, it would be a liability when I reached LA. Unsurprisingly, given its long history of gang violence, Los Angeles was one of the stricter cities in America when it came to owning, and particularly carrying, a handgun. If you were a resident with a spotless record, you might conceivably manage to swing a permit to carry a concealed weapon, but if not, forget about it. Instead, I packed my small case with a change of clothes, my laptop, and a couple of cell phones: my usual one plus a cheap prepay I carried in case I needed a burner.

As I'd expected, it was too late in the day to get a direct flight from Fort Lauderdale to Los Angeles. Instead, I had to settle for a trip via Fort Worth, Texas, scheduled to get into LAX around midnight local time.

I spent the first leg of the trip trying to recall the details of my every encounter with Crozier. It didn't take that long, because there wasn't much to recall: there hadn't been many times we'd been together one-on-one. I hadn't much liked the guy, even early on, and I'd gotten the idea the feeling was more than mutual. That wasn't to say he'd been close to any of the other guys, either. In a company of loners, Crozier seemed to work hard at being the outcast.

Winterlong was not the official name for the operation. It was just one of a series of code names for an operation established in the late 1980s, when the cold war was coming to an end and smaller, more personal warfare was becoming the in thing. It was paid for out of a Pentagon slush fund and given a decoy official title so dull and administrative-sounding that you forgot it as soon as your eyes passed over it in a budget report. The code names were supposed to be refreshed once every eighteen months. They cycled through a few—Royal Blue, Silverlake, Olympia—before deciding that what they'd created was better off not having a name. It was too late, though, because Winterlong had stuck.

Mutual dislike aside, Crozier and I were separated within the team by our respective specialties. It was a small, elite unit, at any one time involving eighteen to twenty operators. Drakakis was the CO, and Grant was his second in command. Below that, the personnel was mostly distributed among three separate but complementary sections: the Signals Intelligence, or SigInt, guys worked communications, covert surveillance devices, hacking and tracking cell phones, breaking into secure web servers and databases. Human Intelligence, or HumInt, covered the people side of the equation: identifying and approaching potential assets and then handling them. SigInt and HumInt tended to lay the groundwork for the third group when it was needed: the shooters. Crozier was in this final group, the team that executed, often literally, the operations that came about through the intelligence gathering and planning of the other two sections. Winterlong ranged far and wide, not tied to any one region or officially designated conflict zone. Usually, we kept to our own activities, deploying and carrying out our operations without the need for cooperating with the CIA or the more visible special operations teams. The advantage was we could go into an area without any underlying intelligence infrastructure and quickly create our own. Occasionally, the Joint Special Operations Command would bring us in on an operation that was already in the planning stages but had been deemed by the brass to be unsuitable for the involvement of the Navy SEALs or Delta, and officially canceled. Too tough for the teams, was how they generally sold it to us. Closer to the truth would be that we were brought in for only two types of assignments: those that required the uniquely wide cross section of skill sets within an extremely compact team and those that required deniability beyond the standard requirements of black ops. The deniability was absolute: when a member of the unit was killed in action, nobody was ever told, not even their families. The dead of Winterlong just disappeared, as though they'd never existed. Perhaps that was why so few of the operators, myself included, had families. We never heard what happened to the badly injured, although I had my suspicions. The upside? The money was great and there was a lot of downtime between assignments.

If you weren't a member of Winterlong, you didn't know about Winterlong. Men trained for years and qualified for some of the most elite fighting teams in the world without ever hearing the name. At the very top of those units, you started to hear whispered rumors of a secret team that was beyond secret. When you were approached to join the unit, it was only after they'd confirmed two things: that you were the best of the best and that you'd accept the assignment.

I didn't fit neatly into any of the three sections. I'd come in on HumInt, my specialty in locating hard-to-find targets, but had quickly developed my skills in the other two sections with Drakakis's approval. There was one other man in the same position, and Drakakis called us his swingmen: we could handle the human and tech work with the best of them, but could also pick up a weapon and operate downstream when called to.

Because of this, I tended not to tag along on the bulk of the shooter operations, except where the job called for it. It was on those sporadic occasions that I came into Crozier's orbit. I guessed I'd been alone with him on no more than two occasions, been involved with him on maybe half a dozen operations. The last of those ops was the catalyst that had started me thinking about leaving.

I changed planes at Fort Worth just after eleven p.m. Pacific: a quick layover, and thankfully both planes were on time. I had no checked baggage to transfer, and my photographic ID caused no problems. The onward flight to Los Angeles was a short one. I spent it looking out of the window, down on the dark patches of landscape and the pincushions of light. I thought about how the LAPD had so much more on its hands than a simple serial killer. I thought about the last time I saw Crozier and then about my own final deployment in Karachi. Mostly, I thought about Crozier's dead-eyed stare and the whispered rumors, and I wondered why the past wouldn't leave me alone.

# 20

The sun had long since set and the light that intruded through the blinds was the dirty sodium yellow of streetlights, but he felt no need to switch on the lamp.

He had left the house for a couple of hours earlier on, but now he was back and watching the live news broadcasts with an interest that almost made him feel ashamed. This had not been part of the plan, not yet. And yet he'd known deep down that it was an inevitability sooner or later.

He actually liked the name they'd conjured up for him this time. He'd had other names in other places: names like *the Woodsman, the Attendant.* It was nothing to be proud of, not really. It only meant he'd been noticed in those places, that he hadn't been careful enough. Most times, he'd completed his task quietly and moved on without a ripple, leaving only questions in his wake. An unexplained disappearance, a random isolated act of violence.

Feeling as though he'd gorged himself on something that was not good for him, he switched the television off and walked across the narrow hall to the other room. He lay down on top of the sheets and knitted his fingers together behind his head. He stared at the ceiling as he thought about the first time. Ninety-six. Three of them had hiked up there, into the mountains, but only two had come back.

The howl of a police siren approaching snapped him out of his thoughts and back to the present. He got off the bed and went to the window, standing at the gap in the blinds until he saw the cruiser flash by without slowing, on its way to some nameless emergency. After the lights disappeared and the noise of the siren faded, he stood there watching the empty street for a minute, wondering about how effective the police would be here in Los Angeles. There was no real danger of them finding him before it was time to move on again, but perhaps it would be prudent to change his approach a little.

The Samaritan lay back down on the bed and knitted his fingers behind his head once again. He wondered how long it would take them to find out about the others.

## 1996

They'd left the Buick parked at a wide spot in the road just before they reached the track. He let Kimberley take the lead, with himself in the middle and Robbie bringing up the rear. Eighty-plus degrees, but the heat didn't bother him. It didn't seem to bother Kimberley, either. Robbie, however, was flagging.

"Screw this," Robbie declared a half hour into the trek. "We're never going to find it. Hey, man, give me the water again."

He hadn't liked Robbie to begin with. He was liking him less and less as the day progressed.

But he shrugged his backpack off anyway, reached into it, and handed Robbie his bottle of water. They had one pack between them, and he'd volunteered to carry it. He supposed Robbie would assume he was doing that to impress Kimberley, and maybe even Kimberley thought that, too. But the truth was he liked to push himself. The hike wasn't enough. The heat wasn't enough. It was always good to push further. Besides, there was another, more practical reason to be the one to carry the pack.

Kimberley stopped and turned around, looking at Robbie with disdain. She was holding a thick branch, using it as a makeshift hiking stick, though in truth it was too short and too thick to be of much real use. "It's up here. I'm telling you." Then she looked straight at him. "How about you? You're not gonna quit on me now, are you?"

He shook his head. "Let's keep going."

Kimberley flashed a wide grin at him, and her chocolate-brown eyes danced. "Didn't I tell you we'd have fun together?"

He nodded slowly and then looked back to Robbie. Robbie was taking another deep slug from his water bottle. Asshole. There would be none left for the return trip at that rate.

By the time Robbie handed the bottle back to him, Kimberley had set off again. She was already twenty yards ahead of them, swinging her branch as she walked. He stowed the bottle in the pack, slung it back over his shoulders, and started walking again. Had he made up his mind to go through with it at that point, as he watched Kimberley stride ahead, masking her own obvious fatigue? He supposed he had. He had already decided this was a day for pushing boundaries.

# 21

After ordering food, Allen called Mike Sanding back. He'd left the office already, but she managed to talk the desk into giving her his cell number.

"I talked to the ME," he said as soon as he answered the phone. "We pulled the files of those two unsolveds we talked about. He actually performed the autopsy on the snitch. We looked at the transcripts, photographs of the wounds. In his opinion, they could have been made by the same weapon in both cases."

"Profile on the weapon?"

"Short knife or dagger, maybe six inches long. A curved, jagged pattern on both sides of the blade."

Allen considered this. "Sounds like what they said here— maybe some kind of ceremonial dagger."

"Yeah, I saw the news—they're saying some kind of black magic shit?"

"Don't remind me. Can I ask a favor?"

"You want to send me the pics of the wounds in LA, see if our guy thinks they're a match, too? No problem, Jess. I already said I might have more to show him."

"That's not the favor. I want you to do what you just said, yes, but I don't want anyone to know about it."

Sanding paused, and she heard him suck air through his teeth. "He's gonna ask."

"I know, Mike. Make something up. Tell him you're working another case and it's need-to-know." The suggestion came out sounding as lame as it was. If the coroner had been paying attention to the news, he would put two and two together.

Sanding thought about it for another couple of seconds and agreed. Hanging up, she knew he had a pretty good idea of what she was worried about. From the hesitation, she had the idea he didn't entirely approve, but he'd go along with it just the same. Mike was a good man, and he'd been as good as his word on her last day with the department—*Anything you need, give me a call.* He'd given her everything he could on this, but she would be on her own for the next part, because there was no one else back in Washington whom she trusted enough to ask the same questions.

The Chinese food arrived at her door fifteen minutes later, and she ate it in front of her computer with a Coke from the refrigerator. She ignored the beers that were in there, still feeling the residual effects from the previous night.

If she was right about the link between the bodies in the hills and the two victims she'd discussed with Sanding, it was likely there would be more Washington, DC victims, probably among the pile of unsolved murders for that year. In the absence of a direct contact from one of those investigations, what she really needed was access to the national crime database. But that would mean leaving an audit trail on the system, and she didn't want to do that if she didn't have to.

Instead, she navigated to the website of the MPDC, realizing the irony of the fact that this was her first visit, despite being a former serving officer with Metro PD. The website hosted a section listing unsolved homicides going back as far as the early fifties. By making the information available to the public and offering rewards, they left the door open for the occasional thousand-to-one chance that someone would come forward with useful information on a cold case.

The older cases were grouped by decade, but each year since the millennium had its own page. She scrolled down a long list of around sixty victims: the year she was interested in had its share of people getting away with murder in the nation's capital.

The list had a name, and usually a photograph, for each victim, along with date and location of death. Each entry could be clicked on for more information about the crime. As Allen scanned the list, she couldn't help but notice how many of the faces were black. Sure, the inner city was more than 60 percent African American, but this roll call of the dead and yet to be avenged was more like 90 percent. She reminded herself that she wasn't carrying out a sociological exercise here and started narrowing her search to the months between August and December. The cases were arranged alphabetically by victim name, and there was no way of sorting, so she had to resort to a pen and paper.

Keeping it to this date range narrowed the search down to a dozen names. She spent time clicking into each one for more information. In most cases, there wasn't too much more detail. Information about the date and time the crime was committed, or the body discovered, along with very basic details of the cause of death. Each record contained a link to a PDF flyer containing the same information and promising a reward of up to twenty-five thousand dollars for information leading to a conviction. The reward flyer also included cell and desk numbers for the investigating detectives, as well as the direct number for their homicide branch.

Twenty-five fairly depressing minutes later, Allen had narrowed the list down to five candidates by eliminating the victims whose cause of death was something other than bladed trauma: mostly gunshot wounds, hit-and-run deaths, even one poisoning. She'd eliminated one of those five— Michael Antonio—because he'd been found alive with stab wounds and had died in the hospital three days later. She was interested only in the victims who'd been killed outright.

The Samaritan didn't make mistakes when he decided to kill.

Allen took a break, made herself a pot of coffee, and then sat down with her four names: Randy Solomon, September twelfth, found at 2:31 a.m. with stab wounds in the 700 block of Delafield Place. James Willis Hendrick, September thirtieth, found with head trauma—nonspecific—in Lamont Park. Audra Baker, October fifth, stab wounds, inside the Fourth Street deli where she worked. Bennett Davis, October seventeenth, stab wounds, the 1200 block of Sixth Street.

The individual summaries on the website hadn't provided much more than the bare bones of information. She knew from experience that there could be a world of difference between two murders recorded under the same cause of death: *head trauma*, for example, covered everything from an accidental concussion that resulted in death all the way up to decapitation. She went back over the four names, typing each into Google in order to cross-reference the dry, factual information on the unsolved site with the reliably lurid accounts in the press or the crime blogs.

It didn't take her long to eliminate two more names. Randy Solomon had been stabbed in the chest following an altercation in a bar, and although there had been witnesses to the killing, the suspect was never found. Bennett Davis had been found facedown in an alley with his wallet missing. There had been only one stab wound—unluckily for Davis, to the femoral artery. He'd bled out in the alley following what looked like a cut-and-dried mugging-turned-homicide. In both cases, the victims had been killed quickly—perhaps even unintentionally—and left where they fell. A different brand of murder entirely from the victims in LA, or the ones she'd discussed with Sanding.

That left James Hendrick, the park victim, and Audra Baker, the deli worker. Other than geography and the manner of their untimely deaths, the two didn't seem to have much in common: Hendrick was a white male office manager in his late forties, Baker a seventeen-year-old black female with a minimum-wage job. But once you got beyond age and race, the similarities soon began to mount up. Even before you took anything else into consideration, the two cases had one important thing in common: the bodies were found in secluded, quiet locations. Locations that were ideal for dumping the bodies of victims who had been killed else-where. Or alternatively, they allowed a killer time to work on his victim.

That common thread made these two victims the best can-didates from the original list of sixty. The additional details Allen had found in the news reports practically sealed the deal. Both were discovered in the morning, having been dead for hours. Both showed evidence of torture; both had had their throats cut. The reports didn't specify a ragged wound pattern, but that was exactly the type of detail that would not be released to the media. It was why she was so pissed about the leak here in LA. It was sound practice: withholding the fine detail so that it could be used to weed out the cranks and to validate confessions. But having spent the best part of a couple of hours tracking down this pair of needles in a haystack, Allen saw it for the first time as a potential disadvantage. The number of homicides annually in Washington had been steadily falling from a peak of nearly four hundred a year in the early nineties, but the numbers were still considerable, and the resources to investigate them finite. With different personnel on separate cases, it was easy for patterns to be missed, particularly when the victim profile was so divergent. And knife murders weren't like gunshot murders—there were no ballistics to precisely match any two killings to a single weapon. The best you could do was to say that two people had been killed by the same *type* of bladed weapon, unless you had the knife itself.

She went back to the Metro PD unsolved website and checked the reward flyers for her two victims. As she'd anticipated, they'd been investigated by different teams in different homicide branches. Finally, she used her personal email account to send links to the Hendrick and Baker cases over to Mike Sanding with a brief explanation of what she wanted. With some smooth talking, he'd probably be able to access the autopsy reports on both victims and run them by the coroner, who would by now have no illusions that he was being asked to judge whether they were looking at the work of a serial killer. That was okay, though, as long as he assumed this was a dormant killer who'd operated in DC two years before and didn't tie it to the case out here in LA.

After hitting send on the email to Sanding, Allen looked at the clock at the bottom right-hand corner of her screen for the first time and was surprised to see she'd been working for more than four hours. She sat back and massaged her eyeballs. It wasn't just a theory anymore. She had three victims of the same killer out here in LA. She'd now identified four similar killings back in Washington, all falling within a period of four weeks in late 2012. She couldn't be 100 percent sure it was the work of the same man, but all of the instincts she'd honed over the past twelve years as a cop told her it was. And she was betting when Sanding's coroner compared the idiosyncratic wound patterns from 2012 with those from LA, they'd have a match.

What the hell did she have here?

Leave aside the tiny remaining element of doubt for a moment. Say the four murders in DC and the three in LA were definitely committed by the same man, what did that say? For a start, it said that this killer was unusual in a number of ways. Serial killers tended to keep to one patch: a familiar city or location. Occasionally, they roamed farther, killing along the route of a particular highway or train track. But this would be something rarer: a killer who struck quickly and lethally in one city and then disappeared, only to turn up in a different city, on the other side of the country and after a gap of more than two years.

It was easy to see how the similarities would likely have been missed had it not been for the coincidence of Allen happening to work two of those apparently unrelated homicides. It was evidence of a smart, calculating murderer. Choosing a range of victim types, varying the exact cause of death and method of disposal, and yet unable to resist using his signature weapon on each one. If it was the same guy, he'd adopted a different approach for the murders in Los Angeles: relying on concealment of the bodies to allow him to carry out his work. And had it not been for the landslide that revealed them, she would not be sitting here now, having made these connections.

She wondered about the two-and-a-half-year gap. Again, from experience, it was rare—although not unheard of—that a killer would be able to stop himself from killing for so long a period once he'd gotten started. Serial killers tended to work themselves into a frenzy, allowing a smaller window of time between each victim until they were caught or stopped in some other way. The easiest explanation was that he'd been in jail. That he'd been arrested on some other, lesser charge and been safely locked away for the past thirty months. That theory could definitely provide a viable lead, if they could come up with recently released convicts fitting the profile.

But it didn't explain why the killer had moved to LA.

As Allen thought it over, a new, more worrying thought occurred to her. Four killings in Washington, DC, followed by a gap of two and a half years, and then three more killings in Los Angeles—that was the theory she'd been working on. But what if that was wrong? What if it hadn't been four killings in one city and then three in a second city? What if there had been more killings, more cities?

What if there hadn't been a gap?

# 22

After landing at LAX, I passed through security and stopped to withdraw some cash. Again, force of habit. If anyone had the interest or wherewithal to monitor activity on the bank account I'd used, it wouldn't lead anywhere too specific, just to an ATM at the sixth busiest airport in the world. I didn't use credit cards when it could be avoided, so I always made sure I had enough paper money with me to last me for a day or two.

The bodies had been discovered off a fire road near Mandeville Canyon, close to San Vicente Mountain. That meant Encino or Sherman Oaks would be the closest parts of town in which to base myself. I happened to know a suitable hotel in Sherman Oaks from my sole previous visit to the City of Angels.

The taxi driver was a tall man of Indian descent. He didn't talk much after taking my destination, and I was just fine with that. The cabdrivers I'd encountered on my first trip to LA had all made a point of complaining at length about the traffic, as though it were somehow a unique feature of the city. In its own way, I supposed it was, if only in its indelible effect on the day-to-day life of everyone who lived here or visited. The freeway wasn't quiet, not even at this time of night, but the trip from the airport took only half an hour or so on the 405. The lack of chitchat allowed me to think some more, to decide on the initial moves I had to make in the morning.

One of my quickest conclusions was that Crozier had not suddenly made the decision to start killing people after a well-earned break. He'd left our common employer a little while before I had made my own exit, which made it just over five years ago. As was the norm, there had been no warning and no notice period. People didn't just leave Winterlong. In my time in the unit, I saw a few depart—either becoming too old or too burnt out. Those people didn't exactly leave. They were just retired from active service. And then, of course, there were those who were killed in action. But Crozier hadn't been phased out and he hadn't been killed in action. He'd just disappeared. Inasmuch as I'd thought about it, I'd suspected Drakakis had finally come to the conclusion that Crozier was too crazy in a way that could no longer be safely harnessed. He'd either been rotated out and into some other team ... or he'd been dealt with permanently. Unfortunately, I now had a pretty good idea that the second possibility hadn't happened.

So I had a five-year gap where I couldn't account for Crozier's movements, ending with yesterday's discovery of the recently buried bodies of three murder victims that looked very likely to be his work. There was no way he'd been sitting around for the past five years playing *World of Warcraft*, so that meant I had to assume there were more bodies buried out there in LA ... or somewhere else.

We arrived at the hotel, a four-story art-deco place just off Ventura Boulevard.

"You sure you wanna stay here?" the cabbie had asked.

"It's old. I can take you to a nicer place a block away."

"No, thanks," I said, shaking my head and handing over cash for the ride. I liked the place, even if it was old. I always prefer old hotels, and not just for aesthetic reasons. There are always fewer security cameras. Fewer ways to leave a trace. Force of habit or superstition again. I checked in as Gil Kane of San Francisco and took the key for my room on the second floor. The hotel might have been old, but it had dipped enough of a toe into the twenty-first century to provide WiFi in its rooms. I wanted to get some sleep before morning, to make sure I was rested up for hitting a few locations I wanted to check, but first I wanted to see if I could find evidence of Crozier's work before yesterday's exhumation.

I opened my laptop and went to the LAPD's website. For a city of Los Angeles's size and reputation, there were relatively few unsolved murders over the preceding five years that I wasn't able to eliminate right away. A lot of gang shootings, a lot of cases where the motive was clear, even if no suspect had been tracked down. That worried me. It meant Crozier had been careful—either by concealing his victims, or by operating somewhere else entirely. If it was the former, there wasn't much I could do about it. I could check the numerous resources for missing persons in the Los Angeles area, but without a confirmed cause of death, I was nowhere.

I didn't even think it would be possible to narrow down possible victim types, because I didn't really believe that Crozier *had* a victim type. I guess he was already technically a serial killer by the time he left Winterlong, albeit in a professional capacity. But if he'd continued that profession on his own time, I was pretty sure he wouldn't be a particularly discriminating killer. It was a rare personality type, but one I knew well: the kind of person who just enjoys the experience of killing. The thrill of taking a life. Therefore, opportunity would be more important than the appearance or age or gender of the victim.

For the moment, I was stalled. Except for one possibility ... I already knew that Crozier was a native Angeleno, almost a rare breed in a city of transplants. The news story about the murdered family sharing his name I'd seen last night had confirmed that. But I remembered one other thing he'd mentioned, on one of the two occasions I'd had something approximating a conversation with him.

In any unit that was frequently deployed overseas, in inhospitable locations, it was common for the men to talk about the things they missed and the things they were looking forward to doing when they got home. Favorite girls or bars they wanted to visit when they got back, things like that. Crozier, as in all things, was a little different. Crozier talked about a guy he wanted to kill.

The individual in question was a sergeant who taught at the Q Course at Fort Bragg when Crozier was trying out for the Green Berets, a few years before our paths crossed for the first time. Crozier held the sergeant responsible for a training accident that resulted in Crozier breaking his arm.

I couldn't remember the name of the sergeant, or if Crozier had even told me it, but I had a location and a rough time frame. I could look for murders or fatal accidents involving army personnel occurring in the vicinity of Fort Bragg within the last five years. I just had to hope that if Crozier had acted on his impulse for revenge, he had done it within the North Carolina state boundary.

It took me less than five minutes to find what I was looking for. It wasn't an unsolved murder. Actually, it wasn't a confirmed murder of any kind, as far as anybody knew. I sat back and looked at the square-jawed face staring back at me from the screen: a service photograph above a news story. Sergeant Willis Peterson, a decorated veteran of Vietnam and one of the best-regarded instructors on the Special Forces program. He'd disappeared en route to work sometime after eight a.m. on Tuesday November 10, 2010, and neither he nor his car had ever been seen again. I found another mention of his name in 2013, when investigators had linked him to a decomposed body found in the woods along his route, but DNA testing had ruled out the match. Suicides were hardly rare among military personnel adjusting to civilian life, or the quasi-civilian life of an instructor, and I got the feeling that all concerned with investigating the disappearance had quietly chalked Peterson's disappearance up to a case of undiagnosed PTSD.

I had another theory, and what's more, I didn't think the second body they'd found nearby was unrelated at all.

In another minute, I had the phone number of Cole Harding, the detective who'd been investigating the body in the woods. The number put me through to his voicemail. I found the number for his squad, dialed it, and found out that he'd be back on shift in the morning. They asked if I wanted to leave a message, and I declined, saying I'd speak to him later on.

It was three in the morning now, local time. Six a.m. by my body clock. I felt frustrated by the little progress I'd made so far. Crozier was out there, maybe getting ready to kill someone else tonight, and I was no further forward.

I decided there was nothing I could do about that for now. The best I could do was to get some rest and recharge my batteries. It looked like I had a start point and an end point for Crozier's movements since 2010. I could build on that tomorrow. I had a phone call to make and a couple of places to visit in the morning. I set the alarm on my phone for seven.

Then I lay down on top of the sheets in a hotel room that was three thousand miles away from the one in which I'd expected to spend the night and closed my eyes.

# MONDAY

# 23

I called again just after seven, using the burner I'd brought with me, and got Detective Harding this time. I told him I'd known Sergeant Peterson from training under him at Fort Bragg. That I'd looked him up on a whim and been shocked to find out he'd disappeared. Harding asked me a couple of innocent-sounding questions to see if he could catch me out, but I dealt with them easily enough. He knew full well he was operating at an information deficit: with all the men that passed through Bragg over the course of a decade, there was no way for a lowly cop to know for sure if I was who I said I was. Besides, I got the feeling he was curious about why someone was calling him out of the blue about a case that was so cold it could give you freezer burn.

"Peterson had a lot of friends, a nice stable family," he said. "Although I guess you would know that."

"You don't think it was a suicide, then?" I asked, avoiding committing to any more than I needed to.

"Well, I would never rule it out, Mr. Blake. You know how it is. A person can seem to be hunky-dory, and then one day they jump in front of an express train. You never can tell. Especially with you military types. No offense."

"None taken. I guess you must have a lot of cases tied to the base, right?"

"We get our share. Nothing quite like Peterson, though."

"How so?"

Harding paused, and I could sense him hesitating. I waited him out. Eventually, he sighed. "You'll appreciate I can't go into the specifics of the investigation, particularly for someone who's not a family member."

"Of course."

"But I've been in this job for going on thirty years. Homicide doesn't just mean homicide; it means any suspicious or unattended deaths, and disappearances that could be deaths, too. You start to get a feel for things. For certain patterns."

He paused, and I said nothing, relying on his frustration with the problem to keep him talking.

"A lot of people around here decided that Sergeant Peterson drove into the woods and ate a bullet. Maybe even his family decided that was the explanation. But I never believed it. Not for a second."

"You sound pretty sure."

"I am sure. Oh, I guess I could rationalize it, talk about how he had a vacation booked and paid for, about how his daughter was expecting his first grandchild, about how he never left a note or gave any indication of wanting to put his affairs in order. But it's more intangible than those things."

"You had a feel for it."

"That's right."

I paused, considering whether to risk the next question. I decided to go all in. I had all the hard facts I could expect to get. If I could get Harding to betray his suspicions, it would be a shortcut to confirmation of my theory.

"You really thought the body you found in those woods a couple of years back was Peterson, didn't you?"

He didn't speak for a moment, and when he did, his voice sounded guarded. Like I'd lulled him into candor over the last couple of minutes, but now the shields were back up.

"Did you see that when you were looking him up? I guess you would have."

"I saw it in the news reports, that's right. But it only said the DNA didn't match. It didn't say if that other body was a suicide."

Silence on the end of the line. I could still hear the office chatter in the background, which was the only reason I knew he hadn't hung up.

"You think there are others out there, too, don't you, Detective Harding?"

Harding's voice was quiet when he finally spoke. "When did you say you were at Fort Bragg again, Mr. Blake? I think maybe we need to meet in person."

"Thanks for your help, Detective," I said, and ended the call. I switched the phone off and removed the battery. I could dump it in the trash later on.

I closed my eyes and pictured a map of the country. North Carolina was almost as far from California as Florida was. It sounded as though Crozier had killed more people than just Willis Peterson there, and he'd had a lot of time and a lot of space to kill many more since then. A man who did not technically exist would have utter freedom to act on his homicidal impulses, as long as he was careful and could rely on a certain amount of luck. Crozier had been careful, all right, but his luck had run out yesterday morning.

Now it was time to curtail his freedom.

# 24

I dressed quickly, in the dark suit I'd brought with me and a fresh shirt. I left the usual telltales in the hotel room, locked up, went downstairs, and left through the main door. I walked to Ventura Boulevard. I turned right and walked until I reached the second-closest car rental place to the hotel.

I didn't spend too long making my decision, choosing a dark blue 2013 Chevrolet Malibu because it wouldn't be too remarkable. I gave the car a quick look over before signing the paperwork. As I'd expected, there were no stickers or plate modifications that identified this as a rental—a legacy of the rash of tourist carjackings that had plagued the city in the nineties. The rental clerk barely glanced at my driver's license, as was usual. It was one of the places that leaves about a quarter of a gallon of gas in the tank, rather than providing a full tank up front. I'd noticed the latter type was almost an extinct breed: a sign of the times.

I was still formulating a plan of action. Crozier would be very difficult to find, even for me. He could be borderline impossible to find, in fact, without either some help or another breakthrough of some kind. Quite apart from his background, he had expert local knowledge of Los Angeles. The murder of his parents and sister—still officially open and unsolved—had taken place in ninety-seven, when Crozier would have been sixteen or seventeen. That meant he had sixteen or seventeen more years of experience of this town than I did, plus however long he'd spent here recently. The first order of business, then, was to start orienting myself, and this was one town in which the only way to do that was by car. The logical place to start was the one place I knew my quarry had been within the last forty-eight hours: the body dump site in the hills.

I filled the tank at the gas station next door to the rental place and scanned the front pages of the newspapers. The *LA Times* carried social media–culled pictures of the three victims discovered in the mountains. The similarity in the three faces was striking and caused me to reconsider my earlier thoughts about Crozier being indiscriminate. He may have been to begin with, but these latest killings suggested he'd developed a type: young, white females with dark hair. I wondered why that was and if it would be unique to LA.

I paid for the gas and a copy of the *Times* and then drove back toward the 405. At first I chalked the morning mayhem up to rush hour before reminding myself that there was no such thing in LA, a town where no one was able to rush at any hour. Eventually, I saw the exit for Sunset and took it, following the route until I reached Mandeville Canyon Road. As I'd hoped, the traffic thinned. Freed from having to focus on moderating gas and brake so that I didn't ram a vehicle in front, or let one behind hit me, my thoughts returned to Crozier.

My conversation with Detective Harding had confirmed my suspicions. The veteran investigator had probably started out investigating the disappearance of Sergeant Peterson open to the possibility it was a simple suicide, or even desertion. But he'd quickly intuited that the sergeant had not disappeared by choice, even if he couldn't prove it. In the absence of evidence of an accident, that left two prob- abilities: kidnap or murder. The lack of a ransom demand, or any other communication, narrowed that down to one probability.

That was why, when a decomposed corpse of similar characteristics and vintage had been discovered in the woods around Fort Bragg, Harding's instinct had been that the body was his missing person. It wasn't, though. It was some other missing person, perhaps yet to be identified, who'd disappeared around the same time and in the same area as Peterson. I knew how the thought process would work for a veteran cop: the non-match against Peterson's DNA didn't make it any less likely that Peterson himself had been murdered. On the contrary, the fact of another dead body in the same neck of the woods made that conclusion even more likely. Harding would have assumed, as did I, that Peterson's body was out there somewhere, and that if there were two bodies, there might well be three, or more. It wasn't about evidence; it was about experience and balance of probability. Patterns, as Harding had admitted to me on the phone.

In the same way, I knew the killer hadn't confined himself to these killings. There would be more out there, waiting to be connected. Maybe a lot more.

The road forked ahead. I'd checked it out on the map beforehand and knew that a right turn would take me on the higher road. I bore right and climbed for about a mile. I'd worked out the approximate location of the dump site by cross-referencing the media coverage, but I realized I'd been wasting my time when I saw the news helicopter hanging in the sky about a mile ahead, like a giant floating signpost. Soon enough, I approached the scene I'd expected. Cars parked on the shoulder. A crowd of people standing at the thin steel crash barrier and looking down the hill. I parked at the end of the line of vehicles and got out. I'd been wearing sunglasses while driving and started to remove them because this side of the hill was in shadow. Then I took a closer look at the crowd at the crash barrier and decided to leave them on.

I looked over the barrier and down the hill and saw the body dump scene. It was easy to identify the three locations where bodies had been found from the concentration of activity around them: uniformed cops and crime scene techs were hovering over each spot. At the bottom of the hill was the road I'd have passed if I'd taken the left turn, only I wouldn't have made it that far because it was blocked. There were two dark-colored vans, a couple of police cruisers, and an unmarked Ford Taurus parked across the road. Dotting the hillside were scars of earth where the ground had been dug up. I could tell the cops were winding down: in comparison to the manpower evident in the helicopter pictures on the news last night, they'd cut it back to a skeleton crew, and there seemed to be no new digging sites at all. One of the cops looked up, staring at the crowd of people thirty yards to my left before turning his head to me. He shook his head and looked down again. I examined the crowd: it was mainly comprised of men in their thirties and forties, most of them wielding cameras. Paparazzi. Again, far from a unique feature to Los Angeles, but one that the city seemed to do singularly well. A couple of them threw casual glances in my direction, but none of them made a move to take my picture. I was pleased, not to mention unsurprised that I didn't warrant a photograph.

I looked back down the hill, taking in all the details that I couldn't get from the text or still pictures or video I'd seen. There's no substitute for visiting the scene of a crime. I could see immediately why Crozier had chosen the spot. It was easily accessible from two separate roads, but not exactly the kind of spot anyone would have any reason to stop and take a look around. The two back roads isolated it from any of the tracks that hikers used in the hills, so there was virtually no likelihood of anybody happening to cover that ground on foot. A dumping ground off of one of the footpaths might offer more seclusion, but it would also be more easily discovered, particularly by dogs. In contrast, there was the risk that a driver might see something while you were digging a shallow grave on the hillside, but again, that was less of a risk at night, particularly if you wore dark clothing and lay down when you heard a car coming.

The nearest of the graves was about fifty feet down from the barrier. The farthest one equidistant between the two roads. It looked like the killer had brought the bodies down from up here, rather than up from down there. Logical—it meant gravity worked with you.

"Getting a good view?"

The sharp voice came from behind me. I turned to see a balding man in his early fifties. He wore jeans and a plaid work shirt. The lack of either a camera or a baseball cap told me he wasn't one of the paparazzi. His casual dress said he probably wasn't one of the cops. I was less certain about the second conclusion. He projected a vibe that said he was used to some kind of authority. I guessed he might be recently retired from the kind of job that would give him that bearing. The thing about him that told me the most, however, wasn't the way he was dressed. It was the look on his face. Angry, but the anger was covering something else.

I nodded down the hill at the police activity, then glanced at the paparazzi before I answered. "Good morning," I said. "Just seeing what all the fuss is about."

The man shook his head. "You're a little late. They already took all the *bodies* away."

The way he said *bodies* sealed it: grieving family member, understandably pissed at people like me and the gentlemen just along the road. People apparently intruding on his grief to make a quick buck or get a vicarious kick. He was fixing me with a full-beam glare. I met it and said nothing for a few seconds.

"I'm sorry. Did you know one of the victims?"

He didn't answer right away. Seemed to size me up. I knew he was doing the same thing I'd done: taking in the way I was dressed, the way I carried myself. I've been mistaken for a cop myself before. It doesn't always hurt. Eventually, he nodded, coming to the conclusion that I might be worthy of closer investigation. "That's right. My kid, Kelly. They told her friend's dad before me; you believe that? My only kid." He looked down at the grave excavation site, and then his head snapped back up to look at me. "Who are you, anyway? You're not one of those vultures, and you're not a cop either."

"What makes you so sure?"

"I was on the force for thirty years, retired last year."

"LAPD?"

"San Diego. You didn't answer my question."

I stuck my hand out. "Carter Blake."

"Dick Boden," he said, taking my hand and shaking it briefly.

"I have a professional interest. My line of work is finding people who don't necessarily want to be found. It strikes me that this is a person who needs to be found."

"You don't look like a bounty hunter either."

"That's because I'm not. I'm more of a ... locating con-sultant."

Boden gave it some thought. "An expensive one, I guess. If you're good."

"Depends on the job."

"And who's paying you to do this job?"

No reason to lie, and in any case, I had the feeling that Boden would know BS when he smelled it. "Nobody," I answered simply.

Boden raised his eyebrows but didn't say anything. He looked away from me, down at the holes in the ground below us again, and his hands balled into fists. "The motherfucker dumped her like trash when he was done with her."

I said nothing. He took a deep breath and closed his eyes, and I could see him mentally struggling to get some objective distance, to put the professional part of his brain to work on this most personal of crises. "And what do you think so far, Blake?"

I took my time before responding, because I couldn't share everything here. I couldn't talk about the fact I knew the killer's name.

"I think this guy has killed before—before any of these three, I mean—so we might be able to do something by backtracking, tagging open and unsolved cases to him. I think he's done it in the past and he'll do it in the future, so that means he needs to be stopped by any means possible."

Boden's eyes flicked up to me at that last remark, but he didn't comment. The personal fighting back against the professional, maybe.

I continued. "The disposal site indicates planning, preparation, and local knowledge. He's a practiced, professional operator who knows the hills."

"Anything else?"

I hesitated. "Yeah. I think he's taking them on these roads. I think he's forcing them to stop and then taking them someplace else."

Although I wasn't looking directly at the men with the cameras, I sensed that our conversation had started to draw their interest. Boden's eyes glanced at them, then he looked at me again, coming to a decision. "You have somewhere to be right now, Blake?"

"Nothing I can't do later."

"Okay." He gestured at a silver SUV parked fifty yards down the road. "Follow me back to my place. It's not far."

# 25

Mazzucco was dead tired. A late night and broken sleep didn't make for the greatest morning feeling.

After dropping Allen at her apartment the previous evening, he'd doubled back and driven back out to Santa Monica. He dropped in on Sloan's, the bar Sarah Dutton had mentioned, and asked them a couple of follow-up questions. The answers were consistent with those they'd already given him over the phone. One of the bartenders vaguely remembered the group but couldn't say when they'd left or whether they'd left together. He was pretty sure they were gone by eleven thirty. No, they didn't have any video. There was a cam over the bar, but that was it. It hadn't covered the area of the bar where the party had been sitting.

After that, he'd driven a couple of different routes from the bar to Walter Dutton's place and turned up four separate gas stations in the vicinity that Kelly could have used. He stopped at each and asked a few questions. In three out of the four, he drew a blank immediately. Nobody remembered serving a girl in a silver Porsche between eleven and midnight. Regardless, he asked for, and got, copies of the security tapes, just in case. He could go through them on fast-wind in the morning. It wouldn't take long, since he knew exactly what he was looking for.

The fourth gas station was inconclusive. The guy who worked Saturday night was on day shift Monday, so they asked him to come back. The boss would be able to email him a digital file containing the security camera footage for the relevant time when he got in. Mazzucco hadn't been optimistic. He decided he'd give them a call back in the morning but that it probably wasn't worth a return trip.

After that, he'd driven back home. Julia had been waiting up for him, against his advice when he'd called. They'd had the usual argument.

"Why the hell are you working so late?"

She knew why he was working so late.

"Were you with her?"

*Her.* She never used Allen's name if she could avoid it. Before he'd partnered up with Jessica Allen, it would never have occurred to Mazzucco to describe his wife as the jealous type. But then all of his partners until now had been male, overweight, and approaching retirement. Nothing like Allen.

It was always like this when he had a particularly late night. Julia kept at him until her anger subsided, and eventually, they went to bed around two. She went to bed, at least. Mazzucco took the couch in the living room. And then Daisy woke up half an hour later and there was a change and a bottle feed and a minor reprise of the argument.

Back on the couch, and sleep had eluded him for at least another hour. He was too mad to sleep. Julia had no cause to be suspicious of his relationship with Allen. Did she? He turned his mind to less complex matters: the day's triple murder.

He'd managed maybe a half hour of sleep and been woken again by Daisy sometime after five. After that, he'd left her sleeping with Julia and decided to get an early start on the day. Halfway to downtown, his cell had buzzed showing a number he did not recognize. He'd pulled over and taken the call. It was the fourth gas station. The guy from the

Saturday-night shift had reported for work, and guess what? He did remember seeing a Porsche and a female driver. Mazzucco told him he'd be there in half an hour.

Twenty-eight minutes later, he was pulling into the gas station. Five minutes after that, he was in the back office with the Saturday-night guy, the manager, and a cup of shitty machine coffee. The manager was cycling through the security footage of the forecourt while Mazzucco talked to the nightshift attendant.

"Just after it started to rain," Mazzucco repeated.

"That's right, would have been just after eleven. News on the radio had just finished."

"And she came into the store?"

"That's right. She paid for ten bucks' worth and went back outside to fill up."

"Was there anybody with her? Anybody in the car, maybe?"

He looked unsure. "No one came in with her. I don't *think* there was anybody in the Porsche, but ..."

"Got it."

It was the manager who'd spoken. Mazzucco looked away from the nightshift guy to the small black-and-white screen on the cluttered desk. The screen showed a paused image: a light-colored Porsche Carrera parked by the back pumps. The time stamp said 23:04. Mazzucco flipped back a couple of pages on his notes and compared the license plate to the one on the screen. It was Sarah Dutton's car, all right.

He asked the manager to run the tape. They watched Kelly get out and lock the car with the key fob. They watched her come into the office. They watched her go back out again. They watched her fill up, unlock the car, and get back in the driver's seat. They watched the car drive toward the camera and then turn and exit the frame.

Just like the nightshift guy said, right there in crisp, silent black-and-white. Except there was one detail that looked off.

"Run it again," Mazzucco said.

The three of them watched the sequence again. Halfway through, Mazzucco worked out what was wrong with the picture.

# 26

It took us twenty minutes to drive to Boden's place. He lived in a modest bungalow in Reseda. There were a few photographers loitering outside, but not enough to count as a mob. We ignored them and headed for the door. I kept my sunglasses on and my head down, but the focus was on Boden. He ignored a few yelled questions, not giving them so much as a glance. I noticed a tired edge to the questions: they'd get bored of being ignored soon, which meant Boden was handling them in exactly the right way. He opened the door and I followed him inside. He waved a hand at the living room.

"Get you a coffee or something? I'd offer you a beer, but I guess it's early."

"I'm fine," I said.

The living room, like the rest of the house, was small and neatly kept. Two leather couches, a coffee table, a bookshelf, and a big-screen TV were the only items of furniture. There were framed pictures on top of the bookshelf. Some of them showed a thin, serious-looking woman in her late thirties, others a dark-haired girl I guessed was Kelly at various stages of her life. Boden caught me looking at them and nodded.

"That's her."

"Your wife's not around anymore?" I asked.

"How do you know that?"

"Kelly's a kid in all the pictures with her. And all the ones of her by herself look like they were taken on film, not digital."

Boden smiled grimly. "You are good, Blake. Mary took off in 2000. Haven't heard from her in ten years. I suppose you could find her, if you put your mind to it."

"Would you want me to?"

"I guess I wouldn't. Maybe she'll get in touch anyway, if she hears about ..." His voice cracked a little and he recovered. "About Kelly."

I sat down on one of the couches and cast my eyes about the room, thinking that I didn't really have a reason for taking Boden's father up on his invitation. I was about as satisfied as I could be that Kelly hadn't been personally targeted by her killer, so it was unlikely I'd learn anything important here. I had a good idea what he was going to ask me, and I knew I'd be turning him down. But then again, you never know exactly what's going to be important.

Boden took his eyes from the photographs and turned to me. His eyes were glassy, the skin around them red.

"So tell me again, what's your interest in this guy?"

"I think I can stop him."

"You don't think the police can handle it?"

I considered the loaded question carefully. "Normally, I think they could."

"Normally?"

"I don't think this guy is normal. I think he'll kill again and then move on before the cops get close to him. If he disappears, we might not get another shot at him."

Boden's eyes narrowed and I wondered if I'd given too

much away, let on that there was a personal element here. But he didn't follow through on the suspicion, if he had one. "Maybe he'll move on anyway, now that they found the bodies."

I nodded. "It's a risk. But I don't think he's done yet."

"You say that as if it were a good thing," Boden said, grimacing. "Blake, I have about twenty-two thousand dollars in a savings account."

I started shaking my head, and he held a hand up.

"Now, I know that probably doesn't sound like a lot to you, and I can't pay you up front, but if you find this bastard, you can have it all."

"No deal."

His eyes narrowed again. "Not enough, huh?"

"That's not it. This one is free."

He didn't say anything for a minute. "And why would you work for free?"

"Call it community spirit."

"Funny way for a consultant to operate." Boden glanced at the pictures of his daughter again. "And what you do with him when you find him. Is that free?"

"I'm not a contract killer."

"You're not a lot of things, aren't you? Not a cop, not a bounty hunter, not a hit man. I'll ask again. What happens when you find him?"

"I guess I'll know when I find him."

# 27

"How long do you need?" the skinny twenty-something tech asked as he looked up from his twin monitors.

Allen considered the question and decided she had no idea. "How long can you give me?"

The tech sat back in his swivel chair and scratched the facial hair he was attempting to cultivate below his bottom lip. "I have a report I need to finish by three o'clock. I could go around the block for a cup of coffee. That usually takes fifteen minutes."

"Could it take twenty?"

He grimaced and looked down at the Lakers tickets Allen had handed him, reading the seat details printed above the barcode. "Section 320. That sounds like the nosebleed section."

Allen narrowed her eyes in irritation. The tickets had cost her two hundred bucks, and he was griping about twenty minutes? She leaned in closer. "I think we're about to have a nosebleed section right here."

Her phone buzzed once for a text message, and she took it out to see if it was Mazzucco. It was from Denny, probably looking to make up after last night. She deleted it unread and looked back at the tech expectantly.

He smirked and got up. "Okay, deal. But if anybody asks, you guessed my password."

"What is your password?"

"Nice try."

The tech disappeared with his Lakers tickets and went in search of caffeine. Allen sat down in the chair and adjusted it before turning her attention to the screen. The National

Crime Information Center, the NCIC database for short, was the FBI's key resource for identifying links between crimes committed across state lines. In other words, it was the ideal tool for the job currently in front of Allen. In the spirit of cooperation, the FBI provided mediated access to local law enforcement in all fifty states. Gaining access to the system wasn't exactly restricted for cops, but there was generally a waiting period and a paper trail. The basketball tickets had removed those barriers, but Allen knew there was nothing she could do about the indelible electronic trail that would be left by her search, should anybody have cause to look for it. She knew the likelihood of Mr. Lakers covering for her was roughly equal to that of his team sweeping the playoffs, but she'd decided it was a risk worth taking. If she didn't find evidence of the killer's work during the gap years, her search would probably go unnoticed. One additional query in the hundreds of thousands run through the system each year from across the country.

If she found what she was expecting to, however, someone else would come looking for the same information, sooner or later. The realization was beginning to dawn on her that she'd need to talk to somebody about her suspicions, and if she wanted to hold on to any sort of involvement with the case, it would have to be soon.

Her phone buzzed, and she picked it up: Mazzucco's number flashed up on the screen. She hesitated a second and decided to let it ring out. She wanted to catch up with her partner to see if he'd had any luck canvassing the gas stations, but she could call him back once the twenty minutes had passed.

It didn't take long to start finding what she was looking for.

It was impossible to be sure without a closer examination

of the individual cases, but when you knew what to look for, a grisly pattern started to emerge. The search was complicated by the fact that she wasn't searching for one kind of crime: she had to consider not just the open and unsolved torture murders over the past two and a half years, but also deaths where the body had decomposed to the point the cause of death could not be ascertained. She also had to consider unresolved disappearances that could fit the profile. Interestingly, she began to see that the variety of the DC killings had not been an aberration. The victim profile in each state seemed to range much more widely than the type the killer had targeted in LA. She wondered if that meant anything.

Allen found potential cases in no less than six states. In each case, the victims had been found in a remote location with torture wounds and at least one cut from an unusual ragged blade. Once again, the victim profile, disposal method, and official cause of death varied, but the ragged wounds remained a constant that was there only when you looked closely.

Even more interestingly, someone had already made one connection between a confirmed murder and a disappearance taking place months apart: a woman in Kentucky and a teenage boy in Iowa. It looked like the killer hadn't been quite as careful in those cases. It appeared he'd used the same abduction method on both occasions—and Allen felt a shiver as she saw what it was. Both victims had stopped for gas late at night, and surveillance footage had shown somebody getting into their unlocked vehicles while they paid. The footage was typically low-quality in both cases, and the suspect kept his face away from the cameras both times, but the reports indicated that the working assumption was that this was the same guy. They'd even come up with a name for him: the Attendant. But then there had been no more similar cases. The leads had dried up, and no one ever proved it was the same guy. Allen thought it was. And she thought it was her guy.

"Time's up."

Allen jerked her head around and saw the tech standing behind her with a large cup of coffee from Starbucks.

"Get what you need?" he said, when she didn't say anything.

"Yeah. And then some."

# 28

After I left Boden's house, I drove until I found the 101 and then headed west, thinking about my next move.

Crozier would not be easy to find. I wouldn't be able to locate him through any of the standard techniques. For a start, I knew he would have left that name behind a long, long time ago. Shedding it like a dead skin, probably as soon as he'd left Winterlong. Phone and credit and vehicle records would be no use to me. He would most likely stay far away from anyplace I could tie to his former life. I knew this because he would have done all of the things I had done to become invisible.

I stopped in Hollywood to grab something to eat, passing a cemetery that gave me an idea for something to check on later. I found a quiet-looking diner on Santa Monica Boulevard and took a seat at the back. I ordered a cheesesteak and a cup of coffee. While I waited for my order, I checked out the few other customers. Another of my habits. There were less than a dozen other patrons, but in a melting pot like LA, this random sample of humanity cut across boundaries of gender and age and race and appearance.

Crozier's appearance, in all likelihood, would be different. I remembered him as a tallish, slender man with unkempt blond hair and an untidy mustache. Almost all of the personnel I'd known in elite units took a fierce pride in their relative freedom from the strict grooming regulations of the conventional military. In a sense, cultivating a scruffy, individualistic look *was* the regulation. I often thought that if you wanted to differentiate yourself as the devil-may-care, nonconformist rebel in your special operations team, the quickest way to do so was to keep your hair neatly trimmed, shave twice a day, and polish your boots every night before you hit the bunk.

At the side of my table was a wooden menu holder that held a couple of regular menus plus a paper children's menu and a little plastic packet of colored pencils. I took the children's menu out and placed it face down on the table, giving me a blank sheet. I used the blue pencil and started to sketch a rough likeness of Crozier the way I'd known him. The hair, the mustache, the general shape of his face and jaw. I had to stop myself from giving him the mirrored shades he wore habitually. I closed my eyes and tried to recall what his eyes had looked like without them, and then I filled them in. I looked at it for a couple of seconds. Not bad, but definitely not perfect either. The eyes were hard to get right.

I started to draw the face again, alongside the first likeness. I kept the general shape, but this time I tried shorter hair and removing the mustache. This one took longer, because it was pure speculation. I didn't even have the dusty mental picture to draw on. When I'd finished, I looked at the new face for a few seconds. The eyes still weren't right.

I looked back at the old one, comparing the two. I sighed. The clean-shaven version looked utterly anonymous, and for a good reason, I guessed. I had no way of knowing how Crozier might have changed his appearance. He could have grown his hair longer instead of trimming it, cultivated a full beard. He could have shaved his head completely, or succumbed to male pattern baldness. He could have started wearing glasses, or even colored contact lenses.

When the police use a sketch artist or a computer to generate a composite image of a suspect and end up with something so generic as to be useless, they call it a ghost. This was worse than that. I didn't even have a ghost in front of me; I had a figment of my imagination. It was—

"Not bad."

I looked up to see the waiter, who'd appeared with my cheesesteak. He was a husky, twenty-something guy in a black short-sleeved shirt.

"Thanks for the critique," I said.

The waiter beamed at me. "He's hot. Who is he?"

I thought about the question for a second. "I'm really not sure."

The waiter gave me a nonplussed look and put the sandwich down in front of me. "Enjoy."

I ate quickly and turned down dessert but asked for another coffee. While I drank it, I checked some local and national news websites on my phone. Nothing much was new.

*The Samaritan Killings.*

I thought about that MO some more. It didn't seem likely that he'd leave the breakdowns to chance, which was just one more element that reminded me of Crozier. One of the *LA Times* pieces mentioned that anyone with information should contact Detectives Allen or Mazzucco in Robbery Homicide

Division. There was an 800 number, too, but I didn't want to call from the cell, since I'd already had to dispose of my burner.

He was out there somewhere. Crozier. *The Samaritan.* I thought back to the quiet, reserved monster I'd been acquainted with, and for the first time since I started in this line of work, I felt a strange sense of apprehension about taking on a job. I wondered briefly if it could be just because this was the first time I'd decided to go to work without a client. Even as the thought crossed my mind, I knew that was bullshit. The Samaritan needed to be stopped, and it probably had to be me who stopped him. That wasn't what was giving me pause.

I'd spent the previous few years being scrupulously careful not to cross paths with anybody from Winterlong. I wasn't sure that my former employers would have made the connection yet, but they would in time, particularly if Crozier was caught, booked, and fingerprinted. If that happened, there would be some difficult questions to answer. Questions that would lead to nothing but dead ends for the cops and probably even the feds, but that would result in other, less accountable people taking an interest in the case. And in anyone else involved.

I knew I could find Crozier on my own. It would take time, but I could do it. It would be safer, cleaner to resolve the problem without ever coming into contact with local law enforcement.

There was only one problem with that. The Samaritan had already taken at least three victims in Los Angeles over a two-week period. I wasn't sure why he'd returned to his hometown, if something personal had dragged him back to his roots, but I was certain that he wasn't done with killing people yet. Killing people here, or wherever he went next, if he elected to move on once again. I would track him down if it took a week or a month or a year. I would track him down and I would stop him, one way or the other. But more victims would certainly die in that time. More Kelly Bodens.

I drank the last from my cup and made my decision. I nodded at the waiter and asked him for the check and one other thing. "Do you know where there's a pay phone around here?"

His face crumpled in incredulity. "What is this, 1986?"

"I'm old-fashioned like that."

He shrugged as though it was my funeral and pointed across the street. "I think they still have one at the 7-Eleven."

Three minutes later, I was speaking to a bored-voiced woman who sounded like she'd been taking the same call all day.

"I'd like to speak to Detective Allen, if he's available."

A sigh. "He's a she. This is about the case out in the hills?" The tone of voice suggested the operator wasn't exactly expecting a major breakthrough from this call.

"That's right."

"What is the nature of your information?"

"I kind of need to speak to Allen about that."

Another sigh, this one more audible. "Name and phone number."

"I'll call back," I said, and hung up. I remembered from a previous job that Robbery Homicide was based out of LAPD headquarters at Parker Center. Another quick Internet check told me they'd moved since the last time I'd been in town. RHD was now based out of the new Police Administration Building, on West First Street. There was another number, which I called.

"LAPD Homicide Special Section, how may I direct your call?"

"Detective Allen, please."

"May I say who's calling?"

"My name's Englehart; she's expecting my call."

There was a pause, and I wondered if that bluff would be enough to get me through, and what I'd say if it did. I didn't get to find out.

"She's not available, Mr. Englehart. Can I take a message, or redirect you to voicemail?"

I kept my voice light, unconcerned. "That's okay. I'll call her back. When would be a good time?"

"I'm not sure about today, but you could leave a message."

I thanked her and hung up. I did a quick Internet search to see if anything came up relating to a female Detective Allen and found a couple of interesting points. The only female homicide cop by that name I could find a mention of was one Jessica Allen. She was a recent transplant to the city and had left her old department in Washington, DC, under lingering suspicion in an evidence-fabrication case that had seen her partner sent down on a corruption charge. The articles on the case in the Washington media mentioned her track record for disciplinaries on minor insubordination matters. On the other hand, her clearance rate on murder cases was exemplary. At any rate, nothing had stuck to Allen as far as the serious corruption investigation went. But I knew there would have been whispers. There are always whispers around something like that.

I didn't know how receptive Detective Allen might be to an offer of assistance, and I wasn't even sure I wanted to make one. From my limited experience of the LAPD, they took a fierce pride in keeping things entirely in-house.

So what next?

It was Los Angeles, so at least I knew one thing: whatever came next would have to begin with a drive.

# 29

Allen and Mazzucco met halfway between their respective starting points, at a deli on Vine Street in Hollywood. They ordered sandwiches and sat on stools at the window. Allen let Mazzucco talk first, knowing she'd need a little time to work up to what she had to tell him.

"So I drove two different routes from the bar in Santa Monica to Dutton's place last night. I passed four gas stations altogether. Three of those places, nobody remembered seeing a Porsche the night before, but I got the security tapes anyway."

"They actually had tapes?"

"You know what I mean. That stuff's all digital now."

"Makes life easier."

"Makes getting the footage easier; doesn't make the rest of the process easier. You still have to watch the damn things. I got the Saturday-night footage from each place emailed to me in a ZIP file. I was going to start looking through it this morning."

"So what about the fourth place?"

"I was getting to that. The fourth place, they asked me to come back today, because the guy who worked Saturday night was on day shift. I'll be honest. I wasn't going to make a special trip out there. But he called this morning and I asked him if he remembered a silver Porsche. Jackpot. Right before the rain started, a girl matching Kelly Boden's description came in and put some gas in the tank, paid in cash. I guess she wanted to make sure she had enough to get her to Dutton's place."

"Only she never made it."

"That's right."

Allen thought about the Iowa and Kentucky cases—the man who'd gotten into the vehicles at gas stations. "Did you find her on the tape?" she asked cautiously.

"Yeah."

"Let me guess—she parks, goes to pay for the gas, and somebody gets into the car, right?"

Mazzucco looked at her, surprised. "Not quite."

"What do you mean?"

Mazzucco took his phone from an inside pocket and tapped into the gallery. "I saved the clip."

He played the clip. It was black-and-white and silent. The camera was positioned over the door of the kiosk, to provide a wide view of the forecourt and a close-up of anyone who approached the door. Sarah Dutton's Porsche was parked in the top right of the picture, the back of the vehicle slightly out of the frame. The overhead fluorescents cast bright stripes on the glass and bodywork of the Porsche. As they watched, Kelly Boden appeared from the driver's side and approached the camera, digging something out of her bag, looking as though she was hurrying.

"Okay. Keep your eyes on the car," Mazzucco said. "I missed this the first time around."

Allen shifted her focus from their murder victim to the Porsche. She had no idea what she was looking for, but then she saw it. It was as though a patch of the shadow beneath the car detached and elongated, just like a puddle spreading. She realized what it was and that the fluorescent lights had shown something beyond the camera's gaze.

"There's somebody on the other side of the car."

As they watched, the new shadow shifted position, then nodded about a little, as though testing the handle. And then the shadow retreated.

"Did she lock the car?" Allen asked.

Mazzucco nodded. "Yeah. You see the headlights blink earlier on, when she got out. I think he tried to get in ... maybe so he could pop the trunk."

"But he didn't manage it."

"Doesn't look that way."

As they watched, Kelly appeared from under the camera, her back to them this time, and jogged back toward the Porsche, examining the unfamiliar keys for the right button. She found it and the lights blinked again. She stood in the blind spot for a minute or so, putting in the gas she'd paid for, and then she got back into the car. She started it up and pulled toward the camera and then curved to the right and out of the shot and on to face the little that remained of her life. Watching it, Allen had a strange urge to rewind the tape to stop her leaving, as though that could save her.

"So he didn't get in the car. We know that," she said. "You can see the trunk and the front seats, and you'd have to go through the front to get in the rear seats. So we're still at square one."

"Not quite," Mazzucco said. "Now we know that somebody tried to get in. That means she was targeted, at least as far back as the gas station."

"The shadow has to be him, right? He followed her from the gas station, got her to stop somehow."

Mazzucco was watching her carefully. "Okay, tell me."

"Tell you what?"

"How did you know there'd be a guy on the tape? Is this about what you said yesterday? How you knew there would be more?"

Allen had seen that look in her partner's eyes before, but only in the interrogation room. She glanced around the deli just in case there was anyone paying attention to them.

There was no one within earshot. No excuses this time. She sighed. "Okay."

He looked satisfied. As though he'd half expected to be disappointed but was pleased she'd made the right decision. She wanted to deck him for that.

"You've seen this guy's work before?"

"Maybe. I think so."

"But I've been your partner since you transferred in. That means I'd have seen it, too."

"Except that this is from before."

His eyes narrowed. "You mean in Washington?"

Allen nodded.

Mazzucco arched an eyebrow. A bicoastal killer? "When?"

"Two years back. Two and a half, actually."

"Who was she? The victim?"

Allen couldn't resist a little smile as the interrogator slipped up with an assumption. "That's just it, Mazzucco. She was a he."

"Go on."

"Gender wasn't the only point of difference," she said. "Age, race, socioeconomic status . . . even the disposal method was different."

"Then I don't understand," Mazzucco said.

"The victim in DC was a black male, at least fifty, homeless and destitute. He was dragged out of the Potomac. He'd been in the water at least a week, so at first it wasn't even clear it was a murder. We never did identify the body. He was one of those ones that nobody missed, I guess."

"Was he tortured?"

Allen shrugged. "Yeah, but even that didn't quite match up. The girl here was cut up. The man in DC was burned."

"You mean set on fire?"

Allen shook her head. "Not like that. He had wounds all

over, but they were all cauterized burns. Like somebody had tied him up and used a hot knife on him. Like I said, everything was different. All except one thing."

"Cause of death?"

Allen nodded.

"Throat cut? Ragged wound pattern?"

"Yeah. Exactly the same cause of death. I've never seen a cut like that before or since. He must have used some kind of special blade. Different from the one he used for the torture."

Mazzucco took another bite out of his sandwich and chewed. He looked doubtful. "So you have two murder cases, two years and two thousand miles apart. Similar cause of death, sure, but ..."

"You've seen a cut throat before, Mazzucco."

"Sure."

"Ever see one exactly like that? Ever see photographs of one like that?"

"No. No, I haven't. But all that means is that two killers used a similar blade. Other than that, you have a completely different victim profile, tortured in a different way, disposed of in a different way, and murdered on the other side of the country."

"I know. Logically, you're right, but this is the same guy. It's not just the throat wound; it's everything. When you take out specifics, there's a lot that's similar. Vulnerable victims, probably kidnapped, tortured, finished off, and then dumped. It's like everything else is window dressing, but the broad strokes are the same."

Mazzucco still looked like he needed time to process this. "You're a Tarantino fan, right?" he said after some thought. At first, Allen thought he was changing the subject.

"I prefer the early stuff, but yeah, sure. What's your point?"

"Tarantino makes gangster movies and kung fu movies and westerns, but they're all Tarantino movies, right?"

Allen grinned. "Exactly. That's what I'm talking about."

"The style beneath the form," Mazzucco said, nodding. "Okay, I get you. But you know nobody else will, right? Not without something more."

Allen cleared her throat and looked down at her own sandwich, mostly uneaten.

"Allen?" he prompted.

"There is more. A lot more."

# 30

It took Allen another ten minutes to bring Mazzucco up to speed. He listened without interrupting too much, and she was glad he didn't seem angry that she'd held this back. When she finished, he thought for a minute.

"You know we have to tell Lawrence, right?"

Allen sighed and agreed. He was right, of course, but she knew all that would entail. They left the remains of their lunch and got back into the Ford. Mazzucco made it to the driver's side first, adjusting the seat way back. Allen didn't object for a change. As they pulled around the corner, Allen saw a blue Chevrolet parked at the curbside. As they drove past, she saw a man in the driver's seat wearing dark glasses. He didn't turn his head as they passed by.

"You know, in a way this doesn't actually change any-thing," Mazzucco said. "This fucker's doing the grand tour, but we still need to stop him here in LA. We still need to work the fresh leads."

Allen nodded, but she was focused on the wing mirror, trying to get a fix on a car she thought was a couple of positions back. The blue Chevy she thought had pulled into the stream of traffic a moment after them.

They rounded a corner and continued east on Sunset, headed for the 101. The two cars behind them stayed on Vine. The blue Chevy made the right onto Sunset a couple of seconds later.

"Take this left."

"What?"

"Just do it. I'll explain in a minute."

Mazzucco braked sharply and swung the Ford down a side street. Allen told him to take another couple of turns until she saw a vacant lot up ahead with a chain-link fence flanking an open gate.

"Pull in here," she said quickly, pointing at the gap in the fence.

Mazzucco complied, pulling through the gap and steering around on the gravel to bring them back facing the road.

"What ... ?"

"Wait a second," Allen said. "Watch out for a blue Chevy."

Twenty seconds later, the Chevrolet flashed by. The driver, still wearing dark glasses, didn't turn to look this time either.

Mazzucco glanced at Allen, the question obvious. She nodded and he tore out of the lot, the tires kicking up gravel as they pulled back through the gate and out onto the street. The Chevy was a car ahead now, moving at the pace of the traffic.

"You want to pull him over?" Mazzucco said, eyeing the light on the dashboard.

"Let's see where he takes us."

They followed him for another six blocks; then he took

a left and an immediate right. Mazzucco was able to keep at least one car between them at all times, but Allen knew they'd have been spotted if the driver in the sunglasses knew what he was looking for.

A block ahead, the lights changed from green to yellow at an intersection, and the Chevy's brake lights lit up as he started to slow. Then, abruptly, its speed increased and the blue car darted off the road and took a turn against oncoming traffic into a multilevel parking structure on the left side of the road. Two or three of the oncoming cars leaned on their horns, and Mazzucco had to wait for them to pass before he could make the turn.

The entrance was covered by a barrier and a ticket kiosk. Mazzucco stopped at the barrier and badged the attendant. "We're looking for the blue Chevrolet Malibu that just came in."

The attendant pointed left and raised the barrier. Mazzucco told him not to let anybody out and drove under the barrier. As it slid back down behind them, he smiled at Allen. "He's cornered now. Care to explain?"

"He's been following us. I'd like to find out why." She buzzed her window all the way down, removed her Beretta 92FS from her shoulder holster, clicked the safety off, and cocked it. She noticed Mazzucco grimacing at the disregard for strict firearm protocol, but he said nothing.

They made a slow circuit of the ground floor, paying attention to any dark blue cars, but not seeing the one they wanted. The circuit took them almost around to the barrier again before they hit the ramp to the next level. Mazzucco bumped up a level, the quiet squeals of rubber on concrete amplified by the walls. They made another slow circuit of the second level. Mazzucco's head turned left to right as he drove. Allen's hand tightened on her gun. She thought about asking Mazzucco why, if they had him cornered, did it feel a little like they were driving into a trap?

The second floor was clear.

They squealed up another ramp and onto the sunlit roof. Allen could hear the low rumble of an engine running around the corner of the line of parked cars. She tried to see between the vehicles and caught a flash of blue. It wasn't moving. Mazzucco gunned the engine and they swung around the end of the line and along the right angle of the roof. The blue Chevy was at a standstill, nose to the parapet of the roof. Mazzucco hit the brakes and brought them to a halt twenty yards from the Chevy. Allen leaned out of the window, both hands on the gun, aiming at the back of the driver's headrest. The angle of the car and its relative height made it impossible to tell if anyone was in it. She snapped her head to the left, then the right, keeping the gun trained on the car. Mazzucco got out on his side, and she heard his gun being cocked. Keeping her eyes on the car, Allen fumbled for the handle and got the door open, stepping out.

"LAPD," she called out. "Remain in your vehicle and place your hands on the steering wheel."

No response.

Mazzucco started to move toward the car, and Allen shook her head.

"I think it's my turn. Cover me."

He opened his mouth to protest, and she took her eyes off the car long enough to shoot him a glare that said, *You know better than to try that protective male bullshit on me.* He did, too, because he just shrugged and aimed his gun at the driver's side of the Chevy.

Allen repeated the warning, louder this time, and moved toward the driver's side, her finger tightening on the trigger, tensing for a sudden movement. She drew level with the car and saw that there was no one in the driver's side. No one in the passenger side or the backseat, either. The engine thrummed away in neutral. She reached through the open window and twisted the keys to kill the noise. Then she opened the door.

"Allen!"

She whirled around, bringing her gun to bear. Mazzucco was facing the same way, his weapon trained on a man who'd somehow gotten between them and their car and was standing with his hands raised in a supremely relaxed pose of surrender. He wore a dark suit, a light blue shirt and the same sunglasses Allen had spotted twice on the driver of the blue Chevy.

"Identify yourself," Mazzucco said, approaching the man, who did not flinch at the two guns pointing at his head.

"Good afternoon," the man said, a thin smile on his lips. "Detectives Allen and Mazzucco, Homicide, right?"

No one said anything for a moment. Allen narrowed her eyes and kept her gun pointed at the spot where the bridge of the sunglasses crossed the man's nose.

"That's right. Now, would you mind telling us who the fuck you are?"


# 31

"You can call me Blake," the man in the dark suit said.

"Blake what?" Allen asked.

"Carter Blake."

"Okay," she said, keeping her gun on him. "Now—how about telling us why you're following two cops?"

"I might be able to help you with your investigation."

"Oh, yeah?" Mazzucco said. "Which investigation's that?"

The man called Blake looked at him as though genuinely confused. "To tell the truth, Detective, I kind of thought they'd have you on this Samaritan thing full-time. Maybe not."

"What do you know about the Samaritan, smart-ass?" Allen said. "And start with a compelling reason why I shouldn't assume you're him."

Blake seemed to consider this. "Well, for starters, I don't think he's stupid enough to walk up to you and introduce himself. Unfortunately." He nodded at the guns, one at a time. "Any chance of ...?"

"Turn around—slowly—and put your hands on the roof of the car," Mazzucco barked.

Blake did as asked, and Mazzucco moved in close, Allen covering him this time. He kicked Blake's legs apart and frisked him one-handed, quickly and efficiently. He pulled a sheet of folded paper out of his pocket, examined it with a thoughtful look, and held on to it. He found a wallet in Blake's back pocket, took it out, and examined the contents. He looked back at Allen and nodded.

"Okay, turn around," she called.

He did as asked once again, and Allen lowered the gun. She kept it cocked, with her finger on the trigger, ready to bring it back into play should the need arise.

"What are you doing here, Mr. Blake?" she said, adopting a more conversational tone.

"I'm sorry if I startled you. The television said anyone who could help with the investigation should contact Detectives Allen or Mazzucco."

"You know what they mean when they say that, Blake?"

"Phone the hotline?"

"Bingo. Running a tail on the lead detectives is not what we'd call our preferred contact method."

"My apologies," he said. "It seemed like it might be the best way to get your attention. Stand out from the crowd."

Mazzucco's eyes narrowed with incredulity. "Are you saying you let us catch you following us?"

Blake nodded, as if that were obvious. "Why else would I drive myself into a dead end?" He lowered his hands slowly and placed them in his pockets loosely before he continued. "Going by experience, I didn't think it would be easy to get an appointment with you the conventional way. But here we are."

"Here we are," Allen repeated evenly.

"What's this?" Mazzucco said, holding up the sheet of paper he'd taken from Blake. Allen glanced at it and saw there were a couple of pencil sketches of a man's face on it.

Blake shrugged. "A hobby. You can keep that if you like."

"Very generous of you."

"So what can you tell us about the killer?" Allen said. "I guess we might as well ask; otherwise the three of us came all the way up here for nothing at all."

"I can help you catch him."

"You don't think we can handle that on our own?" Mazzucco asked sharply.

"I think we can get this guy sooner by working together," Blake answered, plainly anticipating the question.

Mazzucco shook his head. "We don't need any help from armchair detectives. Thank you anyway."

Allen knew from his tone that he was fishing for more background on Blake, hoping to goad him into a reveal. Whatever else this guy was, he didn't give off amateur vibes. He didn't even seem like a private detective. Despite herself, Allen was curious to get to the bottom of this new puzzle.

"Actually," Blake said, unfazed, "I'm a professional. As in, I do this for a living."

"You assist with homicide investigations?" Allen asked. Was he some kind of civilian consultant? If so, why the distinctly unorthodox approach?

"I find people. Usually, people who'd rather not be found. Let me in on this, and I'll find you the Samaritan." He said it flatly, not as a brag or a sales pitch, just with the easy confidence of someone stating the grass is green. That worried Allen for some reason.

She looked at Mazzucco, raising her eyebrows to ask wordlessly if he wanted to say anything else. His expression was passive and slightly bemused. He didn't know what to think of this guy either.

Allen clicked the safety on her Beretta and slid it back into her holster. Whatever else this guy was, he didn't present an immediate danger to either of them—she trusted her instincts that far. So what now? They couldn't very well remain on the rooftop staring at each other, not when there was work to be done. Blake was giving as little away as possible, even when asked questions at gunpoint. He was assuming he'd piqued their interest enough. Two could play that game. She affected a bland customer-service smile and said, "I'm sorry, Mr. Blake. Even assuming your credentials are as impressive as you seem to believe, I'm afraid we don't have room in the budget for additional consultants. I guess we're going to have to make do with our own meager talents."

She glanced at Mazzucco for confirmation and he shrugged. *Too bad.*

"Now," she continued, "if you'd be kind enough to give us a contact number and an address where we can find you if we need to talk to you further, we won't take up any more of your time today."

Blake didn't say anything. His expression was unreadable behind the dark glasses. He took a couple of steps away from the Ford, paused, and started to walk back toward the blue Chevy. He held out a palm as he approached Allen, and she realized she still had his keys. She thought about holding on to them and then realized with annoyance that she had no reason to detain him—she couldn't even get him on speeding, for Christ's sake. She tossed them to him.

Blake caught them in his right hand and his left hand went into an inside pocket. He handed her a plain white business card with a cell number handwritten on it in black ink.

"I'm staying in a hotel," he said. "Just flew into town last night. I'm not sure where I'll be tonight, but I'll answer that number when you're ready to call."

Allen took the card and rubbed it between two of her fingers. The card stock was heavy, expensive-feeling. Apart from that, it gave nothing away beyond the minimum information volunteered by its owner.

Blake looked from Allen to Mazzucco and back again. He removed his sunglasses and looked at Allen. His eyes took her by surprise. They were green, and instead of the amused, playful look she'd expected from the sound of his voice, there was only cold purpose in his gaze.

"I don't want to waste any time, yours or mine, so I'll cut to the chase. If you need a reference, call Special Agent Elaine Banner at the Chicago field office of the FBI. Ask her how she caught Caleb Wardell."

Allen tensed at the mention of the name. It was familiar to her not just as a law enforcement officer, but as someone who owned a television.

Blake continued. "If you want proof I can help you, I'll give you a taster up front. Look up Sergeant Willis Peterson, listed as missing in North Carolina. See if he matches the pattern. Then see if you want to add another state to the Samaritan's travel history."

Allen felt Mazzucco's eyes burn into her. He was thinking the same thing she was: how the hell did this guy know about this? Nobody knew this went beyond LA yet. *Peterson.* She filed the name away even as she opened her mouth to remind Blake that they'd already turned down his offer. He didn't let her get the objection out.

"I'll let you make your inquiries, and then you can give me a call." He started walking toward his car again. "And, by the way, I'm not proposing to charge for my services on this occasion, Detectives. This one's on the house."

# 32

An hour later, they were back on the sixth floor of the PAB, watching as Lieutenant Lawrence closed his eyes and massaged his right temple with two fingers.

"Let me get this straight," he said. "You're telling me that this killer was active in six other states before he got to us. Is that right?"

Allen nodded. "Six at least, sir. I have a bad feeling that once we start looking, we'll find more." *Like in North Carolina, maybe,* she thought.

Lawrence opened his eyes and stared at her hard. "Only it won't be us who'll be looking. Will it? When did you start to suspect this guy was killing across state lines?"

Allen opened her mouth to reply, but Mazzucco cleared his throat and spoke first. "We found out about the other cases a couple of hours ago, when we got—"

Lawrence raised his voice subtly as he cut him off. "The question wasn't addressed to you, Detective, and that didn't answer it in any case. Allen, when did you first suspect this?"

Allen swallowed. "Yesterday, sir. When we saw the first body."

"Yesterday."

"Yes, sir."

Lawrence consulted his watch. "So you sat on this for more than thirty hours."

"I couldn't ..."

Lawrence silenced her with a hand wave. "Explain. What got your attention about the body?"

"The wounds on the Boden girl. They were ... unusual. I'd seen similar marks on a body in Washington, DC, a couple of years back."

"Then a similar blade was used. So what?"

Allen shook her head. "I've never seen a wound pattern like this. And anyway, it wasn't just the wounds. A lot about the two cases felt similar, even with all of the differences. I called one of my contacts back in Washington, asked him to do a little research. Meantime, I checked out Metro PD's open and unsolved cases online and came up with another couple of murders that fit right in with the pattern."

Mazzucco spoke up again. "We agreed that it would be best to make sure of our suspicions before taking it to you."

Lawrence turned his head to Mazzucco. "You went along with this?"

"Yes, sir."

He turned to Allen. "That true?"

Allen glanced at Mazzucco. His eyes were saying, *Go with it.* She couldn't. "It's not true, sir. Detective Mazzucco had no idea about this until a couple of hours ago."

"I thought not. So then you accessed NCIC without authorization and turned up ... what?"

"Another fourteen potential victims across six states."

Lawrence sighed. "And these had not been connected before?"

"Two of them had been, but there was nothing concrete to link the cases: no fingerprints or DNA evidence. A reasonably diverse MO, except for the unique wound patterns. It's not the kind of thing you can query a database on; it needed the same eyes on more than one victim. It needed instinct, not number-crunching."

"So our three-time LA killer has in actuality bagged more than a dozen victims across the country. That is what you're telling me, Detective Allen, isn't it?"

"Possibly more. We have no way of knowing when or where he got started. Not without more manpower on this."

"Which is the only reason you've brought it to me now."

"I didn't want to—"

"Detective Allen, I already told your partner to spare me the bullshit. You didn't want to lose the case to the FBI."

She was silent for a moment. "I wanted to make some headway before they took the whole thing away from us."

"That's not your call to make, Allen. The potential number of victims alone makes this a federal case, never mind the multistate element. We call them in immediately, and they're not going to be happy when they find out you've burned a day of the investigation already."

"I'm sorry, sir."

"No, you're not. You've done exactly what you intended to do. Wrapped yourself so closely in this case that you think you can't be taken off it."

Mazzucco glanced at Allen and back at Lawrence. "Come on, Lieutenant. She's made good progress on this already.

Even if she'd come to you yesterday, I doubt we'd be any further forward. She had nothing concrete yesterday. With all due respect, we have to stay involved."

Lawrence glared back at him. "With all due respect, I don't have to do a goddamn thing I don't want to." He stared at Mazzucco for a moment to make his point and then looked back to Allen. "You've been with us six months, Allen, is that right?"

"That's right."

"You came here with some baggage. A reputation for insubordination, not to mention cutting a few corners."

Allen suppressed a wince. It was the first time Lawrence had referenced her past since she'd been here.

"You probably came here with a lot of ideas about the LAPD, about how we do things. You probably thought you'd fit right in."

"Not exactly."

"I didn't ask you to comment. I didn't think I needed to say this, but clearly I was wrong. This crap won't play, Allen. Not in this division and not on any case I'm involved with."

Allen opened her mouth to apologize again and then thought better of it.

"If you have suspicions that a case is bigger than it appears, you come to me first. You don't go cowboying on your own. I decide what we do and when. Is that clear?"

Allen nodded. "Yes, sir."

Lawrence looked back at her for an uncomfortably long time and then gave Mazzucco the same treatment.

"That'll be all."

The two detectives exchanged a chastened glance and turned to leave the office, and the case. They stopped in their tracks as Lawrence spoke again.

"One more thing."

They turned and waited for him to continue.

"Keep your phones on. I'll need you back in here when I speak to the FBI. Which will probably be soon."

Allen's face brightened. "Does that mean—"

"That'll be all."

The two turned to leave again. Allen was unable to keep the smile from her face. Mazzucco looked exasperated with her, but she thought she saw the hint of a relieved smile around the corner of his mouth, too.

# 33

Briefing Lawrence had taken priority, but Allen and Mazzucco knew what they'd be checking out as soon as they got back to their desks, neither of them happy with themselves for wanting to do it. Carter Blake was an unknown quantity, but with the FBI moving in, Allen thought it might not hurt to have an ally that was a little removed from the investigation. On the other hand, she knew she had to be very careful here. What kind of cop would she be if she wasn't suspicious of a guy who appeared from out of nowhere with highly specific information about a series of murders?

They sat down across from each other, and there was a silence that required filling as their respective computers woke from their slumbers.

"No," Mazzucco said, shaking his head. "I don't like him."

"Neither do I," Allen said breezily.

"Good."

"Great."

There was a pause, and then Mazzucco said, "I'll check out North Carolina?"

Allen sighed and nodded. "I'll take the feds. I guess I'm going to need the practice."

Ten minutes later, Allen was on hold to her third department of the FBI's Chicago office, trying to reach Agent Banner. As she listened to the canned Mozart, she began to regret her earlier words. So far, she'd managed to confirm that Banner existed, at least, and that she had indeed been involved with the race to stem Wardell's murderous rampage in Chicago and the Midwest. In fact, it turned out that she was the very agent who'd stopped him permanently.

She caught the occasional murmur from her partner's side of the desk. Half of the time it was him making the attempt to keep her in the loop, the other half just talking to himself as he worked. By the sounds of it, it looked as though the North Carolina connection was also proving to be worthy of further investigation. Of course, if they did turn up another potential Samaritan case, they'd be turning it over to the boys from the Bureau before they could get anywhere.

Mazzucco looked up. "This Sergeant Peterson is down as a missing person, technically. Missing in the final sense, is what I'm getting. There's at least one other unidentified body in the same neck of the woods, too."

"Anything stick out about it?"

Mazzucco's brow creased. "Nothing to say for sure either way. Probably why you didn't find it. I'm going to give the local chief a call. Guy's name is Harding."

"I hope you have better luck than I'm having."

He grinned and picked up the phone. He dialed a number, looking from the screen to the buttons to check he had it right. He finished and sat back, waiting for the call to connect. As he waited, his eyes found Allen's again.

"You know what I'm thinking?"

"That he's wasting our time?"

He shook his head. "The opposite. But I can think of one very good hypothesis as to why this guy Blake knows the North Carolina case and the Samaritan are connected."

Allen took her time answering. "That occurred to me, too."

Mazzucco's call was picked up, and he turned away, introducing himself to his fellow officer in the Old North State. The tone quickly became conversational, friendly. How different from the brief, cold conversations Allen was having on her own line. She didn't have time to dwell on the thought, though, as the hold music was abruptly cut off midstream and a voice said, "Special Agent Banner."

The sound was tinny, the background noise high—cell phone. Allen, caught by surprise, cleared her throat before introducing herself.

"LAPD, huh?" the woman said. Even with the static, Allen caught the mild, almost disinterested undercurrent of hostility.

"That's right," she replied, taking care to speak with the same tone. "I thought they said you weren't available right now."

"I'm not. But the name you mentioned bought you a couple minutes of my time."

Allen felt a familiar tingle in the base of her stomach. It was the sensation she always got when she could sense a line of inquiry starting to develop—for better or worse.

"I met him an hour ago," she said.

"In LA?"

"In LA."

There was a pause as the person on the other end of the line processed that. "I take it you're working the Samaritan case. Who's our liaison on that?"

Allen cleared her throat. "I don't know yet."

There was an uneasy pause, because neither of them really wanted to be pleasantly shooting the breeze here. Allen ended it by bringing the discussion back around to the subject at hand. "This guy, Blake. He says he wants to help us. I made it clear I had some reservations. He told me to ask you about the Wardell manhunt."

Agent Banner answered quickly and with authority, as though dismissing a subordinate. "If he's offering to help, I suggest you take him up on it, Detective."

"*Suggestion* noted, Agent," Allen shot back.

"Glad I could be of assistance," Banner said. "Good aft—"

"Wait a second." There was a pause, and Allen could still hear the echo and background noise. "Can I trust this guy?"

More silence on Banner's end. If it hadn't been for the crackle, Allen would have assumed a hang-up. Finally, she spoke again.

"I don't really trust anybody, not anymore. But I'd trust Carter Blake with my life."

Banner quickly said she had to go and hung up before Allen could thank her. Her partner had already completed his own call and was looking at her over the partition.

"North Carolina looks solid: cut throat, ragged edges. But that wasn't released to the press."

Allen's phone began to ring again. She hit the button to send it to voicemail.

"You talked to the chief out there?"

Mazzucco grunted in the affirmative. "Apparently, I'm not the first person to call him about it today. No prizes for guessing who beat me to it." He stopped and looked down at his notepad. "Harding investigated Peterson's disappearance and is as satisfied it was a murder as you can be without a body. Then there's the other victim they found—they thought it was Peterson himself at first. Harding told me if he had the resources, he'd have a team of guys digging up those woods, because dollars to doughnuts, there are more bodies out there."

"He may get his wish soon."

"He may indeed. I didn't say anything, but I guess the feds will be speaking to them later on. Harding's convinced that what happened out there five years ago was an undiscovered serial killer at work. He's had nothing concrete up until now. Which only makes me question how the hell Sherlock Holmes back there knows about it."

Allen chewed it over, thinking about Mazzucco's suspicions—which she shared—but also thinking about what Agent Banner had said at the end and the way the tone of her voice had utterly changed when she'd said it.

"He keeps his cards pretty close to his chest," she agreed.

Mazzucco stared back at her, then shook his head. "No. This is a bad idea. I mean, keep tabs on him? Absolutely. As far as I'm concerned, he's a person of interest. But let him in? Work with him? Hell no."

"He gave us a lead. He didn't need to do that."

"He's playing with us, Jess."

"Agent Banner says he's okay."

"Oh, you're bowing to the wisdom of the FBI now? That's quite a switch."

She gave him a withering glance in reply.

"You think there's any way Lawrence is going to go for this?" he asked.

He looked away for a moment, thinking, and she could tell he was being worn down.

"Let's not bother him with this, not right now. We're just following a promising lead."

"You have got to be fucking kidding me."

Allen's desk phone started to ring. She ignored it. She let Mazzucco's question hang in the air and stared him out. He always blinked first when it came to this. When he looked away, she spoke. "Go with me on this. I think we have to talk to this guy."

Before he could respond, his own phone began to ring. He said his name and listened, then said, "Yeah, she's here. I'll tell her," and hung up.

"What?"

"The chief wants to speak to you before the press conference. We'll talk about Blake after, okay?"

# 34

Evergreen Memorial Park and Crematory was the oldest burial ground in Los Angeles. It was situated in Boyle Heights, to the east of the city. I was still getting accustomed to driving in LA, and it took me a while to find the place, which was well off the tourist trail. It was a poor, mostly Mexican part of town, and the further east I got, the more Spanish-language billboards and store signs I saw. After today, I knew as much as I'd ever wanted to about the cemeteries of Los Angeles, after the research I'd had to do in order to track down the specific one that I wanted.

I knew, for example, that if you wanted to see the graves of dead movie stars, Evergreen was definitely not the place. You'd be far better off visiting Hollywood Forever, the opulent boneyard conveniently located just over the back wall of Paramount Studios. That one attracted the biggest and the best Tinseltown corpses, from Rudolph Valentino to Dee

Dee Ramone. The high-end clientele meant that Hollywood Forever also attracted stargazers from all over the world, drawn to the one place where you could absolutely guarantee that the movie stars would stay still for pictures. They shot movies there; they even hosted rock concerts from time to time.

Evergreen Cemetery wasn't like that. Its celebrities were of the minor and long-forgotten kind. Pioneers to Southern California, a few early LA politicians. No one of particular note had been buried there recently. If you went to Evergreen Cemetery, you did so because you wanted to visit a specific grave. Which was exactly why I was there.

The sky was darkening in the east as I entered via the wide sandstone gate on North Evergreen Avenue, slowing down to a respectful pace as I drove along the wide strips of asphalt that wound their ways through the seventy-acre necropolis. The first thing that struck me was that the name 'Evergreen' was a misnomer. There were palm trees dotted here and there, but the overriding color scheme was comprised of dusty browns and yellows. Irrigation was expensive, and these residents had no need of water. The tombstones were arranged in neat rows, following the twists of the access roads. They looked like gigantic lines of dominoes, ready to be pushed over.

The area I was interested in was at the far side of the cemetery. A section that had originally been gifted to the city of Los Angeles by the original owners as a potter's field. As the city grew and swelled, the patch of ground was taken over by the county, and when they ran out of space, they built a crematorium and started incinerating the unclaimed and unmourned indigent dead instead of burying them. With space at a premium, the cemetery bought the ground back from LA County in the mid-sixties, dumped eight feet of fresh dirt on top, and started burying the more recently departed on top of their forebears. The approach was striking in its unsentimental practicality.

When I found the approximate site I was looking for, I parked at the side of the road and got out. I'd passed a few other vehicles on my journey through the cemetery, and even one or two people on foot, but when I looked around, there was no one within sight. No one who was going to give me any problem, anyway. The sun was beginning to sink in the west and was already well below the tops of the palm trees. I started to feel a chill in the air and grabbed my jacket from the backseat before I set off.

It took me another fifteen minutes to find the row I was looking for, but when I did, my eyes homed in on the specific plot. Dusk was advancing by now, and it was difficult to read the dedications on the stones from more than a few feet away, but one grave in particular caught my eye. I glanced around me again, saw nothing and nobody. I looked back down the hill toward the blue Chevy. It was a dark shade of blue, but somehow in the dusk it suddenly seemed bright, out of place among the dust and the stone. I felt a strong sense of unease and chalked it partly up to the fact I'd almost had my head blown off the last time I'd been in a graveyard.

I walked along the row and stopped at the tenth marker from the start. It was a granite headstone, of good quality. Certainly more impressive than anything that would have been provided for any of the original inhabitants of this part of the cemetery. I crouched down to read the inscription. Three different first names: David, Martha, and Terri. All with the same last name: Crozier. Three different dates of birth, all with the same date of death.

*January 4, 1997.*

A Bible quotation below the names and the dates:

*And do not fear those who kill the body but cannot kill the soul. Rather fear Him who can destroy both soul and body in Hell—MATTHEW 10:28*

At the foot of the headstone was the thing that had attracted my attention from the start of the row: a single red rose, the petals folded in on themselves like a fist but still looking relatively fresh. I reached out to touch it, to check that it was as real as it looked. It was. I straightened up again and slowly turned three hundred and sixty degrees. Even in the half-light, the dry, dusty feel of the landscape was evident. The day had been relatively cool for the time of year, but even so, the rose couldn't have been placed there more than a few hours before.

I looked around at the acres of orderly markers. A city of the dead. I still couldn't see a soul, and yet I had the nagging sensation of being watched. Another of those feelings that's difficult to explain but unwise to ignore. I took one last glance at the Crozier family marker and wondered who had picked the inscription. Then I turned and walked back down toward the Chevy, across two layers of corpses.

# 35

"Looking good, Allen."

She didn't look at Coleman. The ever-present undertone of insincerity was there in his voice, of course, but Allen didn't know if it was deliberate this time or if that was just the way his voice always sounded. It was just the two of them and Mazzucco in the squad room. No one to show off to, so perhaps it really was intended as a compliment.

"Glad you approve."

They were rewatching Allen's segment of the press conference earlier that evening on Channel 7. They'd held it in the press room downstairs. Allen had met the LA chief of police for the first time ten minutes before they went on camera. The chief was a solid-built man of sixty, with a cop mustache and a permanently weary look in his eyes. He'd greeted Allen like a longtime friend, asked one or two perceptive questions, and called it good to go.

The chief had opened up the press conference and explained that they were now liaising with the Federal Bureau of Investigation on what had become a far more complex case than anyone could have anticipated. He spoke for five minutes, sounding authoritative and calm despite the fact they'd had to tear up the script a half hour before the cameras were switched on. The chief finished up, brushed off some shouted questions, and introduced the primary detective on the Samaritan case, Detective Jessica Allen.

Watching the recording, Allen kept her face impassive but winced inside as her image on TV began to speak. She hated seeing herself on video, and the knowledge that this piece of footage was being broadcast across the country and around the world did not help with that.

"Good evening," she said onscreen, reading from the prepared statement in her hands. She was pleased to see that the shaking of her hands was not perceptible onscreen. "As you are aware, officers of the Los Angeles Police Department, acting on a report from a member of the public, discovered the bodies of three murder victims buried at a location in the Santa Monica Mountains yesterday morning around eight o'clock. We have subsequently identified the victims as Kelly Boden, Carrie Elaine Burnett, and Rachel Anne Morrow."

Background chatter broke out around the mention of Burnett's name: the TV star. That was why Allen had sandwiched her between the other two vics and read the names as quickly as possible.

"Preliminary forensics indicates that all three women were likely killed by the same individual. Further investigation has uncovered additional cases that we think may be related in"—she paused here and looked up from the statement to meet the camera—"seven different states, dating back as far as 2010."

Theatrical gasps and yelled questions from the assembled pack of journalists. Allen looked back down again and raised her voice over the hubbub.

"The LAPD is now liaising with the Federal Bureau of Investigation on this case. We are pursuing a number of active leads, and we believe the individual is still at large within the Los Angeles area. One of our lines of inquiry suggests the individual is currently targeting lone female drivers, particularly at night. It's possible that he's offering his help to drivers who have broken down in isolated areas. The advice is simple, folks: try not to drive alone at night unless it's absolutely necessary. Make sure you have a full tank of gas, and lock your car when you're filling up. Keep your doors locked at all times, and do not stop for anyone unless it's a marked police car. We urge all citizens to be vigilant and report any suspicious behavior to the telephone number or the email address you can see on your screen."

Allen finished with a "thank you" to indicate she was ready for the questions. The first one out of the pack was predictably stupid.

"Detective Allen, is the Samaritan targeting celebrities?"

Allen watched her face on the screen as she heard the question and was pleased to see she'd kept her irritation under wraps pretty successfully, just making eye contact with the speaker and shaking her head as soon as he'd finished. "We have no evidence to suggest that, no. If you're referring to Ms. Burnett, we don't know that the killer was necessarily aware she was a television personality."

*Which would make two of us*, Allen had thought but did not say.

Another disembodied voice piped up from behind the camera's line of sight. That one was Jennifer Quan from KABC: "The related murders in the other states, did they all have the same MO?"

Allen had needed a second to think, so she had asked Quan to repeat the question.

"Were they all lone female drivers, too? And if so, how has he managed to operate undetected for this long?"

Allen cleared her throat, not wanting to give the little information she had on the additional murders away so freely. "I'm afraid I don't have that information for you right now."

"You mean you don't know, or—"

"Next question."

As Allen watched herself fielding questions on the screen, she started to think about that MO again. If the cases in the other states varied so much, could there be earlier cases in LA that also diverged from this, apparently new, "Samaritan" modus operandi? Cases that did not involve kidnaps from vehicles? Her brief brush with the media had just given her the idea of someone she could approach about this.

Onscreen, she took another question.

"Is the FBI taking over the case? If so, when can we talk to them?"

Allen shot a brief, sarcastic smile at the questioner. Looking back on it onscreen thirty minutes later, she was pleased to see the implicit *fuck you* had come across. Beside her, she heard Coleman snort in amusement at the look.

"You heard the chief," she said, nodding at her superior. "We're working closely with the Bureau on a coordinated investigation with the aim of getting this individual into custody as quickly as possible. The FBI will be coordinating the multistate investigation and assisting the LAPD with the current investigation here in Los Angeles."

That was the party line, and again, Allen was reasonably pleased with the conviction with which she'd sold it. The feds had gotten much more diplomatic over the past couple of decades, and they were touchy about being seen to swoop in and take over every aspect of the big cases. These days, it was all cross-agency task forces, coordinated mixed scenes, and joint communication strategies. That meant that on paper, Allen would keep the three LA murders, with close assistance from the feds. In reality, it was the same old story: the government boys were taking this case, and Allen was welcome to tag along just as long as she played by their rulebook.

The questions went on for another couple of minutes before the chief wound things up and reminded the viewers that they could keep up to date by monitoring the department's

Twitter feed. Watching again onscreen, Allen noticed the visible discomfort with which he said that last line.

Mazzucco turned the screen off and turned to face Allen, giving her four loud claps. "Couldn't have done it any better myself." He smiled.

"Come on, Jon, you hate this shit even more than I do."

"That's what I just said, isn't it?"

Allen smiled. "What time are we meeting with our co-operative coordinated colleagues again?"

"Fuckin' feds," Coleman muttered under his breath as he looked back down at his own, less glamorous case: a seventy-two-year-old woman shot to death during a burglary in Compton.

"Eight-thirty tomorrow morning," Mazzucco answered.

"They were too busy to speak to us today, huh?" Allen mused.

"I offered this evening, but they were fine with the agent's phone conversation with Lawrence. Apparently, they can start moving on this before they need to speak to us. They want to sit in on the psych briefing, and then they'll catch up with us."

"I bet they can start moving without us. They're sending us a message. Me a message."

Mazzucco nodded and smiled. "Don't worry; it is *us*. Same as always. As far as they're concerned, the *us* is not just you and me. It's the whole department."

Allen turned back to the screen, where they were showing helicopter footage from earlier in the day. Mazzucco was right. Us and them. They'd gotten off on a worse footing than necessary, thanks to Allen's reticence, and it wasn't as though the relationship between the two agencies was lacking in friction as it was. She was lucky to still be as involved as she was, and she knew that was down to Lawrence giving her a break. But Lawrence wouldn't be running the show for much longer. She'd be intrigued to find out how involved she'd feel after tomorrow morning's meeting with the FBI liaison.

But before that, she had a call to make.

# 36

"Whoever this is, be warned I am extremely drunk."

From the way the words on the end of the line hazed into one another and the bar music in the background, it sounded like the speaker might just be telling the truth. Allen cleared her throat. "Smith? This is Detective Allen."

Allen heard some shuffling in the background and Eddie Smith's voice returned, sounding a little more sober. "Well, this is an honor. What can I do for you, Detective?"

"I wondered if we could help each other out again."

"I like the sound of that." He sounded immediately interested, and Allen wondered if she was making a mistake. "I caught you on TV tonight. Looking good."

"So people keep telling me. Can we cut the pleasantries?"

"By all means."

"You saw the press conference, so you know about the other Samaritan killings."

"Yep. Pretty impressive, if you're right about all of these other cases."

He actually did sound genuinely impressed, Allen thought. "That's one word for it," she said coldly. "Anyway, I've been thinking about the latest killings out here in LA. It's not public knowledge, but the three victims here ..."

"All look alike," he finished. "You don't have to go to cop school to see that—those three women could be sisters, almost."

"Right," Allen said, caught off guard. She didn't know why she should be surprised that Smith had thought this through. "Anyway, I got to thinking that maybe it's not just the three out here. What if he's killed other people in LA and we haven't connected them?"

"You'd know about it before I would, Detective. Right?"

Allen wasn't so sure about that, but he'd misunderstood her. "I just thought you could go back over your ... portfolio. See if anything jumps out at you over the last year or so, anything we could have missed."

"I know what you're looking for. Distinctive ragged throat wounds, right?"

For the hundredth time, Allen cursed whoever had leaked that detail. "Like that, yes. I've checked on our end, but it's not an exact science. I thought you could take a look at your old photographs."

"Sorry, nothing like that."

"Just like that? How can you be sure?"

"I keep them all with me. Up here."

Allen pictured him jabbing a finger to his head and shuddered at what it would be like to be inside Eddie Smith's mind.

"Right," she said. His media-derived knowledge of the wound patterns reminded her of the other reason she'd called. "Smith, do you happen to know who leaked the details? We could have done without this."

"I'll give you what I have for free, because it ain't much."

"Shoot."

"I heard it was a cop who talked to that reporter. One of the uniforms on the scene."

"We thought so. Don't suppose you 'heard' a name?"

She heard a low chuckle. "Allen, the MSM hates me almost as much as you guys do. Those guys don't come near me if they can help it."

"MSM?"

"Mainstream media."

"What can I say, Smith? You seem such a likeable guy, too."

"Ha-ha. I told you it wasn't much. So when is it my turn to get helped?"

"Your day will come, Smith."

"I feel used."

"Sure you do. Night."

Allen hung up and thought over the conversation. It had been a hunch that hadn't played out, that there might have been other victims in LA that didn't fit the profile of the three bodies in the mountains. Neither Allen nor the other detectives who'd been looking into this since earlier today had turned any up; so if Smith didn't know of any others, it was starting to look very likely that the Samaritan had started work in Los Angeles only recently. But that still didn't explain the new consistency in the type of victim.

The information they had so far suggested that in the other states, the killer had taken between four and six victims before moving on. That meant time was running out. The time they had to catch the Samaritan, and more important, the time they had before another young woman with dark hair and brown eyes was found in a shallow grave.

# 37

The Samaritan drove.

He went out driving most nights, not just on the ones on which he had made up his mind to hunt. It was a comforting routine, setting out before midnight, cruising the streets with the windows down, returning before the first of the morning commuters set out. He hated the days: the long, jammed freeways clogged like old arteries with metal and exhaust fumes and disgusting, sweating people. There was still traffic at night, of course, but one could move relatively freely around the monstrous, sprawling city in the dead hours between the late evening and the early morning. The cars moved efficiently and calmly on the freeways, the drivers less frantic at night, less in a hurry to get to wherever they were going. The surface streets were quieter still, and that was where the Samaritan liked to be.

The mountains, and the maze of twisting two-lane routes that skirted them, had served him well in the past two weeks. Both because of the sparsity of night traffic and the fact that isolation made the prey more uneasy when they broke down, more ready to accept an offer of assistance. That was a happy accident, of course. He had other practical reasons for taking his victims in that area. But he was keeping well away from there tonight, although he would certainly return the next time he had ... company.

The police knew about some of the other killings now. He had not been overly worried when he'd seen the news and had it confirmed they were looking into his back catalog. He'd expected this from the moment he found out that the body from Saturday had been discovered. In truth, he'd been expecting it for far longer than that. He was amazed that his body of work had gone unconnected for such a very long time. Perhaps that had led him to be careless with the burials of these last victims, or perhaps it was merely the comfort of being home again. He'd always been careful not to leave physical evidence, never to use the same firearm twice when he did use one, and even now he knew there would be nothing concrete to forensically connect the cases to one another, still less to connect any of them to him. But then, that was just one of the benefits of being a man who did not exist.

He drove at the speed limit, not paying any more attention than was necessary to the road, watching his surroundings. The darkened storefronts sliding by, the occasional lit-up bar with its regulation huddle of smokers outside, and above it all the dirty yellow night sky, stained that color by light pollution reflecting off the other, more obdurate kind of pollution. And then there was a gap in the buildings and he saw the Hollywood sign shining back at him. He pulled over to the side of the road and turned the engine off. The street sounds from behind him seemed small, lost in the void between him and the hills. He put an arm on the windowsill and remembered the place in the mountains.

A harsh rap on the roof broke the rhythm of his thoughts. He turned his head to see a uniformed police officer, his fist still resting on the roof of the truck where he'd knocked.

"Good evening, sir."

The Samaritan looked for a partner, didn't see one. He glanced in the mirror to see a police cruiser parked twenty yards behind him. Empty, but with the headlights on. The standard words came naturally to him. "Is there a problem, Officer?" Perfect. Just what a normal person would say. He widened his eyes a little, trying to look appropriately nervous.

"Step out of the vehicle, please."

The Samaritan blinked and then unbuckled his seat belt. He opened the door and got out.

The cop asked him to stay there and circled the truck, shining a flashlight over the surface. The Samaritan watched as he reached the flat bed and played the beam of his flashlight over the inside. There was nothing there, just a neatly brushed-out space. The cop came around to the driver's side, extinguishing the light and attaching it to his belt again in a practiced, one-handed move.

He looked to be a lifelong beat cop—late forties, with hair shaved close to his scalp in a way that suggested he was bald under the hat.

"Are you the owner of this vehicle, sir?"

The Samaritan nodded. "Yes."

"License and registration, please."

He hesitated a second too long. The cop, whose eyes had been scanning the interior of the vehicle, stopped and looked at him more closely. The Samaritan looked at the cop's throat. His carotid artery was right there. It would be possible to reach out and render him unconscious in less than a second. He could take him away, make sure that this body was never found.

But a police car would be difficult to dispose of, and the police officer's movements would certainly be traced to this point. Another worry: what if he had already run the truck's plate?

"Is that going to be a problem, sir?" the cop asked, his hand moving slightly closer to the holster at his side.

He shook his head, murmured an apology. He reached in the driver's side window and retrieved the documents from the glove box. Far less risky to play along. It wasn't as if this stop was going to lead to anything.

The cop's eyes held on him for a moment, then dropped to look at the license. The Samaritan kept his hands stiffly by his sides.

"You still live here?" he asked as he read the address.

"Yes, I do."

"Nice place."

"I like it."

There was nothing to worry about. The photograph was his, and although the name was fake, there would be no way to tell that. The license and registration were both entirely genuine, and the vehicle had been purchased and registered under the same name. The cop could confirm that with a very quick check.

In the end it wasn't required. The cop nodded and handed the documents back.

"Thank you, sir. Just a routine stop."

"Not a problem, Officer."

The Samaritan got back into the truck and watched the officer return to his vehicle. He waited for a moment and then realized that the cop was waiting for him to leave first. He obliged, starting up the engine and pulling smoothly back onto the road.

He watched the police car in the mirror until he rounded a corner and lost sight of it, and then he allowed himself a smile. Perhaps it was the brush with authority, a reminder that his time was limited, but all of a sudden, he felt the first stirrings of the urge.

It would be time to hunt again very soon.

## 1996

"Pretty cool, huh?" Kimberley said, smiling proudly.

He didn't say anything, but smiled quickly as he surveyed the small knot of buildings. They were empty and silent, preserved over the years by the relatively temperate climate. A cool breeze was channeled through the corridor created by the buildings. An old sign, suspended by chains from one of the awnings, creaked softly, but otherwise it was quiet.

Robbie had suddenly developed a new enthusiasm, after bitching and moaning most of the way. "How did you know about this place?"

Kimberley pouted theatrically and rolled her head at that. He admired the way her dark hair bounced around her eyes. "I could tell you, Robbie, but I'd have to kill you."

There was a low, partly broken-down fence adjoining the last building in the main row. Kimberley sat down on it first and he leaned against it alongside her, waiting for Robbie to catch up.

"Hey, Robbie, how about a picture to remember today by?" She turned and looked up at him. She was a few inches shorter, even though she had a couple of years on him. "It's a good day, isn't it?" she said to him.

He reached into the backpack again. He moved some of the top layer of contents about—Kimberley's Walkman, some loose cassettes—and found the camera. It was a disposable, the kind people used for casual photography in the years before digital took over. He tossed it to Robbie, who fumbled it and cursed as it dropped to the ground.

"Jeez, at least give me a heads-up."

Robbie took a picture of the two of them and then joined

them on the fence. They sat there for a while, resting and enjoying the quiet for a moment. Then Robbie regained his breath and started talking again. He decided to leave them there and explore further.

There was a big house set on raised ground, a little distance away. It looked more substantial, more ... real than the thin skeletons and shells farther back. It was a wide building with wood siding and a big porch along the front, with a small dormer window set into the center of the roof. When he reached the porch, he looked back. Kimberley and Robbie were sitting on the fence, pointing at the view. He thought about calling out to them but changed his mind. He put his hand on the door handle and twisted it. It was unlocked. He didn't know why that surprised him.

He opened the door, and the smell of dust and stale air greeted him. There was a stairway straight ahead. He remembered the little window and assumed that the stairs led up to an attic room. He climbed them and found a low-ceilinged space with a wide, unbroken expanse of floorboards. There was a small table in one corner, but the space was otherwise unfurnished. The window he'd seen from outside was glassless and looked back down the way he'd just come. He went to the window and put a hand on one of the thin wood partitions. Kimberley and Robbie were still there at the fence, Kimberley throwing her head back and laughing as he watched.

Without realizing it, he'd tightened his grip on the partition, and he was surprised when it snapped in his hand. He stepped away from the window and looked around him at the attic space.

It was what he had been looking for, almost without knowing it. A quiet space. A private space. A house without an owner in a town without a name. A place where he could do things that no one would ever know about.

# 38

I'd checked out of the Sherman Oaks hotel that morning. I was traveling so light that there was no benefit in staying in any one place longer than one night. Everything I had with me fit comfortably in a single bag in the trunk of the Chevy. The manager in the new place told me the room was the best in the hotel, because it was the only one with an entirely unobstructed view of the Hollywood sign.

Perhaps out of a sense of obligation, the first thing I did when I entered the room was to turn out the lights and go to the window. The sign looked white and clean at night, but I knew it would be old and dirty from up close. I also knew they'd erected fences to stop people from getting too close, either to steal a piece of history, or to carve out their own place in it by jumping off the top of one of the letters to kill themselves. I didn't suppose I was the first person to think of it, but it seemed like a pretty good metaphor for Hollywood itself. Look but don't touch. Don't get too close.

I thought about Carol again, for the second time in as many days. I wondered where she'd gone; wondered if she'd headed west, too. Perhaps she was out there in the city, one of the million pinpricks of light in the darkness.

I unbuttoned my shirt and touched a finger to the long, white scar on my chest. Not the stab wound Wardell had given me, but the one that predated it by a few years. The scar hadn't bothered me in a long time, but it had itched all day today. I ran a fingertip down the smooth line of raised tissue.

I watched the Hollywood sign and thought about how it was a beacon that brought people to this town from all over the world. A siren call that lured in the unsuspecting to be chewed up and spat out by this unforgiving town. A city of new arrivals, of people reinventing themselves and their pasts. Prime targets for the Samaritan.

I thought Allen would use the number I'd given her tomorrow. But if she didn't, I had to be ready to draw the Samaritan out.

# TUESDAY

# 39

Almost two days without sleep, and yet Allen somehow found it difficult to switch off when she made it back to her apartment a little after midnight.

She gave up after an hour or so and moved to the living room couch. *Three Days of the Condor* with Robert Redford was the late movie. She watched twenty minutes but found herself unable to concentrate, so she began to look over the case files again. She sketched out a timeline showing the locations of potential Samaritan cases arranged by date. The cases roamed all over the map. Clusters of murders over the span of a few weeks, followed by a break of a number of months, and then a new cluster in a different city. Going back a long time, maybe five years, starting in North Carolina. That got her thinking again about Blake, the guy who'd appeared out of nowhere with an offer of help and an FBI character reference. She knew Mazzucco was reluctant to let him in, but she was starting to seriously consider dialing the number on the plain business card. With the feds now involved, it was the one thing she could hold on to for now, maybe a way to stay ahead of the pack.

She understood Mazzucco's wariness, of course, but she trusted her own instincts. She didn't think Blake fit the Samaritan's profile, and not just because of what Agent Banner had said. There was something about his manner that seemed ... solid? Dependable. And he'd given them the Peterson lead, so he evidently knew his stuff.

And yet, it would be interesting to see if she could rule him out. She spent some time on the Internet and the phone attempting to build up a picture of Carter Blake, and beyond confirming that his driver's license was legit, found it far more difficult than she'd expected. The DL did give her one thing, though: he'd mentioned flying into town on Sunday night, and flying required identification.

At some point, she had finally succumbed to exhaustion, because the next thing she knew she was waking with a start, having overslept by an hour.

When she opened the door to the conference room, she saw that there were three men and one woman around the table: Mazzucco, Lieutenant Lawrence, Lieutenant Anne Whitmore from the chief's office, and another man in a dark suit whom she didn't recognize: the FBI liaison. Lawrence glanced pointedly at the wall clock as she sat down. Even Mazzucco looked a little pissed at her.

"Sorry." She smiled, hoping the bright sunlight streaming through the window didn't highlight the dark circles around her eyes too much. "Still getting used to the traffic in this town."

The FBI guy returned the smile and reached his hand across the table. "You're not from here?" he said, adding, "Special Agent James Channing ... Jim," as they shook. He was in his mid-forties, she guessed. In good shape, broad shoulders, a healthy California tan. No dark shadows under his eyes. He'd probably woken up at five a.m. and gone for a ten-mile run before oatmeal and fruit juice.

"I'm from DC, originally. Metro PD, transferred out here

six months back," she said, keeping it short so as not to aggravate the others further.

Channing nodded. He glanced at Lawrence. "Do we need to ...?" he asked, meaning did they need to stop and bring Allen up to speed.

"I don't think so. Detective Allen knows everything we know." He fixed Allen with a stare. "Probably more."

She avoided his gaze and cleared her throat. This was the last thing she'd wanted, to be on the back foot for this meeting.

"So how's this going to work?" she said, speaking to Channing, her tone deliberately challenging.

Channing blinked and took a moment to collect himself. "This thing is big; I don't have to tell you that. We've had people chasing down possible leads on this killer since Lieutenant Lawrence got in touch yesterday afternoon."

He hadn't taken the opportunity to stress the *yesterday afternoon*, so either he was being very diplomatic about the fact the LAPD had sat on information about a homicide investigation that crossed state lines, or Lawrence had left that part out. She was betting on the latter.

"As I was explaining before you came in, we've now identified potential linked cases in a further four states, bringing the total to eleven states. Potential victims? Over sixty."

Lieutenant Whitmore broke in then. She had dark hair trimmed short, was about five two and of slight build: diminutive in appearance, but with a loud, assertive voice that brooked no dissent. "It looks like the bastard is doing a regular American tour. I hope he's signed up for frequent flier miles."

Allen had met Whitmore only once before and didn't know her well enough to tell if that was a joke. It would make catching the killer a hell of a lot easier if he had been dumb enough to travel using commercial airlines, but given the profile she'd built up already, she very much doubted it.

"We don't know for sure that all of those cases are connected, of course," Channing continued. "Could be fewer, could be more. The best way to find out for sure will be to catch this guy and ask him."

Allen smirked and looked at Mazzucco. "There you go. Why didn't we think of that?"

"Take it easy, Allen," Lawrence said.

The smile faded from Channing's face and he turned back to Allen. She wondered if he was riled and was irritated to see he was being ... patient with her. That was the only way to describe it. "You did a great job making the case-to-case link between here and some of the other states, Detective," he said. "No one's questioning that."

Mazzucco spoke next, probably because he knew Allen would say it if he didn't. "But now the big boys can take over."

Channing sighed, almost inaudibly, but loud enough for Allen to hear and take some satisfaction. He looked at Lawrence, as if to say, *Can you step in here?* No help was forthcoming.

"A little more blunt than I would have liked," Lawrence said after a second, "but I guess that is what we're here to establish, Agent Channing."

"That's not how we work, Lieutenant. We don't see any value in freezing out local expertise. I'm here to liaise—"

"You can skip the five steps of handling local cops, Agent. What does it mean in practice? In this case."

Channing nodded, smiling as though he was glad he was able to talk straight, person to person.

"The Bureau is investigating these murders as one multistate case. Are we best placed to carry out this work nationwide? Absolutely. The homicides on your patch are very recent, and you're already running a very effective investigation, from what I've seen. Do I want to throw that out just because of some historical pissing contest we're supposed to be having with the LAPD? Hell no, I don't. I need you on board. We need everyone on this." He made eye contact with the four of them, finishing up with Allen for the last sentence.

Allen found herself caught between hating and admiring him, because his manner was effective. She could see why he'd been chosen for the sensitive job of liaison to the LAPD. She'd be amazed if he didn't transfer to politics sometime soon with these people skills.

There was a knock on the door and Allen turned around to see Felicia from reception sticking her head around the door, as though she didn't want to open it too far. "Lieutenant Lawrence?"

Lawrence looked up. "The shrink? Send him in."

Felicia closed the door again and returned a few moments later, opening it wide. The consultant psychologist walked into the room. He was quite tall and very thin. He carried a leather briefcase and wore a light gray suit and a matching tie over a crisp white shirt. "Dr. Gregory Trent," Lawrence said, greeting him as they shook hands. "This is Lieutenant Anne Whitmore, from the Office of the Chief of Police, and Special Agent Jim Channing of the FBI. You probably know Detectives Mazzucco and Allen already."

Trent smiled briefly as he shook hands with Allen. She didn't know him, in fact, but she'd seen him around, and she knew how much he billed per hour. She knew Lawrence liked him because he was thorough as well as being fast: a rare combination that enabled him to command exorbitant rates.

When the introductions were done and coffee poured, Trent opened his briefcase and took out a couple of documents. "Before I get going, I'd like to ask you for your take on the perpetrator of these three homicides," he said, addressing all five of them. He spoke with a British accent that had had the sharp edges sanded off by a decade or more in Southern California.

"Actually, it's looking like a lot more than three—" Channing began.

Trent cut him off abruptly. "We'll get to that. My brief was to compile a profile for the unknown subject who killed, mutilated, and buried the three bodies you found out in the Santa Monica Mountains. That's what I've focused on." He paused and looked at each face in turn. "Now, I'm aware that since I was commissioned, it has come to light that the individual responsible may have committed crimes in other jurisdictions. From my appraisal of the additional information sent through to me yesterday evening, I can say with a reasonable degree of certainty that there is a very strong likelihood that you're on the right track with these apparently linked investigations in other states. In fact, it preempts one of my key recommendations. So, with all of that in mind, I'm interested in the primary investigators' take on the killer."

All eyes moved to Mazzucco and Allen. Mazzucco scratched his neck where there was a small patch of razor burn and looked at Allen before answering first.

"Definitely not a first timer was my first instinct, and it looks like that's been borne out already. All three victims bore very similar wounds. No hesitation, no deviation. He wasn't experimenting with anything different, just doing what he's used to."

No one in the room called Mazzucco on his use of the male pronoun, Allen noticed. They were all used to the convention in homicide investigations of referring to unidentified murderers as *he*. It was not just a figure of speech, but also a safe bet, considering the miniscule proportion of women who ended up being convicted for serial murders of strangers. Allen herself would be amazed if it turned out the Samaritan was a woman.

Mazzucco had paused, as though figuring out how he could put the next thought into words.

"It was like the victims had been ... processed. You know what I mean? He knew what he wanted to do and went ahead and did it as carefully and as efficiently as possible. The graves were like that, too: just deep enough to keep them from the coyotes. He got rid of their clothes and belongings and made their vehicles disappear. If it hadn't been for the landslide, we'd have three missing persons cases and we'd still be none the wiser about this guy."

Trent looked pleased but didn't say anything. He switched his gaze to Allen.

Allen cleared her throat, thinking about how to structure her answer to avoid discussing the suspicions she'd held on to for longer than she should have. "The MO for the abductions is starting to look pretty consistent, for these three anyway. He targets lone female drivers at night. Smart, because they're the most vulnerable, the easiest to deal with. At first we were working on the assumption that he gets them to stop somehow, but one of the victims made a call to Triple A, reporting a breakdown before she and her vehicle disappeared. That means it's possible he's finding people who have broken down, offering them help, and abducting them."

"Hence the name you people have come up with for him," Trent said.

"Don't blame us," Allen said. "You know how it is; you can't sell newspapers without a catchy name."

Trent angled his head. "I would argue that it doesn't do your investigation any harm, Detective. If a name brand for our killer helps more of the public pay attention, it makes your job easier in terms of keeping people safe and vigilant."

Allen didn't say anything, but she thought he might actually have a point. "The Samaritan" was a useful-enough name for the purposes of public awareness. It even suggested the situations in which people should be most wary. Assuming he continued to stick to the MO, of course. There was no guarantee that he would, particularly because he'd done things differently in other areas.

Jim Channing sat back in his seat once he was sure Allen didn't want to speak further. "Dr. Trent," he said, doing a reasonable job of covering up his irritation at being interrupted earlier. "I think we'd all be interested in your expert take on the type of individual we're dealing with here."

Trent paused for effect, a twinkle in his eye betraying how much he was enjoying the attention, the weight of expectation. "I've worked in the field of forensic psychology for more than twenty years. I've used my skills to assist this department and others to track down a great many murderers. Bear that in mind, please, when I tell you that I think this individual, this ... Samaritan ... is without a doubt the most dangerous psychopath I have ever investigated."

# 40

In the end, Dr. Trent's report didn't throw up anything they hadn't been expecting in terms of gender, race, or personality type. The thing that surprised Allen was how unsurprised Trent seemed by the revelation of dozens of previously undetected cases in other states.

The psychologist's opinion, having looked closely at all of the information available on the three initial homicides, was that they were looking for a high-functioning psychopath with a strictly methodical approach to his work and a great deal of experience in killing human beings. In terms of a profile, Trent thought they should be looking for a white American male in his thirties or forties. Intelligent, wily and physically strong. From the initial evidence, he thought it was likely that the individual was a native of Los Angeles, as suggested by his choice of abduction method and body disposal site, and further by the fact he'd found a way to make the vehicles disappear, rendering the trail even colder. In the light of the potentially related cases that had surfaced in other states, Trent conceded that his initial opinion of the Samaritan being from LA was open to question but was adamant that he must at least have spent enough time here to develop strong local knowledge. He opined that there was no reason he couldn't have used LA as a base from which to travel to his other hunting grounds.

Trent said that the individual would probably be quiet and reserved, a loner. He would have few close friends but might well hold down a steady job. He would be unassuming but not unapproachable, given his likely abduction process, and it was likely he could be charming when it was required.

The Samaritan would be someone capable of blending into the background, a wolf in sheep's clothing.

Those words had triggered the memory of the encounter on the roof of the parking structure. Open hands and a disarming smile. *I don't think he's stupid enough to walk up to you and introduce himself.*

She'd tried to put those suspicions to one side for now, made herself focus on what the shrink was saying.

The lack of evidence of sexual assault on the female victims was interesting, he thought, as was the quite specific victim profile in the LA cases. He confirmed Allen's impression that the Samaritan was all about the kill: not motivated by sexual aggression, but by the unique thrill of ending another person's life. Trent offered an aside that the disinterest in sex would probably translate to his "normal" life as well, and could suggest a difficult relationship with his mother. He'd smiled disarmingly at that, cracking, "But, then, I have to drop some Freud in somewhere; otherwise people get disappointed." Following on from that, Trent posited that he would not be surprised if the killer's mother—or some other female close to him—resembled the victims.

So far, so routine. But Trent had one other supposition, one that reminded Allen of what the medical examiner had said. He thought it was very likely that the Samaritan had military training. And not just any military training, either.

"He plans these murders carefully," he'd said. "They're not random crimes of passion, although he does enjoy his work—there's no doubt of that. The planning, the setup, the execution, the way he removes vehicles and clothes and personal effects. The care he takes not to leave DNA or fingerprints. That he takes his victims from one place, kills them in another place, and dumps them in a third place. It's like he's sanitizing. Erasing the evidence he was ever there."

"What are you saying?" Channing, the FBI liaison had asked him. "Are you talking some kind of black ops experience? CIA or something?"

"That would fit," Trent had agreed. "A regular serviceman would be much more likely to use a gun. And far more likely to kill people in a spree, rather than one by one. It's the evidence of training and the approach he takes that suggests that type of background to me."

Channing in particular had pushed him on the other cases in the eleven states that had been identified as possibly related. Dr. Trent had reiterated that he hadn't been asked to or had time to look into this in detail, but he was firm that nothing he'd seen so far conflicted with anything he'd gleaned from the initial investigation in LA. In fact, everything he'd read had reinforced his conclusions: an intelligent, meticulous lone psychopath with military training. The possibility of multiple murders in other states merely proved how careful the killer was: roaming far and wide, concealing some bodies, allowing others to be found. He'd operated undetected for at least five years and possibly longer.

Finally, he'd confirmed their assumption that the primary crime scene would be within a three- to five-mile radius of the dump site. Which still left tens of thousands of homes and hundreds of miles of hiking trails to check. Trent's final words seemed to create a tangible chill in the room.

"I'm afraid he won't stop until he's caught. There's no burnout with this type of killer."

As the meeting broke up, Allen checked her phone and found two missed calls: one from Denny and one from Darryl Caine in Traffic. She returned the second one and learned that they'd caught a break: Long Beach PD had reported that Sarah Dutton's Porsche had been found on their turf.

Allen didn't complain when Mazzucco offered to drive,

and they made the journey in almost total silence, both of them processing the information from the meeting they'd just left. Mazzucco broke the silence after fifteen slow minutes on the 710.

"So, basically, we've narrowed it down to an outwardly normal male with psychopathic tendencies." He looked from one side to the other. "I guess he picked the right town."

"The special ops angle is interesting," Allen said. "Remember what Burke said about seeing that kind of thing in the army? It ties in, and it's a little more specific. If Trent is onto something, we might be able to narrow it down that way."

"I thought you said behavioral profiling was a crock of shit."

Allen was distracted, suddenly thinking about Blake again. Blake and his well-informed tip about Fort Bragg. They trained Special Forces at Bragg, didn't they?

"Allen?"

She looked back at him. "When did I say that?"

"Most recently?" He thought about it. "Last week. But you say it a lot."

Allen rolled her eyes. "That's not what I meant. I was just talking about guys like that drawing big bucks for applying the same common sense that you and I use every day. But yeah, okay, I'll admit it. This time he came up with something that *might* be useful."

"Might. You know what the problem is?"

"Same as it was before: narrowing the suspect pool down." Allen looked out of the window as the traffic flew past on the opposite side of the central reservation. "The United States has been at war in various countries for a decade and a half. There's probably more people walking around with the kind of skills and experience Trent was describing than at any time in history."

"Scary, when you put it that way."

"And if we're talking CIA or the SEALs or whatever, we're getting into sealed records territory, government-approved fake identities."

"Maybe Channing will be able to help with that."

Allen looked back at him and smiled over her glasses. "Ever the optimist, Jon." They passed a minute in silence before Allen said, "I think we should talk to Blake."

Mazzucco scrunched up his face. He didn't say anything.

"The Peterson lead looks good, right?"

"The FBI's including it," he admitted, then glanced over at her. "Maybe they ought to include Blake, too."

She told him about her attempts to look into his background last night and that she'd managed to confirm he'd flown into LA only after Boden was killed and from far enough away that it was unlikely he could have been here on the Saturday night. Mazzucco said nothing.

They arrived at the address in Long Beach a couple of minutes later. It was an auto-repair shop. A sign out front told them it was O'Grady's Complete Auto Service and that they worked on foreign and domestic. They went inside and found two uniformed LBPD officers with one of the mechanics: a hulking black guy crammed into blue overalls. Sarah Dutton's Porsche Carrera was up on a hydraulic jack, the tasteful curves of the vehicle obvious under the sheets that had been draped over it.

Allen took her badge out and introduced herself and Mazzucco to the two officers—one male and one female—and the guy in the overalls.

"We got a tipoff this guy had a stolen Porsche," the male cop explained. "We ran the vehicle number from the chassis and it turns out it's the one you people are looking for."

"Whoa," the mechanic interjected, his hands outstretched. "I told you. I don't know nothin' about this being stolen."

The female cop, Officer Danniker, glanced at her notes and back up at the man. "That's right. You said you, uh . . . found it," she deadpanned.

The mechanic had a foot in height and at least one fifty in weight on the cop, but he still withered under her direct stare after only a couple of seconds.

"Yeah, I mean, I know a guy who found it. He brought it in. I was just about to call you guys when . . ."

He tailed off. Allen and Mazzucco exchanged a look, stood back, and let the officer continue embarrassing the guy. They just needed to tie up one piece of information, anyway.

"And this guy you know. Does he make a habit of . . . finding vehicles?"

The guy opened his mouth to say something, then stopped, as though calculating the minimum amount of help he could get away with giving. Allen shot Mazzucco a glance and he obliged.

"Maybe you didn't catch it before, but this is a homicide investigation. We're sure you wouldn't want to impede us in any way. I mean, I can tell you're an upstanding member of the community."

The mechanic looked from Mazzucco to the uniformed officer, his eyes those of a cornered animal. He sighed and nodded reluctantly. "His name is Luis Herrera. You didn't get it from me. He told me some white guy parked it in Watts, got out, and left the keys in and the engine running." He glanced around his interrogators, as though expecting them to laugh at the idea of somebody walking away from an unlocked Porsche in a rough neighborhood, practically inviting it to be stolen.

If Allen hadn't known the provenance of the car, she

would indeed have found the idea ridiculous, but it made a certain amount of sense. How much easier to outsource the disposal of the vehicle. If the Samaritan had done the same thing with the other cars, chances were excellent they had been stripped down for parts or resprayed and sold on. Either way, it would be much more difficult to find them, and even if they did, the best information they could hope to get was where the cars were abandoned.

"We'll need an address for this guy Herrera," Allen said. "I don't suppose he said what this vehicular philanthropist looked like?"

The mechanic drooped his head and looked up at her, playing dumb.

"The white guy who left the keys in the Porsche," she said slowly.

He shook his head. "Nah. Said he was a creepy sumbitch, though."

"Creepy how?"

The mechanic shrugged. "I don't know. Crazy-looking, I guess. I told him you'd have to be." He grinned and then looked at the covered-up Porsche, the grin fading as he remembered that finders wasn't going to mean keepers.

They called in a forensic unit to impound the Porsche. The two LBPD officers were only too happy to pick up Luis Herrera and bring him down to the PAB for Allen to interview. The hunt for the Samaritan was a big deal, and Allen wasn't surprised they wanted a piece of the action, however tenuous. She didn't think it would be difficult to lever some cooperation out of Herrera. It was more than likely he'd have a record long enough that a deal on a charge relating to the theft of the Porsche would look very attractive. She doubted they'd get anything of much use, but it might help to confirm some of the physical attributes suggested by Dr. Trent.

Five minutes later, Mazzucco and Allen were in the car, headed back downtown.

"Dead end," Mazzucco said.

"Huh?"

"If he left the Porsche on the street, you can bet it was sanitized first. We're not gonna find anything."

*Sanitized.* Allen caught that Mazzucco had used military terminology, perhaps unconsciously.

"So what about Blake?"

Mazzucco kept his eyes on the road. Didn't say anything for a minute. "I have to check something out. I think it'll take me a couple of hours. I'll drop you off."


# 41


They made a short detour to pick up lunch at a place Allen liked: In-N-Out Burger. She'd discovered the place not long after transferring, and was proud of her find. She ordered two cheeseburgers and asked for them "animal style"—lots of grilled onions and extra special sauce.

They ate in the car without much in the way of conversation, and then headed straight to the PAB. Mazzucco was cagey about exactly where he was going when he dropped Allen off on West First Street, but that suited her just fine. She promised to check in with him by phone soon and got out of the car, heading toward the entrance doors across the open, triangular plaza out front.

As she neared the main doors of the building, she saw a familiar figure sitting on one of the flat stone benches on the opposite side of the plaza from her. The figure raised one arm in acknowledgment and smiled behind his sunglasses. Allen looked away and at first intended to keep walking but had to stop when she heard her name called.

The tall male jogged across the space toward her, smiling. She kept her expression carefully neutral.

"Hey," he said as he caught up with her.

"What are you doing here?"

"You haven't been answering my calls," he said. As though that answered everything.

"You ever think there might be a reason for that, Denny?"

Denny tried on a confused expression that looked entirely fake. "Is this about the other night?"

Allen sighed. "No. It's about every night. I thought you got the message."

He looked genuinely confused now. "You sent me a message?"

*Jesus.* Had she *ever* been attracted to this guy? She was amazed he had the wherewithal to dress himself in the morning.

"Denny ..." Allen was actually grateful when she was interrupted by her cell phone buzzing. She excused herself and turned her back to him as she took the phone out. She half expected—or maybe just wanted—it to be Blake, but it was a land number with an LA area code. Which meant it had to be work because, unfortunately, everyone else she knew in LA was right here.

"Allen here."

It was Danniker, the female LBPD officer from the garage earlier.

"We picked up Luis Herrera. We're with him at the PAB if you can get down here."

"Great job. I'm right outside, actually. Where are you?"

Danniker told Allen which floor and which interview

room, and Allen thanked her again and hung up, turning back to Denny. He was waiting expectantly, displaying the soulful puppy-dog look that she'd mistaken for depth for too long.

"I gotta go."

"Can I call you?"

"No, you can't. Goodbye, Denny."

She turned and strode toward the doors and didn't look back.


Twenty minutes later, she was sitting down across an interview room table from Luis Herrera. Officer Danniker had remained in the room at Allen's invitation, but was standing back against one wall, leaving plenty of space for Allen to work.

Herrera was tall and solidly built, with tattoos all over his arms. So far, he hadn't been a lot of help, even though he'd rolled over every bit as easily as Allen had hoped when she dangled leniency on the grand theft auto charge in front of him.

"I swear, man, the dude just left it there. Keys in the fuckin' ignition. We didn't even do nothin' to him." Herrera's eyes were wide, his voice imploring, as though he worried they'd never believe that someone would just walk away from a hundred-thousand-dollar car.

Allen reminded him that, just because somebody leaves their car unlocked, it isn't necessarily an invitation to take it—although privately she knew that in this case it absolutely was—and then pressed him for a description of the driver.

Herrera had looked sheepish. "It was a ... white guy?"

"You don't sound sure," Allen suggested.

"I'd, uh ... I'd had a little to drink and ..." Herrera had screwed up his face. "Hat, maybe? A ball cap?"

"Color?" she prompted. "Was there a team logo on it? Lakers? Kings?"

Herrera wriggled for a few more seconds before asking them straight out: "What kind of guy do you want me to have seen?"

Bar the formalities, that was the end of that.

She left the interview room and walked down the corridor to an adjacent room, which was empty. The windows on this side looked out on the *LA Times* building across the street. She stepped inside, took her phone out, and scrolled through her directory until she found a number she'd added very recently. She paused for a second, her thumb over the little telephone icon, thinking the next action through. And then she pressed it.

The call took a couple of seconds to engage; there were three rings of the electronic dial tone, and then a male voice answered.

"Detective Allen."

"Why don't you come on in, Mr. Blake? I think we can find some things to talk about."

# 42

The new headquarters of the Los Angeles Police Department on West First Street was a shiny mission statement that the department had moved past its historical problems and into a bright, new twenty-first-century future. The angular ten-story building looked almost inviting, with its wide expanses of glass and the open plaza out front.

I checked in at the desk and was escorted through a metal

detector and into the building proper. The elevator took me to the fourth floor, and I was led across the expansive Robbery Homicide squad room. A few faces looked up at me with suspicion as I passed through their inner sanctum. My escort pointed out Detective Allen's position in the maze of desks and cubicles. She was at the far end of the room, standing with her arms folded. She had on a similar outfit to the one she'd worn yesterday: a gray suit with a lavender blouse; but today she'd swept her shoulder-length blond hair back into a ponytail. From our brief meeting earlier, and the other information I'd gleaned on her, I didn't think she was the type of person to waste a lot of time fixing her hair in the course of the day.

We shook hands. She smiled, but without warmth.

"Mr. Blake, thanks for coming in." She glanced at the clock on the wall. "You made it here fast."

"I was close by," I said.

She told me to follow her, and we walked through a set of doors and down a corridor with doors down one side. We stopped at one of the doors, and she put her hand on the door knob to open it, stopping at the sound of a loud voice from down the corridor.

"Allen."

We both turned to see a tall, solidly built guy in his mid-forties approach. I heard Allen sigh, loud enough that I could tell she didn't care if he heard it. He wore a gray suit and tie, but just from the way he moved, I got the feeling he'd be more at home in fatigues of some kind. I guessed SWAT.

"Who's this guy?" His tone was confrontational, and he was looking at me even though the question was addressed to Allen.

"This is Carter Blake. He's helping us on the Samaritan.

Blake, this is Captain Don McCall of our Special Investigation Section."

I held out my hand, which was ignored. I hadn't been far off when I guessed McCall was SWAT. I knew a little about the LAPD's SIS team, mostly from reading news stories about accusations of excessive force. SIS was the department's tactical surveillance unit, and they had a reputation for justifying their controversial methods by getting results on tough cases. Sometimes fatal results, for the suspect.

"So who is he? You're not FBI."

"I'm not FBI."

"He's freelance. You got a problem with that, McCall?"

McCall stared at me for a few seconds, but I didn't react. He turned back to Allen, dismissing me. "I wanted to catch you, Allen. When you get a suspect on this thing, you come to me first, before the feds, okay? We can keep our own house in order." He glanced at me again as he said that.

"You'll be the first to know, McCall." Allen's voice was heavy with sarcasm. She really wasn't attempting to hide her feelings.

McCall moved his head sharply toward her, aggressively invading her personal space. I had to fight an urge to put a hand on his chest and push him back, but Allen didn't flinch.

McCall smiled and shook his head. "Whatever you say, Fixer."

He glanced at me again and shook his head before moving on down the corridor.

"Sorry about that," Allen said when he'd gone. "He gets grumpy when he hasn't shot anyone in a while."

Allen opened the door and showed me into a small meeting room with floor-to-ceiling windows that looked out on Spring Street. There was a boardroom table that was slightly too big for the space. There was an iPad and an open laptop on the table—no paper. She walked around the table and sat down with her back to the window. I took the seat opposite.

"I take it your partner doesn't approve of this idea, either?"

"He's looking into something else right now. But I don't know if either of us is entirely comfortable with this."

"I just want to help. I take it you looked into my references?"

She nodded. "I talked to your FBI contact. Detective Mazzucco had a look at the North Carolina connection."

"And?"

"And we're looking into it."

I got the point. I had my foot in the door, but genuine cooperation was going to take a lot more work.

Allen continued. "We also had a look elsewhere. Due diligence and all that. Not that you gave us much to go on. Your cell number is unregistered, no contract. I kind of expected that. There's not a lot else to go on, though, which is funny. You don't seem to leave much of a footprint."

I shrugged as though there were nothing to it. "I value my privacy."

"So it would seem," she said. "The driver's license is genuine, but there's nothing else behind it. No employment or medical history. The address is in New York City; looks like an office building."

She paused, giving me an opportunity to confirm or deny. I said nothing and waited for her to continue, to get this dance out of the way.

"I guess you only have a license because you absolutely have to, these days," she said after a minute. "Not just to drive, but for photographic ID. Difficult to fly or rent a car without that. That's how I knew I could expect to find your name on passenger manifests on inbound flights to LA."

I couldn't help but smile, impressed. Also because this helped to resolve a potential problem for us both.

"It took a little time, but I eventually got a Carter Blake flying into LAX on Sunday night from Fort Lauderdale. I was pleased to find that piece of information."

"I'm glad you did," I said. A look passed between us, and I knew we didn't have to spell it out. The flight records meant that she now had a fair degree of certainty that I had been three thousand miles from LA on the night the Samaritan had last struck. It meant we were getting off to a good start.

Allen moved the laptop to one side and put her hands on the table. "Okay. Before we go any further, I just want to know one thing."

"That sounds fair," I said.

"Why are you offering your services for free?"

I had anticipated the question, of course. The simple answer—because I wanted to catch him—wouldn't satisfy a cop with an inquiring mind, which was to say any cop worth his or her salt. The complex answer, the answer that explained not just why I wanted to catch him, but how I was in a unique position to do so, was out of the question. With that in mind, I had a couple of different rationales for my apparent generosity. Depending on how suspicious Detective Allen was, the first one might be enough. It wasn't even a distortion of the truth, not really. If Allen wanted to, she'd be able to check it out easily enough.

"Bottom line, I'm interested in the case," I said. "Interested enough to come over here and find out more. And yes, I'll be honest with you. I did think about offering my services on a professional basis."

"What changed?" she prompted, watching me carefully.

I hesitated, as though I didn't want to go further. "I drove out to the graves yesterday, just to take a look around. I ran into somebody there. Richard Boden, father of one of the victims. You know that, of course."

Allen didn't say anything. Her face gave nothing away.

I continued. "He was hostile at first, thought maybe I was a reporter, or maybe just a rubbernecker. We talked a while and I explained why I was there. He offered to hire me. I turned him down. I told him this one was pro bono."

Allen smiled, and immediately I knew I'd need to exploit the other angle. "So you're offering to provide your services for nothing, because you wanted to help. Heartwarming."

"You don't believe me?"

"I don't believe anybody would fly across the country to pitch for business and then do the job for free. Not without a better reason than that."

I sighed and lifted my hands up: *You got me.* "Okay, it's not just that."

"Now we're getting somewhere."

"I do want to catch this guy, and I did talk to Boden. But I'm not being purely altruistic here, either. If I help you catch the Samaritan, it's ... You could say it's good for my résumé."

She nodded, although I could still see skepticism. "Like a hotshot lawyer taking on a high-profile case for free, huh? So you can charge the next paying customer a lot more?"

She paused and looked at me across the desk. I looked back at her, saying nothing.

"Okay," she said eventually. "Let's see if you can help."

I got up, put my hand on the back of my chair, and dragged it around to her side of the desk.

"First off," I said, "we should let the FBI do the work on the historic cases. Forget about them for now. We need to focus on now, on Los Angeles."

She looked a little relieved, like I'd taken a weight off her shoulders. "So where do you want to start?"

"Only one place to start," I said. "With the victims."

# 43

"The first one to be buried—the first that we know of—was named Rachel Morrow."

Allen called up the relevant file on the iPad and enlarged the picture—a standard head shot—with a swipe of her fingers. They'd almost certainly gotten the picture from the DMV. It looked like most of those kinds of pictures—a true enough representation of an individual's general appearance, their race, gender, age, hair color, and all the rest of it, but somehow failing to capture the essence of the person. I'd read something a long time ago about why that was. Something about the combination of the harsh lighting and the low-level pressure of knowing that this picture was going to be on an official document for the next five or ten years.

"The accountant," I said.

"Ten out of ten. How'd you know that?"

"The news."

She snorted at that.

"That was an unusual move, by the way," I said. "Releasing the information about the wound patterns to the media."

"It wasn't my move. When I find out whose move it was, I'm going to make sure it's very difficult for them to move without the aid of crutches for a few weeks."

"Got my attention, anyway."

I touched the screen to minimize the picture, looking for

the personal background information. It took me about five times as long as it would have done to turn a page in a file.

"I hate these things," I said. "You don't use hard copy murder books anymore?"

Allen smiled and shook her head. "You mean those blue binders that took up half the office? Some of the older guys are still attached to them. You know, the ones who are out of touch with the modern age."

I shrugged off the dig and handed the tablet to her. "New doesn't always mean better. I like to lay everything out in front of me."

"You're older than your years, Blake."

Allen called up the rest of the information I was looking for with a couple of deft swipes and gave it back to me so I could scan the rest of the file. The background information on the victim, details of her last-known whereabouts, her car, the last people to see her alive. I read the autopsy report. I examined a few of the pictures, focusing on that strange ragged wound pattern. If I'd needed any more confirmation after the news reports, after the cemetery, then here it was. I'd seen those wounds before. I'd seen the weapon that made them. I flipped back to the missing persons report and looked at the date.

"She wasn't even reported missing for a week," I said.

"That's right. Husband was out of town, no kids. Last to see her were the people from work."

"Alibi?"

"Finland."

I nodded, closed the Morrow file, and tapped on the file folder beside it. The name on the folder was Carrie Elaine Burnett. The reality TV star. I scanned through this one. It covered similar ground. Background, last-seen, autopsy. I knew that the three files would all follow the same grim

224

narrative. And the trail for all three victims stopped at the same place: they were all last seen getting into a car at night, and from then it was as though they'd vanished off the face of the earth. Until their bodies were discovered.

But there was one new wrinkle in the pattern with Burnett, because the last contact anyone had with her was not in person; it was by phone, to a dispatcher with the Automobile Club of Southern California, the local Triple A affiliate. I asked Allen about the call.

"That's right. Ten seventeen on the night of the tenth. Her car broke down in Laurel Canyon; she wasn't sure why. She agreed to stay put and wait for the tow truck. It took the driver thirty-six minutes to make it out there. When he arrived, there was no sign of Burnett, or her car. That's how we know the approximate time of the abduction—sometime between ten seventeen and ten fifty-three."

"And that's what gives you an indication of the killer's MO. He finds people at the scene of a breakdown, offers to help, and they're never seen again."

"Like a Good Samaritan, only not so good," Allen said.

"Did you talk to the tow truck driver?"

She rolled her eyes. "Believe it or not, you're not the first person to think of this. As soon as we worked out the MO, that was at the top of our list. How else is he targeting this kind of specific situation?"

"Sorry. I didn't doubt you had."

"Okay. So yeah, we talked to the driver, of course. Iron-clad alibi."

"Iron-clad?"

"Better: digital-clad. Onboard camera backs up his account. He was working all night."

I nodded and sat back from the table, thinking. In standard abduction cases, cops generally look for someone whom the victim would have reason to trust: an acquaintance, or some-body in authority. That wasn't necessarily the case in this scenario: if your car breaks down, you tend to accept any offer of help available. Crozier could be anyone.

"How about the last one, Boden?" I asked. "Same story?"

"We don't know for sure. But there's enough similarities to say it's probable. Both Morrow and Boden were definitely taken while en route somewhere by car. Both were driving alone and at night, both were in roughly the same vicinity. There's one other thing with Boden. We have her on a gas station security camera right before she was abducted. And we think there's someone else on the tape, too."

"You think?"

"You don't see him, only his shadow. We think he tried to get into Boden's car, but it was locked."

I thought about that for a minute. "Do we know if Boden and Morrow broke down, too?"

"No calls to Triple A. But in both cases, the car disappeared along with the victim. So far the only one we've been able to find is the Porsche Boden was driving, and that was a lucky break. The Samaritan should have picked somebody driving a less desirable car."

"Were they members?"

Allen smiled. "You're asking the right questions. No. Neither was a Triple A member."

"Could they have called another breakdown service, or a garage? Any calls to anyone at all?"

"Morrow's husband said she had a prepay cell, like you. No contract, so we don't know who she might have called, if anyone. Boden's phone had been switched off since earlier in the evening. Could be she switched it off herself; more likely, the battery died. You know what cell phones are like these days." She tapped her own phone. "This thing holds a charge about as well as a one-legged rhino."

I smiled at that and tapped into the Morrow file again, scrolling through the personal details. I was looking for something, but I wasn't sure what yet. Then I had it. "Where's the car?"

"I told you. We never found it."

"No, I mean there's nothing about her car in here. What kind of car did she drive?"

Allen looked puzzled, unsure why this would be important. "It was a blue Honda Civic: not exactly memorable. Why?"

"Maybe nothing," I said. "I'm basing this on the assumption that the killer abducted her the same way as he did Burnett and Boden."

"Offering assistance at a breakdown?"

"Yeah. And also the assumption that there was enough of a gap between the breakdown and the abduction for her to call somebody."

"Okay, but since we don't have ..."

"She didn't call Triple A, and she didn't call any of her friends. So unless her cell was also out of charge, she must have called somebody."

I waited for a second and Allen caught up. "Like her regular garage. If it was open."

I nodded. "Exactly. Like I said, it might be nothing, but it's worth a look. Given the resources at your disposal, do you think ... ?"

" ... that we can track down her garage using the vehicle?" Allen asked. "Sure, but it'd be quicker just to take a look at her credit card statements for the last year. If she's taken her car in for a service or a vehicle inspection recently, we can get the address."

"Worth a look."

Allen got up. "I'll be right back." She turned back halfway to the door and opened her mouth to issue some kind of warning.

"It's okay," I said. "I won't go anywhere. I'll take a look at the rest of this while you're away."

Allen departed and the door closed with a *click*. I looked back down at the iPad and cycled through the victim photographs again. Morrow, Burnett, Boden. The three of them had enough physical attributes in common to show this series of killings conformed to a strict type. And that made it unusual in the context of the other killings nationwide. The FBI briefing Allen had been sent by the liaison was saved in a separate folder. I opened it up and found it was short and to the point: a relatively high-level summary, listing open and unsolved homicides and missing persons investigations in multiple states that might be tied to the Samaritan. In all, they'd listed sixty-three cases across eleven states: a one-man epidemic, and one that had gone unnoticed until now. The two North Carolina cases I'd found were included, too, but out of chronological sequence at the end of the document, which suggested they were recent additions. The dates would make them the earliest link in the chain. I had good reason to believe Sergeant Willis Peterson was patient zero in this particular epidemic.

Just going by the summary details, it was clear Crozier had been very careful. Many of the murders were not officially murders at all, but missing persons cases where foul play was strongly suspected. Even if the FBI was correct in tying only half of these cases to the Samaritan, it meant bodies were rotting undiscovered in shallow graves from sea to shining sea. In the cases where the bodies had been found, it tended to be because the killer had made no attempt to conceal them—leaving them in their homes or places of business, or in secluded outdoor areas. The precise cause of death varied, and I wondered if this was as much to do with the urge to experiment as the practicality of avoiding detection. Perhaps the variety in the victim profile was the same—killing two birds with one stone.

But Los Angeles was different, so far. Three young women, all Caucasian, all brunettes. Abducted in the same way, tortured and killed in the same way. I didn't doubt that Crozier was behind these killings, but I wondered if the new consistency meant anything.

I sat back in the chair and wondered how long it would take Allen to confirm whether the lead with Morrow's garage was going to pan out. I thought about what she'd said about the tow truck guy they'd ruled out. After running over it again in my head, I decided she was wrong about one thing. She'd said investigating the tow truck driver had been a no-brainer, because "how else" could he be targeting these women?

I thought back to what she'd said about the gas station and the shadow that looked like somebody trying to get in the car. I knew there was another way.

# 44

*Damn it, Allen.*

Not for the first time, Mazzucco felt like putting in a request to Lawrence for a new partner. He couldn't shake the frustration as he drove to the West LA station on Butler Avenue. As it happened, his old station before he made detective. He'd spent the past couple of hours confirming a suspicion, but he'd been thinking a lot about his partner, too.

*Allen.* He knew what she was going to do. Knew she was going to go ahead and bring Blake into the fold despite his warnings. As soon as they'd confirmed that the guy really did have information they could use, that was all she cared about. And sure, Blake presented an intriguing opportunity that had appeared out of nowhere, but that was exactly why they needed to approach the man with caution—a word Mazzucco was beginning to suspect was not in Jessica Allen's vocabulary. He'd known from the look in her eyes the whole time they were talking in the car that she was going to call Blake. He almost didn't think she could help it: cutting any corners she had to in order to make progress faster. She'd been like this the whole time he'd known her, and by all accounts, for a long time before that. The two of them had never explicitly addressed the rumors, and up until now Mazzucco had liked that just fine. As far as he—if not all of his fellow detectives—was concerned, Allen was a blank page from her first day in the division. Why, then, was she so hell-bent on spilling black ink all over that blank page?

Mazzucco was almost certain that she'd use the time he was over in West to talk to Blake and then present it to him as a fait accompli. So why had he made the trip, then? Federmeyer was a loose end. A loose end that needed tying, but one that could wait. Had he wanted this? Wanted Allen to make the call, but do it alone, so that he could duck the responsibility? He put it out of his mind as he approached the two-story building that was his destination. Such questions were impossible to answer, and dwelling on them was unproductive.

He buzzed at the gate, then drove in and parked. As

luck would have it, the man he wanted to speak to was on the front desk. Federmeyer looked up as Mazzucco walked through the glass entrance doors to the precinct. His eyes registered a split second of surprise, but he covered it nicely with a friendly grin.

"Mazzucco," he yelled out. "What brings a big shot like you back down here? Didn't figure we'd see you again once you made detective. Caught the boogeyman yet?"

Mazzucco shrugged noncommittally. "I can always find a reason to drop by the old place." He did have a reason; two of them, in fact. He decided to go for the noncontentious one first, otherwise he might not get an answer to either question.

"I wanted to check a couple of things with you. About the dump site."

"Shoot," the other man said immediately. "Although, you'll know better than me. Us guys get the glamour job—perimeter security. You know that."

Mazzucco wondered if that was a tell, or simply an innocent comment. Either way, he didn't comment.

"How you getting on with catching the Bad Samaritan, anyway?" Federmeyer asked. "I see the feds stuck their noses in."

"It's not so bad," Mazzucco said. "They get the headache of a few dozen cold cases across the country; we get to focus on the recent ones. All in all, I'd say I'm grateful for the help."

Federmeyer looked a little abashed, as though he couldn't understand why Mazzucco would shy away from a little Bureau-bashing. "Anyway," he said, the smile still in place, but the tone a little colder. "What can I do you for, Detective?"

"Like I said, a couple of things I wanted to check. The kind of things a guy on the scene would probably notice.

Like, did you see any suspicious vehicles around the area? I know we had the media and the paps and the looky-loos, but anything out of the ordinary? The same vehicle more than once, maybe."

Federmeyer shrugged and shook his head. "Not that I saw. Not that any of my guys saw; otherwise I'd know about it. One of the vics' dads showed up a couple of times, but he talked to us direct."

"Richard Boden?"

"That's right, Boden. Turns out he used to be on the job. San Diego police. Decent guy, you know what I mean? Wish we could've helped him."

"You happen to notice a dark blue Chevy Malibu at any point? Or anybody else speaking to Boden?"

Federmeyer took his time, his expression telegraphing how deeply he was thinking. He was making a lot of effort to appear open and helpful. Too much effort. "Can't help you. A couple of the paps got in close for pictures the first time he visited, but he chewed them out good. They kept their distance after that."

"Okay," Mazzucco said. "Let's back up a second. You said Boden spoke to you, and you wanted to help him."

Federmeyer's eyes betrayed his suspicion immediately. "That's right. That's what I told you."

"Anybody else approach you? Anybody else you wanted to help?"

A pause. "What's this about, Detective?"

Mazzucco looked left, then right. A few cops milling around, going to the coffee machine. A couple of grim-faced civilians sitting in plastic chairs near the door. No one within earshot. He leaned forward, putting both hands on the desk.

"I know it was you, Federmeyer. Ragged wound patterns.

You knew we were withholding that, and you sold it to Jennifer Quan at K-ABC."

"That bitch," Federmeyer hissed under his breath. "What happened to protecting your sources?"

"What happened to serious professional misconduct, Federmeyer? That information could compromise this whole investigation."

Federmeyer's tone turned on a dime. "Come on, Mazzucco. We go way back. This ain't no big deal."

"Way back," he repeated. "You never liked me. And I happen to think leaking restricted information to the press, information that could compromise a homicide investigation, is a very big deal."

"Come on, Mazzucco."

"*Detective* Mazzucco. Yeah, it is a big deal when you decide to fuck with my case." He paused, looked at the other man to let him know he was serious. "I'm reporting it to Bannerman."

He turned to leave and Federmeyer yelled after him, "Why don't you get your partner to frame somebody for it, if you're having trouble nailing a suspect?"

Mazzucco froze in his tracks. He turned and walked slowly back toward Federmeyer. Federmeyer pulled himself up to his full height, sticking his chin out. Mazzucco eyeballed him for a good twenty seconds. Long enough for the background chatter to drop away completely as everyone turned their attention to the confrontation at the front desk.

"Just so you know, Lieutenant," Mazzucco said, "Quan didn't give you up. You did that yourself, you stupid bastard. She came out with all the details about the wounds and the nickname from the same source. I knew she got the idea about calling him *the Samaritan* from you, but I needed you to confirm the rest of it. I guess you'd call it *detective* work, huh?"

Mazzucco didn't wait for a response. He turned and walked out, banging the door open on his way. As he approached his car, his phone buzzed with a text message. It was from Allen.

*Meet us at Washington and Crenshaw 30 mins*

Meet *us*. Great.

Damn it, Allen.

# 45

I didn't have to wait long for Allen to come up with an address. Rachel Morrow had used the same garage for her Honda Civic on three occasions in the past fourteen months. They offered a tow service; it was within range of Morrow's likely route home on the night she disappeared, and they were open until midnight on weeknights. All three boxes checked.

We thought about calling ahead and decided against it. Allen said she liked to drop in on people unannounced. It caught people off guard, an advantage any way you looked at it: whether someone was guilty or innocent, it was best not to give them too much time to think, to develop elaborate answers to your questions. I agreed with the approach.

It took forty minutes to make the trip, with me following Allen's Ford all the way. The infuriating stop-start rhythm of the traffic burned time, but made it very easy not to lose her. I thought more about Allen as I watched the back of her head and her eyes occasionally glancing back at me in her mirror. Before we'd left, she had asked a couple more questions about me and my background, which I deflected without too much trouble. I was pleasantly surprised by her lack of curiosity. I decided that once she'd confirmed my credentials, she wasn't too interested in anything else for the moment. From our brief meeting the previous day on the roof of the parking lot, I wasn't so sure her partner would be as flexible.

Detective Mazzucco was waiting for us when we reached the garage, his gray Ford parked curbside with the window rolled down. He spotted us immediately, and I saw him nod to himself in grim confirmation as he saw my car. He got out as Allen parked nose to tail with him. I parked behind Allen's car and decided not to offer my hand as we approached Mazzucco. He stood with his arms folded, glancing at me and then shooting Allen a look that I knew meant, *We'll talk later*.

"How did your errand go?" Allen asked, making no reference to the fact I was there.

"Pretty much as expected. I'll tell you about it later. You want to tell me why we're here?"

Allen glanced at the front of the garage a little way down the street. A red, white, and blue sign emblazoned with PATRIOT AUTO REPAIRS. "Rachel Morrow used this garage. We think she might have called them on the night she disappeared."

The garage sprawled over a wide area. There were several bays, most of them with the doors rolled down at this time in the evening. There were signs everywhere advertising servicing and bodywork and the fact that they offered a tow service. There was a small office appended to the far end of the line of auto-repair berths. They approached it, and Mazzucco pushed the glass door inward, holding it open for me and Allen. The desk was unmanned as I entered. An electronic chime had activated as the door was pushed open, and a minute later a large bald guy with glasses and wearing blue bib-and-brace overalls appeared from the doorway behind the desk. He made us immediately: three people wearing suits and purposeful expressions.

"What can I do for you, officers?" he asked. He was wary, but making an effort to sound relaxed.

Mazzucco produced his badge and introduced himself and Allen. He didn't refer to me at all, and the guy didn't ask.

"Are you the manager?" he asked, once the man had waved their ID away.

"That's right. Anthony Letta."

"Mr. Letta, were you working here on the night of April tenth? It was a Friday."

He thought for a second and nodded. "My day off is Friday. Well, that's when it's supposed to be. I can't tell you how often—"

Mazzucco cut him off. "We're interested in any records for that night. Say between ten and midnight. Specifically, did anybody call for a tow? Maybe they broke down and were stranded."

Letta shrugged. "It's a few days back. I'd need to check the computer."

Allen smiled. "If you wouldn't mind."

Letta tapped his mouse to cancel the screensaver, scratched his chin while he thought for a moment, and then started hitting the keys. He went slowly—hunting and pecking for letters, his brow occasionally creasing as his chubby fingers hit the wrong key and he had to go looking for backspace. I watched Allen and Mazzucco as he worked. Allen kept glancing at her partner, trying to catch his eye, but he kept his own gaze studiously on Letta's trials with the computer.

236

I thought about making some sort of comment to break the uneasy silence but quickly decided against it.

What seemed like a couple of hours later, Letta had a result. "Okay. April tenth?"

Allen nodded. "Between ten and midnight." She wasn't giving too much detail because she didn't have to. She didn't want to lead him to any conclusions or speculations. Just the facts.

"Lemme see . . . Yeah, we had a tow on the tenth. That was what you were interested in, right? Oh, wait a second . . ." He paused and squinted at the screen over his glasses. "No, we didn't. We got a call for a tow around ten forty-five. My guy went out and there was no sign of the customer."

"What was the street?" Allen asked, her voice sounding neutral.

He squinted at the screen again. "Mulholland Drive."

Allen and Mazzucco exchanged a glance, and then she looked back at me, excitement in her eyes.

Letta didn't notice. As far as he was concerned, he'd drawn a blank for us. "It happens. Customer calls up for a tow; then they realize they've just run out of gas, or the car starts up again and they skedaddle, don't even bother calling us." He shook his head.

Allen put a hand on top of the computer screen. "Mr. Letta, did the call come in from one of your regular customers?"

He looked confused. "I'd have to check the—"

"What was the name of the customer?"

He glanced at the screen. "Morrow."

Allen nodded. "Thank you. Now, would you be able to point us in the direction of the employee who drove the truck?"

The three of us braced ourselves for Letta to declare that he needed to engage with the computer once again, but he smiled and shook his head. "That's easy. The bum called in sick today, though, so you'll have to visit him at home."

# 46

I know from experience that some managers and business owners are resistant to giving out the home addresses of employees, even to legitimate law enforcement officers. Letta gave us no such problems. On the contrary, he was happy to turn over everything he had on the driver of the tow truck on the night Morrow had vanished. Tomasz Gryski was an employee he was planning to get rid of anyway. He was constantly late, took too long on callouts, and had an attitude in the bargain. Letta had no idea why we were interested in Gryski and couldn't care less. As far as he was concerned, it was a bonus if it was something that would hasten his departure from the company.

"Gryski," Allen repeated, checking the spelling twice as she noted the details. "Sounds Polish."

"I guess," Letta said, as though it had just occurred to him. "He doesn't have an accent or anything."

"What does he look like?" I asked. Mazzucco shot me a hard look but didn't say anything.

"Tall, about your height, I guess. Dark hair, tanned. In decent shape."

"Has he been working for you long?" Allen asked.

He hadn't been. About a month, and no, Letta hadn't bothered following up on the references. There were a couple of dozen drivers working at any given time, and beyond a small core of longtime employees, the lineup fluctuated constantly. Gryski's work ethic and general attitude meant he would probably be leaving sooner rather than later. Letta provided us with a printout of Gryski's scanned application form, which showed his current address in Arlington Heights, date of birth, previous employment, and social security number. His most recent employer had apparently been a gas station not far from Patriot Auto Repairs.

Mazzucco had one last question—did Patriot receive referrals for jobs from AAA? If so, it meant the same person might have access to the details of both the Morrow and Burnett breakdowns and might even have been able to beat the AAA man to the scene on the Burnett callout. Letta looked puzzled again. "That's right. Sometimes they throw business our way."

We thanked him and headed straight for the address in Arlington Heights. Before we left, Mazzucco called in the social security number—it drew a blank, meaning it was fake. It didn't necessarily mean that Tommy Gryski was the Samaritan, of course, but it meant he had something to hide.

We headed west in a three-car convoy: Mazzucco, then Allen, then me, taking the 10. The sun was setting into the Pacific ahead of us, the rays bouncing off smog particles to create Los Angeles's own version of the aurora borealis.

I had the printed scan of the job application on the passenger seat and took advantage of the pauses in motion to scan it. There was no photo, of course, but the date of birth meant Gryski was an age that Crozier could certainly pass for. Same with Letta's description. Didn't mean it was him; didn't mean it wasn't. I took my phone out and Googled the zip code of the address in Arlington Heights. It was an apartment complex, lots of rooms for rent, probably a high-turnover place. I wondered if we'd find anything at the address. If the social security number was an invention, there was a good chance the address was, too. I switched to maps and brought up a satellite image of the location. I zoomed in and swiped the image around on the screen to get a feel for the territory.

The apartment building was located on West Adams Boulevard. The sun was all the way down as we arrived, the streetlights bathing everything in a yellow sodium wash. The building looked played-out, with a patch of dead grass out front and railings covered with damp clothes left out to dry. Mazzucco had beaten us to the address, getting lucky with the lights on the way. He was waiting for us in the car again. Allen and I parked nose to tail and got out. From close by, I heard an outburst of barking in response to the noise of our car doors.

"Blake," Mazzucco said, reluctantly looking at me for the first time since outside Patriot Auto Repairs. "We'd like you to wait here. We've bent regs enough, allowing you to come in when we were speaking to the manager, but it's not appropriate for you to be knocking on a suspect's door with us. I'm sure you understand."

Allen didn't say anything, just gave me an apologetic glance. She understood that now would not be the time to be crossing any more lines with her partner. I understood, too. It was exactly what I'd expected Mazzucco to do.

"Not a problem," I said. "I'll wait in the car."

"I'm not expecting trouble," Allen said. "If this guy actually does have something to do with the abductions—which is a long shot—there's no way he gave his real address. We're probably about to wake up some old lady."

I nodded, thinking her logic on that was sound. "But at least it means we have a place to start looking for him. And if he doesn't have anything to do with this, he might have seen something we can use on the night he went out to Morrow's car."

Allen's eyes stayed on me a fraction of a second longer

than Mazzucco's as they turned to walk into the building. I got back in the car and watched as the two detectives entered the foyer and hit the button for the elevator. Gryski's apartment—if it was really his apartment—was on the third floor. I waited until the doors of the elevator closed; then I got out and walked down the narrow passageway at the side of the apartment building that led around to the back.

# 47

Allen patted the left side of her jacket as the elevator doors bumped shut, just to reassure herself that her Beretta was still strapped there, ready if she needed it. The apartment building was old, and it had an old, slow elevator to match. She glanced at Mazzucco, who was watching the floors gradually light up on the display.

"I'm sorry, okay?"

"No, you're not."

"He can help us. He's the real deal—look at the North Carolina thing. The feds hadn't even found that one yet."

"I told you, that's what worries me."

"And this is a good lead. We wouldn't be here without—"

"It might not be anything. Even if this Gryski guy knew about Morrow's breakdown, there's no way to tie him to the Boden abduction, for a start, because she had no way of making a call. There are a hundred reasons why people lie to their employers. And, anyway, we'd have found him ourselves soon enough."

Allen said nothing, let him vent without chipping in her two cents for a change.

It seemed to work. After a moment, Mazzucco sighed. "I found the leak. Ed Federmeyer over in West division."

"The guy who knew you from before?"

Mazzucco nodded. "The same. And it's my fault, really. I should have known not to say anything important within his earshot."

Allen was happy. Mazzucco's change of subject meant he was probably ready to draw a line under the issue of her freezing him out of the decision to bring in Blake, for now. She knew him well enough to know he didn't let things go that easily if he was genuinely pissed.

"That fucking asshole," she said quickly. "Did you talk to him?"

"Yeah, told him I'm reporting him to his watch commander."

Allen raised an eyebrow.

"You got a problem with that, Allen?"

"No problem."

Mazzucco sighed. "He'll probably get off with some bull-shit conditional reprimand, anyway."

The elevator pinged and the doors began to open.

"Address is 3E, right?" she asked as they stepped out.

Mazzucco didn't answer. He just slammed her back into the elevator as a figure at the far end of the corridor opened fire on them, the gunshots deafening as they exploded in the cinder-block hallway.

# 48

I saw the muzzle flare on the third-floor balcony before I heard the shots. I didn't think Allen and Mazzucco would have had time to make it to the apartment door itself, so it looked like this was a preemptive attack. That removed all doubt that Gryski had something serious to hide.

I counted five shots. I was already halfway to the foot of the fire escape I'd seen on the satellite images, and I covered the rest of the ground quickly, staying low. The building's street level was mostly parking space, open ground interspersed with concrete support pillars. In the space on either side, between the building and its neighbors, stands of banana plants blocked out the streetlight with their wide, rubbery leaves. I moved to the blind side of the pillar nearest the bottom step of the fire escape and waited, cursing the fact I hadn't been able to bring a weapon. I heard footsteps above on concrete and rapid breathing. Then I heard Allen's voice from above yelling out a warning. The footsteps paused for a second, and I heard another, closer gunshot, followed by two answering shots from higher up. I saw concrete and dust kick up as one of the slugs embedded itself in the paving at the foot of the fire escape, and then a tall figure hurled himself down the last three steps.

I was ready, coordinated my lunge so that I caught him straight across the middle, bringing him down to the ground. He fell down face first, me on his back, and brought the gun around. I was ready and caught it at the wrist. I added my other hand to the struggle and began trying to wrest the gun out of his hand. I tried to look at his face, but it was too dark to see.

I started to pull the gun away and then I was knocked off of him by something big and dark. It was a dog. A big dog: a pit bull, I guessed. I rolled out of the path of its jaws as it tried to gore me, and saw Gryski take off in the corner of my peripheral vision. Seeing the fleeing prey and deciding it was more enticing, the dog went after Gryski, or whoever he was.

"Are you okay?" Allen, suddenly at my side, her gun drawn. I turned and saw Mazzucco following down the stairs.

I nodded. "Are you?"

"Yeah, but only just."

The three of us took off after Gryski. He'd run back down the side passageway toward the street. The dog clamped its jaws around the fabric of his pant leg, but he aimed down and put a bullet in its skull at point-blank range, almost without breaking stride. Allen yelled at him that she was going to fire as we followed, but I knew it was a hollow threat. She couldn't fire blind toward a busy street. I don't know if he knew that, too, but either way he paid no heed to the warnings. We passed the dog, lying dead on the ground as Gryski made it to the street. I remembered its jaws snapping for my face and found it hard to locate my reserves of sympathy.

Gryski plunged headlong across the road, causing a dark-colored SUV to swerve into the opposite lane to avoid hitting him. He made the opposite sidewalk as the horn blasted out and ducked into another alley across the street. A screech of brakes followed by a crumple of steel followed as the SUV slewed into a stationary bus in the other lane.

"Shit!" Mazzucco yelled as we crossed the street. "Go," he yelled at Allen. He made for the driver's side of the SUV, where I could see a woman's head lying against the glass at an unnatural angle.

Allen and I tore past the wreckage and into the alley. It opened out into a courtyard, more apartment buildings facing onto the space on all sides. There were two other entrances on the north and east of the courtyard. Gryski could have taken either. Not speaking, she pointed to indicate that I should take the east route, the one closest to me.

I ran through the arched tunnel beneath the building and came out on a main road. I looked left and right, saw only cars. No one on foot, which made the task easier. There was another row of buildings and the mouth of another alleyway across the street. I started moving across the road when I heard Allen's voice, muffled by distance and obstructions, behind me. She was yelling at somebody, telling them to drop something. I turned on my heel and ran back the way I'd come. As I emerged from the archway into the courtyard, I heard two gunshots in quick succession from the opposite tunnel and ran toward the sound.

"It's okay," Allen's voice called out. "Clear."

I passed through the tunnel and out into another alleyway. Gryski was sitting with his legs drawn up in the corner. His head was bowed, his left hand clutching a bloody wound on his left arm, and his weapon lying on the ground.

"He shot first," Allen said, as she took a couple of steps forward and kicked Gryski's gun farther away. She looked like she was in a little bit of shock, but I knew she'd snap out of it in a few moments.

I knelt down beside Gryski and he looked up at me, seething.

"*Pieprzyć twoją matkę!*"

I ignored the suggestion—my mother's not around anymore, anyway—and examined his features. Pockmarked skin, a hook nose, bushy eyebrows. Blue eyes. Definitely not Dean Crozier. Definitely not the Samaritan.

# 49

"What did he say?" Allen asked, watching as Blake examined the wounded suspect.

"Nothing important." Blake looked up at her. There was consternation in his expression, as though he hadn't found what he'd expected to. Allen was still optimistic. If Gryski was the Samaritan, they might find evidence in his apartment.

"I know you speak English," Blake said, addressing Gryski. "Why did you run?"

Gryski turned his face away from them both. "I want a lawyer."

Blake shook his head and stood up. "Are you okay?" he said, his eyes gliding over the length of Allen's body, looking for evidence of injury.

"I'm fine. I guess he decided it would be safer to try to shoot me than to try to outrun me." She pointed at Gryski's left leg. The fabric of his jeans was torn and there was quite a lot of blood. It looked like the dog had taken a good chunk out of him. When she'd emerged from the tunnel beneath the apartment building, he'd been waiting and had opened fire. The second time he'd tried to kill a cop in as many minutes, and thankfully, his aim hadn't improved any. She was glad she hadn't had to kill him, if only because it meant they would have the opportunity to interrogate him.

"His mistake," Blake said.

He got up and paced around the space, ignoring more insults in Polish and some in English as Allen called in the shooting. As she expected, they told her to stay put and that they'd have uniforms on the scene ASAP. She glanced back down the corridor, wondering what was keeping Mazzucco. Surely he'd have handed over the road accident to paramedics by now. It had been several minutes.

"I have to wait here," she said to Blake. "You should go, check out the apartment with Mazzucco. Maybe—"

Blake was shaking his head. He pulled her a few steps away from Gryski and lowered his voice "I don't think this is our guy, Allen."

"How do—" Allen stopped mid-sentence as she heard footsteps approaching from behind them. She turned to see Mazzucco, a grim look on his face, the phone in his right hand.

He took in the scene, glanced at Allen to check she was okay, then looked at Blake. "Please tell me you didn't."

"It was me," Allen said. "He shot first."

"Jesus," Mazzucco said, breathing a sigh of relief. "Well, at least that's one piece of good news."

"What do you mean?" Blake asked.

"I just took a call from Lawrence. They found an abandoned car downtown. Blood on the seats."

Allen took a second to register what her partner meant. "Burnett's car? Or Morrow's?"

"Neither. This happened tonight."

# 50

It didn't take long for some uniformed officers and an ambulance to show up and take Gryski off our hands. The paramedics treated Gryski's shoulder while the uniforms took statements from Allen and Mazzucco. The chain of events was easy to relay and for them to confirm. Allen and Mazzucco directed them to the secondary crime scene in the corridor outside Gryski's apartment. The officers checked Allen out and told her the Force Investigation Division would have to speak to her in the morning, which was routine for an officer-involved shooting, but that it would likely be a formality, given the circumstances. The ambulance took Gryski to the hospital, where the cops could read him his rights and start to figure out who he was and why he'd run.

We were all set to drive to the scene of the abandoned car when Allen took another call that made that journey redundant: the body of the vehicle's owner had been found dumped in an alley not far from where her bloodstained car was reported.

Forty minutes later, we were at the scene of the Samaritan's latest killing: an anonymous alleyway running between two buildings a couple of blocks from the Staples Center. All of the standard players had moved quickly, according to their designated roles. FBI forensics were on the scene, their work well underway. Uniformed LAPD officers had blocked off a perimeter at both ends of the alley. Traditional media and the paparazzi were jostling for attention. Their airborne corps hung overhead in at least two helicopters that I spotted. Such was the speed of twenty-first century media that I found out the victim's name—unconfirmed as yet—before Allen or Mazzucco, by browsing local news websites. The car had been found abandoned in Valencia Street, a secondary road running between West Pico and Venice Boulevards. A jogger had reported a parked car with the door partially open so the illumination from the dome light revealed bloodstains on the upholstery. The LAPD had locked that scene down quickly, too, but they hadn't been able to prevent the license plate being grabbed by long-lens cameras, illegally checked and matched to one Alejandra Castillo, a clerk from Silver Lake.

We were escorted by one of the uniforms past the barriers and into the alley. Thirty yards in, there was a cluster of activity around the body. There were no surprises based on the information I'd already heard. The victim was a young Hispanic woman. She wore a dark skirt and a white blouse— work-wear, as though she'd been on her way home from the office. She was in a sitting position, propped up against one wall of the alley, as though asleep or drunk. Not that some- one would make that mistake with even a cursory glance.

A waterfall of crimson had stained the front of her clothes below her head, which rested on her chest. It didn't look like there were any other marks on the body, though it was impossible to tell for sure. The blood had pooled on the ground, meaning this wasn't just the disposal site, but the primary murder scene. I counted the points of difference: three significant deviations from the previous LA killings already, just on a first look.

Allen and I hung back on the fringes of the small crowd and let Mazzucco move in close as the representative of the latest contingent to arrive. He glanced under the dead woman's chin and nodded. He turned his head to look at one of the FBI forensics. "Silly question, but preliminary COD?"

"Bets are closed on this one, Detective. Massive exsan- guination from the jugular artery. Looks like one cut, left to right. Perpetrator was probably behind the victim at the time, or he was a lefty. We'll confirm soon enough."

"Any signs of torture? Strangulation or anything?"

"Not so far, but you know the routine: wait for the autopsy."

Mazzucco thanked him and looked up at the two of us. I let Allen speak first. "I don't know about this," she said.

"What are you thinking?" I asked, though I had a pretty good idea.

"Victim is clothed, left at the scene instead of moved and buried, no signs of torture. Big break from the other three."

"That's true," I said. "But the consistency of the three victims in the hills is the exception. Think about the national picture, Allen."

Mazzucco straightened up, brushed alley dirt off the knees of his suit. "Ragged edges look the same," he repeated. "Take a look."

Allen bent down and did as suggested, examining the mortal wound up close. She glanced up at Mazzucco, then at me in affirmation. "I think this is our guy."

"I think so, too," I said.

"It's him, all right."

The three of us turned at the sound of the voice. A tall, sharp-suited agent was standing behind us.

"Channing," Allen said by way of a greeting.

The man nodded at Allen and Mazzucco and looked at me, waiting for an introduction. I got the feeling he'd be waiting a while as far as my two escorts were concerned, so I held out my hand.

"Carter Blake."

"Special Agent Channing," he said, shaking it. He looked at Allen as he said it. An economical gesture. It saved him from coming out and saying, *Who's this guy?*

"Mr. Blake is assisting us with the investigation," Allen said briskly. "As an independent consultant."

Channing seemed to consider it. His eyes flicked from Allen's to Mazzucco's to mine. Then he shrugged. "The more the merrier." He was acting like he was fine with me, but I knew he wasn't. He was just a lot more polished than somebody like that McCall guy I'd met earlier.

"How's your case, Channing?" Mazzucco emphasized the word "your" very slightly. I wondered if Agent Channing would catch it. He did.

"It's all the same case, Detective, remember?" He smiled. "We're pretty sure we've found another couple of Samaritan murders from eight months ago, a small town just outside of Minneapolis." Channing stopped, glanced around, as though to signal that he didn't want just anyone hearing this, and then leaned closer to Mazzucco. "And that's not all. There's a possible survivor we're talking to."

Allen stopped feigning disinterest. "A survivor?"

Channing nodded. "A prostitute. Got into a car with a john; felt threatened when he locked the doors; crawled out of a window when she saw a cop car. He let her go and the cops never got the license plate. The date of the incident was slap bang in the middle of the period the Samaritan must have been there."

"Can we speak to her?"

"Sure," Channing said. "I'll keep you posted."

I could tell Allen was about to protest that, but Channing's phone rang and he turned away from us to answer it.

"Think we'll ever get to speak to this survivor?" Mazzucco said under his breath.

Allen shook her head. "No way. But I guess we'll get the details secondhand. In the meantime, we have enough to keep us occupied," she said, looking back at the victim.

"Same murder weapon, but no torture, and no attempt to conceal the body," Mazzucco summarized. "Why the change in MO? It's been working for him so far."

"Have you ever heard of the observer effect?" I asked.

Mazzucco glanced at me, as though he'd forgotten I was there. "Sure," he said carefully. "By observing something, you change it."

"That's right. You found his dump site; you uncovered the other murders. He knows he's being watched now, and that's changing his behavior."

Allen took a couple of steps back from the body and rubbed her right temple. "Well, it hasn't changed it in any good way."

I turned my eyes from Allen and looked at the slight, motionless figure that had so recently been a living, breathing person—a person who had died to make a specific point.

Mazzucco spoke up. "I think he wants to send us a message. He's not afraid to keep going. He's not going to hide from us."

"Message received," Allen said.

"But this tells us other things, too," I said. "Maybe it tells us more about him than he wants it to."

# 51

At first, the Samaritan could barely believe the evidence of his own eyes.

It had been a minor risk, returning to the alley after the police had arrived, but only a minor one. It was something he'd done before. In a big city like this one, with all kinds of bystanders attracted to the aftermath of violence like moths to a flame, there was plenty of cover. There was nothing to distinguish him from the other people. He fit right in. Even if one of the cops had a moment of divine inspiration and decided to accost, or even search him, there was nothing to tie him to the woman in the alley. No blood had gotten on him when he'd cut the woman's throat. His hands were long practiced, and he knew how to avoid the torrent when necessary.

The only item he had on his person that might raise questions was the magnetic tracker in his pocket. It would be simple enough to palm and drop if he needed to, and anyway, the device was so small and unobtrusive that it could pass for a parking token.

He'd made sure to arrive after the police had set up a cordon, so he could mingle with the crowd on the civilian side and observe them at work from afar. He'd spent a satisfying few minutes watching the comings and goings of the cops and the feds, listening to the speculations of the media people and the civilians around him. He'd been on the point of leaving when an unmarked gray Ford had rounded the corner at speed and parked not far from the crowd. He wasn't surprised by the two people who got out: Detectives Allen and Mazzucco, the primaries assigned to his case. But then a blue Chevy had pulled up behind them and stopped— certainly not a police vehicle. And yet Mazzucco and Allen had hung back, waiting for the driver to get out. There was a flurry of activity among the media as one of the uniformed cops approached the barrier. Some shouted questions, but the Samaritan barely noticed. The driver's door of the blue Chevy opened and a man in a dark suit stepped out.

He was a few years older, and his appearance had changed, but the Samaritan recognized him instantly. It was something about the way he moved, the way his gaze read the street. The man in the suit nodded at Allen, and then his eyes started to sweep over the crowd: a precaution, something hardwired into him. The Samaritan put a hand up to cover his face, masking the gesture by appearing to be scratching his forehead. He turned back toward the alley, looking in the same direction as the rest of the crowd, but out of the corner of his eye he monitored the three new arrivals.

*Him.* What was *he* doing here?

Before the question was fully formed, he had an answer. As soon as the killings across the country had started to be uncovered, he'd known something like this was a possibility. The possibility that someone from his old life would recognize his signature, understand the significance of what he was doing. So this was who they'd decided to send for him. Or had they?

Allen spoke to the cop at the barrier, who seemed to know her. The cop asked a question, looking warily at the man in the suit. The Samaritan took a chance and moved a few steps closer, close enough to make out Allen's words: " . . . helping us out. His name's Blake."

*Blake.* He was calling himself Blake now.

The Samaritan hung back from the crowd after the two detectives and the man in the suit entered the alley. No one noticed him walking back down the street, brushing against the back bumper of the Chevy as he stepped off the sidewalk to cross the street. No one saw the small magnetic device he slipped under the bumper.

# 52

"This tells us more about him than he wants it to?" Allen repeated. "What do you mean by that?" Allen asked.

Blake didn't answer for a moment. He was still looking at the body sitting against the wall, but his eyes seemed to gaze right through it.

"I need a little time to think," he said finally, snapping out of his thoughts. Then he told Allen and Mazzucco he'd call them first thing and, with that, headed back toward the crime scene tape and out into the street. Allen noticed the way Agent Channing's eyes watched him as he passed by, though he still appeared to be engaged in a phone call.

Allen looked back at Mazzucco, who was also watching Blake leave, a thoughtful expression on his face.

"He's growing on you," Allen said.

"I wouldn't go that far." Mazzucco turned back to her. "You could use some downtime too, Jess. You've been working this thing flat-out since Sunday. Not to mention you could have been killed tonight. Why don't you follow Blake's example and get back to this in the morning? I got this."

Allen opened her mouth to object, but the look in Mazzucco's eyes said he'd been plenty accommodating today, and he was standing firm on this one. He probably wasn't naive enough to think she'd go back home and actually sleep, but he could make sure she took a step back. It wasn't the worst idea in the world, all things considered.

Channing had wound up his phone call and was coming back toward the body as Allen made her way out of the alley. She ducked under the tape and ran the gauntlet of media, keeping her head down and avoiding the cameras and phones and recorders thrust in her face as best she could. There would probably be some kind of press briefing once the body was taken away. Probably Agent Channing as well as Lawrence and the chief. It would be interesting to watch on the late news, if only to see who was taking the lead.

Because her eyes were on the sidewalk, she started when she almost walked straight into the chest of a tall man standing on the edge of the crowd. He wore a leather jacket and a red and blue LA Clippers ball cap, and had been so fixated on the activity beyond the tape that he obviously hadn't noticed her coming. Irritated, she grunted, "Police, get out of the way." The man frowned and stepped aside and then turned his attention back in the direction of the alley.

Allen shook her head. The only problem with sealed perimeters was that they had to stop somewhere—she hated dealing with the reporters and the morbidly fascinated bystanders.

She took her phone out and made a quick call for an update on Gryski. He was stable in Northwest Community Hospital and had already been charged and fingerprinted. At that point, he'd admitted to his real name: Stefan Sikorski. The name had been quicker to run than the prints, of course, and had come back suggesting a good reason why he'd fired on them. Sikorski already had separate convictions for burglary and aggravated assault, and at the moment Allen and Mazzucco had arrived at his apartment, he was being sized up as the prime suspect for a local armed robbery.

"Thank you, Three Strikes," Allen groaned. The so-called Three Strikes law had been amended a few times over the years to cut down on incidences of people being sent down for twenty-five for a minor charge like shoplifting, but a third violent felony conviction for Sikorski would have been more than enough for him to fall foul of the policy. Reason enough to fire on two cops, if he thought he was cornered. He'd had nothing to lose.

Allen thanked the officer on the other end of the line and hung up. As she approached her parked car, she heard a voice call from behind her.

"Detective Allen? Come on, just five seconds."

She sighed as she turned around and saw a familiar, smiling face: Eddie Smith. The mutation, as Mazzucco had called him. He smiled apologetically, hands out from his body in supplication.

"Anything you can give me?"

She shook her head. "Sorry, Smith."

"But it is him, right? The Samaritan?"

"I can neither confirm nor—"

"Okay, okay," he said. "How about telling me who the new guy is?"

"Excuse me?"

Smith glanced back toward the alley, then back to her. "The guy in the suit who arrived with you and Mazzucco. He's not a cop, is he?"

"He's helping us out. He's a specialist."

"A specialist?" Smith's eyes were focused, and she could tell this was the real reason he'd stopped her. Personnel behind the barricades was limited to feds, cops, and techs. A civilian was the odd man out. Smith had obviously sniffed a story, a new angle on the case. Allen decided to downplay Blake's involvement. She didn't know him well, but neither did she think he was the kind to do interviews.

"Yeah," she said with disinterest. "You know, profiling stuff. Hasn't gotten us any closer to catching this bastard. I guess we'll check back in with him in a few days if we don't have anything better by then."

Smith pursed his lips and nodded. "Sure. One more question?"

Allen let out an exasperated grunt. She wanted to keep this guy on her side, but there were limits. "One."

He paused for effect and leaned in. "This is him, right? The Samaritan?" The grin broke through at the end as he acknowledged he was pushing his luck.

Allen opened her car door and turned away from him. "Good night, Smith."

# 53

I cruised the streets of downtown for a while after I left Allen and Mazzucco, keeping an eye out for hotels that looked quiet.

LA's downtown district was unlike any I'd ever been in. From afar, the skyscrapers and lights fooled you into thinking it was the hub of the city, and maybe during the daytime that was partly true. But in the evening, the offices closed down and the commuters drove back out to Santa Monica and Glendale and Encino, spreading themselves back out across the city. There were still people around, of course: cleaners, occasional cops and city workers, the homeless, but no crowds. Compared to cities like New York or Paris or London, cities that burst into a parallel nocturnal life after sundown, it was dead. It was strange: a nest of shining skyscrapers and million-dollar businesses by day, a comparative ghost town by night. It reminded me of one of those old horror movies where the inhabitants of a village carry on as normal by day but retreat indoors by dark to shelter from the creatures of the night.

I switched the radio on and cycled through various talk stations until I hit music. Bob Dylan's "Desolation Row." The eerie harmonica combined with the solitary environment brought my mind back to my quarry and his habit of picking lone victims in deserted areas. Before Crozier had returned to Los Angeles, it had been his get-out-of-jail-free card—the lack of witnesses. Some of the people he'd preyed upon had been society's forgettables: bums and prostitutes and addicts. People who could be taken quickly and quietly and were barely missed, if at all. Others, like Sergeant

Peterson, had been missed, but their killer had been careful to leave no trace of them. If there's no body, it's impossible to conclusively decide a disappearance is the result of foul play.

I thought about how the MO had changed subtly in Los Angeles, moving from an almost random victim profile to a very definite type: young, dark-haired women alone in cars. I couldn't be certain from the evidence I'd seen, but I'd gotten the sense he'd spent more time with these victims than with the ones in the other states. I wondered again what that meant. And then I started thinking about how the MO had changed once again, with the newest victim.

Mazzucco had been right, of course. The Samaritan was sending us a message, letting us know he did not back down from the challenge now that his activities were public knowledge. But it did something else, as well. He'd decided not to waste any time with this woman. She hadn't been held for any length of time—had most likely been taken direct from her car to the alley in which she was killed. She hadn't been tortured. She hadn't been stripped of her clothes. He'd made no attempt to bury or conceal her body, despite the fact that there was a nearby row of Dumpsters in the alley. He could have placed the body in one of those and probably prolonged the search for at least another hour or two.

So why hadn't he? The only answer was because he didn't *want* to prolong the search. He wanted this body to be found as quickly as possible. And the only reason for that was misdirection.

I was well versed in identifying misdirection. The people I went after often knew someone would come looking for them, and so they took pains to cover their tracks. They left red herrings; they used false names. If they had any sense at all, they departed from their usual routine, if they had one.

From there, it was a matter of second-guessing the person you were chasing, separating deliberate misdirection from happenstance. I was looking for the same things with the Samaritan now. It meant I had to focus not on what he'd done this time, but on what he hadn't done.

I set my mind to work on that and picked a small, quiet-looking hotel. It had a green neon sign that lit up the street around it in a weird, alien glow. I parked in the basement lot beneath the building and checked into a room on the second floor. I thought about turning on the television and decided against it. I undressed and hung my suit up in the closet on one of those hotel hangers that has a pin instead of a hook to discourage you from stealing it. I took a shower in the dark, wrapped the towel around my waist, and lay down on the bed. I set my alarm for six a.m., deciding I'd call Allen first thing. There wasn't much of a view from the window, just the characterless facade of the building across the street. The green glow from the sign filled the room.

Exhausted from a long day, I began to sink into sleep. I fell immediately into dreams of deserted cities and creatures of the night.


## 1996


He could still hear the murmurs of conversation from outside the house, punctuated by Kimberley's occasional laughter. He shrugged his backpack off and dropped it to the floor-boards, kneeling beside it.

He removed the three bottles of water, tepid by now, and placed them upright on the floor. He removed Kimberley's Walkman and her tapes: Nirvana and Alice in Chains. And

Metallica as well, because she wasn't a grunge purist. He removed her balled-up sweater and placed it carefully beside the bottles and the Walkman and the tapes. Then he reached back into the bag and his fingers closed around the hilt of the knife he'd placed at the bottom of the pack, with some other things. He withdrew it and slid the blade from its leather sheath. It was a Buck Woodsman hunting knife; the hilt was hardwood, with aluminum on the butt and at the guard. The initials *DC* were engraved in the wood: his father's initials. He wondered how long it would take the old man to realize the knife was missing. It was his hope that the first he knew of it would be the next time he saw it up close.

Gripping the hilt in his right hand and listening to the voices outside, he realized how long he'd been waiting for this moment. He'd wanted to be careful, because he had no interest in being caught. But now, a perfect opportunity had presented itself. From things both Kimberley and Robbie had said, he knew Robbie had few friends at Blackstones. Nobody would truly miss him if he happened to disappear. He was seventeen, which was a year into transition age in California. That made a new foster family unlikely to the point of impossible. Kids like him ran away all the time and were never heard from again.

He reached into the bag one more time and withdrew the last couple of items he'd brought with him: a length of synthetic clothesline and a roll of duct tape. He'd brought the latter item to use as a gag, but now he didn't think he would need it after all.

He straightened up and crossed back across the floorboards to the glassless window. The other two were still down there, still sitting on the broken-down fence. He called out to them, telling them to come quick, because he had something to show them.

A minute later, he heard the front door creak open and the sound of Robbie's labored breathing. "We ought to be heading back soon," he said as he began to climb the bare wooden stairs ahead of Kimberley. There was an odd tremble in his voice, like he was nervous or apprehensive about venturing into the house.

Had the kid known what was in store for him then? Of course not. Otherwise he'd never have entered the house. Would never have agreed to the hike in the first place. But perhaps, on some animal level, he sensed the trap that was about to spring shut on him. At any rate, by then it was far, far too late.

He watched as Robbie crested the flight of stairs and looked around him, taking in the attic space, confused that there appeared nothing to see.

"Okay, what ... ?"

Their eyes met, and Robbie tried to make sense of his companion standing before him, stripped to the waist and holding a Buck knife.

"What ... ?" he repeated, and then panic flooded his eyes at last.

He turned to flee and ran into Kimberley, who was coming up the stairs. She yelped in surprise and started to say something to Robbie, but then she saw the knife. Her brown eyes widened and she spoke quietly.

"What's going on?"

# WEDNESDAY

# 54

The phone ringing on the table beside the bed startled me out of a deep sleep.

At first I reached for my cell and for a second couldn't work out why the display was blank. That's when I realized that it wasn't my phone that had woken me. It was the hotel's. I blinked a couple of times to get my eyes to focus and lifted the receiver off the base.

"Hello?"

"Mr. Romita?"

It sounded like the voice of the clerk at the desk. I took a second to confirm that was the name I'd used on check-in. John Romita took over drawing Spider-Man from Steve Ditko in 1966. I like to use the names of comic book creators—unlike actors or athletes, they're not household names to most people, but they're easier to keep track of than a name I've invented out of whole cloth.

"That's right. Is there a problem?"

"I'm sorry to disturb you at this hour, but I have a call from your uncle. He says it's very urgent, I'm afraid." The clerk's voice was a mixture of concern and curiosity.

"My uncle?"

"Yes, sir. Uncle Winter."

I sat up in bed, utterly awake now, as though someone had just tossed a bucket of ice water over me. Quickly, I picked my cell up again, activated the recorder app, and held it to the earpiece. I cleared my throat and tried to sound casual as I told the guy to go ahead and put Uncle Winter through. I must not have done that great of a job, because the clerk paused before transferring the call and said, "I'm sorry, sir. I hope it's not bad news."

I didn't think it would be anything but. I wasn't disappointed.

There was a long pause. I heard street noise, tinnily reproduced: a cell phone. And then I heard a soft, familiar voice that sounded like a cross between a mortician and an accountant. "Good morning. I have to say, you're a man of many names."

I got off the bed and stood up, cradling the base unit in my other hand as I walked across the room as far as the cord would allow. I kept to one side of the window and peered out onto the green-lit street one floor below. There was no one there that I could see. I scanned the darkened windows of the office building across the street, saw no movement.

"I could say the same about you," I said.

Another pause, and then the cold voice. Slow, deliberate. "I'm pleased you've decided not to waste time by feigning ignorance of who I am. I always appreciated that about you, Blake. Your ... directness. I take it you'd prefer I address you as Blake? That is, rather than—"

"Blake is fine."

"Blake it is, then. I see you're keeping busy." There was a condescending lilt to the voice that made me want to reach through the phone line and grab the speaker around the throat.

"You haven't been too idle yourself. Where are you now, Crozier? Are you close by? I don't suppose you've held on to the old name, either."

"Don't be ridiculous." I wasn't sure which question he

was responding to, but then I hadn't exactly expected him to give me his address.

I backed away from the window and scanned the room for signs of entry. None jumped out at me, and the thin strip of tape was still across the door where I'd left it. That was good.

"So don't get me wrong, I appreciate the call. Nice to hear from you after all these years. But I have an early start tomorrow, so how about you get to the point?"

"The point? The point was just to confirm it was really you. It seemed somehow . . . unlikely. You working with the police."

"Believe it."

"So I was right. You're not with our mutual friends anymore."

"Not for a long time."

"Then why are you doing this, Blake? Why interfere in something that's not your concern?"

"Interfering in things that are not my concern is sort of my mission statement."

He paused again, and I thought I could hear the sound of a low-flying aircraft in the background. Takeoff not landing, I thought. When he spoke, he sounded almost confused. "Surely you, more than anyone, should be aware of the dangers of interference? You know what I can do to you."

"I'll take my chances. Because you know what I can do, too."

"Walk away now, Blake. Fair warning."

"Too late for that."

"A pity. But suit yourself."

The call was cut off, and I slammed the handset back down on the base. I ran across to the window and looked out, trying to get a view of the sky. No dice. The tall building across the way left only a small rectangle of predawn sky visible directly above. I moved back across the room, flung the door open, and ran down the corridor to the fire escape door at the far end. I pushed the bar to open it and stepped out on the steel walkway. There was a clear view west from here. The vast sprawl of much lower buildings that reached all the way to the mountains. I saw a passenger jet rise and disappear into the clouds. I scanned the rest of the horizon and saw no other aircraft. Too early for the morning rush.

I ran back into the hotel room and switched on my laptop. I replayed the recording of the Samaritan's phone call, focusing on the background noise this time, instead of our conversation. The plane I'd seen had taken off from LAX, and I was pretty sure it must be the same one I'd heard in the background. From its position in the sky by the time I made it out onto the fire escape and the volume of its engines on the recording, I knew the call had to have come from somewhere very close to the airport, probably directly under the flight path.

I closed my eyes and tried to ignore the shifting feeling of unease awoken by the voice on the recording. I heard street noises, the intermittent sound of cars passing by. A yelled greeting from someone to another in the background. Nowhere too remote. I shook my head. If the Samaritan was as smart as the man I'd remembered, he'd have made this call from somewhere far removed from his hideout. But then again, everybody makes mistakes. And it was a place to start.

And then I heard it. Overlapping a fraction with his voice as he said, *Don't be ridiculous.* A ringing bell. A very specific kind of bell. The kind that sounds outside of a firehouse when the doors are opening, to alert people to get the hell out of the way because the fire truck's coming.

I got on the Internet and looked for fire stations under the flight path. There was only one.

# 55

I don't ordinarily appreciate being woken by a telephone call from a serial killer at a quarter to six in the morning, but on this occasion it had gifted me an advantage. The LA traffic was manageable at this hour. I used the GPS on my phone for the quickest route and made it to the fire station in Inglewood within twenty minutes.

The street was four lanes wide and unnaturally quiet. I parked directly across from the firehouse. Like most structures in Los Angeles, it was low and wide. Two big shuttered doors closed off the twin bays out front, looking like the garage on a suburban house blown up to double-size. Out front, the Stars and Stripes hung limp in the still air from a pole, beside another pole with a klaxon and lights that were primed to flash to alert traffic when the fire trucks were pulling out. I examined the rig and tried to estimate how far from it my midnight caller might have been standing. Probably not too far, I thought.

Then I became aware of a low rumble building in the west, and it took a moment before I realized what it was. The noise grew closer and louder until I looked up to see another passenger jet pass a couple hundred feet above my head. The morning rush beginning to get underway. It continued climbing, and the noise of the engines faded and the silence flooded back into the void.

I looked around me. There was another anonymous low and wide building across the street behind a six-foot fence. There was an intersection a hundred yards away, and beyond that the street turned residential: bungalows and apartment buildings. I started to walk toward the intersection, looking from side to side. A man approached from the opposite direction, his eyes darting away from me in discomfort as I openly stared at him. He gave me a wide berth as he passed by, probably thinking about how the crazies come out this time of night.

And then something made me turn around. I looked back down the street, the way I'd come, and saw another man standing beneath a streetlight, his face in shadow. A man who wasn't moving. A man who appeared to be staring straight at me.

I started walking toward him, picking up speed with every step. He straightened and took a step back. I quickened my pace again. He bolted.

I broke into a run, gradually closing the gap. I thought about yelling after him and then asked myself what good it would do. The street was empty and silent, the sounds of our footsteps cracking off the sidewalk the only noise. He ducked to the left, and I saw him disappear into a building. As I got closer, I saw it was a parking structure, like the one I'd met Allen and Mazzucco inside a couple of days before.

I heard footsteps on stairs, climbing not descending. I made the pedestrian entrance to the structure and saw a flight of concrete steps to an upper floor. I took them two at a time and came out on the second level. The ceiling was low, supported by thick concrete pillars. The space was square, a couple of hundred yards on a side, bordered by solid walls on the east and west sides and half-height walls on the north and south that left a large, open gap beneath the ceiling for air to circulate. It was around half full with cars, which meant plenty of places to hide.

The parking spaces were arranged in double rows, with aisles between wide enough to allow vehicles to pass one another. I picked the middle aisle and started walking down it. I kept my eyes open and my ears alert. I moved my head from side to side, checking the spaces between cars, making sure not to spend too long looking in one direction.

I got to the halfway point between the entrance stairwell and the north wall and then stopped and listened. I stood still for a full minute, not moving. I heard nothing, but I knew he was in here with me. There hadn't been enough footsteps for him to have ascended to the next level. I waited another minute. I could wait all night if that was what it took.

But then the air was filled with noise again. Louder than the jet had been, in the close confines. A car alarm: the horn blaring and echoing and amplifying off the concrete walls and the low ceiling. A black SUV in the last row before the solid east wall was angrily flashing its headlights. It was a demand for attention, a beacon to home in on. Which was exactly why I ignored it.

Instead of running toward the black SUV, I dropped to the floor and looked under the parked cars in the direction of the east wall. He was there, a shadow against the fluorescent-lit concrete, low crawling toward the half wall on the north side of the building. He realized he'd been spotted and rolled to his feet, still with two double rows of cars between him and me.

I edged between two cars in the first row and crossed the aisle as he made for the north wall. In the light, I could see him better, though his back was to me. He wore jeans, a dark coat and a green ball cap. He looked to be the right height and build. I dived through the final two rows of cars and out onto the space along the east wall as he reached the north wall and swung a leg over it. He hauled himself over and dropped off the edge, my hands just missing his as he let go. I looked over the edge and saw him hit the ground and roll fifteen feet below. The parking structure backed onto a narrow maintenance road, about ten feet wide, and then there was a chain-link fence beyond. He kept his head down, and all I could see was the top of the ball cap. He took a run at the fence and caught it halfway up, scrambling up it with agility. The top of the fence stopped a couple of feet below and ten feet across from my position.

I took a step back and judged the gap between the wall of the parking structure and its ceiling, and the distance to the fence. I jogged backward a few steps and took a run at the wall, crouching low to avoid the ceiling and kicking off the top of it, trying to hurl myself horizontally across the gap.

I had judged it just right. I hit him just as he was cresting the fence, and my momentum knocked us both over on the opposite side. The impact knocked out my angle and all of a sudden I realized I was dropping toward hard asphalt face-first. I got my arms up in front of my head and tried to angle my body, twisting my legs toward the ground and doing just enough to save myself.

I felt a blunt pain as I touched down and immediately started calculating the damage. Broken ankle, or perhaps broken leg. Six weeks in plaster. If there were another six weeks in my future, that was.

My quarry had had better luck than me, managing to grab hold of the fence on the way down and hang on. He dropped off and landed on three points as I tried to roll over and onto my feet. A stabbing pain in my left ankle dropped me back to the ground again.

He circled me cautiously, like someone moving past a wild dog. He was looking right at my face, but the streetlight directly above us cast a long shadow from his ball cap over his face and halfway down his chest. He lingered for a second, as though coming to a decision, or thinking of something to say. And then he took off again across the lot.

I rolled onto my side and started to get up again, putting all my weight on my right foot. The fenced area enclosed a patch of land and a weather-beaten two-story warehouse. There was a battered sign on the front that was obscured by an almost equally battered sign that read FOR RENT, providing a phone number.

As I watched, my target reached a fire door in the side of the building. A couple of seconds later, he had it open and was inside.

Gingerly, I tested my left foot, putting a little weight on it. My ankle hurt like hell, but it wasn't broken; just a bad sprain. I started to limp toward the warehouse.

# 56

The man in the hat had closed the door behind him, and when I tried the handle, it was locked. I wondered about that for a second: had he had time to pick the lock in the moment I'd seen him fumbling with the door? I didn't think so. That meant somebody had accidentally left the door unlocked—which seemed a little convenient—or somebody had deliberately left the door unlocked. Perhaps even the same somebody I was chasing.

The entire half hour from the end of the Samaritan's phone call until now had been one long period of frantic activity. I'd barely had time to think, only to act on instinct. One action after another, following the trail, narrowing down the options. It was only now that my options had been reduced to one clear pathway that I took a second to wonder if I'd been meant to follow this trail all along. It was almost too simple: one action after another, leading to an inevitable conclusion. And, as I'd been so quick to brag a little earlier in the night, the Samaritan knew what I could do.

Either the Samaritan had been a little careless and a little sloppy, or he had been very careful and very well organized. I thought about how I would engineer this situation if I were him. I decided that it wouldn't be so difficult—the trick would be to make sure it didn't seem too good to be true. If I was right about this, then it meant I was about to walk straight into a killer's trap.

I put a little more weight on my sprained ankle. It still hurt, but it was solid enough. I considered my options. I could call Allen and have her come out here herself—or better yet, with backup. But that would take time. There was probably more than one exit from the building, and I could be in only one place. There was still a chance that this wasn't a trap, that the warehouse was a dead end. Perhaps the Samaritan hadn't watched for the five forty a.m. to Newark taking off before he dialed the number of my hotel. Perhaps he hadn't called in a fire in this neighborhood to 911 a moment before.

I reached into my pocket for my wallet and located the appropriate size pick. Ten seconds later, the lock had been sprung. I held my breath, turned the handle, and gently pulled the door toward me. The rusted hinges screeched, but only a little.

I got the door open all the way and stood on the threshold, listening. My eyes could just barely make out shapes and hard edges within, so it wasn't all the way dark. The air that escaped from the doorway smelled musty, abandoned. From somewhere inside, I heard a brief flapping of wings. And something else. I had to move my head closer to the doorway to confirm I was really hearing it. Music. Something old-time, from the thirties or forties. A crooner tune. I took one step and then another into the darkness.

It took a second for my eyes to adjust further, but I soon realized there was just enough light to make out my immediate surroundings. I glanced up and saw the reason why: a big hole in the corrugated roofing thirty feet above me was letting in moonlight and a reflected glow from the streetlights. Ahead of me was a corridor lined with plywood walls. I guessed that the open-plan warehouse floor had been partitioned into separate rooms—offices or workshops or something. About twenty yards ahead of me down the corridor was a metal stairway that led up to a second level spanning only half of the interior space. I couldn't be certain, but I thought that was where the sound of the music was emanating from.

I blinked a couple of times to hasten my eyes' adjustment to the dark and scanned the concrete floor ahead. It was pitted with holes, weeds were sprouting up in some of the corners, and there were piles of scrap metal and machine parts lying abandoned here and there. I started walking toward the stairway, making sure to avoid the pitfalls and keeping my tread as light as I could with a sprained ankle. As I walked, I passed doors that led off into the partitioning. I tried a couple of them and found them locked. I reached the foot of the stairs and looked upward.

The music was louder here. It sounded like Bing Crosby, or someone of that vintage. I hadn't figured Crozier for a fan of old-time pop music. The stairs looked rickety, the guardrail missing on one side. I put a cautious foot on the first step and settled my weight onto it. It held without complaint, so I proceeded upward. I'd made it almost to the top when a flash of movement burst in front of my face. I rocked backward on my heels, grabbing the guardrail, before I realized I'd been startled by a pigeon. Or rather, we'd startled each other. The bird flapped upward before gliding through the torn opening in the ceiling.

I let a slow breath out and paused to listen. Nothing but my heartbeat and the music. I climbed another step and saw a thin line of light in my sight line, which was just above the level of the upper floor. The light was shining through the gap at the bottom of a stack of wooden pallets. I made the top step and moved onto the upper level. The platform was floored with rigid boards suspended from the roof beams, rather than supported from below. The stacks of pallets created a high wall directly in front of me. The light and the music were coming from farther back. I saw a narrow gap in the pallets thirty feet to my left. It required sidestepping along an empty strip of floor no more than eight inches wide, with no fence or guardrail to separate me from a twenty-foot drop. I put my free hand on the pallets and started to move carefully toward the gap. I glanced down and realized that the partitions had no ceilings of their own. It was like looking down into a wine box divided into squares by crisscrossed cardboard. In the dim light, I noticed that some of the boxes were empty, and some were filled with unidentifiable shapes.

Another couple of birds took flight as I disturbed their sanctuary. I could be as quiet as I liked, but if there was anybody waiting for me behind the wall of pallets, the birds would be giving him all the warning he needed. I took comfort in the fact that neither the music nor the light had been switched off.

I made the gap in the pallets and stepped gratefully in off the ledge. There was a narrow corridor twenty feet long and a foot wide between the stacks. The light spilled out from the far end. It was a small, dull light, probably from a low-wattage table lamp. I saw something else, too. A dark red stain pooling out from the source of the light. The music stopped and there was a moment of utter silence. I was almost relieved when another tune kicked in.

I recognized the song from somewhere, though I couldn't identify the voice of the crooner, who'd probably died of old age thirty years ago. It was all about the girl of the singer's dreams. I walked toward it, my eyes flicking from side to side for any ambush point that might be concealed in the wall of pallets. I glanced above me and saw nothing but a corrugated ceiling, pendant lights with shattered bulbs hanging every few yards. As I got closer to the blood pool, I could see that it was starting to coagulate, but only just. That meant it had been spilled relatively recently.

I made the corner, paused, and stepped out into the light. *Shit.*

There was a woman's body on the wood floor. She was nude and was lying on one side, her wrists bound with rope. I could see deep incisions on her back and on the backs of her legs. A blood-soaked mop of blond hair covered her face like a shroud, but it didn't obscure the ragged gash across her throat. I cursed out loud and fought the urge to break something. A voice in the back of my head spoke in a measured, matter-of-fact tone: *This one is on you.* The Samaritan, far from backing down at the challenge, was escalating his activities. This particular victim, whoever she was, had died because of me. To send me a message.

I took my attention from the body for the time being and surveyed the rest of the scene. Someone had created a hidden grotto within the stacks of pallets. The space was about ten feet by fifteen. The light came from a battery-powered lantern that had been placed on one of the horizontal beams supporting the ceiling. There was a small office desk in the far corner. There were three items on the desk: a cheap stereo, from which the music was coming; a heavily bloodstained chamois cloth; and something that looked a little like a small black leather briefcase that was open on its hinges but facing away from me. Attached to one of the ceiling support beams near me was a stub of rope, severed just below the knot. I didn't need to look back at the corpse's bound wrists to know that the two lengths of rope would match. The bastard had hung her up while he had his fun.

I looked back at the body. The victim was tall and blond, different body type from the first three victims. Another deliberate choice, I thought. It fit perfectly with my working theory on what the Samaritan was trying to do.

I maneuvered around the body, being careful to avoid the pool of red, and approached the desk. I reached into an inside pocket of my jacket and took out a pair of surgical gloves. I put the gloves on before I reached out and hit the off button on the CD player, cutting off the singer in the middle of another declaration of undying devotion. I turned my attention to the briefcase, only it wasn't really a briefcase. It was more like a box with a leather cover. I'd seen boxes like that before, and I had a pretty good idea what it would contain. I reached out and took hold of the open lid, using it to swivel the box around so I could see the contents. The interior was lined in red velvet and there were shaped depressions that snugly held a collection of knives. Scalpels, paring knives, boning knives. Like a hunter's blade set mocked up to look like a surgeon's kit. But no surgeon would have had a use for the largest blade in the case.

It was an ornate dagger called a Kris, a ceremonial blade of Javanese origin. It had a gilded handle with swirling patterns on it. The blade was eight inches long and curved back and forward in a jagged pattern. The razor-sharp edges glinted in the lamplight. The weapon held an odd attraction. I wanted to pick it up and feel its weight, test the sharpness of its blade. I ignored the impulse, just on the unlikely chance that the Samaritan had left his prints. Even if he had, I reminded myself that they wouldn't do any good.

I was so absorbed by looking at the blade that I didn't notice the sound of approaching rotor blades until they were practically overhead.

I heard a smash of glass from one of the windows downstairs, followed by a thud of something heavy hitting the concrete floor. It was followed by a second sequence of the same. I moved quickly back to the narrow corridor that looked back toward the warehouse floor and saw two fat clouds of smoke rising to the rafters. The Samaritan had trapped me, all right, just not in the way I was expecting. I batted the battery lamp off its perch and it crunched on the ground, plunging the death room into blackness. From outside, I heard a screech of feedback from a megaphone and then a gruff, commanding voice.

"This is the LAPD. You are surrounded. Lay down your weapons and come out of the building."

# 57

"Hello?" Allen was still only semi-awake when she hit the button to receive the call from Mazzucco—she had been worried it might be Denny again—but his next words shook her out of the sleep haze immediately.

"I just spoke to McCall—he says they got a heads-up on the Samaritan. They're surrounding an old warehouse down in Inglewood. They're making the incursion right now."

Mazzucco's voice was strained, and she could sense his controlled anger.

"What the *fuck*?"

"Ow. You don't need to yell, Jess. I know. He says they tried to get ahold of us earlier, but—"

"Bullshit. I've had my cell beside me all night."

"Me too. Jess, we can talk about it—"

"Got it. Just give me the address and I'll meet you there. Gimme a sec." She hunted around for a pen and something to write on. "That *fucker*."

"I know."

She located a makeup pencil and scrawled the location of the warehouse down on an unopened bill from her cable company. Without bothering to say goodbye, she hung up and threw on the clothes she'd been wearing the previous night. There was no time for niceties.

She took the 405 south. The sun was not yet up, but the early-morning traffic was already beginning to harden the arteries that crisscrossed LA. The whole drive, she was fighting to forget about how much she wanted to rip Don McCall's stupid goddamn head off and focus on what was important. Who had provided the lead on the Samaritan? How did they know they needed to treat it seriously? How had McCall managed to steal it from under them? Her next thought was of Blake. Had he somehow managed to track the killer down to his lair? Maybe he'd been the one to call it in.

She thought not. She'd known Carter Blake less than a day, but she was a good judge of character, and her every instinct told her he was a straight shooter. He might hold back on some things, but she was certain he wouldn't deliberately cut her out of the loop in favor of a moron like McCall.

She saw the blue lights glancing off windows and walls before she turned the corner into the street the warehouse backed onto. Mazzucco's car was already there, along with multiple police cruisers and two of McCall's tactical vans. A helicopter hovered above the scene, its search beam flitting across the low rooftops. She parked and ran to the barriers. McCall was there with one of his men. Mazzucco was there, too, actually jabbing a finger into McCall's body-armored chest to make his point.

"What the hell is this?" she yelled at him.

McCall turned to look at her. He couldn't keep the smug grin off his face, or perhaps he didn't even feel like trying. "What do you know, Allen? I guess I *was* the first to know, huh?"

Something about the way he said that brought Allen up short. The look in his eyes said he was withholding other information from her and was having a good time doing it.

"This is not your investigation, McCall. It's not even ..." She looked at the warehouse and immediately recognized a clusterfuck in progress. McCall had deliberately frozen everyone else out and the blame would probably come back to her as the lead. "Where's SWAT? Where's the fucking FBI?"

"As I was just saying to your partner, take it up with Lawrence. We got a call; we had to act. You snooze, you lose."

"We're going to talk about this later," Allen said. "Just tell me what the fuck is happening."

For a second, McCall looked as though he was considering not responding, but then thought better of it. Perhaps he felt he could afford magnanimity. "My guys just went in. We got the two entrances, front and back. We tossed in some flash-bangs and some smoke grenades. Anyone's in there, they'll be out here soon."

"You just went straight in?" Mazzucco asked.

Allen shook her head. "Of course he did. What did you expect, subtlety?"

"Hey, fuck you, Fixer," McCall said. "Now back off, cupcake. We got work to do."

Allen snapped. She launched herself at McCall, but was caught around the waist by Mazzucco, who'd plainly been anticipating the explosion. McCall's man, late to react, inserted himself as another layer in between the two of them and McCall.

"You heard the man," he said stonily, eyeing the pair of them.

Mazzucco fixed Allen with a glare. "Later."

She nodded and relaxed, jutting her chin at McCall's flunky as she allowed Mazzucco to move her a couple of steps backward.

McCall had moved a few steps in the opposite direction. He put two fingers to the earpiece on his headset. "Rooker, sit-rep."

Allen backed away and looked at the building. And then she realized she'd forgotten all about somebody in the heat of the moment.

"Where is he?"

"Where's who?" Mazzucco replied.

"Where's Blake?"

McCall heard her and grinned. "I forgot to tell you the other thing, Allen. Our caller gave us a name, too."

# 58

I moved back down the tight corridor between the pallets and glanced over the edge of the drop. The smoke was already filling the warehouse. It looked like they'd fired smoke and stun grenades in from the windows on both sides. Had I been on the ground floor, I'd be blinded or severely disoriented. As it was, the Samaritan's little makeshift death chamber had effectively insulated me from the explosives.

The smoke had already engulfed most of the open portion of the ground level, rising and expanding and starting to fill the small partitioned rooms. It was like standing halfway up a mountain and seeing the morning fog fill the valleys below. I saw movement toward the rear door, the one I'd come in by. I huddled close to the nearest stack of pallets and tried to focus on the movement. In another minute, the smoke would be thick enough to blind me to anything further than a couple of feet in front of me, but for now I was elevated enough to make out shapes and disturbances in the smoke below. I could make out at least four figures entering from the doorway, where the smoke was thinner. I caught small details that added up to trouble. Body armor. Riot helmets. Assault rifles. A SWAT team. LAPD, most likely, or perhaps FBI. Either way, it was very bad news for me.

I remembered the SIS guy I'd encountered earlier. McCall, that was his name. If McCall's men followed his lead, they'd be the type to shoot first, ask questions never. If I'd guessed their numbers at the rear entrance correctly, that meant the same number again approaching from the front entrance. Minimum: eight trained men with Kevlar and grenades and M4s, versus one unarmed guy wearing a nice suit.

I glanced around my immediate surroundings, knowing I had bare seconds to do so. I saw nothing that could help me. I looked up at the roof and remembered the gaping hole in the ceiling. I found the spot and dismissed any idea of escaping that way. It was fifty feet out from my position, more than a thirty-foot drop to the solid warehouse floor. The nearest steel rafter was ten feet from the hole. Even if it hadn't been, I could still hear the chopper's rotors thumping away directly above me, its search beam glancing through the hole and the second-floor windows every so often. Behind me was a tight corridor and then a brick wall: a dead end with a dead body.

If I was getting out of here, it had to be from the ground level.

I looked back toward the position of the four men who'd entered at the back. It was getting tougher to see them all the time, but I could see they were beginning to spread out, covering the open-plan area at the back of the warehouse. I heard low voices as they called out code words. The smoke finally reached me, my already limited visibility beginning to gray out. I crouched down, gripped the edge of the platform, and swung myself over the edge. I took a deep breath and let go, allowing myself to drop blindly into the void. I hoped I'd memorized the configuration of the partitions below correctly.

I landed hard on the concrete floor, making sure to favor my right side. I couldn't avoid banging the sore ankle pretty hard, though, and I had to stifle a grunt as my shoes cracked off the surface. I heard a yell, a three-round burst of automatic fire, the splintering of wood. None of it too close to me. I waited and exhaled. I guessed I had dropped into the second row of boxes, meaning the guys out there would have to clear the first row. *Nice going, Blake*, I thought. *You've bought a whole extra couple of minutes of remaining unperforated.* I could see a little better down here. As I'd hoped, the partitioned workshops or offices or whatever they were, were fouling the dispersal of the smoke. Some of it was seeping through, but visibility in here was much better than out on the floor.

The immediate space around me was square, about ten by ten. The walls were also ten feet high, making this a big square wooden box with no lid. And me, the Jack, waiting to be sprung. The box was virtually empty, the bare wood walls showing holes and scuffs where shelves or bulletin boards had hung. There was a door that I knew had to open out on the central corridor. Since I didn't have too many other options, I carefully pushed the handle down and pulled the door open. I had a vague idea about getting farther back into the nest of partitioned rooms, but beyond that I was out of ideas. All I knew was that the longer I wasn't shot or cuffed, the better. The smoke was much thicker in the corridor. I turned in what I was reasonably sure was the opposite direction from the men who were approaching from the warehouse floor and started to walk deeper in.

Visibility was worse than ever now. I could barely make out my own shoes. I bore close to the side of the corridor, tracing my hand along the wall and marking the doors as I passed by. I was starting to think it was about time I picked one of the doors when I heard a yell from some unknown distance behind me.

"Freeze!"

I didn't stop to think. I was alongside one of the partitions that happened to have a bare doorframe. I ducked inside the box before the voice could follow up with further instructions. There was no gunfire. I wondered if the yell had been a bluff. Perhaps he'd seen something, a whisper of movement, but he couldn't possibly have gotten a clear view of me and my position from any distance, not in this smoke. I looked around my newest box. It was harder to see in here, the absence of a door meant the flow of the smoke had not been restricted the way it had elsewhere. Still, visibility was far better than it had been in the corridor. This box had been an office. There were shelves on the wall and a steel file cabinet with the drawers removed. There was a desk along one wall, and a broken swivel chair had rolled into the center of the room.

The voice rang out again from outside. The same voice, I was pretty sure. A clear, commanding tone, just like the one he'd been trained to use.

"Come out with your hands on your head. I will shoot you."

I decided it probably was a bluff, but an informed one. The guy out there had seen *something*; he just wasn't sure what. If the something had been a someone, it was a safe bet that someone was hiding in one of these rooms. My hunch was backed up when I heard a door being kicked in, maybe four boxes down. Twenty seconds later, I heard another one. He'd be taking the methodical approach. Room by room. I heard the voice again, lower this time, conversational. Talking to one of the others over his headset, I guessed. More bad news.

A lull and then another door kicked in. Next door, I was certain of it. This guy wasn't waiting on his backup, probably wanted to nail the bad guy all by his lonesome. I expected there'd be another one or two along soon, but probably not all of them, not yet. I was betting one of the teams had ventured upstairs. I wondered how long it would take them to discover the body.

It hadn't taken him long to clear each room, so I knew I was down to seconds. I stepped up onto the desk, being careful not to make any noise, and listened. I heard scuffing of boots, something small being knocked over in the next unit, probably with the barrel of a rifle. I waited to hear the retreating steps. I gave him time to get back out into the corridor, and then I grasped the top of the walls and lifted myself up and over, trying to balance speed with making as little noise as I could manage. A simple maneuver, under normal circumstances—up, over, and drop. I landed in the adjacent box, making sure to touch down on my right foot. Immediately, I moved to the door, which my pursuer had helpfully left opened. I moved into the corridor and waited.

Five seconds later, the guy appeared at the adjacent door, his head turned slightly in his planned direction of travel: the opposite direction from me. He was decked out in standard tactical dress: a black uniform, body armor over the chest, a black helmet and visor. I hit him in the throat with the blade of my right hand. It took absolute precision—I had to make sure I struck in the narrow gap afforded by the body armor and the visor, and I had to hit him hard enough to stun him immediately. But the real precision was in judging how hard to hit for a stun, rather than a killing blow.

The cop made a gagging noise and dropped to the floor, his helmet smacking off the concrete with a crack, his Bushmaster M4 clattering on the ground. I crouched beside him and touched the same hand to his neck, this time checking for a pulse. I found it and wasted a couple seconds to make certain he was still breathing, and then I stripped his sidearm out of its holster. It was a Beretta. I checked the safety and tucked it into the back of my waistband, and then I took off down the corridor.

There was one last door at the end of the corridor. I opened it and found myself in a narrow corridor, this one defined by the last wall of the partition block and the brick wall of the warehouse itself. I'd been hoping for a fire exit that had been missed in the rush to surround the place. What I found was a large split-door hatch in the floor. The hatch was locked, too, with a rusting padlock that looked reassuringly old. Reassuring because it didn't feel like I was following the Samaritan's script this time: he would have used a fresh padlock. This lock was worth spending a little time on. It was old and cheap enough that I knew I could have simply shot it off, but I wanted to avoid signaling my location while my pursuers still had an entire warehouse to search. I got my wallet out again and took out a couple of the smaller picks, testing one, then the other. The second one I tried was the right size. Out of habit, I counted off the time in my head as I worked the lock. Six seconds. Not exactly world-beating, but it would do.

I unhitched the padlock and opened one wing of the hatch. Below, it was pitch-black. No ladder. How deep could the basement floor be? Not too deep, I hoped. There was a rung on the underside of the hatch door, which would allow me to close it behind me. I positioned myself on the edge of the drop, then grabbed the rung and pulled the door most of the way closed, allowing myself space to slip through the gap. I gripped the edge with one hand and kept ahold of the rung with the other as I shuffled my body into the drop. Just before the hatch door slammed shut on my fingers, I let go of the edge and reached my hand up to join the other one holding the rung. My feet dangled in the air as I hung suspended from the underside of the closed hatch. I'm six feet even, and my arms are about thirty inches, shoulder to fingertip. That meant the drop had to be at least eight feet. I tried to raise my left foot a little higher than my right, and hoped to hell it wasn't too big a drop as I let go.

The good news was that my feet hit solid earth a heartbeat later. The bad news was I didn't manage to protect my injured ankle. A fierce stab of pain shot up my leg and I dropped onto my back, grabbing the ankle. I rubbed it for a few seconds until the pain dulled. The ground felt uneven and dusty beneath me. I got my phone out and hit the flashlight app, directing it upward at the closed hatch to confirm I'd fallen only a matter of inches.

After the past twenty minutes of darkness and smoke, it was like staring into the sun. I blinked the glare of the light out of my eyes and cast the beam around me. I was in the foundations of the warehouse. The ceiling was about ten feet above me; the giant slabs of concrete supported by steel crossbeams. The brick walls came all the way down here to the foundations, and the floor was hard-packed dirt. Any illusion I'd had about this warehouse being the Samaritan's primary workshop were dispelled, because this would have been a far better location than the second floor. Light and sound would be well contained; day and night would appear the same to a prisoner. But there were no shackles, no bloodstains.

I hadn't been meant to find my way into this part of the warehouse. If the Samaritan had taken the time to look down here, he'd have made sure there was no escape for someone who made it this far. I played my flashlight beam across the nearest wall again. There was a gap where some of the bricks were missing. I walked closer and confirmed my hope—I could see the basement of the neighboring building through the hole. I tugged at one of the bricks at the side of the gap. It was loose. I hit it with the heel of my hand and it moved an inch or two. Much looser now, it took almost no effort at all to work it free of the wall. I heard another burst of gunfire from above as one of the tactical guys opened up on a pigeon or a threatening shadow. I heard footsteps on the concrete floor a little way off.

I started working at the other bricks at the edge of the gap.

# 59

It was almost an hour after the initial incursion by McCall's team before the warehouse was finally cleared for Allen and Mazzucco to enter. The sun began to rise in the pale blue sky, bathing the streets in a golden glow.

A lot had happened in that time. Ray Falco, one of McCall's men, had been found unconscious but otherwise unharmed in a corridor within the maze of office units in the building. McCall's team had followed the trail to find the point where their suspect had made his escape: a rupture in the wall that led through to the adjoining basement. By the time it had been discovered, their quarry was long gone. Finally, the second team had made a more grisly discovery: the mutilated body of a young woman.

Like Alejandra Castillo, this one didn't match the physical type of the bodies they'd uncovered on Sunday, but the handiwork was unmistakable. And this time the Samaritan had left behind some of the tools of his trade. Perhaps he'd been interrupted, Allen thought. Or perhaps that was just what he wanted them to think.

Her gloved fingers held the knife carefully by the guard that separated the blade from the hilt. The wickedly sharp, curving blade glinted in the light. With her other hand, she took out the sketch the ME had come up with based on the earlier wound patterns and compared them. The blade was a dead match.

The coroner investigator was the same as the one who'd carried out the preliminary examinations on Sunday.

"Looks like the same guy, all right," he said, as much to himself as to anyone else. It wasn't like anyone had much doubt of that. There were other speculations that were more disputed, however.

"At least we know who it is now."

Allen looked up to see that Don McCall had joined them on the upper level. Evidently, he'd extracted himself from the heated discussion with the first two FBI agents on the scene. Channing wasn't there, not yet, but Allen didn't doubt he'd have something to say about being cut out of the loop. *Join the club*, she thought wryly. McCall had come up with a young-looking uniformed cop from outside. He sounded angry and defensive, as though daring someone to criticize his team for letting the suspect escape. Allen rolled her eyes and put the knife down on the table carefully before turning to face McCall.

"I told you, it's not Blake," she said. "The Samaritan's playing you, McCall. It must have been him who called in the tip. It's way too convenient; even you have to get that."

"Oh yeah?" McCall said. "I just talked to Falco, and his description of the guy who sucker punched him sounds *exactly* like the guy I met downtown. With you. I gotta hand it to you, Allen. You got close to the perpetrator real quick. Pity you didn't notice."

"That's what you're basing this on? That's bullshit—"

McCall cut her off. "That's not all. Tell her what we just found, Officer."

He was addressing the cop on his left-hand side, though he kept his eyes on Allen. The cop was in his mid-twenties, still a little green around the gills. He cleared his throat. "Uh ..."

"Tell her about the car."

The young cop cleared his throat again. "Uh, that's right, Detective. We found a blue Chevrolet Malibu parked one block over. It's a rental. Rented in the name of Carter Blake two days ago."

McCall raised his eyebrows and opened his palms toward Allen in a *satisfied?* gesture.

Mazzucco glanced at her but said nothing.

Allen's mind raced. It couldn't have been Blake who'd killed this woman, but the circumstantial evidence was certainly starting to build up. Only it was built on a shaky foundation: an anonymous call that was way too on the money.

"Maybe he was here," she said after a minute. "It doesn't mean he's our guy."

McCall shook his head in amusement. "You don't even know what you did, do you? You brought a fucking serial killer in to help the investigation into his own crimes. You're done, Allen."

Mazzucco had kept quiet until now, observing the dialogue, but now he picked his moment to speak. "She's right."

Allen felt a surge of gratitude, but the look on her partner's face told her he wasn't doing this out of loyalty to her—not just out of loyalty to her, anyway—but out of a gut instinct that all this was just a little too neat.

Mazzucco had stepped forward, holding eye contact with McCall. "We get an anonymous call that tells you where to catch our killer in the act, and that doesn't strike you as convenient? Not just 'Hey, I saw something suspicious' but an anonymous caller that happens to know the suspect's *name*? What the hell did he do, ask Blake to fill in a survey? This is bullshit, McCall. You're playing into his hands."

McCall got in even closer, the mask of amusement disappearing. "This killer fucked with the wrong people. We'll get him before the day's out. Dead or alive."

Allen shook her head. McCall had just revealed more than he'd intended to. Maybe he thought Blake was the Samaritan, maybe not. It didn't matter. All that mattered was that Blake had hit one of McCall's guys and added insult to injury by managing to escape. That was what mattered to McCall, and it meant he'd happily throw his weight behind an investigation that was about to career off on the wrong track, just to get even.

"You asshole, McCall," Allen said, letting her full contempt for him show for the first time. Her phone began to buzz, and she was only vaguely aware of McCall yelling something back at her as she looked at the screen. All of a sudden, McCall's abuse didn't seem to matter. Lieutenant Lawrence was calling.

# 60

In a gray, windowless room on the other side of the country, a small but solidly built man named Davis put down his coffee and picked up the phone on his desk on the second ring. The voice at the end of the line sounded panicked, told him to get to a television or on the Internet.

Davis was puzzled. "What's happening?"

The voice told him it would be easier for him to see for himself. Ten seconds later, looking at the website of the *LA Times*, he was forced to agree. He hung up without preamble and scanned the story. His eyes kept darting up to the picture at the top, as though he needed to reconfirm it for himself. This was bad. Potentially very bad. His guy on the West Coast had all but confirmed that it was Crozier killing people out there. Crozier was a problem, sure, but one that could be dealt with. This new development couldn't help but complicate things.

He had to speak to Faraday; that much was clear. He didn't look forward to the conversation. Faraday was in New York this morning and would not appreciate the interruption. He dialed the number for the New York office, and the call was answered by a young-sounding female voice.

"Director's office," came the mandatory greeting. No "Good morning," no "How can I help you?" and certainly no named company or department. Davis identified himself and said he needed to speak to Faraday and that it was urgent. There was no acknowledgment. A click and thirty seconds of silence: no hold music, of course. When the line came back to life, Davis heard another female voice. This voice was a little more mature, more assured, and much colder.

"I'm in the middle of something, Davis. This had better be good."

"It's about Los Angeles."

A pause. "Arrangements are in hand, Davis. You kn—"

"I'm not talking about Crozier. Not just him. The police have just released a picture of their suspect."

"Don't keep me in suspense, Davis."

Davis closed his eyes and steeled himself. And then he said the name. Just two short words, but he knew they would change everything.

# 61

As she'd expected, the call was a summons. Allen left Mazzucco at the warehouse and headed back downtown, fighting the rush hour. Lawrence said nothing as she opened the door to his office. He didn't invite her in, didn't even nod in the direction of one of the chairs. He just stared at her until she came in and closed the door.

Allen steeled herself and walked a couple of steps into the room. Lawrence kept the stare going.

"Lieutenant—"

Lawrence cut her off with a wave of his hand.

"Save it. Just explain to me why you decided to bring a civilian in on the investigation into a series of murders that now appear to have been committed by that fucking civilian." As he spoke, his voice, outwardly calm at first, rose to the point that he was practically yelling the last three words at her. Allen was taken aback. Before now, she hadn't thought Lawrence capable of losing his temper like this.

"Lieutenant, this is a setup. Blake isn't the Samaritan."

It was Lawrence's turn to look mildly taken aback.

"So why did we find his rental car parked outside the damn torture chamber? Why did McCall's man give a description that fit him like a wetsuit?"

"I don't know that yet. All I know is that it's pretty convenient that we get an anonymous call to go to this address, saying it was the Samaritan. Who made the call? How did he know?"

"That's an interesting point, but in the meantime, I got a better one. Where the hell is Blake? If he's innocent, where is he?"

*Good question*, Allen thought. She'd tried calling his cell a couple of times, but it had gone to voicemail. If Blake was smart, and she knew he was, he'd have dumped the phone, or at least switched it off as soon as he exited the warehouse.

"Maybe he's shy. Maybe he doesn't like that his name and description are being circulated as a person of interest in this case. Think about it, Lawrence. The Samaritan has been operating under the radar for years. We've finally got a lead on him, and he's rattled. So he throws us a nice big distraction to keep us occupied. We won't find a shred of DNA evidence on that body in the warehouse, just like the others."

"Why are you so convinced Blake is clean?"

Allen sighed and related her attempts at due diligence: the call to Agent Banner, the flight times that proved Blake had been three thousand miles away when Kelly Boden was murdered. Lawrence looked less than convinced, but she knew that he wasn't 100 percent convinced the other way, either. He couldn't be: he was a good cop with thirty years' experience. He knew better than she did that perfect tip-offs rarely came in without a reason.

Lawrence listened, and when she'd finished, he sat back in his chair, folding his arms across his chest. "This isn't your first black mark with me, Detective Allen. Explain to me why I shouldn't put you on suspension right now."

"Come on, Lieutenant."

"What would you do? What would you do in my position, huh? I've got a loose cannon withholding information from official channels, sharing other information with unauthorized civilians ..."

"I'd give them a suspension," Allen admitted. "Once the case is through. Because I'd need somebody chasing down the real killer while everybody else is distracted looking for the guy who's been framed for it."

Lawrence stared back at her. His expression was impossible to read. Finally, he said, "I'm sorry, Allen."

"Lieutenant ..."

"You haven't given me any damn choice. You understand that, don't you?"

Allen swallowed. "I know, sir."

"The FBI is pissed. I had Agent Channing on the phone ten minutes ago, asking why the hell we kept them in the dark about the warehouse until the operation was in progress."

"That wasn't my—"

"I know that, Allen. But they also wanted to know why they didn't know about Blake. They wanted to know why we apparently have them on a do-not-call list, and I had no comeback to that." He paused and shook his head in frustration. "They're going to use all of this to take over this thing. You know that, don't you?"

"I'm sorry, Lieutenant."

"Two weeks' suspension without pay, effective immediately." He held out his palm, indicating the area of his desk nearest Allen.

Without a word, Allen took her Beretta from its holster and placed it on the desk, then took out the leather wallet that contained her badge and ID and placed it alongside the gun. She turned to leave, stopping as Lawrence began speaking again.

"I'll leave it to you to speak to Mazzucco. Let him know you're off the case. Better it comes from you. I expect you'll have arrangements to make."

Allen turned around and looked back at the lieutenant. He had turned away from her, was staring at his computer screen, pointedly not looking at her. Did he mean what she thought he meant? Her own words came back to her: *I'd need somebody chasing down the real killer while everybody else is distracted.*

"See you in two weeks, Detective."

Allen smiled. "Yes, sir. Understood."

# 62

As soon as she stepped out into the corridor, Allen reached for her phone and saw that she had a new message. As she'd hoped, it was from Mazzucco. It simply said, *Call me ASAP.*

She took the stairs down to the foyer, heading outside. As she walked, she wondered if she'd read the subtext of Lawrence's words all wrong. She decided it didn't really matter, because she knew what she had to do. She walked ten paces from the building before dialing Mazzucco's cell. As she listened to the ringtone, she stared up at the towering City Hall building across the street.

Mazzucco picked up. "How'd it go with Lawrence?" he asked, in lieu of a hello.

"He suspended me for two weeks."

Mazzucco paused. "Can't say I'm surprised, exactly. So what are you going to do?"

"He told me to call you, and that he'll see me in two weeks."

"Allen ..."

"I think I'd like to spend my vacation time with you. What do you think about that?"

"Is there any point even telling you what I think about that?"

"Probably not. Blake's not our guy, Jon."

"I know that."

That caught her by surprise. "You do?"

298

"I like to think I'm a pretty good judge of character. That, and you're right about this anonymous tip. It's a crock."

Allen grinned, thanking God for Mazzucco's cool head for once. "How'd it go with the owner?" When Allen had gotten the call to go to Lawrence's office, Mazzucco had volunteered to check out the warehouse's listed owner, one William J. Carron.

Mazzucco sighed. "All right. I got down here a half hour ago—had to hammer on the door until I got Carron out of bed."

"And?"

"And he's the owner, but that's as far as it goes. He said he hasn't been down to the warehouse recently. He bought it in an auction in 2007, had the idea of turning it into luxury apartments."

"Luxury? In *that* part of town?"

"Hey, it was before the crash. Anyway, he can account for his movements last night. He was drinking in a bar down the street with a buddy until closing time, then asleep at home with his wife until I woke him up. He was pretty surprised when I told him there was a dead body on his property."

Allen shook her head. "Another dead end."

"I hadn't finished yet, Jess. After I told him about the body, I asked if he was sure he hadn't been down there recently. He remembered that he'd been there briefly about six months ago, to show a prospective buyer around."

"And?"

"And he can't recall too much. I get the feeling this guy would have trouble describing last night's dinner. All he remembers is it was a guy and he seemed kind of interested, but that he never heard back from him afterward."

"I don't suppose he could recall a name?"

"Even better. He was drawing a blank, but I kept at him,

kept saying we'd really appreciate it if he could give us something. He went and had a look at the notepad he keeps by the phone. Luckily, he hadn't had too many calls in the past year. The phone number was still there. There was a name too—Dean—though that doesn't exactly narrow it down."

"Cell or landline?" Allen asked, praying for the latter.

She could hear the smile in his voice as he answered. "Landline. It's registered to an address in Santa Monica." He paused, teasing her. "I guess you don't really need to know this, you being on suspension and all ..."

Allen grinned. "Just give me the address, you jerk."

# 63

Mazzucco was parked curbside a few numbers down from the address in Santa Monica when Allen got there. She parked behind him and they got out simultaneously. The houses were fairly uniform: single-story detached units with spacious front yards. The only variations were in the paint jobs—white or pastel shades—and the yards—immaculate or scruffy.

It was an unusually crisp morning, the sun straight ahead of them, low and bright. They kept their sunglasses on, and no words were exchanged between the two as they approached number 2224. It didn't look abandoned, not exactly.

It didn't look much different from the other houses. This one was a pastel blue, in need of retouching. The yard was overgrown, the white picket fence out front in dire need of being torn down and replaced. The only reason Allen didn't assume it had been left to rot was the fact the windows weren't boarded up. The blinds were all closed, however. She felt a shiver as she looked at the house. Something about it felt wrong. Which, perversely, meant it felt right as a piece of the puzzle. Maybe the biggest piece so far.

She looked at Mazzucco. He didn't say anything. He didn't need to. It would be difficult to explain to a civilian, but something had clicked into place. All of a sudden a lead they'd been careful not to get too excited about had started to look very good indeed.

The gate was virtually off its hinges, but somebody had made sure to close and latch it the last time they'd left or entered the property. Mazzucco unlatched it and had to lift the gate clear of the ground to get it to open. He led the way up the flagstones leading to the glass-paneled front door. Allen kept her eyes on the windows, looking for a twitch of the blinds.

When they reached the door, Mazzucco hesitated before knocking. Allen knew what he was thinking, and opened her coat to show him her empty holster. Mazzucco shrugged and withdrew his gun. He raised his left hand and knocked three times, hard and loud. A cop knock, impossible to ignore. They waited a minute. Two minutes. Allen watched the windows.

Mazzucco raised his hand to knock again and let it hang there as they heard the noise of a car approaching, the engine decelerating. They turned around and looked in the direction of the noise. There was an overgrown bush on that side of the yard, its leaves so thick and wide that it would obscure the whole yard if you were approaching from that direction. A green Dodge appeared from behind the bush, clearly halfway into the maneuver of swinging in to the curb to park in front of the house. The driver, like them, was wearing sunglasses against the glare. As soon as he spotted the two figures at the door, he corrected, swinging back into the road and easing off the brake for a split second as he took a closer look.

Allen started moving back toward the gate, her free hand automatically reaching for her badge before she remembered she didn't have that either. As she did, the driver of the green Dodge made up his mind and floored the accelerator, kicking the vehicle back up to speed with a screech of tires.

She yelled out "Stop!" as the car vanished out of her field of vision. She raced out to the curb, but by the time she made it through the gate, all she could see was the back of the Dodge disappearing around the corner a hundred yards up the street.

"Shit!"

Mazzucco was beside her. "You get the plate?"

She shook her head. It was no good running back to their own cars; the driver of the Dodge could be a mile away by the time they could get turned around and as far as that corner.

Mazzucco took his phone out and quickly called it in, giving their location and asking for a rush on the bulletin—a green Dodge Charger driven by a lone male, probably white or Hispanic.

"Let's see if we get lucky," he said as he finished the call.

"Doubtful," Allen said. "Guy looked like he knew how to make a clean exit." She looked back at the house. "I'm more interested to see if we get lucky with what's inside."

Mazzucco hesitated a second and then followed her back to the front door. He folded his arms as Allen picked the basic lock on the front door. She glanced up at him as the catch clicked back and saw a smile playing at the edge of his lips.

"Aren't you going to say something disapproving, at least?"

Mazzucco shook his head. "I think we passed that point when I gave you the address, didn't we?"

Allen smiled and nodded.

"Anyway," he continued, "depending on what we find in there, we can leave everything untouched and come back when we can get a warrant."

"You've been spending too much time with me. What happened to by the book?"

Mazzucco reached forward and pushed the door handle down with the back of his hand, swinging the door open. "If this is his place, he could be keeping somebody inside. I want to make sure before we do anything else."

Allen held out her hand in an *after you* gesture and watched him step over the threshold. She liked that about Mazzucco—he was all about the rules right up until the point they got in the way of doing the right thing.

It was dim inside; no lights had been left on. Even so, the blinds were thin enough and cheap enough that there was no problem seeing around. It smelled a little damp and musty, but the stench of decomp Allen had been bracing herself for was absent. That was a good sign, but it didn't necessarily mean they weren't going to find a body. Back in DC, Allen had been involved with a homicide investigation involving a corpse that had been double-wrapped in plastic shower curtains and hidden beneath the floorboards of a bedroom closet for three years, unbeknownst to the unfortunate current owner of the house.

There was a short hallway with four doors on either side. They checked them methodically: living room, kitchen, bedroom one, bedroom two. At the far end was another door with a frosted glass pane—the bathroom. It didn't take them

303

long to make a cursory search to confirm there was nobody in the house—held against their will or otherwise. In fact, other than the fact that the bed in one of the bedrooms was made up and there was some food in the refrigerator, there was very little evidence that *anyone* was living here. And yet someone was. Someone who drove a green Dodge Charger, most likely.

Allen eyed the phone on the bedside table, likely the one used in the call to the warehouse owner. A slipup, for sure, but an understandable one. If the occupant of the house really was the Samaritan, he probably hadn't counted on his number being remembered all these months later, even if the police ever had cause to look into it. She got the feeling that this morning's framing of Blake had been an improvisation—a deliberate attempt to throw the authorities off the scent, but not necessarily one that had been planned very far in advance.

She noticed that something was trapped under the base of the phone. The edge of something flat, like a flyer or a business card. She pulled the sleeve of her jacket over her hand and moved the phone back an inch, revealing the edge of a photograph. She weighed the risks, decided *screw it*, and moved the phone the rest of the way. She picked up the photograph, being careful only to touch the edges.

It was a real photograph. Meaning, not a digital pic printed on glossy paper, but a picture taken by a real camera and developed from real film. It was obvious not just from the feel of the paper and quality of the image, but from the fact that it was clearly a decade or two old. The colors had faded a little in the intervening years, and there were scuffs and marks on it, as though it had been taken out and looked at regularly, perhaps moved around from place to place.

It showed two teenagers sitting on a fence: a boy and a

girl. Neither looked much older than sixteen, and if Allen had had to guess, she'd have said the girl was older than the boy.

The boy looked tall for his age. He had short dirty-blond hair, and his thin, angular face looked as though it was a couple of years away from needing to shave more than once a week. He wore sunglasses, a white T-shirt, and khaki shorts that came down to his knees. The strap of a backpack was slung over his right shoulder.

The girl was the one who drew Allen's attention, because she had a very familiar look. Brown eyes and dark hair cut in a style that suggested to Allen that the picture had probably been taken in the nineties. Style aside, the hair and the eyes and the features reminded her of the three bodies they'd found in the Santa Monica Mountains. No way was this a coincidence.

She wore DIY jeans shorts cut off halfway down the thigh and a faded black T-shirt with a yellow smiley face with crossed-out eyes on it. Allen had seen rock kids wearing those shirts before and knew it probably related to some band.

It looked like a summer's day somewhere reasonably warm. Could well have been California. But it could also have been a lot of places with a warm climate. There wasn't much to see in the foreground, and the background was mostly obscured by the side of some kind of building. It looked like a bar or a diner, because the tubing from a neon sign was visible in the window, although it wasn't switched on. She could make out the letters *S*, *T*, *E* and the start of something that looked like a *V*. Steve, maybe? Steve's Diner? In the extreme left of the picture, she could make out scrubland and blue sky.

She heard her name called from another room and slipped the photograph into her pocket.

She found Mazzucco in the other bedroom, on his knees in front of a closet. He was wearing his gloves, and he'd carefully removed the lid of a medium-sized box that had evidently been sitting just inside the closet. Allen had seen boxes like this before in the files. Boxes that contained a specific combination of everyday objects that would only ever be collected in one place by a very specific type of person.

Mazzucco rattled off the inventory. "Plastic zip ties, duct tape, a knife, some gauze. For a blindfold, I guess."

"A torture kit."

Mazzucco nodded. Allen had been about to tell him about the photograph, but watching him kneeling by the closet, she found herself remembering an eerily similar scene, not so long ago. Another partner, another house belonging to a vicious criminal. She said Mazzucco's name quietly.

He looked up at her. "What?"

"This thing could end up going the wrong way for me, depending on what happens. I just wanted to tell you something before ..."

Mazzucco looked uneasy. "Before ..." he prompted after a moment.

"Well, just in case. We might not be partners this time next week. I wanted to tell you about the thing in DC."

"The Victor Lewis case? Allen, we don't need to talk about this."

"No, we do. Lewis was guilty as hell. You need to know that. Only we didn't find what we expected to find in the house. Bratton—my partner—decided to change that. He planted the victim's necklace in Lewis's closet."

Mazzucco said nothing, waited for her to continue.

"I didn't know he'd done it at the time. I thought the bust was clean. Somehow, Lewis's attorney found out what had happened. There was an investigation. Bratton and I were suspended. He came to my house and told me what he'd done, begged me to say I'd seen him find the necklace, fair and square."

"But you didn't," Mazzucco said.

"How did you know that?" Allen asked, surprised.

Mazzucco shrugged. "Like I said, I'm a good judge of character."

"I didn't tell anyone that he'd confessed to me, but I didn't back him up either. In the end, they'd have nailed him anyway. A rookie reported seeing the necklace in the victim's home when we searched it after the murder. Only it never showed up on the inventory because Bratton took it."

"You did the right thing, Allen."

"Did I? I always thought, no matter what, you back up your partner's play. And then when I was put in that situation, I . . . I just thought . . . we have to be better than them, you know?"

Mazzucco nodded. "Still, you could have made things easier on yourself by burning Bratton, but you didn't."

"Just because I wasn't going to help him plant evidence doesn't mean I wanted to help send a good cop down." She gave a humorless laugh. "Turns out, half the cops in the department assumed I was in on it and got away with it; the other half assumed I threw my partner under a bus. So ninety-nine percent of my fellow cops ended up hating me anyway. I picked the worst option."

"Not from where I'm standing, you didn't."

She said nothing for a minute. Then, "Thanks, Jon."

"For what?"

"For being the one percent."

"Always happy to be right," he said, looking a little uncomfortable at the uncharacteristic display of emotion between the two. He looked back down at the torture kit.

"Let's put this back the way we found it and call it in." He looked up at her. "You find anything?"

She remembered the photograph and held it out to him, being careful not to touch the surface. "I don't know. Maybe."

He examined the picture and looked back at her expectantly. "The girl fits with the profile." He nodded.

"It looks like he's been keeping this around," she said. "What do you think it means?"

Mazzucco shrugged. "Could mean a lot of things. Maybe they're both victims. Maybe the kid in the picture is him. There isn't a lot to go on here."

"You recognize the location?"

Mazzucco looked again and shook his head. "Should I?"

"I don't know. I was thinking it could be somewhere around here. The light and the colors are right for Southern California. There's something familiar about it. I just can't put my finger on it."

"It could be around here," Mazzucco agreed. "Then again, you get blue skies and dust in a lot of other places. Could be Brisbane, Australia, for all I know. Are you going to put it back?"

"Okay. Okay." Allen took her phone out and snapped a couple pictures of the original before replacing it on the bedside table. Then the two of them went back outside, closed the door, and called it in.

# 64

The warrant didn't take long to come through. Being part of an ongoing federal investigation had its benefits after all.

Only, Allen wasn't officially part of the investigation anymore, so she made a strategic retreat to her car, leaving Mazzucco waiting at the house. Before long, the unassuming dwelling was crawling with LAPD and federal agents. Not too long after that, the first of the news helicopters arrived overhead, attracted by the activity like flies to a fresh piece of carrion. Allen sat in the car and drummed her fingers on the steering wheel, frustrated not to be able to be inside. She thought about what they'd found in there, about the man in the green Dodge. Occasionally, she thought about her conversation with Mazzucco. She hadn't intended to tell him about it. She hadn't intended to tell anyone about it, ever. And yet it felt like a weight had been removed from her shoulders. Mazzucco had told her she'd done the right thing, and for the first time, she'd allowed herself to give that idea some credence.

She wondered why it was she could never meet a guy like Mazzucco in her personal life. Instead, she seemed to be stuck with one long line of Dennys.

At around eleven thirty, Mazzucco appeared on the street and headed toward her.

"Got a minute?" he asked.

Allen leaned over and opened the passenger door, and he got in and started bringing her up to speed.

The torture kit had been quickly found, along with an unregistered Smith & Wesson SD40 pistol and a dozen or so boxes of ammunition. On a work desk in the second bedroom, they'd found the cannibalized remains of some electronic devices, along with a full complement of miniature tools for working on them. Mazzucco said that one of the techs had identified some of the parts as belonging to some high-end bugging and tracking devices. In the wastepaper basket beneath the desk, they'd discovered pages from recent editions of the *LA Times*, with rectangular holes where pictures and articles had been cut out of them, as though for a scrapbook. It didn't take long to confirm that the missing clippings were from articles about the Samaritan. But the scrapbook, if there was one, was nowhere to be found in the house. Evidently, he was keeping these clippings at his other place. That summed up the bad news: they were still missing the primary crime scene; there was no sign that anyone had been killed or even held in the house.

The good news was that there were plenty of recent, usable prints all over the domicile, suggesting that the Samaritan had not expected this hideout to be blown. A perfect set of prints had already been lifted from a fresh carton of milk in the fridge and was even now being rushed to the lab. The FBI guys wanted to run the prints, and Mazzucco hadn't argued. The result would come back a whole lot quicker, and given that the Samaritan had been operating nationwide, it was as likely they'd get a match from some other state as one from a Los Angeles crime scene.

Mazzucco had stuck around long enough to be satisfied the techs were doing a good job and had left them to it. He had paperwork to file downtown, and besides, he'd heard Agent Channing was on his way over. He got out of Allen's car and said he would give her a call if anything came of the BOLO on the Dodge.

Allen watched him leave and then considered her options. It was pointless to stick around here without being able to officially take part in the investigation, but she wasn't sure where else to go either. The focus was here.

She checked her phone for missed calls, half expecting some kind of message from Blake, but the screen was blank. She'd just put her key in the ignition when a knuckle tapped softly on the window. She started and looked up to see Jim Channing staring back at her, a vaguely amused look in his eyes. She had an urge to turn the key and drive away, but she resisted it. Instead, she turned the engine off again and got out of the car.

"I heard you were ..." Channing began.

"I am," Allen said. "But it's a free country, and I can take a drive wherever I like."

Channing shrugged. "Anyway. This was good work, Detective. You got a look at the suspect?"

"Excuse me?"

Channing broke out the disarming smile again. "My mistake. What I meant to ask was, did Detective Mazzucco see anything and relay that information to you?"

Allen cleared her throat. If Channing was holding her link with Blake against her, he wasn't showing it. Not yet, anyway. And why should he? She'd basically done him a favor, effectively highlighting the professionalism of the FBI's conduct in comparison to her own.

"Not much of one. Male, Caucasian, probably. Dark glasses and a hat. There's a BOLO out on the car; it was a green Dodge Charger. So far, nada. Not exactly a surprise. This guy's made cars disappear a couple of times before."

Channing, who had been gazing along the street toward the house, looked back at her.

"So you think this guy could be an accomplice?"

"An accomplice?"

"Working with Blake."

She thought about going along with it for a quiet life. Not for the first time, she chose the path of greater resistance. "Blake isn't our guy. I think he was set up."

Channing looked back at her for a minute, refusing to take the bait by reacting too quickly. "Then where is he?"

"Where would you be, if half the cops in the city were looking for you and your face was on the morning news for something you didn't do?"

He didn't hesitate this time. "I'd be turning myself in. I'd be trusting in the LAPD to hear me out and establish my innocence, so they could move on to other lines of inquiry."

"Goddamn, Channing. And you can say that with a straight face, too. I'm impressed."

"Come on, Detective. He was caught in his den with a body. Dead to rights."

"In response to a suspiciously well-informed tip from an as yet unknown person. A person I suspect may have been the guy living in this house. And anyway, if it was his den, why did they find evidence of only the one murder? We still need to find out where he took the others."

"He has multiple safe houses. Maybe this is one, too. Maybe the prints we're running at the moment are Carter Blake's. Maybe the guy in the green Dodge was Blake. Can you rule it out? Tell me honestly."

Allen felt bile rising in her throat. Channing had let the good-humored mask slip a little there, had slipped too easily into condescension on that last shot. She took a deep breath and said, "I've got somewhere else to be."

She opened the car door again, got back in, and started the engine. She didn't look up when Channing rested his arm on the windowsill and said, "You certainly do, Detective."

She didn't want him to see her face. Didn't want him to see that he'd hit a nerve. Because she couldn't do it. She couldn't swear that the guy in the shades and the hat could not have been Blake.

# 65

As she drove away from the Samaritan's safe house, Allen suddenly realized how fried she felt. With everything that had happened since Mazzucco's early-morning phone call, it felt like she'd pulled a full shift already.

Since she'd be unwelcome at headquarters anyway, she decided to stop off at her apartment to make some coffee and something quick to eat. She spent the journey trying to shake the doubts Channing had put in her head. If Blake really was the Samaritan, if he had killed the victim in the warehouse, then who had called in the tip? Added to that, she knew from the flight details that Blake physically could not have killed Kelly Boden. But that didn't rule him out for any of the other murders. Not even the girl in the alley last night. Maybe he could have killed her before meeting Mazzucco and her at Gryski's apartment. It would be ballsy, but that was one attribute this killer certainly had in spades.

So perhaps Channing's idea of an accomplice was on the money. Two men carrying out the murders, allowing Blake to be in Florida while his colleague murdered Boden. It wouldn't be the first such setup.

And yet it felt wrong. It was ridiculous, but she felt as though she knew Blake already. Even more ridiculous, she trusted him.

She cast around for something else to occupy her mind and alighted on the picture she'd found at the house. She waited until the traffic inevitably bunched up and took advantage of the pause to look at the copy she'd taken on her phone. A boy and a girl and a building. Somewhere warm, a desert climate. Maybe LA, maybe the surface of Mars. What was the nagging feeling of familiarity about the picture, then? She looked again at the faces. Young, fresh-faced. Although the hair color was different, there was a mild similarity about the features, as though they could be related—brother and sister, cousins perhaps. Her smiling, him looking serious.

It was no use. Given the vintage of the image, there was no way the two people in this photograph still looked much like they did here. If they were even still alive. Given her physical similarity to the Samaritan's first three LA victims, Allen thought that was particularly unlikely in her case.

A chorus of angry horns erupted behind her and she looked up to see the traffic had started to move again. She flipped the bird to the closest car almost automatically and put her foot down on the gas pedal again.

By the time she reached her apartment, she decided a hot shower would be more beneficial than the cup of coffee. First, though, she went into the bedroom and took the box containing her personal gun out from the drawer beside the bed. It was a Beretta 92FS, the same model as her depart-ment-issue weapon. She loaded it and slid it into the holster. That matter taken care of, she undressed, tossing her clothes carelessly on the bed, and walked back down the hall to the bathroom. She stepped into the shower cubicle, turned the water on, and stepped under the stream.

She closed her eyes and let the jets of water bounce off her face and cascade down her body. She saw the photograph again, as though it were projected against the backs of her eyelids. Where did the weird sense of familiarity originate?

She was almost positive she'd never seen either of the kids in the picture before.

And then it hit her. It wasn't the people; it was the building in the background. The neon sign that was switched off, or maybe broken: S-T-E something. She opened her eyes and wiped the water out of them with the thumb and index finger of her right hand. The rest of the word spelled out in the neon tubing did not read *Steve's Place* or *Steve's Diner* or Steve's anything. It read *Stewarton's*.

She knew this even though she'd never seen the building with her own eyes. She felt a twinge of doubt, wondering if this was a trick of memory, something she'd remembered almost correctly but subconsciously twisted to fit the sign in the photograph. No, she was 99 percent certain. And there was an easy way to make that a hundred.

Allen turned the shower off and stepped out of the cubicle, grabbing a towel and briskly wiping the moisture from her skin and hair. She wrapped it around herself and walked through the open bathroom door into the hallway. As she turned in the direction of the living room, she happened to glance at the front door.

Something wasn't right.

She froze mid-stride and looked at the door until she worked out what it was: the lock. When she'd come in, she'd let the door close again on the latch, the way she always did. But she could see from the position of the handle on the latch that it hadn't just clicked into place and stayed that way. The handle had been twisted around and, when she looked closely, she could see that the second dead bolt had been engaged. The door was double locked, and she hadn't done it. She never double locked during the day, only at nighttime.

Her breath caught in her throat as she stood in the hallway, occasional drips of water from her still-wet body tapping softly on the wood flooring.

Someone had unlocked the door, entered the apartment, and then double locked the door again. You couldn't engage the dead bolt from outside, so that meant that someone was still in the apartment, with Allen. And that someone would have known she was in the shower and would know she'd just turned the shower off.

She listened. There was no sound but the occasional drips on the floor and from within the shower cubicle. She glanced left and right down the hall. On her left was ten feet of hall and then the door to the bedroom. On the right, the kitchen on one side and the living room at the far end. She made her mind up quickly to head for the bedroom, for one very good reason: it was where she'd left her clothes, and with them, her gun.

She moved slowly. One foot and then another, alternating between looking straight ahead and casting furtive glances over her shoulder. She resisted the temptation to run, because she didn't know if she'd be running into the arms of the intruder, if he'd decided to wait in the bedroom. A shiver traveled along the still-moist and suddenly cold flesh of her back as she thought about the implications of that: of the choice to lie in wait in her bedroom.

She wondered how long it had been since she'd stepped into the hall and noticed the dead bolt. Realistically, she knew it could not have been more than a minute or so, but it felt like an hour. Whoever was in here would have noticed the hesitation and that she hadn't made any noise since.

Allen realized she was still holding her breath as she approached the bedroom door, which was open. Had she left it that way? She couldn't remember. She got within a foot of the door and stopped to see how much of the room she could see in the gap between the door and the jamb. A frustratingly small field of vision, was what. There was no one in her line of sight, but that didn't mean there wouldn't be someone standing by the window, or standing on the blind side of the door.

What she could see was part of her unmade bed. She could also see her coat discarded on top of the duvet, a bump showing where she'd tossed her shoulder holster before dropping the jacket on top of it. She reminded herself not to start feeling too relieved—there might still be someone standing between her and the gun. She glanced behind her and let the held breath out slowly and silently. Another breath and she opened the door, eyes scanning the room even as her hands made straight for the bulge under the jacket. She ripped the jacket off the bed as her eyes swept the room to confirm it was empty.

But then she heard the hard click of a shoe stepping onto the wood floor of the hall behind her, joined a second later by another. She looked down at the holster, guessing she probably had time to get the gun out, disengage the safety, and be covering the door before—

Allen stared down at the bed in disbelief. The leather holster and shoulder strap was still there, approximately where it had landed ten minutes ago.

But the gun had vanished.

# 66

"Afternoon, Agent."

Agent Jim Channing looked back at the doorway of the house that was being virtually taken apart by his agents and saw Detective Mazzucco standing there, cradling a sandwich bag in one hand and two cups of coffee in a cardboard drinks holder in the other.

"Looking for Allen?"

Mazzucco hesitated before answering. "Allen's on suspension."

Channing smiled. "She happened to stop by. You just missed her, in fact. She said she had someplace to be."

Mazzucco said nothing. His eyes flickered to either side of Channing, as though not entirely sure whether to believe him. Then he shrugged and nodded at the cups of coffee. "I guess I have some going spare, then," he said, holding the tray out for Channing to take one. He accepted the offering with a nod.

"How we doing here?" Mazzucco asked as Channing sipped the coffee.

Channing suppressed a grimace as he realized the latte had at least three sugars in it, but swallowed anyway. "Not a lot to find," he said, casting his gaze around the hallway and into the bedroom. "Besides the torture kit—which, of course, could be explained away by any halfway-decent defense attorney, if it ever gets that far—all we know is that somebody's been living here for a while and that they seem to lead a pretty spartan existence. A couple days' worth of food in the refrigerator, nothing fancy. A few books, including the Bible, some clothes and some electronic odds and ends.

Nothing to suggest anybody was ever held here against their will—no blood, no female personal effects, nothing like that. We looked up the name on the lease and found out there wasn't one. This place was repossessed by the bank in 2009 and hasn't been inhabited since. I guess there are enough of these empty places these days that the banks don't notice a few squatters, huh?"

Mazzucco took a sip of his coffee and said nothing, waiting for Channing to continue. A classic interrogation technique. Channing dry-swallowed to try to get the sugary aftertaste out of his mouth and depressed the raised buttons in the plastic lid, as he habitually did. He decided to take the same tack as he had with Allen, see how it went down with her partner.

"Tell you the truth, Detective Mazzucco ... Jon, is it?"

Mazzucco nodded slowly, as if reluctant to confirm or deny.

"I'm not sure this lead is going to take us anyplace. I mean, sure, the connection with the warehouse down in Inglewood is interesting, if it was the same guy ..."

Mazzucco cut in sharply. "And what about the guy in the green Dodge, hightailing it as soon as he sniffed cop?"

Channing shrugged as though he didn't have a particular dog in this fight. "It's a good point. Definitely worth investigating. But if the guy's living here illegally, that's reason enough for him to pull a fade, isn't it?"

Mazzucco had opened his mouth to reply when Channing felt a tap on his shoulder. He turned and saw it was Agent Moreno, a tall, twentysomething woman in her first year out of the academy. She looked serious, as though something had caught her by surprise for the first time on this job.

"What have you got for me, Isabella?"

Moreno looked uncomfortable, glanced at Mazzucco, who was watching with fresh interest.

"It's about the prints, sir. We heard back from the lab." She inclined her head toward the living room of the house, suggesting that Channing might want to speak in privacy. He was intrigued, but he didn't want to break the moment with Mazzucco by overtly freezing him out. He nodded at the detective and smiled at Moreno.

"It's okay. You can go ahead. We're all on the same team here, right?"

Moreno's discomfort seemed to heighten. She stared at Channing for a moment longer before relenting. "The lab followed what they tell me is the standard procedure, albeit with a rush. They ran the prints through the local databases first, checked out anything held by local law enforcement." She glanced at Mazzucco as she said this.

"And?"

"And the search triggered a DR17."

"A DR17?"

"It's a flag, in this case from Homeland Security. It means forget you asked."

Channing's eyes narrowed. All of a sudden, he was starting to regret having this conversation in front of Mazzucco, but it was too late now.

"Okay," he said, making sure to keep his voice even and unrattled. "So what happened when we ran them using the national database?"

"That's the weird thing, sir. They put the prints through the VICAP database next." The acronym stood for Violent Criminal Apprehension Program—a nationwide database used to map similarities between violent crimes crossing state lines, available only to the Bureau and cops who put their request in writing and ask nicely.

Moreno continued. "We got a hit on the prints there and

a little more information. But I'm told we can expect a call from somebody in DHS."

"Well, who is he?" Channing prompted, careful not to betray how impatient she was making him. He expected she was about to tell him that the prints matched one of the murders in another state. He was not prepared for what she actually said.

"He's a dead man, sir."

"Excuse me?"

"Dean Crozier, born right here in LA in 1980, signed up for the army in ninety-eight, KIA 2004 in Afghanistan. He's been dead for over a decade."

Channing glanced in Mazzucco's direction, wishing he could erase the cop's memory of the previous three minutes. Mazzucco's face was impassive. He took another sip of his coffee as he watched the show.

"But that doesn't make any sense. Those prints come from this house. They're all *over* this house, the same prints. They were left here by somebody recently."

Moreno stared back at him wide-eyed, as though worried that he wanted her to explain this apparent impossibility on the spot.

"Thank you, Agent," Channing said, dismissing her with a strained smile. Moreno gratefully turned away and headed outside.

Mazzucco watched her as she went. He raised his eyebrows at Channing. "First time I heard of a legally dead squatter."

Channing put the sugary coffee down on the floor and approached Mazzucco. Mazzucco didn't move, didn't back off, just returned his gaze and let the hint of a smile play over his lips.

"We'll get to the bottom of this, Detective. Meantime, our number one priority is still tracking down Carter Blake."

"Let me guess. No progress on that, either?"

Channing let the implied insult go. "Your partner seems to have gotten quite attached to this guy."

"She tell you that?"

"She has a habit of doing her own thing. Isn't that right?"

Mazzucco said nothing for a minute, then looked away. "I think I'll head back down to headquarters. I need to check in with the lieutenant."

Channing smiled. "Be careful, Detective. It's easy to be led astray, particularly when it's your partner who's doing the leading."

Mazzucco nodded and turned back toward the doorway.

"Enjoy the coffee, Agent."

Channing watched Mazzucco's back as he walked down the path toward the sidewalk and waited until he'd vanished from view. Then he took his cell phone out and dialed a number that he'd added very recently. There were a couple of rings, and then a gruff, harried voice answered.

"McCall."

"Captain McCall, it's Agent Jim Channing, FBI."

"Oh yeah?" The voice betrayed surprise, along with immediate suspicion.

"How's your guy doing, the one Blake assaulted?"

"He'll live. You make a habit of expressing your concern for on-the-job injuries, or is this a social call?"

Channing smiled. "Actually, I wanted to get your opinion on one of your colleagues. Jessica Allen."

# 67

I sat back on Allen's leather couch, trying to rub some sensation back into the left side of my jaw while I waited for her to come back through.

After a minute, she appeared at the door, having wrapped a hand towel around her wet hair and quickly dressed in jeans and a T-shirt. She didn't look any less pissed off than she had a couple of minutes before.

"You want some ice or something for that?" she asked curtly.

I shook my head. I'd let her take the swing at me; figured she deserved it.

"What the hell are you doing breaking into my apartment, Blake? I thought you were *him*."

"Seems to be a lot of that going around."

"Where's my gun?"

I nodded at the television table, on top of which I'd left her gun after taking the precaution of moving it from where she'd expected it to be. Given her violent reaction to seeing me, I decided it had been a sensible precaution.

"I was worried you might not give me a chance to explain."

Allen kept her eyes fixed on me as she crossed the room and picked the gun up. She ejected the magazine and checked the load, then clicked it back into place. She didn't point it at me or anything, but I noticed that she didn't put it down again either.

"So explain."

"You want to sit down, or—?"

"I'm fine."

"I didn't kill the girl in the warehouse. I got there ten

minutes before the cops did—it was a setup. That must have crossed your mind, right? The guy you're looking for isn't that sloppy."

"Let's say I thought there might be more than meets the eye. Keep going."

"Somehow he found the hotel where I was staying. He called me up last night, wanted to talk."

"He called you. The Samaritan called you."

"Yeah. I think he tailed me from the scene of the first murder last night, the one in the alley."

"Wait a second. Why would he be interested in you? You're not even an official part of this investigation."

I'd been hoping she might not pick up on that.

"I think he noticed I was helping you. He decided to check me out and then decided I was a nice, expendable individual who wasn't any kind of cop and wouldn't be believed if I was found in a warehouse with the latest victim."

Allen waited to see if I was going to say anything further. When I didn't, she brought the gun up to cover me and moved over to where she'd left her cordless phone on a shelf of the bookcase. She picked it up, eyes still on me, and began to dial a number.

"What are you doing?"

"I'm calling it in. I'm going to tell them I'm holding Carter Blake at gunpoint and I'd like them to come get him."

"Wait a second. I thought you believed me."

"I didn't say that. I had some doubts about the way things went down at the warehouse. But I don't believe a goddamn word of what you just said."

"It's the truth, Allen. He tracked me down, called me up, and led me to the warehouse like an idiot. I was so eager to nail him I wasn't thinking clearly."

"That's not the part I'm talking about, and you know it.

Whoever set you up didn't pick you at random. And you didn't pick this case at random either, did you, Blake?"

Neither of us spoke for a moment. And then she dialed three more digits, the tones sounding like a discordant advertising jingle.

"One more digit, Blake. I press it, and time's up."

"Wait."

She held a finger poised on the last button, turned her face to me expectantly.

"What gave me away?" I asked.

Allen didn't put the phone down, but she did move her finger away from the button. "I never really bought the idea you'd come all the way out here on a whim. You showed up within hours of the story hitting the news. That tells me you wanted in on this badly."

I kept my mouth shut. The first rule when you're in a hole: stop digging.

"I parked my suspicions, though, because it seemed like you were on the level about doing this for a living, and your references checked out. I thought you could help us. The clincher was last night."

"The tow truck driver?" I asked.

She nodded. "You knew Gryski wasn't the Samaritan the second you looked at him. How did you know that? He fit the profile and he resisted arrest using deadly force. Exactly like a cornered killer would behave. But you knew it wasn't him as soon as you saw his face. Call it a cop's instinct, but I knew right away—your body language changed as soon as you didn't see the face you were looking for. Which means you know who we're looking for, don't you?"

"It's not that simple."

"Make it simple."

I felt like smacking myself in the head in the hope it might knock some sense into me. Twice in the last twenty-four hours I had painfully underestimated the people I was dealing with. Crozier first, and now Allen. Brute force and luck had gotten me out of the first tight spot, but I didn't think either could rescue me from this situation. Only some level of mutual trust could do that.

"You said you checked me out after we first spoke," I said.

"I tried to. I didn't come up with a whole lot, besides your FBI friend."

"That's right. And no offense, but you could have a lot higher clearance than you do and you'd get the same results. I'm a free agent now, but that wasn't always the case."

"I figured," she said. "So what? CIA, NSA, something like that?"

I shook my head. "Smaller than that. I worked for a very secret, very well-funded group that carried out difficult work in places the United States wasn't always supposed to be."

"You mean some kind of black ops? Deniable assassinations, that kind of thing?"

I didn't say anything.

"It fits with the blank slate, I guess. Is Blake even your real name?"

"It is now."

"Don't get cute." She hit the cancel button on the phone and replaced it on the shelf, lowering the gun again. "So what's your connection with our mystery man? You obviously know his face and his methods. Was he on some kind of kill list? Was he the one that got away?"

"Nobody got away, Allen. And I'm afraid it's much worse than that."

She looked puzzled for a moment, and then she understood. "He was one of yours."

"His name was Dean Crozier. I don't know what he's

calling himself now, obviously. He tended to work at the business end of our operation. He enjoyed his work a little too much."

"Do I want to know the details?"

"Probably not. He wasn't the only one who enjoyed killing, but he was the one who seemed to want it more than anything else in the world. You want to know what brought me into this, Allen? The same thing that brought you in. I recognized his signature: the torture marks, the ragged wounds."

"He was using the same knife back then?"

"Yeah. It's called a Kris. Your people would have found one in the warehouse. I don't think it's his only one."

Allen put the gun down on the coffee table and sat down next to me. "Anything else?"

"He's from LA originally. That was the other reason I knew it was him. His family was murdered back in the mid-nineties. The case was never closed. He used a plain old hunting knife for that one. He joined the army after that and found his way into our little club a few years later. By the time he was cut loose, he'd served his apprenticeship. That's when the killings started stateside."

"What was the first one?"

"Fort Bragg. The very first murder was a sergeant who'd pissed him off in basic training."

"Peterson, right?" Allen asked. "The name you gave us. That matches up. The feds identified a couple of cases earlier than that, which they thought could be connected, but Fort Bragg is the first one with the ragged wounds, on the body they did find. Maybe he was worried the sergeant could be traced back to him, so he killed the other guy to make it look more random."

I shook my head. "He couldn't be traced. He wasn't

worried about that. Crozier wants to kill, period. Peterson just gave him a place to start that was as good as any."

We sat in silence for a couple of minutes before another question occurred to me—one I'd been thinking about earlier. "Did you identify the second victim from last night? The one at the warehouse?"

Mazzucco had brought her up to speed back at the house. They'd ID'd the victim after her roommate had reported her missing and her car had been found parked near the warehouse. "Yeah. Erica Dane, she lived half a mile from the warehouse. She worked nearby, never made it home last night." Allen stopped and thought something over. "Three bodies out in the hills: Boden, Morrow, and Burnett. Two last night: Castillo in the alley and Dane in the warehouse. That makes five killings in this cycle."

"Five that we know of."

"Exactly. That's what I'm worried about. What if he's done with LA, Blake? You've read the report from the feds on the other ones. Hell, you probably knew most if it before they did. The average victim total in each area was usually five or six."

The thought had crossed my mind. If we were judging the Samaritan's behavior purely on his track record to date, it would be a concern: that he'd vanish once again, only to pop up someplace else six months or a year from now, probably being cautious enough that no one would know it was him until he'd moved on again. But this wasn't like the other cases: there were a couple of key differences.

"He'll stay a while longer. He's not done yet."

"Is this your observer principle thing again?"

"Yes, it is. By observing his methods, the ways he operates, we've changed them. He might have stopped, moved on, but he's gone the other way. He's stepped up the intensity. And now you know about the other thing: his connection with me. His plan last night worked pretty well, on the face of it—he has everybody looking for me instead of anywhere that might lead to him. But that won't be enough for him, because he wanted me beaten and contained, and he didn't quite manage either. He won't leave until he resolves things between him and me. He knows I'm too dangerous to leave in the game. He's been operating with impunity up until now. If he walks away from LA, he'll be looking over his shoulder for me until I find him again. And I would find him again."

"You sound pretty sure of yourself."

"There's one other thing, too."

"What's that?"

"I think LA was different even before those bodies were discovered. I think he came back here for a reason. And I think the murders last night were meant to distract us from that."

# 68

Allen thought about it for a second. "This is about what you said earlier, right? About this Crozier guy being from LA originally. You think there's some kind of personal connection."

"I'm sure of it," I said. "Something—or someone—brought him back here after all this time." I saw a flicker in her eyes that told me she was matching what I was saying with some other information. She knew something I didn't. "What is it?"

She hesitated, and I thought she was going to hold it back,

whatever it was. But then she changed her mind, maybe coming to the same conclusion I had a few minutes before: that we could get further by sharing what we knew.

"We found the owner of the warehouse. His alibi checked out, but he told us he remembered a guy looking the place over a few months ago. First potential buyer in a long time, so it stuck out for him. We went to talk to the guy, but he hightailed it when he saw us. The house was a foreclosure, but someone had been living there. Someone who kept a spare torture kit and some high-tech tracking equipment."

I was quiet for a second. "The house ... was it in Santa Monica?"

Allen nodded slowly and told me the name of the street.

"That's where Crozier lived twenty years ago."

Allen puffed her cheeks out and blew out as she processed it. "So what did you mean about the distraction? Besides pinning everything on you, I mean."

"I started thinking about it after I left. The victim in the alley—Castillo—was the first victim since the bodies in the hills were found. It was the first victim he left intending it to be found."

"So he was conscious of being observed on this one."

"More than that. He has an urge to kill; that's a given. But I believe Castillo and Dane were more about sending us a message than satisfying a compulsion."

"Mazzucco said that, too; he was showing us he's not scared."

"Not just that, though," I said. "He made sure we'd know both of the murders were his. The MO with the abductions from vehicles, the ragged wound patterns. But last night I kept thinking about what was different, not what was the same."

"That's easy: the first three were buried, and the last two he barely even attempted to conceal."

"What else?"

"The first three were all held for a while and tortured before they were killed. He didn't have time to do that with Castillo. It was rushed."

"That's what we were meant to assume. But still, he took risks killing and dumping Castillo near so many people. Risks that he was careful to minimize when he dumped the first three bodies."

"By burying them up in the hills, where he knew he wouldn't be disturbed. But he wanted the two bodies last night discovered, remember? To send us a message, and to frame you, in the case of Dane."

"It's more than that. What's been missing from the first three murders all along?"

Allen paused for a second to think. "A primary crime scene."

"Exactly. The first three victims were all abducted in one place, tortured and killed in a second place, and dumped in a third. We've never seen the second place."

"I know where you're going on this, Blake. I took a course on geographical profiling at the academy. It looks like Boden and Morrow were both abducted on Mulholland Drive, Burnett on Laurel Canyon Boulevard. All three within a five-mile radius of the dump site. Odds are ..."

"That he killed them someplace close by."

"And that's why he made sure we found the last two victims miles across town: to distract us, like you said. When you look at it that way, it almost confirms it rather than hiding it." Allen stopped and rubbed the side of her head. "We were already working on the assumption that he's keeping a torture house within a few miles of the dump site. Only problem is narrowing it down."

"The place in Santa Monica would be close enough," I said.

She was shaking her head already. "It wasn't that house. It was clean. That's just where he's been holed up." She stopped, and I saw her shiver almost imperceptibly. "His ... workshop is someplace else."

I massaged my knuckles, the frustration welling up inside of me. "And that could be anywhere within easy reach of the dump site. Could be another house. Could just be a hidden, sheltered place in the mountains. There are lots of old trails up there. A shack or a cave, maybe."

Allen went to her bookcase and dug out a map of the Greater Los Angeles area that she'd bought when she moved in. It only reinforced the scale of our task. There were a dozen separate neighborhoods within the general area in which we were looking. Some of the main hiking routes were marked out as well, but I knew there would be countless unmarked trails as well. As my eyes traced the thin, winding lines that snaked through the hills, I thought about other mountainous trails I'd seen, in locations worlds away from this one, in Waziristan and Kashmir and Peru. The more I looked at the map, the more I became convinced that Crozier's bolt hole was somewhere in the hills. Somewhere it would be hard to find him, harder still to corner him. A place where he'd be in his element. I told Allen about my gut feeling and she groaned.

"Needle in a damn haystack, then. You ever been to LA before now?"

"Only once, and only for about a week."

"Great. Then we have less than a year's experience of this town between the two of us. Beyond what we've seen in ..." Allen trailed off before she could finish the thought.

"What is it?"

After a second of gathering her thoughts, she began to explain. She told me about the photograph she'd found in the Samaritan's safe house in Santa Monica and showed me the copy she'd made on her phone. I examined it. The reproduction was pretty good. It showed a boy and a girl standing in front of a store or a bar with some scrubland in the background. But I wasn't paying any attention to the background, not at first.

"That's him," I said quietly.

"Crozier? Are you sure?"

"Not a shred of doubt. He's younger here, but that's him. He was a killer when this was taken, even if he hadn't killed yet." As I uttered the words, a grim thought surfaced. "Allen—who's the girl? Have you identified her?"

She shrugged. "I hadn't even ID'd Crozier until you just told me. I thought they might be related. Could she be a family member?"

"I don't think so. He killed his parents and sister, but I've seen a picture of them. The sister had blond hair, green eyes. Not brunette with brown eyes like this one."

"Then who is she?"

"I don't know. But I think we should find out, because she—"

"She matches the profile on the first three," Allen finished. "We noticed that, too. You think maybe she was the first? That she's the reason he's picking women who look like that?"

I didn't say anything, but I thought Allen was probably on the right track. With an effort, I moved my focus from the two faces to the background of the photograph. The building and the landscape were fairly anonymous. Nothing stuck out to me. The partial read on the sign could be enough, if we were lucky. "It looks like it could be somewhere in the hills.

We can narrow this down. Check if there are any businesses called Steve's or anything else beginning with S-T-E in the vicinity. This is twenty years old, of course, but ..." I broke off as I saw Allen was shaking her head.

"I know this building, Blake."

"Then why didn't you—"

"I know it, but I don't know exactly where it is." Allen stopped and considered her words before continuing. "I remembered in the shower, was just coming to confirm it before you decided to scare the crap out of me. I've seen the building, but I've never been there."

Allen disappeared again and returned holding a colorful rectangular object. She tossed it to me and I caught it. It was a DVD case. Some obscure romantic comedy from the eighties that I'd never heard of. It starred one of the lesser members of the Brat Pack and an underwear model.

I looked back up at Allen. "Seriously?"

She nodded.

Allen put the DVD in the player and we hunched down in front of the television screen. She hadn't seen the movie in a few years, so she had to skip forward to find what she was looking for. About halfway into the picture, the visuals switched from a city setting to a more rural environment. The bickering hero and heroine, handcuffed together, were on the run from some drug dealers for some reason and had holed up in a small town. I recognized a lot of the establishing landscape shots even though I, like Allen, had never seen them with my own eyes. I recognized them because they had been well-used shooting locations for television and movies for the best part of a century. They'd built sets for westerns and thrillers and *Star Trek* episodes out there. And 1980s romantic comedies. Allen found the scene she wanted and froze the picture. The underwear model was in the middle

334

of an argument with the Brat Packer, her mouth open in suspended animation. In the background was the building from the photograph. The neon was illuminated here, and you could see the whole word: *Stewarton's*. Not a *V*, a *W*.

"A lot of times, they just abandon the sets once they're done. It's cheaper than tearing them down."

"Any idea where this exact one is, or was?" I asked.

She shook her head. "But we can find someone who will."

"Allen, this investigation has more holes in it than a sieve. If you bring in the rest of the department and the feds, it'll get back to the Samaritan. Maybe before we can get out there."

She smiled as though I'd made a joke.

"What is it?" I asked, confused.

"I couldn't bring them in even if I wanted to. I'm on suspension."

"That's on my account, I guess."

She nodded. "And now I'm compounding it by harboring a murder suspect." She must have seen something in my face, because she frowned then and said, "You looked into me, didn't you?"

I shrugged. "You checked me out, didn't you?"

She had no answer to that, so she asked another question. "How come you didn't ask me about the thing in DC?"

"Because it wasn't my business, and it has nothing to do with this case."

She looked at me for a long minute, and I thought she was going to talk more about it, but then she went back to the previous subject. "I wasn't talking about taking out an ad in the paper about this; I was talking about going to my partner."

"Mazzucco? Can you trust him to keep his mouth shut?"

"We don't have to worry about that."

# 69

Mazzucco had been at his desk for ten minutes and was in the process of pulling all of the information he could find on any and all Dean Croziers in LA City and County when his phone rang, displaying Allen's cell number. He picked up, eyes on the screen in front of him.

"I was just about to call you. Where are you?"

"I'm at my apartment," she said. There was something a little odd in her voice, an artificial brightness, maybe. Another person wouldn't have caught it, but that was the advantage of working with someone day and night for six months straight.

"Are you with someone?" Mazzucco asked.

There was a very short pause before Allen answered in the negative, but it was enough to confirm she was lying. She was with Blake. Mazzucco knew he wasn't the killer, but he also knew harboring him could end Allen's career. He put it out of his mind for the moment.

"Listen, Channing's people put a rush on the prints from the house. You're not gonna believe this."

"Try me."

"The prints came back flagged by Homeland Security— God knows what that's about. Anyway, they used the FBI golden ticket and got a hit. Only it came back saying the prints belong to a dead man."

There was a pause, and Allen's voice sounded a little strange again. Hesitant. "What was the name?"

"Crozier. Dean Crozier."

Allen said nothing. Mazzucco continued. "I'm checking him out right now. Guy was in the military, which fits the profile. Killed in action, in fact. But these were recent prints, Allen. They took a set off the fucking milk in the refrigerator. I mean—"

"What else do you have on him?"

"Well, get this. His family was killed in ninety-seven. Murdered. Crozier was the prime suspect, but he walked. No evidence."

"Son of a bitch," she said quietly.

"Allen, are you listening to me? The guy we're looking for's been dead for eleven years. Only somebody forgot to tell him that. What gives?" He remembered that Allen had called him and asked her if she had anything new on her end. He was expecting her to say she'd heard from Blake, but what she said took him by surprise.

"Actually, I do have something. A lead on the photograph."

It took him a second to remember. "The one from the house this morning?"

"Yeah. I know where it was taken, Jon."

He listened as she explained about recognizing the building from an old movie, about how she knew they sometimes left old sets standing out there in the mountains.

It sounded promising. "We're still looking for a primary crime scene within reach of the dump site," Mazzucco said thoughtfully. "Probably somewhere secluded and out of the way. That would fit."

"That's where he is, Jon. I know it."

"We need to go to Lawrence with this," he said before another thought occurred and he grunted with displeasure. "Shit, we probably have to bring Channing in on it, too."

"And tell him what? That we need to send a SWAT team down to some old derelict building because it reminds me of something I saw in a movie?"

"You have the photograph from Crozier's safe house."

"No, I don't. The FBI has it, remember? Because you and I did not jump the warrant and carry out an illegal search."

"Jesus ..."

"And besides, they still don't know who was in the house. They're still focused on Blake."

Mazzucco sighed with frustration. He couldn't argue that point, but again he felt himself getting sucked into Allen's favored course of action against his will. "So what's your alternative?"

"We check it out ourselves first. The only problem is, these places aren't on maps. They aren't real places at all. So I thought if you happened to know someone we could ask ..."

"I can do better than that," Mazzucco said, not without reluctance. "I might be able to talk to somebody. Somebody who would know where to look."

"Sounds like a plan, partner."

"Don't push it, *partner*. As soon as I get anything like confirmation our boy has been hiding out up there, I bring everybody else in. We can work out what our excuse for being there was later."

"You're the boss."

Mazzucco snorted at that and told Allen he'd call her back. He scrolled through the numbers in his phone, looking for a man he'd known back when he worked in West LA. Darrick Bromley had been a twenty-five-year veteran with the department and had taken on a lucrative consultancy gig in his retirement: providing advice to movies and TV shows. He dialed Bromley's cell and spent a minute or so on pleasantries before getting down to business. He described what he was looking for, the rough area where he thought it might be and the name of the movie Allen had mentioned.

"You know, there are a lot of these old sets out there, Jon," Bromley said after a long pause.

"I understand," Mazzucco said, his heart sinking. Plan B was to start looking at satellite images and checking off potential locations one by one. But then Bromley laughed.

"Sorry, I couldn't resist. Yeah, I know the one you're talking about. I've been there, in fact. It was still around as of a couple of years back. It's not far from a hiking trail." He thought for a minute. "You know where the old missile sites are?"

Mazzucco was confused for a second before realizing that Bromley was talking about the decommissioned cold war–era missile defenses that circled LA. "I know some of them. There's one up there at San Vicente Mountain, right?"

"That's the one. You go all the way to the end of Mulholland and bam, you're there."

Mazzucco felt a jolt of electricity. Mulholland. Allen was right: this was it. Bromley gave him rough directions from the decommissioned missile site to the old set, and Mazzucco told him he owed him a beer and hung up. Two minutes later, he'd zeroed the position using the satellite view on Google Maps. It was a couple of miles from the missile site. Straight along one of the fire roads and then down a half-mile of dirt trail. Within easy reach of both Mulholland Drive and, by using an off-road vehicle, the dump site.

He picked up the phone and tapped on Allen's number in recent calls. In the pause while he waited for the line to connect and the dial tone to kick in, he thought about the hesitation in Allen's voice when he asked if she was alone.

# 70

While Allen got ready to leave, I taped up my injured ankle with a bandage from her first aid box. It helped quite a bit, made it so it didn't hurt so much to put weight on it. After that, I made a pot of coffee, all the while thinking more and more about the two teenagers in Allen's photograph. Crozier and someone else. I thought she represented something important we'd all missed. Mazzucco called back less than ten minutes after Allen had hung up on her call to him. I was impressed. She wrote some notes down and gave him her personal email address so he could send a link over.

"That has to be it," she said firmly. I could hear the excitement in her voice. I knew that exact feeling intimately: the feeling when a promising lead opens up and you can feel the solution getting closer. "Yeah, I can find it. I'll see you there soon."

She hung up and turned to me. "This is it, Blake. It's in exactly the right place." Without waiting for an answer, she moved over to the computer and, a minute later, we were looking at a perfect satellite view of a dusty plateau surrounded by ridges and with three groups of buildings. She was right. This had to be it.

"When do we leave?" I asked.

She was shaking her head before I'd finished the sentence. "Forget it. *We* don't."

"What do you mean?"

The remote for the TV was on the coffee table and within reach. By way of an answer, she picked it up and turned on the television. Rolling news again, only now the ticker was sliding past under a very familiar face. They'd used the picture from my driver's license. Words like *dangerous* and *wanted* and *manhunt* jumped out at me from the scrolling red-on-white type.

"You're an extremely wanted man, Blake. I don't know how you made it this long without being caught, but you're staying here until we get this guy."

I opened my mouth to protest, but then I remembered there was something I could go to work on right here and backed off. "You'll call me if you need me?"

She hesitated. "Sure."

Before she left, I asked her to text me her phone picture of the photograph from the Samaritan's house. I took a look at the pair of teenagers in the picture, focusing on the girl this time.

I had a hunch the girl in the photograph might still be alive. And I had to find her before that changed.

# 71

The Samaritan didn't mind waiting.

He'd located his target's car first and then found himself a position equidistant between it and the door to the stairwell, one that was situated in one of the blind spots of the two CCTV cameras in the underground lot.

Over the last two decades, he'd become very accustomed to long periods of waiting followed by short, sudden bursts of action. Not only could he endure long waits without irritation, but he had grown to look forward to them as periods of reflection. He used them to reminisce over past exploits, to analyze every aspect of a recent kill. To identify mistakes and missed opportunities.

The past few days had seen too many of both. The bodies of the three women being discovered had been unfortunate, but the involvement of the police hadn't unduly concerned him. It had happened several times before: in Fort Bragg, in St. Louis, in Kansas City. The authorities hadn't gotten close to him any of those times, although in KC they had forced the decision to cease his activities and move on. The problem here was a little more complex. For one, the LAPD was larger, better resourced, and more experienced at looking for people like him than any other police department in the country. And this was before the involvement of the FBI was taken into consideration. The Samaritan had never faced pursuers so blessed with resources and manpower before now. He wasn't sure exactly how the connection had been made with his previous work, but it hadn't truly surprised him. It had always been inevitable that someone would start to uncover the others, sooner or later.

The involvement of the man who now called himself Carter Blake had been by far the most dangerous development. Blake had already caused him real problems, and would certainly cause him more, assuming he managed to continue to elude the police. He hadn't been surprised in the least that Blake had managed to escape his little trap, but the primary objective of shifting the focus of suspicion to Blake had been accomplished. It had been the only logical course of action, turning Blake's greatest advantage—the similarities between the two men—into a liability for him.

But the necessity for quick action had caused him to make his first unforced error, unwittingly sacrificing the house in Santa Monica. He assumed the cops had located it through his viewing of the warehouse. He'd considered several similar properties upon returning to the city, but that one had been the best prospect for his purposes until he'd decided on a more suitable base. It was only after he'd set things in motion with Blake that he remembered he'd used the landline to make the appointment with the warehouse owner. He'd thought it unlikely that the owner kept much of a filing system, but it seemed he had been mistaken.

Had this been any other time and place, Blake's involvement alone would have been enough to make him cut his losses and leave. But he couldn't do that, not just yet.

He'd been careful to keep his eyes on the door to the stairwell as he thought things over, and he brought his full attention back to the here and now as he heard the sound of a woman's shoes clacking on the concrete stairway behind the door. He settled back into the shadows as the door opened and Detective Allen appeared from within. She was putting her phone back inside her jacket, evidently having just completed a call. She let the door swing shut behind her and started walking across the basement parking lot to where her car was parked. The Samaritan watched her, being careful not to move. She looked preoccupied, in a hurry. He saw the slight raise in her jacket on the left side and knew she was carrying. He glanced at her pant legs and saw undisturbed lines on both—she wasn't carrying a backup piece strapped to either calf. As she passed within ten feet of him, he stepped forward and said her name.

Allen stopped with a jerk and her eyes darted to his face. Her expression relaxed a moment later.

"What are you doing here?"

The Samaritan widened his lips in an approximation of a smile. It always felt strange, unnatural. "I was worried about you."

"Worried? About me?" Suspicion in her voice. He wasn't surprised by that.

He nodded, changing his expression to adopt a serious, earnest look. "That's right. It's this Blake guy. It's all over the news now. I started to think he might come after you."

Allen nodded, as though thinking this over. "Okay. Thanks, I guess. I'm fine, though. Blake probably left town already."

He took a step forward. She began to back away, and he saw her eyes darting to the security of her car, only feet away. Did she suspect? Had he overplayed his hand?

"You're sure? You're really okay?"

"I'll catch up with you later," she said. "Gotta run."

He said nothing as she turned and hurried toward her parked car, unlocking it with the remote as she walked. The Samaritan's eyes made a quick surveillance of the deserted subterranean space as she retreated. If she did suspect, it would be better to take Allen out of the picture right now. It would be easy enough to close the distance between them as she stopped to open the door and get in. He could move very, very quietly. He'd be on top of her before she knew anything. He could touch the steel of his blade to the soft pink flesh of her throat and force her to climb into her own trunk. Or he could kill her right here and leave her to bleed out and be discovered by the next resident who drove in.

Allen reached the door and fumbled with the handle. She cast a glance back toward him and got in.

No. The Samaritan fought back the building urge. He closed his eyes and breathed in through his nose, out through his mouth. He'd already created problems by acting impulsively. An impromptu abduction or murder, without laying the groundwork first, would be foolish. Particularly when he knew he would be satisfying the urge soon enough.

344

He relaxed his body and simply watched as Allen started the car, pulled out of the space, and drove toward the exit ramp, out of harm's way. For the moment.

# 72

I sat on the couch and watched Allen's television for a little longer while I gathered my thoughts. I wasn't really paying much attention to what was being said, but I absorbed the important stuff. It was being emphasized that the FBI were searching for a man named Carter Blake who had been identified leaving the scene of an ongoing investigation in Inglewood. By the looks of things, they'd only just released the information that another body had been discovered in the warehouse and it was being tied to the ongoing Samaritan investigation. The FBI guy, Channing, had addressed the press and refused to be drawn when asked directly if he could confirm the man they were currently hunting was the Samaritan.

"I can say he's a person of interest, ladies and gentlemen. You'll draw your own conclusions."

Wonderful. The more I saw of Channing, the less I liked him. I got the feeling he was the type of guy who wouldn't worry too much about trifling concerns like guilt and inno- cence if it meant he could close a big case and bask in the glory. I knew they'd never be able to prove I'd committed any of the murders—because I hadn't—but I'd been around enough manhunts to know that the suspect sometimes doesn't live long enough to get to that point. Allen had been right: the safest place for me to stay was right here.

I shut off the TV and found Allen's computer at the other side of the living room. The girl in the photograph was important. Not because she looked like the three victims in the hills, but because they looked like her.

Staring at the picture, I knew that she was the reason those women had been chosen. From the start, I'd wondered what had brought Crozier back to his home turf after all this time. When his MO had shifted subtly from random murders to a far more consistent victim profile, I'd known on some level he was rehearsing, maybe building up to a specific person. The choice of Castillo and Dane as the latest victims—both of them diverging a little from that profile—had reinforced that suspicion the same way the locations of their deaths had told me he was trying to shift attention away from the dump site in the hills. The Samaritan was trying to distract my attention like a three-card monte sharp. Don't look there; look over here.

But the photograph gave the lie to that. The girl in the picture shared a mild likeness with Crozier. A cousin, perhaps, or a half sister. The clincher was the fact he'd kept it so long. It was important.

It hadn't occurred to me to check if Crozier had any other family in LA. The articles I'd been able to dig up had all reported that the entire family, minus him, had been killed.

Fifteen years ago, I could never have found what I was looking for in anything less than two days, probably involving a dozen phone calls and a trip to the Hall of Records. Now I could do better sitting in somebody's living room and tapping on a keyboard for a while.

Within five minutes, I'd mapped the key points in Crozier's life from birth to six months after the murders of his parents. None of that directly gave me what I needed, but it did tell me where he went to high school. Thirty seconds on the school's home page gave me the archived yearbooks for the last half century. I flicked through the relevant years, easily finding pictures of Crozier and his sister, Terri, each time. Then I went back and looked more closely, hoping for a break. In the ninety-six edition, I got it. The girl from the photograph. The hair was tied back, but the eyes and cheekbones and smile were all the same. There was a name—Kimberley Frank—and a quote: *Better to burn out than fade away.* The posed nihilism was at odds with the beaming picture. Given the date, I was betting the Neil Young reference came by way of Kurt Cobain's suicide note. It fit with the Nirvana T-shirt in Allen's picture.

Five minutes later, I had the connection. Kimberley Frank was Crozier's half sister on the paternal side. David Crozier had fathered her with another woman around eighteen months before his son was born. Her mother had died when she was two, and she'd spent the next twelve years in foster care before winding up in a group home called Blackstones. While there, she'd enrolled in Crozier's high school in 1996, and—I guessed—somehow they'd discovered their connection. A connection that meant that Kimberley Frank was the sole blood relation to have survived the family massacre in ninety-seven.

Five minutes after that, I had everything else I needed, including an address in Los Angeles. In Santa Monica.

The street running parallel to the one where Allen had found the safe house.

That final detail turned an urgent search into a critical one. I took my phone out and called Allen's number. It went to voicemail, and I left a short message without identifying myself.

"Allen. Regarding the picture, you might want to look up a Kimberley Frank. Quickly."

I gave the address, hung up, and considered my next move. Allen had been right about me lying low, I thought again. Without a doubt, the safest thing for me to do was to stay put.

Yeah, right.

I switched the computer off and walked through to the bathroom. I looked in the mirror to compare what I saw there against the driver's license photo I'd seen a few minutes before on the television screen.

The driver's license was the only identification I had. If I could get away with it, I wouldn't have even that. It was the bare minimum official documentation I had to have in order to move reasonably freely.

The guidelines for the photograph are pretty stringent, aimed at ensuring consistency for facial recognition software, but even so, you can manipulate those guidelines to make sure the resulting image is of as little use as possible. Ironically, the requirement to keep a neutral expression helps you to look a lot less like you. A smiling face is far more characteristic than the kind of blank, dead-eyed stare that I was only too happy to provide. I'd also prepared for the photograph by letting my hair grow a little longer than I usually keep it and cultivating a four-day growth of stubble. In contrast to my usual dress habit of a jacket and a shirt, I'd worn a faded black T-shirt under a hoodie. Throw into the mix the fact that I'd aged three years since registering the license, and I was already well on my way to looking like a different man than the one in the picture.

I found a box of disposable razors in the bathroom cabinet and some rose-scented shaving gel—the type that comes in a pink can and costs double what they charge for the men's version, despite it being exactly the same product. In another couple of minutes I was clean shaven and had brushed my hair back neatly. At worst, I looked like the accountant big brother of the guy in the driver's license photo. You'd have to look close to see even that resemblance, I hoped.

I thought about leaving the way I'd come in, through the parking area beneath the building, where I could borrow one of the parked cars. Reluctantly, I decided against it. On balance, stealing a car was more risky than taking a cab. I put my sunglasses on and took the elevator down to the ground floor, where I left by the street entrance. I started walking. Just being a pedestrian in LA made me stick out, and I started to feel more and more exposed. I wondered if it wouldn't have been better to risk stealing the car. A red Ford passed by me a little too slowly and I had the sense of the driver glancing at me. I hoped it was idle curiosity rather than recognition.

A minute later, a taxi appeared with its hire light on. Gratefully, I stuck a hand out and got in the back. I gave the cabbie the directions and hunched down in the seat, watching the deserted sidewalks as we crawled through the late-afternoon traffic.

# 73

The 101 was moving relatively smoothly for a change, and it was a few minutes before the traffic bunched up and Allen had the time to glance at the screen and see the missed call from Blake. She dialed into her voicemail, listened to the short message, and hung up. She thought about the weird encounter in the parking garage a few minutes before. If she hadn't been so worried about someone finding Blake in her apartment, she'd have been more forthright, told her concerned visitor not to hang around her place like that. Putting the incident out of her mind, she dialed Mazzucco's desk number again, hoping she'd catch him before he left.

It rang five times, and Allen was about to give up when the call was answered. But the voice was not Mazzucco's. It belonged to one of the last people Allen wanted to hear from: Joe Coleman, the squad-room comedian.

"Allen," he said, and she could hear the smirk in his voice. "I heard you'd been a bad girl."

"I don't have time for this shit, Coleman. Do you want to help me out, or do you want to hang the fuck up and forget I called?"

There was a pause, and then he spoke again, sounding chastened but curious. "What do you need?"

Allen talked quickly, told him to access the DMV record for a Kimberley Frank of Santa Monica and to email the details through to her. She hung up without waiting for a response, immediately wondering if she'd made a mistake by trusting Coleman even this far. But then a minute or two later, her phone pinged for a new email. She tapped into her emails by touch, keeping her eyes on the road, and then glanced down at the screen.

The email contained a picture of an older but easily recognizable face. No question about it. It was her—the girl from the Samaritan's photograph. And then the picture vanished and Blake's number flashed up again.

"Allen?" There was echo and muted traffic noise in the background, like he was in a car.

"I'm here. I told you to stay in the apartment. You're too—"

"Forget about that right now. Did you check out Kimberley Frank?"

"Yeah, looks like the girl from the picture, all right. But

how do we know Crozier even has this woman on his radar? Okay, the photograph shows they've met, but so what?"

"She's his sister, Allen. His half sister."

That brought her up short. If Crozier had killed his family, it made sense he'd want to finish the job. "But if he did kill his family out of some kind of grudge, why not take care of her back then?"

"You're forgetting something. He was a first timer back then, most likely. He'd planned the murders, and he was smart enough to get away with them, but he was still in the frame. You kill your own family and there's no way to avoid that suspicion, no matter how smart you are. Even if he'd wanted to, he couldn't have killed the sister back then, not while the heat was on. Three months later, he'd joined the army. Maybe everything up until now was just working his way back to this point. He's come full circle."

As he spoke, Allen thought about the two pictures of Kimberley Frank, separated by more than a decade and a half but united by common details. Female, Caucasian, brunette. Appearance: twenties to early thirties. Just like Boden, Morrow, and Burnett.

"He's obsessed by her," she said, as much to herself as to Blake. "That's why the first three victims looked the way they did. He's killing her over and over again."

Blake started speaking again, but Allen told him she'd call him back and hung up. She'd received a new text message while on the phone to Blake. It was from Mazzucco: *Found the road. See you soon?*

Allen grimaced, weighing her options. The next exit was a mile away. She could drop off the 101 and backtrack toward Kimberley Frank's address, but it would take her at least twenty minutes. And Mazzucco was already well on his way to the abandoned set. She couldn't be in both places at once.

She picked the phone up again, intending to call Dispatch before remembering that she wasn't officially on the job right now. Instead she dialed Coleman's number again. She told him to call it in and arrange for whichever patrol car was closest to go to Kimberley Frank's house and bring her into protective custody. Then Allen changed her mind. She asked Coleman to tell the uniforms to hold Kimberley at the house until she arrived.

She slowed and took the exit. Mazzucco could handle himself for a little longer. Kimberley Frank had just become the priority.

# 74

The taxi had almost reached Kimberley Frank's address by the time I ended my conversation with Allen. I assumed she was arranging for a black-and-white to head straight here, so I knew I would have to move fast. I raised my voice and asked the cabbie to slow down, so we were coasting at fifteen miles an hour as we passed the house. I wanted to give the place the once-over before getting closer.

No cars parked directly outside, no one in the front yard. I told the driver to let me out three doors up and handed over the fare, telling him to keep the change. He was a young, Middle Eastern guy in his early twenties who smiled and then looked more closely at me as he took the bills.

"Are you famous or something? You look kind of familiar."

I pushed the sunglasses higher up on the bridge of my nose. "You got me. *American Idol*, a couple of years back."

He looked doubtful at first but then smiled again. "That must be it. Hey, is Simon Cowell really—"

"Worse," I said and made a hasty retreat out of the backseat. I slapped the side of the cab and waited for it to vanish around the next corner before I headed back along the street to Kimberley Frank's house.

As soon as I got within twenty feet of the front door, I felt a dull ache in the pit of my stomach. It was ajar. People didn't deliberately leave their doors ajar in Los Angeles, even in a relatively safe neighborhood like this one. I got close, my senses attuned for noises and flashes of motion, and nudged the door open with my shoulder, being careful not to touch anything. It swung open with a creak and unveiled what looked like the aftermath of a violent struggle: furniture upended, a broken vase, a phone lying on the ground, its cable ripped out of the wall, a shattered cell phone on the ground not far from it. There was no sound from within.

I was about to step over the threshold to make sure when I heard the sound of a police siren approaching fast. I backed away from the door and glanced around me. There was a path around the side of the house bordered by a low fence separating this lot from the next. I ducked down the side, vaulted the fence, and made my way into the neighboring backyard. Thankfully, it was empty. There was an old six-foot-high corrugated iron fence at the back. I scrambled up and over, into a narrow access road that ran between this street and the next one over. My feet landed on the opposite side just as I heard the police car come to rest outside the Frank house.

I ran down the access road to where it came out on the street. I needed a car, fast. My eyes scanned the street for a good prospect. It was a reasonably affluent area, so there was no shortage of new and nearly new vehicles parked curbside.

But that was the problem: newer cars had newer security features. They were a little more difficult to break into—a lot more difficult to hotwire. I needed something old. And then I saw it. A couple hundred yards from me, diagonally across the street. Not old—*vintage*. A 1973 Chevrolet Camaro Z28. Red with twin vertical black stripes down the hood. Under normal circumstances, way too nice a car for me to consider stealing. But I was in a hurry, and these were not normal circumstances.

The Samaritan had taken his last victim, and there was only one place on earth he could be going.


# 75


The location of the abandoned town set wasn't on any GPS, of course, because it wasn't a real place. Nevertheless, by using Darrick Bromley's directions together with Google's satellite imaging, as well as a good old-fashioned map, Mazzucco had been able to plan out the route with a fair degree of accuracy. He'd even found pictures of the abandoned set on one of those Hidden LA websites, so he knew what it would look like on the ground. He had an LA road map in the car, the book open to the page he needed on the passenger seat.

The first part of the journey was straightforward: along the entire length of Mulholland, past the last clutch of houses, and on to where the road entered the San Vicente Mountain Park. Mazzucco took a left turn onto the West Mandeville Fire Road, which took him past the LA-96 Nike Missile site. He followed the curving road for about a mile, looking for the next turn on the left. When he found it, it took him onto a narrow road that led upward. He slowed down and hit the trip meter under the odometer as he took the turn. There would be no signposts for the next part of the journey: all he had to go on were Bromley's directions and the photographs from the website. By cross-referencing with the satellite images, he had worked out that the dirt track leading to his destination was situated at approximately two and a half miles along the length of this road.

As the trip meter clocked up toward 2.5 in tenth-of-a-mile increments, Mazzucco began to slow down, watching the right-hand side of the road for evidence of pathways. At 2.6, he saw it. A tight dirt track, unsurfaced and almost obscured by bushes. If Mazzucco hadn't been going so slowly and hadn't been on the lookout for exactly this, he'd have passed right by and been none the wiser.

He stopped the car and got out, examining the concealed entrance. There were multiple tire tracks, crisscrossing one another and traveling in both directions. The tracks looked reasonably fresh. Fresh enough to tell him somebody had used this road since the rain on Saturday night, anyway.

He took his phone out and sent a text message to Allen. If she was coming straight from her apartment, she'd be here within another twenty minutes. The problem he had with waiting here for her was the same as the problem he'd had with waiting for the warrant: there could be somebody up there who needed his help now, not in twenty minutes' time.

His phone buzzed in his hand, and he tapped to open the message, expecting it to be Allen. Instead it was his wife, asking, *ETA for dinner? X*

Mazzucco felt a twinge of guilt. He'd barely thought about Julia or Daisy all day. Quickly, he tapped out a reply, telling her not to wait for him. If Allen was right about the old set, they might be able to shut the Samaritan down today.

Maybe then things would cool off a little and he could start getting home on time for a change. Maybe.

He considered getting back in the car and driving onward along the track but decided against it after a moment's thought. If he'd calculated right, the set was less than half a mile along the track. He could cover that on foot in a few minutes. That way, he wouldn't risk alerting anyone who happened to be up there with the noise of the engine.

He'd give the place a quick once-over and wait for Allen if it looked like he'd need the backup. Mazzucco took a second to check his gun, locked the car, and started walking up the rutted dirt road into the wilderness.

# 76

Allen was on Santa Monica Boulevard, about a mile from Kimberley Frank's house, when her phone rang again. There was evidently some kind of holdup up ahead, because traffic had come to a dead stop instead of its usual jerking progress. As she checked the display and saw it was Blake again, she heard faint ambulance sirens behind her. Probably some kind of accident up ahead, then. She hoped it hadn't prevented the black-and-white from getting to Kimberley Frank's place. And then Blake's first words to her made that academic.

"He's got her already."

"What?"

"I was just at Kimberley Frank's place. She's gone, and it looks like she didn't go quietly. We need to get out to the mountains. I'm on my way there right now."

"In whose car?" Allen asked, then quickly interrupted his

answer. "I don't want to know. Okay, Mazzucco's out there now. We can catch up with him. I was on my way down to Frank's house ..."

As Allen spoke, the ambulance passed by her in the other lane. When the blare of the siren dropped away again, she thought she could hear others approaching, too.

"Where will I meet you?" she said when she could hear the sound of her own voice again.

"Remember the old missile site we saw on the map?" Blake said after a second.

"Sure. Make it twenty minutes."

She hit the button on the dash to activate the light and siren and pulled out of the line of traffic, making a U-turn and putting her foot down.

# 77

Captain Don McCall was parked in the Universal City Overlook. He knew Allen was headed for the address in Santa Monica, but he was playing the odds by staying around Mulholland. He wasn't really interested in Allen anyway, only Blake. Channing's suspicion that Allen was still in contact with the fugitive had been dead-on, and his instinct that McCall was the best person to find out more had been similarly well founded. It was just a pity from Channing's point of view that he'd never see the benefit. McCall's cell rang again, displaying Rooker's personal number. Both of the men he'd trusted enough to let in on this surveillance had been warned to keep things strictly off the grid. He picked it up and held it to his ear, not saying anything.

"Captain? We got another call on the subject's phone. She's not headed to the address in Santa Monica anymore. It looks like she's setting up a meet this time."

McCall smiled. "Same voice on the phone?"

"Same unidentified male. They're both headed out to the mountains."

"Where's the rendezvous?"

"Unconfirmed. They said something about a missile site, which I think could be ..."

"I know where they're going."

"Do you want me to ... ?"

"Negative on that," McCall said quickly. "I'm going to observe the meet personally. I want to tail them and see where they're headed after this. If I need backup, I'll call you."

There was a pause. "Captain ..."

"Did I ask you for an opinion?"

"Understood, sir."

McCall hung up and switched his phone off. In the time he'd been sitting here, the sun had begun to set, so he removed his dark glasses and started the engine. He had a head start on both Blake and Allen, but he wanted to be prepared.

# 78

The light was ebbing out of the sky as Mazzucco approached the crest of the hill, keeping low. Beyond the crest, the ground fell away into a flat hollow that extended half an acre to the north. The set was built on this plain.

Once upon a time, it must have been quite something to look at. There were three main clusters of buildings. The nearest, and largest, was a mock-up of a main street. Most of the storefronts were just facades, and some of them had collapsed over the decades. A couple of them, however, had been built all the way back and had roofs. Mazzucco guessed those had doubled as interior sets, too. At the far end of the street was the bar from the photograph Allen had found: Stewarton's. It was one of the facades, nothing behind the surface. Mazzucco heard a low creaking sound and took a couple of seconds to find the source: a wooden sign hanging by a single chain from one of the fake buildings, swaying slowly back and forth in the breeze.

Despite the sad state of the forgotten make-believe town, Mazzucco found himself strangely impressed by the craftsmanship, the attention to detail. He realized it was because they didn't do this sort of thing anymore. These days, the filmmakers would pick a real-life town that was close enough to what they wanted, and some computer nerd would CGI the rest.

A little way off to the side of the main street was a barn. The paint on the sides had probably once been a vivid red but had long since flaked and peeled and faded to a brown the color of dried blood. The corrugated sheet metal on the roof had buckled and fallen in on itself, never designed to last. The other building was on the opposite side from the barn, out past the end of the main street.

It was a house. Mazzucco had never seen the movie Allen had spoken of, but based on the size of the house, he assumed it must have played a central role. It was one of the finished buildings. From a distance, it looked just like a real dwelling. It seemed to have weathered the years better than the rest of the town. It was a wide structure topped out by a gently sloping roof with a dormer window in the center. Along the front was a long porch. Once Mazzucco's eyes had been drawn to the house, he held his position for a minute or two, watching it for signs of . . . what, exactly? There was no movement around the building, but straining his eyes to look at the patch of dirt track along the front, Mazzucco thought he could make out depressions in the soft ground. A vehicle had been parked there recently.

He'd switched his phone to silent on the way up the track. If the Samaritan was here, the last thing he wanted was a ringing phone giving him away. He examined it now and found a text message from Allen. She'd been delayed but was on her way again. The last sentence of the message read: *Bringing a friend along.*

Mazzucco knew exactly what that meant, but standing on the edge of the abandoned set, he couldn't honestly say that he was sorry Blake would be joining them: when it came to a situation like this, three was definitely better than two. Or one. But it didn't change the fact that he needed to confirm whether there was someone being held in the barn or the house.

He rose to his feet and started to descend the road that led down into the set. After a moment's consideration, he opted not to walk down the main street. Too many windows, even if what lay behind most of them was an inch of plywood. Instead, he walked along the strip of ground between the back of one side of the street and the barn. As he drew level with the barn door, he noticed more tracks on the dirt outside. He stopped and glanced around him. The air was still. From this side, the row of stores manifested as a blank wall buttressed by long beams of wood. He turned his attention back to the barn. Though the wood siding was rotted and holed in places, the double doors were firmly closed.

Mazzucco approached them quickly and looked closer. They weren't shut tight. One of the doors was warped, as though it had once been locked or barred but had been prized open. There was a gap between the two more than big enough to get his hand into. He did, and pulled the door. It swung open, the bottom edge scraping off the dirt floor. Mazzucco raised his gun, covering the opening.

It was dark inside. There were no windows, and what light there was came from the section where the ceiling had collapsed. The space was about fifty feet square and was mostly empty but for some rotted hay bales stacked at one end. Mazzucco assumed they'd been just for show and had been abandoned at the end of the shoot like everything else. Likewise, he thought the lack of natural lighting was a deliberate choice by those long-ago set designers. As Mazzucco's eyes gradually adjusted to the dimness, he saw that there were two vehicles inside, parked over on the opposite side from where the remains of the daylight came in via the hole in the ceiling. They looked alien in their surroundings, because they were both relatively clean and relatively new. The nearest vehicle was familiar: the green Dodge they'd seen a few hours before.

The other one was a pickup truck, also green in color, though a darker shade. A California license plate. As Mazzucco approached it, he saw that there was a towing rig with a rolled cable at the rear. Perfect for offering a helping hand to a stranded driver. This had to be it: the Samaritan's truck.

Mazzucco kept his gun trained on the windows of the pickup as he got within a couple feet of it. He couldn't see any sign of anyone inside, but that didn't mean there was no one there. As his hand reached out for the handle, he froze as he saw what was on the front seat. A digital SLR camera and a canvas shoulder bag. He stood there for a second, wondering what it was that struck him about the equipment, and then it came to him along with a dull, sick feeling in his gut.

He reached his left hand into his jacket and pulled out the sketch he'd taken from Blake the other day. The two versions of a face he'd penciled on the back of a menu. Something about the face had seemed familiar. It was why he'd held on to it. He straightened out the piece of paper with one hand, and all of a sudden, the haze cleared and he realized who it was in the picture. It wasn't an exact likeness. In fact, it looked like the halfway point between the kid in the photograph and someone else. Someone close to home. It seemed glaringly obvious now.

He was about to reach for his phone to call Allen when he heard the noise.

He stopped and listened. There it was again: a muffled banging sound, as though somebody was kicking something. Somebody trying to attract attention. The sound wasn't coming from inside the barn, but from outside. He couldn't be sure, but it didn't sound close enough to be emanating from anywhere on the main street.

Mazzucco turned around and ran back toward the door. The last of the evening sun outside made the dark space on either side of the door even darker. He was two steps away from the threshold when a piece of the darkness on the left side came to life and slammed into him, right across the bridge of the nose.

Mazzucco rocked back on his heels and another blow slammed down on the back of his neck while powerful fingers like steel cable twisted the gun from his grasp. He was twisted around and he felt his knees give way. He dropped to the ground and saw his own shadow and that of someone else cast in the rectangle of light from the door. He started to turn around, and an arm clamped around his upper body. He reached up with both hands to wrestle himself out of the grip when he realized there was a more pressing problem. Specifically, the touch of sharp steel against his bared throat. Mazzucco froze and relaxed his arms.

"I'm a cop," he said quietly.

"I know," a voice whispered, as though there were anyone to overhear.

And then there was a jerking motion and a sound like a hose being cut. Mazzucco flashed on Julia back at home, eating dinner alone. Daisy. The last thing he heard was the whisper.

"You shouldn't have come here."

# 79

Allen had just glanced at the speedometer as she came out of another curve on Mulholland Drive, so she knew she was doing at least fifty when the back tire blew out. As the car lurched toward the side of the road, her eyes widened and her hands whitened around the wheel as she tried desperately to persuade the two-ton hunk of steel to remain on what now seemed a hopelessly narrow strip of asphalt. She tried to yank the wheel left, succeeded only in sending the car into a skid. An oncoming vehicle swerved as she swung out into the opposite lane, missing her by inches. The car pulled out of the skid but now she was lurching toward the edge again.

The Ford slipped and slewed toward the crash barrier at the edge of the drop, and she knew she was about to cut through it like a sledgehammer through balsa wood.

And then the three remaining tires caught some traction

on the surface and obeyed the steering wheel at last, altering the car's suicidal trajectory so that it smashed into the barrier at an angle of forty-five degrees—closer to side-on than straight. Allen felt the metal of the barrier buckle as she rammed into it, but it held. The car screeched along its side against the barrier, a fountain of white-hot sparks erupting against the windows.

Allen's eyes widened still further as she saw that the barrier came to an end not too far ahead. She yanked the wheel to the left again, but the car stayed its course, its wheels seemingly locked into position.

And then the landscape outside began to slow just in time. The screeching lowered in pitch and the geyser of sparks dwindled as the barrier ran out, and then the view out of the windshield came to rest at an odd angle, as though somebody had tipped the world a little onto its side.

Allen blinked a few times until she realized it was the car that was at a strange angle, not the world. The red setting sun glared into her eyes. The engine was still running, although coughing intermittently. She reached for the keys in the ignition to turn the engine off and the car shifted again, tipping still farther to an angle.

Allen froze and held her breath. She swiveled her eyes to the side as far as they would go, not daring to move her head and risk another lurching motion.

The car was precariously balanced on the edge of the steep slope; the wheels on the driver's side actually off the ground. The crash barrier had only covered the tight curve of the road, tapering out as the road straightened. It had been just long enough to prevent her from skidding off the edge, but now she was one wrong move away from the car toppling sideways off the edge anyway.

Slowly, ever so slowly, she reached down and used the

ball of her thumb to eject her seat belt. She issued an involuntary cry as the belt released and her body listed slightly to the side and something creaked on the precipice-facing side of the car.

She closed her eyes for a second and told herself to calm the hell down. Panicking and rushing was absolutely not the way to get herself out of this situation in one piece. She opened her eyes again. Slowly and deliberately, she turned her head from the drop and focused on the door handle. Just as slowly and just as deliberately, she raised her hand and moved it until it was resting on the door handle. So far, so good. She started to push the handle to the point where it would release the door, trying to do it softly, with two fingers. Soon she realized the mechanism was too stiff for such gentle treatment. She put four fingers against the handle and pushed a little harder. A muffled squeal sang out from somewhere off to her side.

She gritted her teeth and pushed harder, feeling the handle move back even as the car started to tip in the opposite direction. The mechanism opened with a pop and she continued the forward motion without pause. As the door began to swing up and open, fighting gravity, she felt the equal and opposite reaction of the car beginning to shift over onto its left side, rocking across the fulcrum. She was aware of the wheels lifting farther off of the ground and was surprised to find herself noting with a detached clarity that the tilt had passed the point of no return.

Warped metal screamed as she continued pushing the door open. She braced her foot on the dash and pushed her body forward, out of the door. Her arms and the side of her head slammed off the asphalt as the car rolled away from her, ripping the skin on her legs, the mouth of the doorway trying to drag her down with it like a great white shark devouring its prey. She clawed her hands on the road and tried to dig her fingertips into the surface as the motion of the toppling car gained an inexorable momentum and began to flip up and over. She screamed out as her foot caught on something and she felt herself being pulled backward.

And then her foot slipped out of the shoe and the car fell away in a torrent of noise and breaking glass.

Allen lay facedown on the road, eyes closed, until the smashing and crunching had stopped. She opened her eyes and slowly got to her feet, wincing as she realized her left foot had been sprained as her shoe had been torn off. She hobbled to the edge, looked down the slope, and saw the decimated remains of the Ford a hundred feet below. Suddenly, the pain in her foot became insignificant. Allen limped to the opposite side of the road—the safe side—and puked. She shuffled to the side a little and then sat down feeling marginally better.

It took her a couple of minutes to collect herself and to take stock of her options. She'd narrowly avoided certain death, but there was still a job to be done. The only problem was, how was she going to do it? She still had her gun, but her phone had been lying on the passenger side of the Ford. Even if she was in any shape to make a descent down the slope, the phone would probably be in several pieces right now. No way to call Blake or Mazzucco. No way to cover the remaining miles to the Samaritan's lair on foot, not with her ankle in this shape. It was getting darker, the setting sun almost gone in the west.

She heard the vehicle before she saw it. The low growl of a diesel engine. A cautious driver taking it slowly on the curves. And then it appeared up ahead. A green pickup truck, a lone driver. Headlights on. Allen stared at the oncoming vehicle for a long moment and then placed her good foot on the road and started waving him down. The pickup angled itself out toward the center of the road and Allen thought he was going to blow by without slowing, but then the driver eased off the gas when he got within thirty yards of her. The pickup passed by her, slowing down. She saw a male driver wearing sunglasses. The pickup's brake lights blazed again, and it came to a full stop at a wide point in the road. After a second, the driver's door opened and a man got out.

Allen squinted her eyes to confirm what she was seeing. Mazzucco's words from Sunday came back to her: *Fucking new mutation.*

The man took a couple of steps forward, a puzzled look on his face, and then he began to smile. "Allen?" Eddie Smith called out, the tone of his voice suggesting that he didn't believe it either. He began to stride toward her. "What are you—" He stopped as he saw that she was limping, and then he registered her bloodied and scratched arms and the fact she had only one shoe. "Jesus! Are you okay? What happened?"

Allen took a moment to breathe and collect her thoughts. She nodded her head in the direction of the destroyed Ford at the bottom of the slope. "Car trouble."

Smith crossed the road toward the drop and looked down. He looked back at Allen, then back down at the drop, then back at her.

"*Shit,*" he exclaimed. He turned and walked back toward her, offering his hand for her to lean on. "Come on. You need some help."

She was shaking as she looked up at him. He was wearing a green baseball cap. The brim cast a shadow over his face in the twilight.

"Yeah, I think I really do."

# 80

The Samaritan had a head start on me, and there was no way to know how big of a head start. All I knew was that he had Kimberley Frank, and she was going to die if I didn't stop him. I was pinning everything on Crozier heading back to his hideout in the mountains. Allen had said that she and Mazzucco had narrowed down the location of the abandoned set in the photograph and had given me rough directions, but I was glad we'd arranged to meet en route.

Not for the first time, I worried that the abandoned set was a red herring. Basic geographical profiling dictated that his hideout would be in that vicinity—the relative proximity of the burial site of the original three victims made that likely. But that didn't mean the Samaritan had definitely picked that specific location.

Nevertheless, it was all we had to go on, because of the photograph. Crozier had held on to that one photograph across two decades and God knows how many conflict zones. That told me the site would have significance for him. The photograph looked like it had been taken on a carefree teenage jaunt into the mountains—a hike, or a mountain biking expedition, perhaps. They'd found a forgotten piece of Hollywood and spent some time there.

It didn't take much more of a leap of logic to arrive at the fact that the photograph itself was talismanic. He'd kept the image close to him all these years, probably memorized every color and line and detail. The place in the hills would have remained in his mind all this time. The location made practical sense, too: it was a remote, forgotten place that provided shelter and privacy for the dark work he was planning. I didn't think anyone alive really knew Dean Crozier, not anymore, but the time I'd spent with him in Winterlong probably gave me as good an insight into his psyche as anyone. That was how I knew the movie set was where he was headed.

I kept within five miles an hour of the speed limit as I traveled along Mulholland once again, the pinpricks of light beginning to appear in the vast carpet of the city as the sun sank ahead of me toward the western horizon, streaking the sky with swathes of purple. Someone once said LA is the most beautiful city in the world, if viewed at night and from a distance. I thought that was about right. The movie star dream palaces began to get fewer and farther between as I put more and more miles between myself and LA, until the road opened up and I felt I had really left the city behind.

I thought about the origin of the Samaritan's name. The parable of the Good Samaritan told of the road from Jerusalem to Jericho; a route so fraught with danger from bandits that it was known as the Way of Blood. It was there that the Good Samaritan had saved the stricken traveler. This time, the Samaritan had created his own way of blood. I let my foot down harder on the gas pedal as I guided the car through the twists and turns.

A couple of oncoming cars passed me, and at one point I passed a green pickup truck that had stopped by the roadside. I could see two people inside. I didn't think to look closely at them. Later on, I would wonder how things would have gone had I taken more of an interest in the green pickup.

I kept my eyes peeled for the landmark Allen had talked about, and soon it came into view: a mushroom-shaped structure built into the hillside by the road, about thirty feet tall. Like our intended destination, it was an abandoned relic of the past; one of sixteen air defense locations set up around the city during the cold war. The site was a cylindrical tower topped with a wide, overhanging platform. The approach off the main road led you through the remains of a checkpoint. The pillbox was still there, as were the stern warnings against unauthorized personnel. But there was no one manning the checkpoint, and there were no gates to enforce the signs. I pulled into the access road and followed it up a slope, past the tower to the parking lot at the top. Unauthorized personnel were encouraged these days—the more recent signs welcomed tourists and advised them to ascend to the platform to take in the stunning 360-degree views of the mountains and the Los Angeles Basin.

To my surprise, the lot was empty. I had expected Allen, with her head start, to be here by now. It had been her idea to meet up before going any further, and I had concurred. I was all too aware of whom we were going up against, and I wanted as much backup as was available.

I pulled into one of the parking spots and left the engine running. I took my phone out and dialed Allen's number again. No answer. Not a good sign. I cast my eyes back toward the main road, looking for approaching vehicles, but saw nothing. I couldn't wait much longer—not while the Samaritan had a prisoner. A prisoner that I hoped was alive for now. It would probably take me longer to find the old movie set by myself, but it was better than twiddling my thumbs waiting for Allen to get here.

I sighed and put the parking brake on. I had a lot to think about, but it wasn't much of an excuse for not having any idea someone was approaching the car until I heard the voice.

"Get out of the car, Blake."

Slowly, I raised my hands. I turned my head to the left to look out the open window. There was a nine-millimeter Kimber Solo pistol pointed at me. I recognized the owner.

"McCall, right?"

The bulky cop was wearing a Kevlar vest over a black T-shirt and was doing a professional job of covering me with the pistol: two-handed grip, steady aim, not close enough for me to reach. He answered me by jerking his head, wordlessly repeating his initial command. I kept my eyes on the muzzle of the gun as I slowly reached down with one hand and opened the door. He took a half step back, anticipating that I might try to slam the door into his legs. I hadn't planned on doing anything of the sort, but it was interesting to note his precautions. I wondered how he'd found me, and for a brief moment considered the possibility that Allen had given me up. I dismissed that thought a nanosecond later. Leaving everything else aside, I got the impression she and McCall hated each other with a fierce purity. He'd be the last person on the planet she'd help out like this. At least, not intentionally.

"Keep 'em high. Step out of the car slowly and put your hands on your head."

I did as instructed. As I got out of the car, I risked taking my eyes off McCall and the gun long enough to glance around the lot. It was still empty. I could see no one on the road, no one on the observation platform above us. No backup, no marksmen.

"Where's the rest of the party?"

McCall smiled. "I'll call them soon. You don't need to worry about that."

I didn't like the sound of that. But as long as McCall seemed to be willing to converse with me, I thought it would be a good idea to keep that going.

"You know, I didn't kill the girl in the warehouse. I didn't kill anybody."

"Sure, Blake. You just happened to be there. Ray Falco says hi, by the way. He's the cop you sucker punched."

Looking at him, I knew McCall didn't give a shit whether I was the Samaritan or not. He didn't care because he knew the only thing he needed to know about me: that I'd punched out one of his guys and I'd gotten away from his team. Humiliated him in front of the feds. He had no intention of bringing me in. He was going to shoot me in cold blood and claim I'd resisted arrest. And there was nothing to stop him. He was a cop, I was a wanted fugitive, and the nearest witness was probably a mile away. If it turned out I really was the Samaritan, he'd be a hero. If I wasn't? No big deal. I was a regrettable victim of circumstance.

I considered my options. They were not numerous. So I asked him another question, partly to buy time and partly because I wanted the answer.

"How'd you find me?"

"You can thank your buddy Detective Allen. We call her the Fixer downtown. Did you know that?"

"I guess you have to call her something. Besides twice the cop you'll ever be."

McCall's eyes narrowed. Not the response he'd been expecting. "Don't you want to know how she gave you up?"

I shrugged. "I don't think she did."

"Think again."

"I think somebody hacked her phone. We set up this meet over our cells. Never a good decision if you can avoid it, but in this case we couldn't."

"You're a smart guy, Blake. You know what happens to smart guys?"

"Yeah. They use dumb guys to do their dirty work. Hacking Allen's phone in case she was in contact with me was an intelligent move. Too intelligent for you. Who's pulling your strings, McCall?" I already had a pretty good idea. Agent Channing—he'd suspected Allen was harboring

372

me and had used McCall to spy on her. He'd miscalculated, though, because McCall had no intention of including anyone else in this.

McCall tightened his grip on the gun and gritted his teeth. "You are so fucking dead. You know that? I'm gonna put a bullet in your fucking brain and they'll pin a medal on me. I'll ..."

"Of course you're going to shoot me, McCall. It's not like you have any other option. I mean, I beat the crap out of Falco, and he wasn't ten pounds overweight and twenty years past his prime."

It was a life-or-death gamble with fifty-fifty odds. Like betting everything on red at the roulette table. McCall was either going to do the smart thing and put a bullet between my eyes, or he was going to rise to the bait. His finger tightened on the trigger and his nostrils flared, and then he slowly lowered the gun, sliding it into the holster.

He took a step forward and swung his right fist into my stomach. I had already decided to let him get in a couple of good blows: I would give him confidence, stop him from reconsidering the decision. I tightened my stomach muscles but still, it felt like being slammed in the chest by a fencepost. My goading of McCall had been designed to produce this reaction, but he really was a lot stronger than he looked. I anticipated his follow-up move and rolled with the punch that came from his left. His third blow came a split second faster than I'd anticipated, and he managed to land a solid punch just above my left eyebrow. I fell back a step and wiped blood out of my eye. Three solid hits in less time than it takes to tell it. McCall knew it, too. The smile was back on his face.

"Not so talkative now, huh? You got more smart comebacks for me, Blake? Let's hear 'em."

I shook my head. "My mother always told me to be nice to the elderly."

Wham. Another hammer blow to the stomach. I tensed again and my stomach muscles absorbed a lot of the force, but I didn't want to take another one like that if I could avoid it. I dropped to the ground, doubled over. I hoped he wasn't a Marquess of Queensberry guy; it would screw up my next move. McCall didn't disappoint me. Instead of offering a hand to get me back on my feet, he took a step back and aimed a hard kick at the side of my head. I blocked it with a forearm and then blocked a second, keeping my eyes locked on his feet and timing the moves. When the third kick came at me, I was ready. I grabbed his boot with both hands and twisted it around hard, yanking him off his feet. The Kevlar he was wearing meant it was useless to hit him on the upper body, so I chose a lower target. I summoned up all the anger I'd suppressed during the last few blows I'd taken and channeled it all into my right arm as I punched him in the balls. McCall screamed and kicked out again. I dodged backward and launched myself at him, landing on top of him and nailing him straight across the bridge of his nose with a right.

His hand went down to the holster and came back up with the pistol. One problem: he wasn't out of my reach anymore. I grabbed his hand at the wrist and pushed it back as he squeezed the trigger and the gun went off between us. I smashed my forehead into his nose again and brought my other hand up to join the first one, smashing his hand off the ground until I felt a couple of bones break and the pistol slipped uselessly from his hand. The fight wasn't out of him yet, though. He slammed his left fist against the side of my head, hard enough to make me see a white starburst that temporarily obscured his twisted, hate-filled face. I still had a pretty good idea of our respective positions. I squeezed his broken hand with my left hand. As he screamed out, I let go with my right, brought my arm up, and slammed my elbow into his face. Once, twice, three times.

I blinked the vision back into my eyes and saw that McCall had stopped fighting. He was still breathing, although it came out of the bloody hole where his mouth was with a rasping sound.

I kept ahold of the gun and carefully got to my feet, watching him the whole time in case he was playing possum. He wasn't. The second or third of my elbows to his head had sent him deep into dreamland. I wiped some more blood out of my left eye and looked around. Still no one around, still no Allen.

I certainly didn't want to risk McCall coming to and following me, so I took a few seconds to pat him down. I found his backup piece—a compact Ruger .380—strapped to his ankle and put it in my pocket. I found a set of car keys. He'd probably parked down the road a little, out of sight. I bunched them up and threw them off the top of the hillside in the direction of the San Fernando Valley. Then I unlaced his boots, removed them, along with his socks, and tossed them as far as I could in opposite directions.

Before I left, I did my good deed for the day. I put the bastard in the recovery position so he wouldn't choke on his own blood. As I headed back to the Camaro, I wondered how McCall would explain this situation. I decided that he probably wouldn't mention it to anyone ever again.

# 81

The man Jessica Allen knew as Eddie Smith listened as she told him where she wanted to go and then nodded. "Yeah, I know where it is. You're meeting somebody up there?"

"My partner," Allen said flatly. She was looking straight ahead as they followed the course of the road.

The Samaritan smiled and kept driving. Not too fast, not too slow. There was no need to rush. She'd asked him to drive her in the very direction he wanted to go. Although, of course, he wouldn't be dropping her off at her requested destination. The place he had in mind was a little farther away, a little more secluded. The dusk was closing in on them now. He clicked on his full headlights.

There was silence for a couple of minutes. He'd been absolutely right to be concerned: between them, Allen and Blake had worked it out. Or rather, perhaps not all of it, but enough to bring them out here, to where it had all begun.

The Samaritan glanced over at Allen and she looked instinctively away. Still jumpy from what had very nearly been a fatal crash, perhaps. Or did she suspect something? She'd been cagey earlier in the garage, as well. It didn't really matter though, not now. It was too late for them by the time they were sitting beside him in the passenger side. He felt a flutter of excitement in his gut at what was to come. Allen would be an indulgence. An unscheduled bonus. He'd followed her in the hope she'd lead him to Blake, but there had been no sign of his old comrade in arms. No sense wasting a trip, however. And he had no doubt that Blake would mourn her loss. Another reminder of who was the better man.

"You're lucky to be alive," he said. Allen said nothing,

probably not wanting to think about the crash.

It was true, she really was lucky to be alive. The small explosive charge he'd placed inside the wheel well was intended only to disable the car, not to cause a fatal accident. He hadn't counted on her driving this road like a lunatic. He was glad she'd survived. For the moment.

As the road curved around, the platform of the observation tower loomed into view, about a mile or so distant. In another minute or two, it would be time to let the mask slip.

He'd been giving the matter of dealing with Allen some thought. Usually, it was enough to lock the doors and keep on driving. The other women out here had all reacted in the same way, progressing through the same steps in the process. Had he been the academic type, he could have written a self-help book on the stages of dealing with one's own imminent murder. First, there was confusion, transitioning quickly into disbelief. Then fear. Then bargaining. From there, things diverged somewhat from the traditional stages of grief. They never had time to get depressed, and he was reasonably sure none of them ever progressed to anything like acceptance. Instead, they seemed to bide their time, perhaps hoping some unlikely circumstance would arise that would allow them, somehow, to escape. He was always mildly surprised that none of the victims seemed to move on to the use of force, to make a last-ditch effort to effect an escape. Soon enough, they all looped back a step to fear.

He harbored no illusions that the standard pattern would hold for Detective Allen. As he turned off Mulholland and passed the boundary for the San Vicente Mountain Park, he rehearsed the sequence actions in his mind. He would pull to a stop and wait until she turned away from him to open the passenger door. Then he would say her name casually, as though she'd forgotten something, and when she turned back to him, he would hit her full in the face. If she was still conscious after that, he'd take the time to bind her hands for the remainder of the journey. Then the fun would begin.

"Smith."

The Samaritan turned his head and found himself facing down the barrel of Allen's Beretta nine millimeter. Despite his surprise, he was impressed. He had glanced in her direction immediately beforehand and she'd been looking out the window. She must have drawn and aimed the weapon in a fraction of a second.

"How fucking stupid do you think I am?" she asked.

The Samaritan said nothing. He saw no reason to attempt to continue the pretense. That would be demeaning. He let the cop talk as his mind worked out a solution to the current problem.

"You just happen to appear at my parking garage, and then all of a sudden you just happen to be there right after I get a blowout? Only that wasn't a blowout. I heard a pop before I heard the tire blow. You rigged it, didn't you?"

"Very good, Detective," he said. "I apologize. I certainly didn't mean to insult your intelligence."

"Nice cover, I guess. A photographer. Lets you return to the scene of the crime without suspicion."

An astute observation, the Samaritan thought. But that wasn't the only advantage to posing as Smith. The ability to speak to contacts within the LAPD had been a bonus when the first three bodies were discovered. He'd been reassured to discover how little they knew, before Blake decided to stick his nose in.

Allen was shaking her head. "I should have known earlier. You slipped up the other night, on the phone. I just didn't realize it until now. You knew the LA cases were different from the others because the victims looked so alike. 'Like sisters' you said. Only we hadn't released any details of the murders in the other states, so as far as anyone knew, all the victims looked like that."

"You're right; that was sloppy," he said, growing more impressed with Allen even as he admonished himself.

"What have you done with Kimberley Frank?"

He smiled. He guessed this had been Blake's discovery. "She's alive, Detective Allen. You might get to meet her, in fact."

He'd slowed down as they talked, but now the entranceway to the missile site was approaching on the left-hand side. He let his foot drop a little on the gas pedal, and the needle began to climb.

Allen leaned closer until the gun was pressing against his temple. "Stop the car. Now."

"Okay."

The Samaritan yanked the steering wheel hard to the left, timing it perfectly so that the car slammed into one of the solid concrete gateposts at the entranceway. Allen's side of the vehicle took the brunt of it, but both of them were flung forward and back violently as the truck smashed to a stop. A secondary jolt bounced them forward again as the truck's back wheels, which had lifted off the road on the abrupt impact, came back down to earth and bounced. The gun had been jolted from Allen's hand and had landed in the footwell. Her head lolled to the side, stunned. The Samaritan decided not to take any chances. Before the detective could shake off the effects of her second crash in the space of half an hour, he reached his right hand across and pinched the carotid artery. Just long enough to knock her out; he didn't want her impaired in any way for later.

She opened her mouth and her eyes rolled toward him,

and then they rolled upward and her head dropped against her chest.

The Samaritan opened the driver's door and got out of the truck, surveying the damage. The passenger side of the hood was caved in around the solid concrete gatepost, and from the way the vehicle had come to rest, he could tell he'd snapped the front axle. He cast a glance up at the parking lot but saw no sign of anyone waiting. Had anybody been there, they would surely have come running at the sound of the crash. There were no other cars parked up there, meaning he'd have to make the rest of the journey on foot.

He pulled Allen out through the driver's side and laid her down on the road. Then he retrieved his kit from a compartment in the flatbed of the truck and bound her hands tightly with a zip tie, opting to leave her ankles free. He had no objection to carrying her across the remaining distance, but if she happened to come to, it would be quicker if she was able to walk. And then he bent, gathered his arms around her at the waist, and straightened up, heaving her limp body over his shoulder. He had a couple of miles to go, so he started walking at a good pace. He had another guest, after all, and he didn't want to keep her waiting.

# 82

Detective Mazzucco's still-open eyes stared up at me from the dirt floor of the barn. It looked like his killer had cut his throat from behind. The ragged gash across his neck was sickeningly familiar. I was still holding the pistol I'd taken from McCall. I tucked it into the back of my belt and knelt down beside the dead cop.

I felt a strong urge to find a sheet or something to drape over Mazzucco's body, or at least close his eyes, but I knew I couldn't. Forensic considerations aside, I didn't want the Samaritan to know somebody had been there. He was nothing if not prepared, so I didn't want to give him any extra warning if I could avoid it. I patted the body down and found nothing of import. His gun and cell phone had clearly been taken by his killer, disposed of as far from here as possible. I looked up and scanned the immediate area around the body. The interior of the barn was almost pitch-black in the twilight, but the body had been close enough to the door that I could examine the area well enough. The only thing I found, funnily enough, belonged to me. In his coat pocket, I found my sketch of Crozier from a couple days before. Why had he kept it?

I stood up and glanced back out the doorway. I listened for sounds: a distant engine, perhaps. Nothing. I looked back down.

I examined the position of the body and thought about it. Rigor had yet to set in, which meant Mazzucco had been dead less than a couple of hours. The light would have been better when he'd come in here, so it would have been harder to surprise him. And yet I knew he'd been ambushed, from the lack of defensive wounds on his hands. If he'd been facing toward the door when he died, did that mean he'd been on his way back out of the barn when he was jumped? What had attracted his attention?

I cast a last glance at Mazzucco's body and decided it was time to check out the house I'd seen at the far end of the set.

I exited the barn and moved to a point where there was a gap between two of the facades that made up one side of the main street. From here, I had a clear view of the access road, which came over the crest of the hill. I watched and listened for a minute. Nothing. I began to worry that the encounter with McCall had delayed me enough to miss the Samaritan entirely.

I stepped away from the gap and looked up at the house. It was dark enough by now that I'd have expected a light to be burning if there was anyone in there—a lamp or even a candle. Perhaps there would be nothing there, or worse, perhaps he'd already killed Kimberley Frank and departed for who-knew-where. There was only one way to find out.

I approached the house warily, watching the windows for any hint of movement. I circled around the rear to see if I could enter the house around there, but then I discovered there was no back door, or even back windows. Although the house was a real structure, it evidently needed to be seen only from the front.

I completed the circle and stood before the three steps up onto the porch. No sign of life or light at either of the two windows flanking the door. I stepped up onto the porch and put a hand on the doorknob. It was locked. I was about to get my picks out when I heard a muffled banging from inside the house. It sounded like somebody kicking or stamping on something. Somebody who couldn't speak but wanted to attract attention. Somebody who could be badly hurt, perhaps.

I took a step back, lifted my right foot, and slammed it into the door alongside the knob. I felt a crack as the jamb split, and then another kick sent the door bursting inward. It was as dark as a crypt. I made out a large hallway, big enough to accommodate the film cameras, with two doors leading off into each side of the house and a wide staircase leading to the upper level. It was hot inside, as though the house had spent all day absorbing the warmth of the sun and was reluctant to let it go. Hot, and with a familiar stench. The smell of old blood.

There was a brief silence and then the banging started up again, with greater urgency. It was coming from the upper floor. I raced up the stairs, which creaked and moaned as though unused to traffic. I came out into an open-plan attic. The last of the twilight came in through the single window, revealing a large, low-ceilinged room, with the roof support beams exposed. Hanging from one of them was a set of manacles.

I heard rapid breathing from the far side of the room, in the darkest corner. I walked forward, and my eyes began to adjust to the shadows. A young, dark-haired woman was there, gagged and blindfolded. She wore black slacks and a white shirt. She was bound at the wrists with a plastic zip tie, her hands in her lap. She had drawn her knees up against her chest, and her head was angled toward me, as though straining to hear. Even with her face obscured, I recognized her as Kimberley Frank.

As she heard my approaching footsteps, her breathing quickened. Through the gag, I heard three muffled words, unmistakable as "Oh my God."

"It's okay," I called out as I approached her, my eyes scanning the space, looking for unexpected surprises. The floorboards were bare but looked as though they had been painted or varnished. The room was empty and unfurnished but for a hardbacked wood chair and a small table. "My name is Carter Blake, Kimberley. I'm here to help."

The gag was tight. I worked the knot for a second until it loosened and then let it fall down around her throat like a neckerchief. Then I slipped the blindfold the other way, taking it off. Her brown eyes blinked up at me. They seemed oddly calm, as though she was studying me with a detached curiosity.

"How do you know my name?"

I didn't answer, too busy looking at what was on the table. It confirmed that this place was not just used for keeping prisoners. There were knives and blades and saws of all shapes and sizes. There was another doctor's case identical to the one I'd seen in the warehouse. Handcuffs and wire. Tools. It was then I noticed that the finish on the floor was uneven in patches and realized that the boards were not stained with paint or varnish, but with blood. Almost the entire floor had been washed with it at different times. The variation in the shades and concentrations, as well as the volume that must have been expended, told me that this was the room in which the Samaritan's first three victims had died.

There was one other thing on the table, and though it seemed innocuous, it chilled me more than any of the tools of murder. It was a thick, binder-sized photo album. I had a good idea what would be inside of it. I put a hand to the leather cover and stopped when I heard the urgency in Kimberley's voice from across the room.

"You have to hurry up. He'll be coming."

She was right. We had no time to waste. I selected a short blade from the table and went back to the corner where Kimberley was sitting.

"You don't understand. He'll kill you. He's my half brother. I thought ..."

"That he was dead?"

She looked surprised, but held her wrists still while I used the knife to saw through the zip tie. I examined her wrists. There was minor abrasion, but they didn't look too bad, considering.

"Can you walk?"

384

She rubbed her calf muscles and nodded uncertainly.

"Then let's get the hell out of here."

I bent down and put one of her arms around my shoulders and stood up, supporting her as we moved toward the stairs. She was shaking violently, the vibrations conducting their way out of her and through my own muscles like an electric current.

"How did you know—?"

"Just concentrate on walking," I said, trying to keep my voice calm and soothing. "We can talk about it later, okay?"

She swallowed and focused on one foot after another. She kept talking, probably couldn't help it. "He killed my dad, years ago. His mother and his sister, too. The cops knew it was him, but ..."

"It's okay, Kimberley. We're getting out of here. It's over."

"No. You don't understand. He's insane."

I saved my breath and started to ease Kimberley down the stairs. We'd made it about halfway down when she was seized by a cramp in her leg. She cried out and stumbled to the side, putting all of her weight on a section of the step that had succumbed to dry rot. The wood crumbled beneath her and she slipped out from under my arm, tumbling down the last few stairs. Thankfully, she didn't have far to fall. She landed on all fours in front of the open door.

Quickly, I descended the rest of the stairs and crouched down to check that she was all right, turning my back to the front door for a second. Her face looked up at me, and I saw her eyes widen even as I became aware of a shadow falling over the two of us.

I spun around and felt something smash across the side of my head. I dropped on my back and caught a glance of a tall figure silhouetted against the evening sky before the black clouds rushed in from the sides of my vision.

# 83

As I began to swim out of the haze of unconsciousness, I became dimly aware that the voice I'd been hearing wasn't part of the scrambled collage of sounds and images scrolling through my subconscious. The voice sounded regretful but philosophical. I was having trouble following what was being said, as though my brain were rebooting, having to work out how to parse English again. And then something clicked into place and I heard three words, spoken quietly from very close.

"Quite a mess."

I kept my eyes shut and tried to backtrack through my memories to work out what was happening, because I didn't think it was anything good. The last thing I could remember was helping Kimberley Frank up off the ground, and then ... it came back to me. The Samaritan filling the doorway and a simultaneous blow to the side of the head.

It was like typing in the correct password. All of a sudden, my senses started to operate again. I felt nausea and a throbbing pain on the left side of my skull. The dull sounds of birds and far-off traffic noise made me think I was somewhere outside, but the dank, mildew smell spoke of an interior. Sensory input from elsewhere: my hands were behind me, the inside of my wrists tight against a wooden post or pillar. I felt my skin contact that of someone else, as though the two of us were tied back to back. The barn. We were in the barn.

I heard someone crouch down beside me and whisper in my ear, "Come on, Blake. A conscious person's breathing is quite different from someone who's still out. You know that as well as I do."

I opened my eyes and saw the Samaritan staring right back at me. He'd changed. He had lost a lot of weight, had more lines around the eyes. He was clean shaven, and his hair was trimmed neatly in a buzz cut. His eyes flicked to the side of my head and he touched a finger to the place where my head hurt. I flinched as a lightning bolt of pain stabbed into me, and then his finger came away bloody.

"It was always your problem, Blake. Always too interested in other people's business."

"I guess neither of us has changed much, Crozier."

He blinked. "Don't call me that."

"You prefer the Samaritan now? Is that it?"

"I prefer nothing. I'm nothing and nobody. You should understand that."

I remembered the hands nestled against mine. I assumed they belonged to Kimberley. They felt warm, which was a good sign. I moved my bound hands upward against them to see if I could get a reaction from the owner and winced as sharp plastic scraped my wrists: I guessed he'd used a zip tie. Better news than wire, but only if I could manage to get some space to work with it. That wasn't going to happen, not with the position he'd tied us in.

"Kimberley?" I called. "Are you okay?"

The Samaritan's lips drew back from his teeth in amusement. "That's not Kimberley," he said.

It took me a second before I realized who was there. "Allen?"

Silence from behind me. The Samaritan smiled in acknowledgment.

"She's still unconscious. Genuinely unconscious, that is. We'll need to wake her up soon, though."

"Where's Kimberley?"

My question was met with a strange laugh from the

Samaritan. He gave no other response. I decided to keep him talking, since conversation was currently the only tool I had at my disposal. "Why are you doing this?"

The Samaritan's features creased in a look of disappointment. "Blake." The word was an admonishment.

"Yeah, I know—you live to kill. Very impressive. But why her? What did your sister ever do to you?"

Now a look of confusion crossed his face, as though the answer was plainly obvious. "She made me the man I am today."

I heard movement behind me. Not Allen, who was still unconscious, but someone else. Footsteps. A second before the slight, graceful figure passed into my field of vision, I felt a cold shiver as I realized just how wrong we'd all been.

"You," I said simply.

Kimberley Frank's face stayed impassive, but her eyes smiled. "My hero," she said.

## 1996

Dean Crozier made no attempt to chase after the fleeing boy as he stalled in his rush to the staircase. Robbie's voice was panicked as he pushed against Kimberley, trying to get past her, not understanding yet why she was still blocking his way.

"What's going on?" he repeated. "What's going on? You're brother's a fuckin' psycho. That's what's going on."

"Oh," Kimberley said, her brown eyes looking from Robbie to her newfound brother, the brother she'd discovered she had only a couple of weeks before. "Is that all?"

Robbie looked back at him, then at Kimberley, and then

made a bolt for the stairs again. Kimberley was too fast for him. She brought the makeshift hiking stick down hard on the back of his neck.

Robbie cried out and staggered forward. Crozier moved quickly, getting on top of him with his knee between the boy's shoulder blades. He put the knife down, yanked Robbie's hands behind his body, and started wrapping the clothesline tightly around his wrists. Robbie struggled, but though the two boys were only months apart in age, he was no match for Crozier's strength.

When he'd finished, he let him drop to the floor again. Kimberley's eyes were bright, excited. It would be her first time, too, after all. Talking about it, planning it, had been exhilarating, but now it was actually happening.

Kimberley stepped around Robbie and picked up the Buck knife from the floor. She put her left hand on Crozier's cheeks and kissed him softly on the lips.

"Are you ready, brother?"

# 84

I heard the noise of steel singing as it was pulled from a leather sheath, and the blade was in the Samaritan's hand. The Kris. The wicked, curving blade gleamed in the moonlight through the door like an oversized piece of jewelry.

Kimberley held her hand out, and the Samaritan gave her the knife, a soft smile on his lips. She crouched down in front of me and stared into my eyes. She touched the point of it to my throat and pressed gently. I felt a sharp prick as it punctured the top layer of my skin. I didn't give her the satisfaction of wincing, just kept my eyes on hers.

"Listen to me, Kimberley. You don't need to do what he says. We can ..."

She smiled and shook her head, and I realized I'd gotten this back to front. I replayed the last couple of minutes. The submissiveness in the Samaritan's body language as he'd handed the knife over. The beatific look in his eyes as he watched his sister holding the blade to my throat. *She made me the man I am today.*

"It's you," I said. "You're the Samaritan."

"I wouldn't go that far, Blake," she said. "It's both of us. You could call it a family business."

My eyes flicked over to Crozier. His gaze was fixed on the knife against my throat. I wondered if he was eager to see blood spilled, or worried that he wouldn't get me to himself.

I looked back at Kimberley. "The other killings across the country ..."

"Can't take the credit for those. Those were all down to this brother of mine. Quite an endeavor, wasn't it? And quite a compliment."

I looked from Kimberley to her half brother. I'd noticed that Crozier hadn't uttered a word since Kimberley had begun speaking. An interesting family dynamic.

She continued. "I had gone a long time without ... indulging, Blake. More than ten years. And then I received a letter from him. It told me what he'd been doing. How he thought often about when we were kids. He told me to look out for his work, that he'd leave little messages for me that only I could see. He told me one day he'd come back for me. And he kept his promise."

I turned away from her, being careful not to move too fast with the point of the knife against my Adam's apple. I addressed Crozier directly. "I guess she wears the pants in this relationship. It's encouraging to see, actually. It's about time the homicidal maniac community embraced gender equality."

She looked irritated, but more by the fact that I'd addressed Crozier rather than what I'd said, and opened her mouth to say something. I kept talking to Crozier.

"So why are you picking victims that look like her here in LA? Maybe some repressed sibling resentment?"

Crozier smiled and shook his head. "It won't work, Blake. You can't make me angry." He approached and crouched down beside his sister before me. He put a hand on her shoulder and moved his head forward, closing his eyes and smelling her hair. "Those others, they didn't belong here."

Kimberley smiled modestly at him as he said this, as though receiving a romantic compliment from a lover. She looked back at me, her eyes suddenly all business again. "Cut the cop down," she said, speaking to her brother but still looking at me. "We can take her up to the house first."

Crozier took another blade out, a smaller one this time, and put a hand on my back, pushing me carefully forward. Kimberley moved the blade back a couple of inches so it didn't puncture my throat all the way. That would spoil the fun.

I felt Allen's body shift as Crozier worked on the zip tie. The knife cut through and she slumped off of me. The weight of her body on top of my bound hands had been cutting off some of the circulation, and now the feeling started to ebb back into my wrists and hands. I winced as I started to feel the plastic edges cutting into me. But now that the weight on my hands was gone, I had an opportunity.

Allen mumbled, beginning to come to as Crozier scooped her up and swung her body across his shoulders, carrying her in a fireman's hold. He waved his free hand at the open doorway. "You can listen while we attend to her. Unfortunately, time is of the essence, but I'll make sure it's a memorable experience. Perhaps you can use the time to picture yourself in her place."

There was no point arguing with insanity. I decided to appeal to whatever vestiges might remain of the logical, practical soldier I'd known. "You don't have time for this. Allen and Mazzucco will be missed immediately. The cops will track them down soon."

"Your point is?"

"Let Allen go. Do what you want with me."

The Samaritan's mouth twitched in amusement. "Do you honestly think that you matter, *Blake*?" This time, he said my name with mocking emphasis, as though to remind me of how transient all of this was. Names, faces, lives.

Kimberley pressed the point of the Kris a little farther into my neck, as though considering my suggestion. I held still and felt a drop of blood slide down toward my collar.

"Don't worry. We'll be back in a little while," she said.

And then the blade was gone, and so was Kimberley, and so was the Samaritan.

# 85

I waited until I had heard the sound of their steps retreat far enough outside that I could be sure they were gone. Crozier had clearly been in a hurry, because he'd chosen the quickest and most efficient way of restraining Allen and me. Binding us to a fixed object rather than spending time hog-tying us. I guessed he'd chosen not to bind my hands in front of me because he knew that would leave a lot of ways I could be dangerous. So under the circumstances, he'd picked the best way to do it.

But now that they'd removed Allen and her body weight was no longer bearing down on my wrists, I wasn't quite as securely tied as I had been a few minutes before. I now had a small amount of space for movement. I pulled my knees up toward my chest and dug my heels into the floor. At first there was no movement, and the ties just dug deeper into my wrists. I adjusted the angle slightly and managed to slide my back up the post. A minute later, I'd manage to push myself up so that I was standing with my back to the post. I braced myself against the imminent pain and closed my eyes.

Then I started to move my wrists up and down against one of the corners of the post. The sharp plastic rubbed and cut and tore at the flesh on my wrists, but I kept the rhythm going, feeling the plastic start to warm as it rubbed against the edge of the old wood. Blood ran from the abrasions and mingled with the sweat on my hands, making them hot and slippery. Splinters from the post joined in the agony, stabbing into my flesh as I rubbed the plastic up and down. Just at the moment I thought I was going to give up, the plastic snapped and I fell forward, just breaking my fall with my forearms. I stood up and glanced at my wrists. They were torn and bloody.

I heard a scream from the direction of the house. It was Allen.

I didn't waste time looking for my gun, or Allen's. The Samaritan and his sister would have made sure not to leave them anywhere near us, on the off chance we did manage to get loose. I started for the door and then froze when I heard another, closer sound.

Footsteps.

# 86

Quickly, as silently as I could manage, I moved to the side of the barn door, holding my breath though my lungs were fighting for air after the exertion of breaking free. No sooner had I made it into position than the sound of boots stopped just outside the door and I heard breathing. Without knowing where exactly he was standing, I couldn't be sure if the post where I'd been tied up was in his line of sight. I heard Allen scream again and my blood ran cold. It took every ounce of willpower I had not to move, to keep still, keep holding my breath.

And then Crozier stepped through the doorway. The split second of confusion in his body language told me that for the first time tonight, I'd gotten lucky. He hadn't been able to see the bare post from outside. Maybe he'd just stopped to look back at the house and savor the sounds of Allen's pain. I didn't particularly care. I charged into him from the side, wrapping my arms around his waist and bringing him down hard on the floor. He was still holding the Kris, and he hung on to it even as I slammed him to the ground.

His bright eyes fixed on mine as I landed on top of him. My senses went into crunch-time mode. Everything was in slow motion. I saw his fist tighten around the hilt of the Kris even as his body contacted the ground. All my instincts told me I ought to deal with the knife first. Block it, grab it, get it away from him.

I ignored those instincts. I wanted to cause him pain more than I wanted to avoid it myself. I hit him hard in the face, feeling teeth give way behind the flesh of his lips. It was a solid blow with no time for defense. I hit him so hard that it took most of the energy out of his simultaneous thrust with the blade. He'd been swinging around to stick me in my left side. Instead, his wrist contacted my left arm and the six-inch curved blade finished its travel in thin air, an inch behind my shoulder blades. I hit him again and again. I realized I'd been pulling my punches earlier with McCall. This was something else. I'd never hit a human being this hard before. I didn't think I'd even hit a bag this hard before. I wanted to pound his face into the dirt until there was nothing left.

But somehow he took it. Before I could hit him a fourth time, he'd gotten his left palm under my throat and was squeezing. I saw the blade glint out of the corner of my eye and realized he was about to bring it back around again. I shifted my weight and got my left forearm up in time to block the strike. The impact of our arms contacting felt like I'd been hit with a bat. I was off balance now, and as he bucked under me, I started to slip off of him and winced as my injured ankle twisted under his body. He managed to scramble to one knee as I fell back. I heard the blade sing through the air as he swung it back around, backhanded. I kicked off the ground to avoid the arc of the blade, not quite getting out of range as the razor-sharp steel parted the cloth of my shirt. I glanced down at my stomach as I fell backward, seeing blood, but not a deep cut. An inch or two closer, and I would have been picking my intestines off the floor.

He got to his feet and lunged at me, firmly on the offensive now. His face was a fright mask of hate. Blood poured from his shattered mouth and his flattened nose. I rolled aside as he brought the blade down and then blocked his arm again on the follow-up. I knew I'd been lucky to parry the two close swipes so far and that I couldn't expect that lucky streak to continue. Before he could pull back for another cutting swing, I grabbed the hand holding the Kris with both hands and started to twist, trying to wrest it from his grip. He held firm, his eyes burning into me from the bloody wreck of his face. He got his other hand in my face, his fingers clawing for my eyes. I couldn't let go of the knife hand to protect my face, so I did the best I could, angling my jaw upward and jamming my eyes shut tight. Navigating blind now, I focused all of my energy on the hand holding the knife. Forget about taking it from him. Give it back to him instead.

I switched the tactic from twisting to pushing. Crozier, utterly focused on holding on to the knife with one hand while trying to gouge my eyes out with the other, wasn't prepared for this. Too late, he gave up on my eyes and brought his left hand back for reinforcement. But by that time, I'd already pushed the point of the blade an inch into his throat. He gagged and tried again to pull the knife back, but I got the heel of my right hand to the bottom of the hilt and drove the blade up, up. I felt hot blood course down my arms as I kept the pressure on.

His throat made a horrible gurgling sound, and his eyes rolled white, and then, only then, did his hands relax. I pushed his body to the ground. As I wiped the blood off my hands, I remembered that there was no time to rest. It might already be too late to save Allen.

The night air was cool on my skin as I tumbled through the door of the barn. I could see lamplight burning in the attic room of the house. The screaming had stopped, but I could hear low voices emanating from the glassless window. A one-sided conversation. Kimberley was taking a break, perhaps selecting a new tool.

Ignoring the sharp lances of pain that dug into my ankle with every other step, I ran for the door and found it open. I was on the second stair when I heard the first gunshot from above.

396

# 87

I froze on the stairs at the sound of the first shot. I gripped the handrail at the sound of the second. Two shots so close together that they almost had to be into a single target.

Allen. I was too late. Kimberley had killed her.

My mind raced to process the new information. It didn't make sense. They liked to torture their victims, make them suffer. Crozier and his sister had wanted me to listen and be powerless to do anything before it was my turn. Even if Kimberley had decided to put her out of her misery, she wouldn't have used a gun. I got the feeling the final killing stroke was Kimberley's job, and I didn't believe she'd pass that up for any reason.

The next sound told me she hadn't. I heard a gasp and the sound of faltering footsteps. Kimberley appeared at the top of the stairs, a long, thin knife coated with blood in her hands. I tensed to defend myself, but then I saw there was no need. A trickle of blood ran down from a hole in the center of her forehead, as though someone had turned on a faucet. Her eyes rolled in her head and she crumpled to the floor, her head tilted back over the stairs. Her eyes stared down at me from there, dead. It was then that I noticed there was blood coming from underneath her too, from her abdomen.

I inched up the stairs toward her, keeping my head down but angling myself so I could see into the room. The first thing I saw was Allen. Her shirt had been stripped off. She was hanging from the manacles I'd seen earlier on. Her upper body was bloodied by a number of cuts. It was impossible to tell how many there were because the bleeding was so profuse. She wasn't looking at me. She was staring at something or someone out of my line of sight. I took another couple of steps up so that I could see most of the second floor.

The person who'd executed Kimberley was standing a couple of steps back from the stairs, facing Allen, not looking in my direction. He held the gun that had killed Kimberley in his right hand. He looked very calm, in good shape. Mid-twenties, solid build, around five eleven. He had an almost preppy air about him: short dark hair, thin-frame glasses, jeans, and a black tennis shirt. He looked like a junior doctor on a weekend break in the country.

Allen hadn't noticed me either. Her eyes were fixed on her apparent savior. I guessed he'd been drawn to the house by her screams.

"Thank you," Allen said, sounding out of breath. "How did you—?"

The man in the glasses said nothing. Then he raised his gun again and pointed it at Allen's head.

# 88

"Stop," I said, stepping up the last stairs and fully into the attic room.

The man's head swiveled back to me. His gun stayed on Allen. His brown eyes blinked behind the lenses, dispassionately assessing the change to the dynamic of the situation.

"Carter Blake, isn't it?" he said.

"Do I know you?"

"No. You were before my time."

I looked down at Kimberley's body and the position of the

bullet holes. One dead center at the breastbone, one between the eyes to finish the job. Professional.

"Winterlong," I said.

"I've heard a lot about you."

"How's Drakakis?"

He blinked again. "Not here anymore. Where's Crozier?"

"Dead. In the barn." I gestured toward Allen. "We're just leaving."

He kept his gun on her, shook his head briefly. "This is a deep clean. No witnesses."

I glanced at Allen. She glanced at me and then back to the man with the gun. "Who the hell is this guy, Blake?"

I didn't answer and took a step toward the man in glasses. He didn't react, so I took another and another until we were five feet apart.

"Don't come any closer."

"If you pull that trigger, you die next," I said, flexing my bloodied hands.

His eyes dropped to my hands and back up my blood-soaked upper body, all the way to my face. "I don't see a gun."

"I won't need one."

"*I'm* the one with the gun."

"You've heard about me," I said. "You know you can't kill me."

"Maybe things have changed."

"Maybe."

We stood there for a minute, watching each other. I decided to help him make the decision. "The cops are coming. You don't have time for this. She doesn't know anything, anyway."

He took his time, kept the gun on Allen and his eyes on me. And then he raised the gun and clicked the safety back on. He walked back toward the stairs, eyes on me the whole time. I half expected some kind of parting shot, like "This isn't over" or "Be seeing you," but none was forthcoming. The brown eyes behind the glasses adhered to me until he reached the stairs, and then he was gone.

I walked across the room, glancing back at Kimberley's body. The blood coming from the exit wound underneath her was pooling and seeping into the floorboards, adding a fresh coat to the other patches of dried gore. I took my jacket off and hung it on Allen's shoulders. She kept her eyes shut tight, flinching when my hands touched her.

"It's over now," I said quietly.

# 89

Once I'd cut Allen down, I examined her wounds. She needed medical attention—there was no doubt about that—but she'd live. The cuts were superficial, calculated to inflict pain and blood loss rather than mortal injury. The Samaritan and his sister had liked to take their time. I found my gun and Allen's on the table beside the rest of the knives and tools, along with a cell phone that I guessed was Crozier's.

I took a second to open the photo album and immediately regretted it. Hundreds of pictures of the Samaritan's victims. Males, females, all ages, multiple races. Alive, dead, wishing they were dead. I was no stranger to death, but this went beyond even my experience. Steeling myself, I leafed to the back and found the most recent pictures. Boden, Burnett, and Morrow. Kimberley was in some of these ones, taking part in the torture with a zealous glint in her eyes. I remembered the urgency in her voice the first time I'd gone near the book and realized why she'd stopped me.

"What is it?" Allen called.

I swallowed and closed the cover of the album, knowing that some of those images were burned into me for good. I walked back over to Allen and helped her toward the stairs. We stepped across Kimberley's body and descended to the ground level, emerging into the fresh night air.

"Are you okay?" I asked.

Allen was shivering, but she nodded. "Where's Mazzucco?"

I shook my head. "I'm sorry."

She didn't blink, just asked, "Where?"

I pointed in the direction of the barn. Part of me thought I should tell her to stay put, that she was in no condition for this, but the look on her face gave me second thoughts.

I followed her across to the barn, a few paces behind, and let her go in by herself. A couple of minutes later, she appeared at the doorway again. My jacket was no longer around her shoulders, and I knew she'd draped it over Mazzucco's face.

She didn't look at me at first, just took a deep breath and looked back at the make-believe house with its single lit window.

"You mind explaining to me what the hell just happened, Blake?"

"We got it wrong. Kimberley wasn't the target. He was killing those women as a tribute to her. She was helping him. I think she probably helped him kill his family, too."

"So she was the reason he came back to LA, just not in the way we thought."

"There's always something you don't know," I said.

"What about the guy with the gun? Was he from ... before?"

I nodded. "They don't like people drawing attention to them. If Crozier had been caught alive ..."

"Unwanted attention. I get it. What about his prints?"

"That ship's sailed, remember? They already ran the ones from the house. This is damage limitation."

She nodded. "Thank you, by the way."

I didn't say anything. All things considered, I didn't think Allen should be thanking me for anything.

She leaned back against the barn and closed her eyes. She held her hand out. "Give me the phone." I handed it to her. She turned away from me and made the call. When she was done, she turned back to me. "They'll be here soon. You should go."

I looked her up and down. She looked reasonably okay. She was one tough customer. But still ...

Seeing my hesitation, she raised her voice and yelled, "Go! If you're here when they get here, I can't protect you."

Reluctantly, I nodded and left her standing by the barn, waiting for the cavalry.

I walked quickly in the opposite direction from the road. Going back to where I'd left the Camaro was out of the question, even if the cops weren't en route. I pictured the map of the area, remembering that there was a road roughly five miles west, across country. I oriented myself with the stars—you could actually see them up here—and started walking. An hour and change later, I came upon the road I'd been looking for.

I stepped off the dirt and onto the asphalt and started walking east. If I remembered the map rightly, I would hit the northwestern edge of Los Angeles in another ten miles. Once I got there, I could find a bus station and put as many miles between myself and LA as possible. But for now, it was a clear, crisp night: a good night for walking. I would reach my destination in three hours or so. Unless, that was, some Good Samaritan stopped to offer me a ride along the way.

# TWO WEEKS LATER

Another day, another cemetery.

I watched the burial from a distance, from a bench close to the perimeter fence. A small group had come to see Kelly Boden committed to the earth beneath a perfect blue California sky. Her father, some extended family members, Sarah Dutton, and two young men in black suits who I guessed were the boyfriends of Sarah and Kelly. And Allen. It hadn't been that long since the night at the Samaritan's house, and I thought she'd probably flouted doctor's orders to be here. It didn't surprise me in the least.

As I was thinking this, she happened to turn her head in my direction. She spotted me, held her eyes on me for a moment, and then turned back to the service. It was a little eerie, the timing of it, as though she'd picked up a telepathic signal from me or something.

I looked on as the minister said a few words, his Bible open in front of him. I was too far away to hear exactly what he was saying, but I'd attended enough funerals that I could probably recite the words myself.

Finally, the two boyfriends and the father and one of the other male relatives took up an end of rope each, and slowly lowered the coffin into the grave. A real grave this time. I didn't know how much these things mattered to you once you were dead, but it had to be better than an unmarked hole in the Santa Monica Mountains.

The small crowd began to disperse, breaking off in different directions to the various gates. Allen lingered behind, talking to Richard Boden. They spoke for a few minutes, and at the end, he reached around Allen and gave her a brief hug. They shook hands and Boden walked away to join the rest of the mourners.

Allen turned to look at me again, seemed to think something over, and then started to walk up the hill to where I was sitting.

"I didn't think I'd see you again," she said. "Didn't think you were the sticking-around type."

She sat down beside me and we looked down the hill at the fresh grave.

"I'm not," I said. "But I wanted to check in on you, see how you were. The hospital wasn't an option, but I figured you'd show up here."

"You really are good at finding people who don't want to be found."

"I guess I deserved that."

She turned to me, head angled in mild apology. "Sorry, Blake. None of this was your fault. And I'm fine ... thanks to you."

I could see the end of a partially healed scar on the side of her neck, protruding above her shirt collar. She touched a hand to it, and her eyes flashed with an irritation that reassured me ten times more than her words. "Don't look at me like that, Blake. I'm not a freaking basket case."

"Sorry," I said.

She sighed, loosened her posture a little. "Okay, the dreams aren't great."

"That'll happen."

"It'll get better in time though, I think," she said. "It helps to know it's really over. That they're both dead."

"I'm sorry about Mazzucco."

"Me too. He and his wife have a baby, you know. A little girl."

I didn't say anything. There didn't seem to be anything to say. The ripples of devastation caused by Crozier's madness seemed to keep on spreading. I knew they'd be felt for a long time yet.

"Boden wants to thank you."

"What did you tell him?"

"Nothing too specific; don't worry. But more than I told anybody else. You're still technically wanted for questioning."

I nodded. "Nothing I can't handle."

I knew the LAPD and the FBI would still want to speak to me if they could, but there was no longer any kind of active manhunt. The evidence at the house was more than enough to prove that the murders had all been committed by Crozier: acting alone at first and latterly with his half sister.

Allen sighed. "Give them a week and they'll get over it. The LAPD just cleared six murders. Nine, including the ninety-seven case. The feds will be closing cold cases across the country for the next couple of years. Nobody's shedding any tears for Crozier and his sister. The case is a slam dunk; no need to overcomplicate the narrative."

I smiled. Allen was probably right about the cops and even the feds. I was a loose end, but not one that would trouble them for long, not with the Samaritan finally out of action. But there were other people who would be wondering about me. People who weren't so easily satisfied.

The press coverage surrounding the whole case was predictably intense. The official story was that there had been some sort of records glitch in Afghanistan, which explained how Dean Crozier had apparently risen from the dead. I wondered if that was guesswork by the authorities, or the official story that had come down from on high. It didn't matter either way, just a plausible explanation for something that would never be publicly explained.

No one would ever know exactly where Crozier had gone when he came back to America. The only traces he left in those early months and years were the bodies that had sometimes waited years to be discovered. What was clear was that he'd returned to Los Angeles eighteen months ago. He'd set up the identity of Eddie Smith to give himself a cover, to let him get to know the city and its law enforcers again. All the while, he'd made brief trips to other parts of the nation, staying a week or two, killing with impunity, and then returning to LA, unsuspected.

I corrected Allen on one point. "The LAPD didn't clear those murders, Allen. You did. You kept focused; you found the murder house. It was excellent police work. Next time any of them gives you any shit, you remind them of that."

"That I fixed the Samaritan, huh?" She smiled.

She held out a hand, and I took it in my own and shook it.

"Good working with you, Detective."

"Likewise. Maybe we'll do this again sometime."

"For your sake, I hope not."

She smiled again and stood up. I watched as she walked back down the hill and toward the main cemetery gate without a backward glance.

I waited there a while longer, feeling the sun on my face and thinking about dreams. About scars and about the past: the things you carried with you, no matter how far you tried to run.

In time, the shadows lengthened and one of the cemetery workers appeared by Kelly Boden's grave and started to shovel the displaced earth from the pile back on top of the coffin. He moved with practiced ease. The job would be complete soon, and the new grave would begin to blend in with all of the others. But I would be long gone by that time.